CW01496701

RONALD A. RYBERG

THE BABINGTON PLOT

AN ELIZABETHAN CONSPIRACY

Based on real events

To my daughter Patricia, without whose
invaluable help this book would
have never been possible.

To my wife Martha, for
her permanent support.

To my son Percy, who helped me
with many suggestions after
reading my first draft

To my grandson Matías,
who decided it should be published
and took care of everything necessary to do it.

PART I
GENESIS OF THE PLOT

CHAPTER I
CAPTAIN JOHN FORTESCUE

On a gray foggy morning in November 1584 Captain Fortescue cut a fine figure as he walked the streets of London. He was very handsome, 40 years old, tall and dark complexioned, with a shaved face except for a thin black moustache. That morning he was wearing his best doublet. The doublet was the garment used by gentlemen on top of the shirt in those days. Doublets had tight fronts and backs and ample sleeves. The doublet Fortescue was wearing that day was not in one piece but elaborately cut in strips, His fine cape was laced with gold and he had silver buttons on his hat. As always, he carried his rapier and a matching dagger. His rapier had a thin thrusting blade with two sharpened edges along its entire length to make it a cut and thrust sword.

He accidentally met an acquaintance; a fellow called Bernard Maude, almost as tall and well dressed as himself.

'I was just thinking I should look you up, Bernard. Are you free to accompany me this morning?'

'Sure John, why not? I was just on my way to look at a horse that was offered to me a few days ago. I can do that any other day, if you think I'll be useful to you this morning.'

'I'm planning to take fencing pupils, so that I'll have to move to some place that has ample room to give fencing classes.'

'You're good at fencing, but you're no master.'

'Few beginners are willing to pay expensive lessons with a master. I can teach beginners. Meanwhile, I can take lessons with a master to improve my technique, but I must practice a lot with someone at my own level, like you. That's why I wanted to contact you. How would you like to practice fencing with me two hours a day, almost every day?'

'With that kind of practice I would become a master myself. I like the idea of becoming a very good swordsman, but two hours a day is too much. How about taking one-hour lessons with Rocco Bonetti, three days a week for two months? Also one hour a day practice between ourselves, four days a week for as long as we can, except when either of us is away from London.'

'Excellent Bernard. It's a deal. Now come with me to look at three places being offered for rent that appear to be suitable for what I want.'

Five years before the casual meeting between Captain Fortescue and Bernard Maude, in an area called Black Pool a tall young man knocked at the door of a farm house. A middle-aged woman opened the door and exclaimed, 'my black Foskew' when she saw the man that had just knocked.

A young woman came running from behind and supported the woman, who had almost fainted and started to fall.

A strong big man with a black beard came to the door to look at the stranger standing there.

'Who are you?'

'My name is John Ballard and I've come to see Master Oscar Fortescue, but apparently this is not the right time for a visit, since this lady is not feeling well.'

'She was shocked at seeing you, Sir. You look a lot like a son of ours that was killed in the war in Scotland, 20 years ago. He was only 16 when he left home and he would have looked like you if he had reached the age of 35 or 36.

Black Foskew his playmates used to call him, and that's what my wife said when she saw you. He was dark for an

Englishman, like you and me.'

'I'm sorry I shocked your wife, Sir.'

'Nothing to be sorry about, young man. We like to remember our son, and it's a rare opportunity to see what kind of a man he would have grown to be if he had had the chance. He was killed in Scotland during the siege of Leith. A French army was stationed in Leith in support of Regent Marie de Guise governing Scotland in replacement of her young daughter, Mary Stuart. She was in France and had just married François, the 15-year-old French Dauphin. Lieutenant John Fortescue arrived as part of an army of 6.000 English soldiers under the command of Lord Grey de Wilton. In an unsuccessful attempt to storm Leith, John's superior officer, a captain, was killed and John was made captain to replace him. One night, ten men led by my son were surreptitiously inspecting the walls of Leith to find a weak point to mount a second attack. Just then, the French came out in force, killed or wounded everyone in the English party taking the wounded inside the walls, including Captain John Fortescue.'

At this point, Oscar Fortescue remained silent for over a minute to calm down. Then he continued.

'Leith was never taken, but after the Treaty of Edinburg was signed the French left. We expected our wounded son to be returned, but the French declared he died and was buried in a common grave with all English and Scot prisoners. Not only did we lose our son, but we don't even have a grave to visit.'

'The worst part is that we lost our son to help establish Protestant rule in Scotland, but he was a Catholic, like all of us.'

It was Mrs. Fortescue who had spoken now, after recovering and joining her husband.

Mr. Fortescue jumped and stood up when he heard his wife.

'Silence woman. Master Ballard will think we're traitors.'

'Not at all,' said Ballard. 'Like you, I'm a loyal English Catholic. And I'm not just a Catholic, but a Catholic priest. I was told that you were good Catholics and I came here hoping to get your help. The Jesuit Order, that I have joined, sent me to England to give comfort to the Catholic faithful, like you, that are prevented from assisting mass and practicing their religion.'

'There's no doubt that we will help you, Father Ballard,' said Mrs. Fortescue.

'I gladly accept your help, but it must be very clear to you that there's a price on my head and I will not abuse your kindness staying longer than necessary. I've been supplied by my order with papers as John Stone, to cover my real identity; but these are forged papers and eventually I'll be discovered and sent to the gallows. The people that help me must know that I came here to help Catholics, not to compromise them.'

Mrs. Fortescue now spoke with a strong voice.

'You can throw away your forged papers. We'll give you a cover with legitimate papers. You're not John Stone anymore. You're not John Ballard either. You're John Fortescue. You lost your memory when you received a blow on your head and were captured. The French took advantage of you and took you to France as a French soldier. Only a few months ago you recovered your memory, escaped to England and returned home. We'll go to see Sir Wilfred Lawson, High Sheriff of Cumberland, the highest local authority in this area, who'll certify that you're Captain John Fortescue, back home after all these years. Oscar knows Sir Wilfred quite well.'

'But your son had friends and they'll immediately realize I'm someone else.'

'Charlie and Bill were the best friends of our son. They're good Catholics and will be glad to help a Catholic priest. If they say that you are John Fortescue, everyone in Black Pool will believe it. All you have to do is to invent a good story for your years in France, when you didn't know your own identity.'

'Do you speak French, my son?'

'Yes, Sir. I studied for the priesthood in France and I've been a priest in France for many years. I'm beginning to think that Mrs. Fortescue story is believable.'

'My name is Annie, but from now on you must call me Mom.'

'And you should call me Father. But you must work on a change of personality. You're a serious man while our John had a very outgoing extroverted personality. Charlie and Bill will help you to behave like John Fortescue.'

'If the Jesuits have given you some money, you should spend it on clothes. Our John always dressed very well.'

'My testimony as John's sister, will also contribute to prove your new identity,' said Helen Fortescue, who had also been present since John Ballard entered the house, 'as well as that of my husband, who's a good Catholic.'

Everything went exactly as Anne Fortescue said and every person living in the Black Pool area was convinced that the newcomer was John Fortescue, who after recovering his lost memory had rushed back home.

There were many Catholics in the area of Black Pool, Cumberland, in the North-West corner of England. The Fortescue couple explained to their Catholic friends that before recovering his identity his son had become a priest. As a Catholic priest he had a significant flock of faithful that, because of the Recusancy Acts, outwardly adhered to the Church of England. They attended the evening mass given by John Fortescue every Sunday in a barn of the Fortescue farm that had become a secret church.

Anne Fortescue felt she had recovered the son she had lost years ago. John Ballard rapidly assumed the extroverted personality of the man that he was replacing and became extremely popular in Black Pool, not only among the Catholic faithful but with everyone he met. The hard farm work made him a much stronger man that he had been before. He went out riding on horseback every day and his friends Charlie and Bill taught him fencing.

The years John Ballard resided at the Black Pool farm of the Fortescue family were among the best in his life. They were marred only by the news of the execution of his best friend, Father Edmund Campion. Also, two young priests, that he also knew well, were executed with Campion. Several more executions of priests followed.

The year 1583 was also spoiled by sad events. In February, Oscar Fortescue died suddenly of heart failure. Six months later, Anne Fortescue fell ill and after three weeks she passed away too.

In 1584 John Ballard decided that it was time to move on and that he should travel to France to talk with his superiors in the Jesuit Order about a new assignment he had in mind. With his identity of John Fortescue he applied for a permit to travel to France, which was rapidly granted.

An elegantly dressed gentleman entered Clermont College, the first Jesuit establishment allowed in Paris. At the entrance, he said he was Captain Fortescue and requested to see Father Edmond Auger. Half an hour later he was led to the office of Father Auger, the maximum authority of the Jesuit Order in France with the title of Provincial of France.

'Good morning, Father Provincial.'

'Good morning, Captain. What can I do for you?'

'Don't you recognize me, Father Auger?'

After Auger examined his visitor carefully, he said, 'I've been in contact with you before, but I can't remember the circumstances. Give me a few minutes to think.'

After a few minutes, he exclaimed: 'Just what our order needed, a swashbuckling Jesuit!'

He stood up and walked towards his visitor with extended arms. 'I'm so happy that I must embrace you, my son. I thought you were dead. We never heard of you after you landed in England. Your face hasn't changed except for your silly moustache, but I didn't recognize you immediately because of your stance and the way you walk. Your personality has changed so much, that makes you appear to be a different person.'

'I had to assume the personality of a dead man to use his identity as my cover. After five years it has become my personality. My identity as Captain John Fortescue is a perfect cover that includes a family and lifelong friends.'

Father Ballard then told his superior everything that had happened since he landed in the northwest corner of England, five years before. He talked for nearly two hours giving full details of everything.

'My son, you've performed your duty to give comfort and the support of the Church to the Catholic faithful in England for many years, at great peril to your life. Happily, you're now back in a Catholic country where you can be a normal priest again.'

'But I'm still needed in England and I have a perfect cover that shouldn't be thrown away. In fact, I came back here to ask your permission to move from Black Pool to London in a new assignment.'

'You're stretching your luck, young man. There's a man called Francis Walsingham that wants to capture and execute every Catholic priest in England. He's been very successful so far. He has a wide net of informers and London is precisely the place from where he operates.'

'I know that very well. Also, that he falsely accuses every captured priest of plotting to kill Queen Elizabeth to replace her with Queen Mary Stuart. If you give me the assignment I request and he captures me, I will not be falsely accused.'

'Why not? He dared to accuse your good friend Edmund Campion, who was very well known in England and even had had contact with the queen when he was in Oxford.'

'Yes, he would accuse me if he should capture me, but what I mean is that his accusation would not be false. I want to go to England to organize two teams, one, lead by me, to kill Queen Elizabeth and a second one to simultaneously free Queen Mary Stuart.'

'No John, you're a priest and I'm a priest. I cannot send you to England as an assassin.'

'When you recognized me, you used an expression I liked. You said I was a swashbuckling Jesuit and that was what the order needed. A swashbuckling Jesuit can lead a group of seven or eight determined Catholics to kill Queen Elizabeth and can organize another group to free Mary Stuart.'

'I meant it as a joke. I had no idea of what you had in mind. I will not send you to England as an assassin.'

'I also have an alternative idea. I thought it was unlikely that you would agree to let me kill Elizabeth, but I had to try. Could you send me to London to aid and comfort a relatively small group of Catholics? These few people might develop plans to replace a Protestant queen by a Catholic one. Working with a small group I shouldn't be noticed by the spies working for Walsingham.'

'Pope Pious V accepted the Ridolfi Plot and wanted the English to replace Elizabeth with Mary Stuart. He ex-communicated Elizabeth to encourage the formation of Catholic groups with plans such as those you've just explained. The current Pope, Gregory XIII, thinks the same way about England. We, Jesuits, must support all initiatives that come from the Papacy. You've done your homework and I cannot refuse your request. But I must make myself very clear. You can only act as advisor of your group but cannot be an active member. You cannot participate in any of the two teams you have in mind.'

'Thank you, Father Provincial.'

'I'm accepting your request with great sorrow. I feel I'm sending you to the gallows. You and your small group will be crossing the path of a man that has detected and sent to death everyone plotting the replacement of Queen Elizabeth by Mary Stuart.'

'Do you really think so? Walsingham uncovered three plots, the Norfolk Plot, the Campion Plot and the Throckmorton Plot. Both of us know that the Campion Plot never existed. The accusations against Francis Throckmorton were an obvious sham with no proof except a confession signed under torture. He was supposed to have plotted an invasion of French Catholic troops led by the Duke de Guise in a series of meetings with the Spanish Ambassador. Apart from the fact that Throckmorton's meetings wouldn't be of much help to the Duke de Guise if he wanted to invade England, it's totally unlikely that he would involve himself in a war against the Protestant English. He is already fully involved in a war against the French Huguenots.'

'I'm perfectly aware that the idea of an invasion of England by forces of the Duke de Guise to depose Queen Elizabeth is absurd. I'm afraid that the Duke de Guise might be planning something similar but to depose King Henri III, my king. The king's younger brother, François, Duke d'Anjou, has died recently. This death makes a Huguenot, Henri III, King of Navarre, next in line to the French throne. The Duke de Guise, leader of the Catholic League, does not accept this situation. In such delicate conditions my king has designated me as his Father Confessor, a position in which I must advise him about all matters concerning our Catholic faith. I've accepted and I've resigned as Principal of France of our order. I'm staying only until my replacement is named, since

I have to devote myself full time to the service of the king.'

'I'm shocked by the news, but certainly the king has elected the best possible Father Confessor. In any case, continuing our conversation, I see that you agree with my belief that the Throckmorton Plot never existed and was invented by Walsingham. If he obviously invented the second and third plot of the three he uncovered, he must also have invented the first one. Walsingham is very good to detect the plots he invents and to arrest priests that expose themselves for several years giving masses attended by hundreds of people. In my new assignment, I'll give mass only to a small group of not more than twenty people that will know me as Father Ballard. To everyone else, I'll be Captain Fortescue.'

'You'll need funds to carry out your plans. Our order will not provide you with any funds, but James Beaton, Archbishop of Glasgow and Ambassador of Queen Mary Stuart in France, has access to a fortune that Mary has in Paris. It can be expected he should be happy to provide funds for the liberation of his queen. I'll arrange for Archbishop Beaton to meet you here so that you can explain your plans and request the funds you'll need.'

'Perhaps I should be the one to visit the archbishop.'

'No. Walsingham has many spies in Paris and I'm sure he's checking everyone that visits Archbishop Beaton. You should remain in Clermont College as long as you stay in Paris. You're now taking a most dangerous path and your plans must be kept in the utmost secrecy, known only to a handful of strictly selected men that you'll advise. Of course, you must realize that when requesting funds from the archbishop you should only talk about your plans to set Mary Stuart free, without any mention of your other idea.'

Twenty days after his first meeting with Father Auger, John Ballard returned to England and went directly back to the Fortescue farm. He told those that knew his real identity that the Jesuit Order had given him a new assignment in London and that he would move there soon.

After talking with his friends, Ballard was ready to install himself in London but he did not go directly from Black Pool to London. Instead, he travelled for nearly two months to several places, to visit English noblemen that Father Auger had told him were Catholics that could be trusted. He told all of them that Queen Mary Stuart would be freed soon and that it was very important that all Catholic English noblemen should rise in rebellion right after she was freed. They should demand that the Scottish Queen should be officially declared to be the rightful successor of childless Queen Elizabeth. After the completion of this task Ballard settled in London as affluent Captain Fortescue, without telling anyone that he was a Catholic priest.

One week after he settled in London, while he was eating lunch at the Dragon and Unicorn pub, a very elegantly dressed gentleman approached his table.

'Are you Captain Fortescue, Sir?'

'Yes, I am.'

'I'm pleased to meet you, Captain Fortescue. I'm Roland Chateneuf and I work at the French Embassy in London. The Ambassador, Monsieur Michel de Castlenau, Sieur de Mauvissière, has requested me to contact you.'

'I was expecting to be contacted at this pub. Please take a seat at my table.'

Once seated, Chateneuf spoke in a very low voice.

'I have funds for you that have been sent from France. Please give me your London address.'

After Ballard gave the address, Chateneuf continued.

'Tomorrow morning I'll give you the amount Archbishop Beaton has sent. I understand he arranged the amount with you.'

'That's correct.'

'I've been told that you may need additional funds in the future. If you should need more funds you can find me at this pub the 10th of every month between 4 and 5 o' clock in the afternoon.'

One afternoon, near the end of January 1585, a young man presented himself at the large house where Captain Fortescue gave fencing lessons. A middle-aged housemaid attended him.

'My name is Gilbert Gifford and I would like to see Captain Fortescue.'

'The captain is busy right now but will be available in about half an hour.'

'Is it all right if I wait for him here?'

'Certainly, and you can sit down in any of these chairs until he comes.'

Twenty minutes later Captain Fortescue came into the entrance hall accompanied by Bernard Maude, who went straight to the door to go out.

'Goodbye, John.'

'Goodbye, Bernard.'

Captain Fortescue addressed the visitor as soon as Maude left. Gilbert Gifford was a young man in his early twenties, of medium height, slightly overweight, with brown hair, brown greenish eyes and a pleasant, shaved face.

What can I do for you, Master Gifford? Are you interested in taking fencing lessons?'

'I'm here to assist you in your work in England, Father Ballard. Archbishop Beaton sends me. I bring a letter sent to you by Master Charles Paget, assistant of the Archbishop, explaining everything about me, including the fact that I've been ordained as a deacon by Cardinal de Guise in Rheims.'

John Ballard was shocked to be addressed as Father Ballard, since no one had used that name in England for many years. In Black Pool, even those that knew he was a priest addressed him as Father Fortescue, while in London no one knew he was a priest or that his real name was Ballard. The priest recovered in less than a second to behave again as self-assured as usual and read the letter.

'Very good, I see that you studied in Rheims, at Douay College and also for some time in Rome, at the English School.'

'In a few months, Archbishop Beaton will send you more men that can be trusted. In the meantime, I must help you to establish contact with Queen Mary Stuart. All contact with her has been interrupted since the execution of Sir Francis Throckmorton. But now I'm worried about something else. Do you know well the gentleman that just left?'

'Bernard Maude? I've known him for a relatively short time, but I like him. I could say that he has become a great friend after I moved from the north of England to London.'

'Does he know you're a priest?'

'No one in London knows that I'm a priest, except you, now.'

'I'm glad to hear that. I'm not totally certain that your friend works for Walsingham, but someone that looks like him does. When I arrived in London on board a ship that came from France, a group of Walsingham's men came on board to check several passengers, inspecting all their belongings. One tall man in that party did look like the gentleman that just left. I was scared to death because I had on me the letter that I just gave you. I had it under my clothes, against my skin, but I was not picked for inspection and they didn't even search my luggage.'

'I can't believe that Bernard would work for Walsingham,

but we must check.'

'I must follow this man to see if he goes to Whitehall Palace, where Walsingham has his office. Until then it should be better that he doesn't meet me.'

'I must show you this place now. Do you need a room to stay? There's plenty of room in this big old house.'

Gifford had expected to be invited to stay with Father Ballard and he had planned to accept the invitation, but now decided to decline after looking at the very poor state of conservation of the house Ballard had rented.

'Archbishop Beaton provided me with some funds before I left France and I've already made arrangements for my stay in London for some time. Perhaps later I should move here, if it is convenient.'

Father Ballard then showed Gifford the place he had rented, which had several halls large enough for fencing practice.

'This must have been a magnificent mansion many years ago, Father Ballard, but is in a rather sorry state right now. I understand Archbishop Beaton has provided you with ample funds to get established in London. Why didn't you rent a house in better conditions?'

'I rent this house at a much lower price than I could rent any other I've visited and it's perfectly suitable for what I need, ample space for fencing lessons, large rooms where the group of devote Catholics that I must gather can meet and living quarters for me and for any other in the group that may need a place to stay in London.'

'As a Jesuit priest you made poverty vows and what you say makes sense. But you're pretending to be Captain Fortescue and no retired Captain that moves to London after receiving an inheritance, would have rented a house in such a state of disrepair.'

The priest was embarrassed by the veiled admonition received from someone half his age.

'Perhaps you are right and I should do some repairs to cover appearances.'

'I've an idea. I have references about a man that works as a carpenter but is actually a "Jack of all Trades" and can do all sorts of repairs. In his youth he was a soldier that fought for Queen Elizabeth in Scotland, just as you're supposed to have fought. He's a widower with no children and lives alone in a rented room that probably costs him most of what he earns. I'll go to meet him. If after meeting him I consider him adequate, I'll bring him here to make arrangements with you. You can offer good wages to him and a room in this house. He can work full time to make this residence more suitable for an affluent retired Captain.'

'Now that you tell me I realize that you're absolutely right. I need a man to work here every day to fix all that needs to be fixed, starting with the leaky roofs.'

Late in the evening of the day when he visited Father Ballard, Gifford was looking for a man called John Savage, in the miserable London neighborhood where he lived. After nearly half an hour asking questions, Gifford knocked at the door of the room where Savage lived. A suspicious man opened the door just a narrow crack and looked at Gifford from the inside.

'Who are you and what do you want?'

'My name is Gifford and I'm looking for John Savage to offer him an opportunity for profitable employment.'

'I'm Savage, come in,' said Savage after checking that the well dressed, not very strong young man standing next to his door was alone.

After entering, Gifford noticed with pleasure that the modest room used by Savage was clean and neat. The room was furnished only with a table, a chair and a bed.

'Before you start talking about the job you're offering, you should know that I already earn a very good wage with the furniture maker that employs me, 16 pence a day.'

Gifford did not believe it was true that Savage was earning as much as he was saying, but he had not come to argue.

'I'm not the man that can give you a job so that I cannot discuss wages with you, but I don't believe that the wages you're used to earning will be a difficulty. A friend of mine is a retired captain, Captain Fortescue. He fought against the French in Scotland. He was badly wounded and captured by the French. He lost his memory and the French took advantage of that to take him to France instead of releasing him when the war was over. His family believed he was dead, but in 1579 he recovered his memory, escaped from France and returned to the farm where his family lived. Last year, both his parents died. As he inherited some money, he left the farm to his sister and settled in London. He has rented a large house where he gives fencing lessons. The large house used to be a mansion many years ago, but now has leaky roofs and is in a bad state of disrepair. I suggested to the captain that someone that's able to do all kinds of repair jobs should live at the house and make it a more suitable place for him to live and give fencing lessons.'

'I remember Captain Fortescue, a tall man as dark as I am. I was not directly under him when I was a soldier, but I met him and liked him. He's about the same age I am. He was a lieutenant and was made a captain only a few days before the French wounded him and then took him prisoner. I thought he was dead and I'm glad to hear that he's alive and well. I'll be most pleased to go to see him, even if he cannot meet the wages I earn.'

'I can pick you up here tomorrow evening and take you to see Captain Fortescue. At what time do you want me to come?'

'Six o'clock in the evening would be fine, if you agree.'

'Excellent. I'll be here at six o'clock sharp.'

John Savage was a man that in 1579 had sworn to God he would kill Queen Elizabeth. In 1584 he was going to meet a man that was planning to organize a team to kill her.

CHAPTER II
CHURCH IN THE ATTIC

Let us go back to 1579. The same day that in Black Pool Father John Ballard was offered a new identity as Captain John Fortescue, in London Anthony Babington went to give his condolences to a good friend, Peter Thornwell, who had recently lost his father. Peter's father, Thomas Thornwell, had been Baron Mountcrest, so that now his friend had become Lord Mountcrest.

Anthony was a thin, 17-year-old youngster of medium height, soft features in a round face, brown eyes and light brown hair. When he reached Peter's house the butler took him to the drawing room where he found Michael Hussley, Peter's best friend. Michael greeted Anthony warmly. He, like Peter, was four years older than Anthony and had always had a protective attitude towards him. He was almost two meters tall, thin but very broad shouldered, with short blond hair and light blue eyes in a face with regular features and a distinctive square jaw with a dimple in the center.

'Peter will be with us in a moment', said Michael. 'We arrived in London rather late last night and I stayed here for the night.'

'Thank you for coming so promptly to see me, Anthony', said Peter entering the room and giving Anthony a warm hug.

Peter was a bit taller than Michael, was also thin but athletic and had an oval face with regular features, short dark brown hair and intense blue eyes.

'I'm so sorry', said Anthony. 'Not only had I always liked Lord Mountcrest, but my mother told me that he and my father were great friends.' Anthony's father had died several years ago.

Anthony and his two friends were from Dethick, in the north

of England. The three of them talked about their mutual friends in the north, with Anthony asking questions while Peter and Michael told him news about his friends. After several minutes of conversation Anthony told Peter about Father Campion.

'Peter, if at this time of bereavement you should wish to talk to a Catholic priest, I have come in contact with a truly remarkable one, Father Edmund Campion. I can arrange a meeting with him if you wish.'

The three friends, like most noblemen in the north of England, remained in the Catholic faith, but to comply with the Recusancy Acts had to appear to be members of the Church of England. Non-compliance meant property confiscation and imprisonment. It was the same policy that in Spain the Catholic rulers applied to a large and prosperous Jewish community. In Spain, Jews had to appear to be Catholic.

Earlier this year, 1579, Anthony had joined a secret society of young men formed to protect the handful of Catholic priests that were attending the need of laymen prevented from attending Catholic services publicly. As a member of the secret society he was put in contact with Father Campion, a well-known former Deacon of the Church of England that had gone to France to become a Catholic priest. Ballard was not the only English priest sent to England by the Jesuits. Several priests were sent and their capture was one of the priorities of Sir Francis Walsingham, Principal Secretary of Queen Elizabeth. He had created the first counterintelligence service in history and had a wide net of informers both inside and outside of England.

'Anthony, you should know that I don't feel about the Recusancy Acts as strongly as you do. Of course I resent them and I would prefer to attend Catholic services if I had a choice. I don't agree but I can understand the political motivations, which are the same in all countries, Protestant or Catholic. Every time rulers have tried to allow both

Protestants and Catholics to practice their faith, bigots have made chaos. But we are English, we have a Parliament, eventually Parliament will repeal the Acts and we Catholics will be allowed to practice our faith. But yes, I'm most certainly interested in meeting Father Edmund Campion. He made quite a good reputation for himself during the time he was in Oxford. I had no idea he'd returned secretly to England.'

'He will celebrate Mass in a private home tomorrow at 7 in the evening. If you come one hour earlier, you'll be able to talk with him. I'm leaving the address in a slip of paper that you should destroy after memorizing its contents. But I don't understand what you are telling me about the political motivations of the Recusancy Acts.'

'Do you mean that you don't understand what I said about bigots making chaos every time the ruler tries to reconcile Catholics and Protestants?'

'Yes, that's what I mean.'

'I could spend all day giving you examples in full detail, but I'm a busy man and I've been out of town for over two months. I will just tell you that fanatics from the majority have killed those in the minority in such cases. One attempt to reconcile Catholics and Huguenots in France ended in what is called the Saint Bartholomew Massacre. It started with many Huguenots killed in Paris on Saint Bartholomew's Day, continued in Paris for weeks and extended to other French cities for months. In the end more than 10.000 Huguenots were killed. We Catholics are in the minority in England. How would you feel about more than 10.000 Catholics killed here?'

'French Catholics and Protestants are at war right now.'

'Yes Anthony, their Seventh Religious War. I understand that you want to be a lawyer like Michael and myself. It is then important that you should study the recent history of Europe from the time of Henry VII of England and Isabel I of Spain.

In the fifteen hundreds, the cinquecento, as the Italians say, we're living the most important time period in history. But everything started towards the end of last century.'

Peter and Michael arrived at the address given by Anthony at 6 pm.

'Good evening, may I see Father Campion,' said Peter to the elderly gentleman that opened the door.

'Good evening, Lord Mountcrest, Master Hussley, I'm Jonathan Darcy and was expecting you. Please follow me and I'll take you to see Father Campion.'

Peter and Michael entered a well-furnished large house following the gentleman that opened the door. The old furniture was all heavy oak. They went up massive oak stairs and entered a large hall. It had about a dozen chairs near the walls and in the center only a ladder placed under an opening in the paneled ceiling.

'Kindly go up this ladder to the attic. Father Campion is waiting to see you.'

The two young men ascended the ladder, reaching a very large attic lighted only by the feeble evening light coming through a sizeable window at one end of the room. At both sides of the attic the low tapering roof did not leave enough standing room. In the center there was plenty of room and about 50 people were already there talking softly in several groups. An altar with a white mantelpiece had been placed at one end, near the large window. Two rows of long wooden benches almost filled the entire attic. An aisle was left between the two rows and in this aisle was the opening through which Peter and Michael had entered the attic.

A man, that was part of a group of four talking near the altar, left the others and approached the two friends with an extended hand.

'I'm Father Campion', he said, ' Anthony told me that you

were coming and he also told me of your recent loss, Lord Mountcrest.'

Father Campion was in his early forties, tall although not as tall as Peter and Michael, had short brown hair, a thin moustache and a very short shaggy beard around his face.

'I'm honored to meet you, Father', said Michael, ' but I should leave and let you talk alone with Peter.'

Michael left Peter so that he could talk freely with the priest and proceeded to examine the attic that was going to be used as a church for today's services. He looked at the window, a lattice window in which small pieces of glass were held together by strips of lead. It was partially open. He looked outside and saw that it gave to a relatively small backyard covered with grass that had a shed next to the limit with a similar backyard of a neighboring house behind. They were in a house with neighboring houses attached on both sides. He was concerned about being in a place from which it was very difficult to escape, while being engaged in an illegal activity most severely punished by law. Furthermore, in charge of the arrests and of bringing culprits to justice for this type of activity was Sir Francis Walsingham, who had informers that monitored everything that might pose the slightest danger to the queen.

Michael decided to examine the roof. He opened the left side window pane widely. He stepped onto the lower edge of the window, got out to a wide windowsill and from there grabbed the edge of the roof with both hands. Being a very strong man, he easily lifted himself to get on top of the roof. The side of the roof where he was formed a V with the roof of the house next door. The cleavage between the two roofs was the only place where those attending the mass could hide if Walsingham's men should barge in. Of course, he and Peter could escape easily going from one roof to the next until reaching a place where they could climb down unseen by those that would arrest them. But they could not leave all the others, so hiding in the cleavage was the only option.

Michael came back into the attic through the window. Several men looked at him with obvious astonishment. One youngster, about 16 or 17 years of age, approached him. 'Hello, I'm Charles Tilney, a friend of Anthony's. I've been examining the roof and perhaps you reached the same conclusion I did. The only places to hide, if worse comes to worst, are the cleavages between the roof of this house and those of the two neighboring houses at its side.'

'I'm Michael Hussley and yes, I agree with you about the only places to hide. But if those that are looking for us reach this clean attic they'll know the place is being used for large gatherings. They will continue looking until they find the crowd using the attic.'

'We agree again. I have four boxes full of dust to spread all over after we leave, if we should have to leave, that would make the place look as if it hasn't been used in 40 years. You must have noticed that we haven't cleaned the spider webs in the ceiling. But this is only a precaution. The dust may be used some day, but not today, the first time that mass will be given in this attic. Our Dutch brothers in Amsterdam have a Church in the Attic (1) that already has been operating for several months with no problems.'

'Sir Francis Walsingham is not in Amsterdam, but here in London. I'm glad that you already have four boxes of dust here since it's quite probable the house will be raided this evening. If that's the case most of those assembled here are incapable of getting to the roof without help. My suggestion is that everybody should line up to go to the roof, half of them this side of the window with me going to the roof and you helping them to stand on the windowsill. From the roof I can lift everyone standing on the windowsill and place him or her on the roof. My friend Peter and Father Campion can go to the other side of the window, with Father Campion helping them and Peter lifting everyone to the roof.'

'Excellent. Our plan was to have two of us lifting people to the roof on this side and another two on the other side, but you and your friend are big and strong enough to do it alone.'

Peter was still in deep conversation with the priest and Michael examined the crowd in the attic. Almost everybody was sitting now and most of the long wooden benches in front of the altar were now full. Michael estimated there were about 80 people waiting for the mass, mostly young men and a few women.

When the priest left Peter to put on his vestments for the mass, Peter took a seat on one of the last two benches and Michael sat next to him.

'I saw that you went through the window to explore the area, Michael. Can you tell me anything?'

Michael then told him briefly the plan he had discussed with Charles Tilney.

'I'm afraid you're right and we will be raided this evening. There are nearly one hundred people here tonight. To get such a large crowd Anthony and his friends must have made more than 300 invitations. With so many people involved someone in the large web of Walsingham informers must have heard about it. It was a mistake to come here, but I'm still glad I had my meeting with Father Campion. He's the most spiritual man I ever met. I really needed his words.'

The mass started and all whispered conversations ceased.

Earlier that afternoon Sir Francis Walsingham, Principal Secretary of Queen Elizabeth, was interrogating a suspect. Walsingham was a tall man in his late forties, of dark complexion, aquiline nose, dark brown eyes, brown hair, moustache and a very neat small, pointed beard covering only the chin. He was wearing black clothes, as was his custom.

'My dear Mr. Savage, you can talk to me freely and you can leave as an unharmed free man. No friend of yours knows that you're here and after you leave none will know you came. I have a responsibility to make sure that no Catholic group is planning to kill our queen to put Mary Stuart on the throne. We know that you have Catholic sympathies. That's no crime and I respect your sympathies, but I also know that a Jesuit priest called Edmund Campion entered this country illegally, is in London today and will give mass this evening for Catholic sympathizers like you. According to our information, you've been invited, so that you must know the address. Please give us that address.'

John Savage was in his early forties, short but strong with a barrel chest, of swarthy complexion, dark brown eyes and hair. His working man clothes contrasted with the elaborate gentlemen outfit of elegant Sir Francis.

'I know nothing. I used to be a Catholic during the reign of Queen Mary because that was the law. I am a Protestant now because Queen Elizabeth says that's the law now. I'm a poor man. I was a soldier and fought for Queen Elizabeth in Scotland. I'm not a highly educated man that knows the religious difference between Catholics and Protestants, but I prefer Protestants for the Queen of England rather than Catholics for the Pope of Rome.'

'Mr. Savage, you have three choices. The first one is to continue with your denial of any knowledge of a Catholic mass. The second one is to tell us the information that we need and then leave. And the third one is to join us and get well paid for your services.'

'Oh, thank you Your Excellency, I can start to work for you immediately.'

'I'm glad to hear this. You can start right now giving us the address of the place where they will give the Catholic mass this evening.'

'I' can't do that because I don't know anything about any mass, but I'll start to work on it right away.'

'I'm afraid that's not good enough. Someone else will

continue this interrogation.'

Walsingham rang a bell and two men came in. 'Take this man to talk with Tim,' said Walsingham to the two men.

Walsingham was upset for failing to obtain the information he needed. Savage was going to be tortured now, in case he did know the address they needed, but the Principal Secretary actually believed his claim that he did not know anything. He never expected good information from torture. It was the ancient method of the stick and the carrot, the combination of menace and bribery that gave good results. Torture was necessary for the very unusual cases of someone that wanted to play hero, but tortured men usually told lies, anything to stop the pain. Of course, the best use for torture was to obtain a confession from someone that had to be eliminated and there was no proof against him, but it was generally useless to obtain information. Savage might give an address that would result in a complete waste of time.

Half an hour later the two men that had taken Savage away came back. 'Savage said he doesn't know the address because he wasn't invited,' said one of the men, 'but that the mass will be given in the home of Jonathan Darcy, who lives near the Black Dragon pub. We'll go to the pub right away to investigate the address."

'That's not necessary', said Walsingham, 'Jonathan Darcy is on our surveillance list because he is a son of Thomas Darcy, beheaded because of his involvement in the Pilgrimage of Grace. I'll give you the address in a minute. Twenty men headed by Jones should go there to arrest everyone in the house. I'll finish some paperwork here and will arrive a bit later.'

John Savage had been trying to figure out some name to give to his interrogator when he was shown the rack, but not even one of all the people he knew in London had an entire house to live in. After the interrogator started to stretch him, causing great pain, he remembered someone pointing to an old fellow in the pub.

'That's Jonathan Darcy, the son of a beheaded traitor.'

That Jonathan was well dressed and must have a big house in the neighborhood of the pub, so that Savage accused him to stop the torture and the pain.

He had no idea that it was precisely in the home of Jonathan Darcy that Father Campion had just started mass.

When the party of 20 Walsingham men reached the house of Jonathan Darcy and Jones banged the entrance door with a series of hard blows, Anthony Babington rushed up the ladder and with head and shoulders emerging from the trap door shouted, 'we're being raided, place the cover on this opening immediately.'

He came down the ladder, removed it and took it to a window opening to the small garden. From the window he lowered the ladder to the garden, where it was taken by one of his friends, Thomas Salisbury, who rapidly took it to the shed.

Jonathan Darcy opened the door, introduced himself to Jones and was going to ask what he wanted when he was pushed aside by Jones, falling to the floor. Anthony and his friend Thomas were already on the ground floor and were also pushed aside by Jones' people dispersing in all directions and searching every room of the house.

Jones stayed in the entrance hall. After a few minutes they all started to return to the entrance hall.

'There's no one upstairs,' said one of the men.

'There's no one here on the ground floor either, except for these three,' said another one.

Anthony and Thomas had helped the elderly Mr. Darcy to

stand up again. The three of them were standing near the entrance door.

'Do you have a basement here?' asked Jones to Darcy brusquely.

Before Darcy had a chance to answer one of Jones' men said, 'I've been there with three men and there's no one in the basement.'

'Jim and I have been in the shed at the end of the backyard and there's no one there either.'

Jones addressed Darcy. 'Why are there no servants here?'

'Because today is Sunday, I'm a dutiful member of the Church of England and I gave the day off to the three servants that work here.'

The entrance door had been left opened and Sir Francis Walsingham walked into the house.

Jones addressed his superior. 'We haven't found anyone here but these three. The elderly man is the owner of this house, Jonathan Darcy. We checked the basement, the ground floor, the top floor and the tool shed in the backyard.'

'You haven't mentioned checking the attic. From the street I could see that this house has a very large attic,' said Walsingham.

'We didn't see any entrance to the attic,' mumbled Jones, obviously embarrassed.

'You should have told Darcy to show it to you' said Walsingham. Then he turned around and faced Darcy. 'Please show us the entrance to the attic, Master Darcy.'

'I inherited this house ten years ago when an uncle of mine died. There must be an entrance to the attic, but I was never told about it. I never opened another entrance because the house is much larger than I ever needed, particularly after my wife died last year.'

'Don't you worry; we'll open one for you right away.'

Walsingham turned around again to face Jones. 'To open an entrance to the attic all that's needed is an axe and a ladder.'

'I brought an axe,' said Jones.

'There's a ladder in the tool shed,' said one the men that had been there.

'Bring the ladder upstairs,' said Walsingham to the man who had just talked. 'Let's go upstairs. Jones, bring the axe and one of your strongest men.'

Then he turned around and faced Darcy. 'Please stay down-stairs but don't remain standing, of course; go to a hall where you can sit and wait for me.'

Walsingham reached the upper floor and spoke to Jones again. 'I want to examine the ceiling in every room. Perhaps I may detect the hidden trap door to the attic.'

When he reached the hall with the paneled ceiling he said, 'the trap door to enter the attic must be here.' He was right since the trap door was at the center of that ceiling and included four panels, but it was impossible to detect any difference in the edges of the panels.

'I can't find the trap door, so we must open another entrance with the axe. I don't want to damage this nice ceiling. In any case it's easier to open a hole in a room where the wooden planks of the floor of the attic are in plain sight, as the ceiling of the room we just left.' The man bringing the ladder was already there. Jones strongest man started his work with the axe as soon as Walsingham indicated where they should open a hole in the ceiling. He elected a place where a very large knot in the wood weakened the plank.

Walsingham had expected this raid to be a failure. Under torture Savage had to come up with the address of a house and the Principal Secretary thought it was likely he did not know anyone that had a house. He had said that the house was near the Black Dragon pub and this house was quite far away from that pub. In the pub someone must have pointed out Darcy to Savage, perhaps telling him he was the son of a beheaded traitor. That was someone Savage figured should have a house and he could accuse to stop the torture. A glimmer of hope was given by the ignorance claimed by Darcy about the entrance to the attic. Maybe he wanted to postpone the inevitable, but it was also possible he really never bothered to learn about the entrance to the attic. Very soon his men would enter that attic to find out if there really was a crowd to be arrested there.

In about 15 minutes the strong man using the axe had opened a hole sufficiently large to go through and he entered the attic with a lighted candle.

'There's nothing here except spider webs and dust,' he shouted from the hole.

'Go up there to confirm,' Walsingham told Jones.

Jones went up the ladder to the attic with a lighted candle in one hand. The hole through which he entered was in a place of the attic where the height of the roof was low and full of spider webs that clung to his face, hair and clothes. He had to crawl on hands and knees to get to a place where he could stand, getting dust all over him.

He walked along the full length of the attic and was satisfied it was completely empty. There was no light coming through the window, because night had fallen. He came back to the entrance hole and climbed down the ladder.

With face, hands and clothes very dirty he said, 'it's like the old man told us. This dirty attic is empty and hasn't been used in many years, much more than ten years I would guess.'

Walsingham usually checked personally everything he was told by his men, but he also was very neat and well dressed and had no desire to get as dirty as Jones going to the attic. He accepted the result of Jones' examination that confirmed what was said by the man that entered first.

If Walsingham had found the trap door that was un-detectable in the paneled ceiling, everything would have been different. If he had entered the attic without getting dirty, after finding a window there would have told a couple of his men to go to the roof and would have imprisoned Campion and all those hiding there. Jones had seen the window but had paid no attention to it and did not even mention it to Walsingham.

Darcy's ploy of not indicating the entrance to the attic worked out much better than could have been expected. The idea was just to give more time to those attending the mass to go to the roof, but if Walsingham had entered the attic through the real entrance those hiding in the roof would have been found out.

The factor of luck was that the knot in the wood that weakened one plank, was in a place that made Walsingham make the decision to open an entrance in what resulted to be an uncomfortable place to enter the attic.

Walsingham went back downstairs with his men. He entered the large hall where Darcy and the two youngsters waited for him sitting on armchairs. He sat in front of Darcy.

'You must excuse us, Master Darcy. We received false in-formation that indicated that a Catholic mass was being celebrated at your home. Surely you understand that it was necessary to check if this was true.'

'Of course I understand, Sir Francis, and you and your men are certainly excused for any inconveniency to me.'

'Regrettably, we also damaged the ceiling of one of the rooms to go to the attic.'

'That's entirely my fault. There must be an entrance to the attic somewhere and it was very foolish of me not to find out. I'll make a new entrance using the hole your men made with an axe, so that no damage has been done.'

'And who are the two young men that are here with you?'

'One is Anthony Babington, a grandson of my late brother George. Anthony has always treated me as if I were his grandfather. Since I never had any children his devotion has been a great comfort to me. This evening he came so that I wouldn't have to have supper alone. I'm a widower and the house servants have the day off today, being Sunday. The other boy is his good friend, Thomas Salisbury.'

Walsingham wrote both names down in his notebook and next to Anthony's name he wrote, "descends from a traitor". Next to the other name he put, "friend of above".

When Walsingham left Darcy's place he spoke to Jones. 'I'm going home now. Let Savage go free. He's no Catholic, has been a soldier of the queen that fought for her in Scotland and was accused by someone with a grudge against him. That's the problem with a network of informers; sometimes instead of informing about enemies of the queen they inform about their own enemies. Savage had to use his inventiveness to stop the torture and must have remembered over-hearing something about Darcy in the pub. He was perfectly justified for inventing a lie. It was not a complete waste of time for us since it's convenient to check on sons of traitors once in a while to keep them straight.'

John Savage was on the rack, still in pain, since after he gave an address the tension on his limbs was not relieved. Obviously, they had gone to check on the address and he wondered what would happen after they found out he had lied. Would they kill him immediately or would they continue to torture him? He hoped they would kill him with no further torture.

His interrogator had looked at him and said. 'Enjoy the suspension of your torture while it lasts. The stretching will continue. You're a very short man and I'll make you grow.'

The interrogator left and Savage was alone for nearly two hours. He wondered how on earth he had come to be in such predicament. He had never been involved in any religious discussion with anybody.

Then he remembered. A week ago, while he was drinking with friends in the pub, a fellow leaving while talking to two men pushed him aside rudely to get to the door and half the beer in his mug was spilled to the floor. A discussion followed and he struck the fellow in the mouth with a clenched fist. The fellow fell to the floor with a bloody mouth; his friends lifted him and took him out of the pub.

The stranger he struck down must have been one of Walsingham's informers and he took his revenge sending him to be tortured to death in an interrogation he could not answer.

When Tim, the interrogator, came back he looked upset. 'You lied to me and I don't like liars. If you couldn't answer you should have let me continue with the stretching until the pain made you faint.' While talking, Tim continued to stretch Savage. 'And I have received incredible orders. I should let you go unpunished.'

In spite of the orders he received, Tim continued to stretch Savage for a while. Then he released all the tension in the rack and started to untie Savage.

John Savage could not believe what was happening. He thought it could be another twist to make him suffer, raising hopes for freedom before his execution. But just in case, it was important to look at Tim with great attention. He had to engrave Tim's features in his mind, because if he really was set free he would look for Tim to kill him.

In an instant he swore he would kill three people. Two were Tim and the drunken idiot that had taken revenge accusing him of being a Catholic that might be plotting to kill the queen.

The third one was not Walsingham. If he was left to go free, it would be because Walsingham had pardoned his life, so in return he would pardon Walsingham's life.

John Savage swore to God that he would kill Queen Elizabeth.

CHAPTER III
COURIER

Anthony Babington kissed his young wife and left his house to go to Lincoln's Inn, where he was studying law. Shortly after the narrow escape from prison when Walsingham's men raided the home of Jonathan Darcy, he went back to Dethick to marry his childhood sweetheart, Margery Draycott. Both of them were only 17 years old. To study law he did not go to a University like his older friends, Peter and Michael, both of them Oxford graduates. Instead, he returned to London where he could enjoy an active social life while studying at his own pace. He was accepted at one of the four Inns of Court, Lincoln's Inn. The members of the Inns of Court were all experienced men of the law, but the inns also took students that were taught by members. They studied not only law, but how to sing, dance and play instrumental music. Most students also had their lodgings at the Inns of Court but Anthony, being a married man, could not do so. Anyway, he often dined at Lincoln's Inn.

Jonathan Darcy, an uncle of Anthony's mother who was a widower with no children, after being ill for several weeks had died the previous month. He left in inheritance his large London house to Anthony, who had always been very close to him. With many friends and acquaintances, a large house and the important yearly income left by his father, Anthony was starting a brilliant social life in London with his beautiful young wife.

Just after he entered the Lincoln's Inn building, where he was taking lessons, he met a fellow student, Henry Dunn. He also was a member of the secret society for the protection of Catholic priests. The two friends went outside of the building to the large park surrounding the institution to talk for a while, since it was early for the class they would attend that day.

'Is father Campion still in Berkshire, Henry?'

'I was with him in Berkshire two weeks ago. He's constantly on the move between Northamptonshire, Oxfordshire and Berkshire. No one knows where he is until he appears suddenly. This is the best way to protect those that give him refuge in their homes.'

'The Privy Council is now worried about him. They have declared that he recently entered the country with treasonous rather than religious purposes, now in mid-1580, after they had been chasing him for almost a year.'

'Father Campion told me he knows that he'll be captured and probably executed since he cannot be always on the run. But he's been ordered to come here for spiritual support of the Catholics that are prevented from practicing their faith. He's preparing a statement called "Challenge to the Privy Council", explaining the true reasons for his coming.'

'He must be wrong about his capture. There are many like us that can protect him and other priests.'

'Are you forgetting Anthony that it was only by a difference of a few minutes that he wasn't captured last year, when about one hundred people escaped through a window to sit on a roof?'

'How can I forget it? I was sitting in front of Walsingham when he told Uncle Jonathan he was giving up the search.'

'But we should talk about more cheerful things. My father has just agreed with me about the fact that if I'm going to be a lawyer, I should know Paris well. I must apply for a travel permit and, if I get it, my father will give me the funds I need. Would you like to join me?'

'Perhaps I should take advantage of the fact that Margery and I have no children yet to make a trip with her right away. And Paris is just the place for that trip. Yes, I would love to join you and I'll apply for my permit tomorrow morning.'

Three weeks after their conversation in the park of Lincoln's Inn, Anthony Babington, his wife Margery and his friend Henry Dunn were traveling across the English Channel from London to Boulogne Sur Mer in a three mast Dutch flyboat fitted for passenger traffic. It was a ship light enough to navigate rivers and coastal waters and seaworthy enough to cross the channel. The French did not allow passenger ships to go to Calais, a port that had been an English enclave on the coast of France for many years.

The accommodations for the short crossing were not too comfortable. Anthony obtained a place for Margery and him to lie down in a very small cabin, but Henry only had a place to sit on a hard bench.

Upon arrival they rented horses to travel to Paris. 18-year-old Margery was as good a rider as her husband, perhaps even better. In her father's estate she used to ride astride, but in front of strangers she could ride sideways on a side-saddle for ladies.

She brought her own side-saddle in which she was facing directly ahead with her left foot in a stirrup and her right leg also on the left side with her knee over a horn in the front part of the saddle. It was much better than olderside-saddles on which women had feeble support and had to turn to look ahead rather than sideways.

In the 16th century roads were just dirt tracks. People travelled by horse. Some rich people rode in carriages, but these were very uncomfortable because they did not have springs and roads were very bumpy. It was worse in France than in England, where they constantly had men repairing roads. Anthony, his wife and his friend travelled with a group of riders since lonely rides on roads were very dangerous because of the assaults by highwaymen. They tried to find enough young travelers to travel fast, but they had to settle for a mixed group that travelled at the leisured pace of about 10 leagues (50 km) per day. It was a 50-league trip that required 5 days. Margery was the only woman rider in the group since all the other women sat behind their husbands, holding on to them to stay on the horses.

Anthony, Margery and Henry spoke fluent French like most educated members of the English nobility. They enjoyed the 5-day ride along the French countryside, crossing through quaint little villages and having tasty lunches and suppers.

Sleeping quarters were the only drawback, since at the inns they rented space for sleeping at rather stiff prices in bedrooms with 6 to 10 beds, and each bed was for three people. Anthony paid for one extra space each night so he and Margery were not uncomfortable, except for the fact that they had to sleep fully dressed. Henry had to share his bed with strangers and it wasn't too bad, except for the time it was his turn to sleep in the center.

The fifth evening they arrived in Paris. Henry went to the home of a French nobleman that was a friend of his father, who had made arrangements for him to stay there. Anthony did not have time to make any arrangements since he had made the decision to travel only three weeks ago. He had written and sent through a friend a letter to Monsieur Jacques Babton. He told him about his visit to France and requested information about a suitable inn where he and Margery could stay in Paris. Since there was not enough time for a reply, Anthony indicated he would visit him as soon as he arrived in Paris.

Jacques Babton was the 25-year-old grandson of Robert Babington, younger brother of John Babington, Anthony's grandfather. Robert emigrated from England to France after the executions of those that participated in the Pilgrimage of Grace (2). This way the Babington family was split into two branches, the descendants of John, who lived in Dethick, England, and the descendants of Robert, who lived in Paris,

France. For phonetic reasons, the name of the French branch was converted to Babton, name that rhymed with Danton and sounded quite French.

'Anthony and Margery, I'm so glad that you came to visit France and that I can meet you personally,' said Jacques as soon as he entered the drawing room where the young couple had been led by the butler. Jacques spoke these words in perfect English, since although his mother spoke no English, his father had always talked to him in the language of Robert Babington.

'This is my wife Suzanne. I'm afraid she speaks no English but she's in full agreement with me when I tell you not to even think about going to any horrible inn. We have a room ready for you. You're family and we want to spend as much time as possible with you during your stay in Paris.'

'Margery and I speak French and we can speak French when Suzanne is present,' said Anthony in French. 'We're delighted to accept your invitation since this will allow us to participate in the life you're living here, in France, with a Catholic king, without the problems we have in England with our Protestant queen. She not only doesn't allow us to assist to Catholic services but forces us to attend Protestant ones.'

'We've invited several of our friends tomorrow evening, so that they can meet you,' said Jacques, 'and you'll find that they are not too fond of Henri III, our Catholic king. Another Henri, the Duke of Guise, is the Catholic leader that we follow.'

After this brief conversation Anthony and Margery joined their hosts in a light supper.

'What's this?' Margery asked this question looking at a silver artifact placed on the left side of her plate.

Suzanne answered. 'That's a fork. Watch me when I start eating using it. After this evening you'll never have meals without using forks. Henri III brought them from Poland and now they're used by all the nobility and the upper yeomanry.'

'Forks,' said Anthony, 'I heard about them in London from fellows that had been in France, but I'd never seen one.'

After supper, Anthony and Margery, very tired by almost a week of travel, were free to bathe and sleep in a comfortable bed in the fine guest room that was prepared for them.

While Anthony and Margery were sleeping soundly in the home of Jacques Babton, two men in their mid-thirties were talking about them in the streets of Paris. One was tall and thin, the other stocky and rather short; both wore elegant clothes, totally black.

'We only have three more inns to check to find Babington and his wife,' said the tall one to the other in English, while they were walking hurriedly.

'The instructions we must follow are to find them. The other places we've been checking were too expensive. I'm confident we'll find them in one of these last three.'

'I don't share your confidence, since according to the information received Babington should have gone to an expensive inn. My conclusion is that he must be a guest at a private home.'

'That's not possible; he applied for a travel permit less than four weeks ago and he arrived at Boulogne Sur Mer several days ago. He didn't have time to make any arrangements.'

In the evening of the next day, well rested Anthony and Margery were enjoying the party that Jacques and Suzanne had prepared to introduce their young English relatives to their Paris friends. When asked about the situation of English Catholics in Protestant England, Anthony started requesting Jacques' friends not to repeat to anybody what they would hear. He was afraid Walsingham might have informers in Paris reporting on English visitors. Then he told his Church in the Attic narrow escape from prison.

Anthony was as fluent in French as he was in English and told his experience with flair, keeping his listeners in suspense.

'It's very noble of you to do what you're doing for the Church,' said a gentleman called Antoine, Marquis of Chandon, 'but now that you are a married man you cannot continue to put your life and your possessions at such high risk.'

The Marquis of Chandon was a heavy-set man in his fifties, recently married to Suzanne's younger sister.

'I intend to slow down my Church related activities and to devote myself to the study of law. Father Campion is no longer in London, so that I'm no longer responsible for his safety. But I've received so much from God that I feel obliged to give something in return.'

'Jacques may have told you that one of Anthony's great grandfathers on his mother's side, Baron Thomas Darcy, gave his life for the Church,' added Margery.

'I'm marveled to listen to you two speaking French as well as if you had been born in France,' said Ivonne, Suzanne's sister.

'I learned French at the same time I learned to speak English,' answered Margery. 'I used to have a French governess since I was a baby and always spoke French with her and English with my parents. I must tell you that I used to spend much more time with my governess than with my parents. Anthony has more merit in learning French well, since he was taught it in school.'

'I had very strict French teachers and almost all my school mates speak it as well as I do. It's very important to learn French well since it is not only your language but the international language of all Europe. I've met Germans, Italians and Russians in London that spoke English poorly and preferred to talk to me in their fluent French. 'Now you must tell me, about King Henri III. Jacques told me that most of you don't think very highly of him.'

The Marquis of Chandon spoke now. 'Let me tell you about Henri III, since probably I'm the only one in this room that appreciates his high intelligence. You may have heard, in England as well as in France, that he is foolish and effeminate. That's not true at all. He's very intelligent, much more than the two elder brothers that preceded him as Kings of France, François II and Charles IX, and more intelligent than his younger brother, François, Duke d'Anjou. And he's not effeminate at all but a man who has had many mistresses and was deeply in love with Marie de Cleves. When he came back from Poland to become King of France after Charles IX died, he intended to get married with Marie de Cleves. This beautiful woman was married to another Henri, the Prince of Condé and Henri III, as the new king, had made arrangements with the Church to have that marriage annulled. Unfortunately, Marie became sick and died. Henri was so much in love with her that he suffered a depression and the coronation had to be postponed for almost a year until he recovered. Henri's mother, Catherine de Medici, acted as Regent in the meantime. Two days after the coronation Henri married Louise de Lorraine, a woman that looks almost as if she were Marie de Cleve's identical twin.'

'How can you say that he is not effeminate? What about his mignons?' interrupted another guest, Pierre Reveille.

'I was just about to explain that now, to everyone here and not only to our English visitors. There's a group of several unsavory characters of dubious morals and strange behavior that Henri calls his mignons, which accompany him every- where he goes. Henri says they're his friends. When he went to Poland he took them with him. On some occasions groups of six to eight mignons go out to have fun raising hell in a tavern. A couple of times a few of them have rode in carriages along the streets of Paris dressed in women's clothing. Several of them have effeminate behavior but all of them are very strong and, what's more important, are master swordsmen that practice constantly and never go out without their rapiers. They carry pistols too and are excellent marksmen. Henri says they're his friends. Two or three might be his friends, but as a team they're his employees, the men in charge of his personal security that we could call his bodyguards.'

'Why does he say they're all his friends?'

'The main reason is that he doesn't want to make public that he fears for his life. Furthermore, Henri has another twisted reason to make all these men appear to be gentlemen. If he believes that someone poses a danger to him, he sends one of his mignons to pick a fight and challenge him to a duel. A rapier or pistol duel with a mignon is a death sentence without a trial. The regular guard of soldiers he now has as the King of France cannot arrest and kill men without a trial.'

'But why does he think he needs so much personal security?'

'Nobody knows, but I have a theory. Catherine de Medici was a follower of Nostradamus, a seer that's said to have predicted the death of Catherine's husband, Henri II, because of an accident during a tournament. Catherine requested Nostradamus predictions about the life of all her children. My guess is that Nostradamus predicted that Henri would be assassinated, that Catherine told Henri this prediction and that Henri is doing everything possible to prevent his assassination.'

'Antoine, you've given me an entirely new perspective on our king, but I see him as sinister now,' said Jacques.

'Eleven years ago, when he was only 18 years old, Henri was in charge of the royal army that defeated the Huguenots. In one battle Huguenot leader Louis, Prince of Condé, surrendered and was taken prisoner. After the end of the battle, Condé was shot dead by an anonymous soldier. It's widely believed that Henri ordered the assassination. It's also widely believed that he took part in the killings of the Saint Bartholomew Massacre. Henri III is a dangerous man to have as an enemy, but that does not stop another Henri, the Duke de Guise, from doing everything possible to embarrass him showing the French that he's more powerful than the king. The two Henries are on a collision course that I'm afraid may result in civil war, on top of our Wars of Religion.'

A servant announced that dinner could be served as soon as everyone would be seated at the table.

'One great advantage of Paris over London today is that we use forks, thanks to Henri III that brought this important innovation from Poland. Yesterday evening we introduced Anthony and Margery to forks,' explained Suzanne while everyone was going to the dining room.

'Most Englishmen that travelled to France recently brought forks back to England, but they're not available in England yet. I plan to take forks with me for our household and for a couple of friends. But you've mentioned several times that Henri III was in Poland when his brother Charles IX died. What was he doing there?' asked Anthony.

The Marquis of Chandon spoke to answer. 'He was King of Poland. Poland is not a hereditary kingdom; instead, kings are elected for life. When Charles IX died, Henri de Valois had been recently elected by the Polish-Lithuanian Parliament as Henryk Walezy, King of Poland and Grand Duke of Lithuania. Catherine de Medici negotiated this arrangement with the sister of the previous king. In return, Henri had to marry that woman, who was 28 years older than him. When it became possible for Henri to be King of France instead of King of Poland, he escaped from Poland, fortunately just before the scheduled marriage with the older woman.'

While Anthony and Margery were about to start dinner at the house of Jacques Babton, the two somber looking Englishmen that were trying to determine where the young couple was lodging in Paris were dining in a tavern.

'I've investigated and I can tell you that no families named Babington nor Draycott live in Paris,' said the tall man.

'I've checked and there is no Darcy or Dunn family either,' 'We'll have problems if we cannot locate Babington.'

'But using our wide net of Parisian contacts we should be able to locate him. He must be moving around and meeting people.'

Anthony Babington certainly moved around the three weeks he spent in Paris with his wife, having a very interesting social life in addition to visiting the Notre Dame Cathedral and several churches, in or near Paris, with historical traditions such as Saint Germain des Pres, St. Etienne du Mont and the St. Denis Basilica, where they saw the tombs of all French kings since the 10th century. What he and Margery liked most, after managing to be allowed to enter, was the Sainte Chapelle with its marvelous stained-glass windows.

Two days before their return trip, Anthony and Margery went to see a play in a rather small court used to play ball, late in the evening, with light given by oil lamps. They went with Henry Dunn, invited by his Paris host, Louis Chatenau, who came with his wife, Marianne. The play was a farce and was not too funny. There was room for only a small audience of aristocrats and wealthy people. Half of the seats for the audience were empty. Margery, Anthony and Henry told Chatenau they had enjoyed the play very much, but in fact they only enjoyed seeing that English theater was far superior.

After the play, Chatenau invited them to have dinner in a Paris restaurant. He was a big, tall man about 50 years old, a little overweight but strong and healthy, that used long hair but kept a shaved face. His wife was a few years younger, hardly ever spoke and was pleasantly plump.

'I'm very glad to hear that you enjoyed this play because I didn't,' said Chatenau. 'But I'm sure that you'll enjoy the next place I'll take you, the newest Paris restaurant there is, La Tour d'Argent (3). It's so new it hasn't been formally inaugurated yet. This is because they want Henri III to be present at the inauguration and he hasn't accepted the invitation yet. In the meantime, it's a private restaurant for gourmets like me. It's the first restaurant in the world to use forks and that's why it's so important that King Henri III, who introduced forks in France, should be the first to use forks in a public restaurant.'

'This is not a restaurant,' said Anthony after dinner, 'it's a temple to gastronomy. I've had several delicious meals in Paris of which the best one was at your own home, Seigneur Chatenau, but this one is out of this world.'

'English theater might be better than French theater for the time being,' answered Chatenau, 'but French cuisine is so much better than English cuisine that no comparison is even possible.'

The day before the start of the horse ride to Boulogne Sur Mer to take the ship back to London, Anthony was talking with Jacques. He was telling him how much he and Margery had enjoyed his hospitality and how pleased they were of their visit to Paris, when the butler interrupted them.

'Two gentlemen at the door wish to speak to Master Babington,' announced the butler.'

'Send them in,' ordered Jacques.

'My name is Thomas Morgan and my companion is Charles

Paget,' said the taller of the two men that entered. 'We're assistants to James Beaton, Archbishop of Glasgow, who's the Ambassador of Queen Mary Stuart to the King of France.'

'We've been looking for Master Babington since his arrival in Paris because we know that he has been a page of Queen Mary Stuart and is very devoted to her,' added the shorter fellow.

Seeing that Anthony was about to answer, Jacques grabbed his shoulder to keep him quiet and said to him, 'don't speak Anthony.' He then addressed the two men.

'I'm Master Babington's host in Paris and also his lawyer in France. Here in France, he will not answer any of your questions. You may say what you wish to say to him and he'll consider and evaluate his answer at length and might send you an answer from London through proper channels.'

'We need to send correspondence to our prisoner queen. We believe that Master Babington, who's been her page, knows reliable people at Sheffield Castle where she's being kept prisoner that can deliver the letters to her,' said the taller man. 'Furthermore, I was hoping that Master Babington would take with him a letter from Archbishop Beaton to Queen Mary that I have here with me.'

After hearing Thomas Morgan's request that Anthony should travel to England carrying a compromising letter with him, Jacques' face became flushed with indignation. Making an effort to contain his anger he spoke to the two visitors very slowly in a low voice.

'It's absurd that you should ask Master Babington to take the risk of being sent to prison, tortured and perhaps executed for taking to England a letter that can go to the French Embassy in London, carried by any of the several diplomats that travel constantly between Paris and London. If Master Babington wishes to send you an answer, he will do so through a French diplomat. Good day gentlemen, the butler will escort you to the door.'

Jacques called the butler and the two very embarrassed Englishmen were shown the way out.

'Don't ever answer to these two scoundrels. They might or might not work for Archbishop Beaton, but I believe they're Walsingham's agents setting you up.'

'You are right, Jacques. Thank you for taking care of this matter so swiftly.'

Regardless of his words of acceptance of Jacques opinion and advice, Anthony was thinking about Mary Stuart, the beautiful helpless prisoner queen and what a great honor would be to be her courier. Once back in London he would have to check about Thomas Morgan and Charles Paget. Also, he should find out if after three years he still had the necessary contacts at Sheffield Castle.

But he decided to do everything possible to obtain the incredible honor of becoming Mary Stuart's courier.

CHAPTER IV
THE CAMPION PLOT

Sir Francis Walsingham was talking in his office to several members of the staff he used for searches and arrests.

'There are about 20 papist priests here, in Protestant England, preaching papist doctrine as if they were in Italy. They go everywhere they please and your duty is to arrest them and bring them to justice, but you're doing nothing, the months go by, they continue preaching and not even one of them has been arrested.'

The men listened in total silence. They knew that after several months with no results it was no use telling the Principal Secretary any details of the strategy they had followed.

'There are four priests that are particularly seditious because they preach to Protestants and must be arrested soon; these are Edmund Campion (4), Robert Parsons (5), Alexander Briant (6) and Ralph Sherwin (7). The papist doctrine they preach is subversive. The pope has excommunicated our queen, has declared she's an illegitimate daughter of King Henry VIII and has called her an illegal queen. The four papist priests pose a great danger to Queen Elizabeth. If you don't arrest at least one of them within a month, all of you will have to start looking for new jobs. Now go and start to work, all of you except Jones.'

When Jones was alone with him, Walsingham spoke to him in a very low voice.

'Jones, what I'll request you is strictly confidential. You mustn't discuss this with any of your colleagues or with anyone else. I want you to contact Sir John Branche, Lord Mayor of the City of London, in my name, to request him to set free one criminal, no one in particular but one that you pick to work for us.'

After a pause Sir Francis continued. 'The ideal man would be a murderer that hasn't been sent to trial yet but would surely be condemned to death in a trial. He would be highly motivated. If he doesn't perform well, he would go back to prison and then to a death sentence. If, by any chance, there are several men in this condition you should select the one you consider the most intelligent.'

Sir Francis waited for a question or a comment by his subordinate. Since Jones remained silent, he continued.

'This murderer, to be set free at our request, will be strictly controlled. Of course he cannot commit any crime while working for us. If he does, he must know he'll suffer a fate much worse than any he might have suffered under the London authorities. You'll be the only one to deal with this criminal since I don't want to have any contact with him.'

Jones listened without speaking a word and Walsingham continued.

'Edmund Campion moves between Berkshire, Oxfordshire, Northamptonshire and Lancashire. Our people follow him, but never find him because when they get where he was, he has already moved to another county. I want a spy that will wait in Berkshire for him. In my experience, criminals can be excellent spies. Our criminal spy should befriend a large amount of people, should become a regular visitor of Berkshire pubs all over the county, should have enough money to invite others to drink beer with him and should pretend to be a Catholic. When Campion surfaces in Berkshire our spy will arrest him in my name. Understood? That's all, you may leave now.'

'There's something I must tell you, Sir Francis.'

'Yes, Jones'

'Tim, our interrogator in the palace, has died. He was killed by a thief last night, near his home.'

'How was he killed?'

'He was stabbed in the abdomen several times, left to bleed for some time and then his throat was cut.'

'That's unusual for a thief. I think that's vengeance, not robbery. The killer must have wanted his victim to suffer and to hear why he was being killed. Possibly he cut his victim's throat only because someone approached. If Tim was robbed, it probably was just to make revenge look like robbery. I think we had a similar case a few months ago.'

'Yes, now that you said it I remember. Our informer Dan Smith, died the same way late last year.'

'An informer last year and a torturer now. It makes sense to think that someone wanted to get even with both of them, but those sent to Tim for interrogation end up dead or in prison.'

'Not always, Sir Francis. You indicated yourself that John Savage should be set free when he was on the rack, after having sent us to look for Edmund Campion in the wrong place.'

'John Savage, I remember him well. I even like the man. He should be working for us. He was accused by Dan Smith of being a militant Catholic who was invited to the mass given by Campion in London. He was no Catholic and had no idea of what he could tell Tim to stop the torture. He finally invented a story based on something he overheard in a pub. Tim must have been displeased with my orders and must have continued the torture for a while before releasing Savage. In revenge, Savage killed the informer and the torturer.'

'Should I arrange for the arrest of John Savage?'

'No, we might find we can use Savage sometime in the future. Both Smith and Tim deserved what happened to them, but you must locate Savage and keep him under surveillance.'

A couple of weeks after their return from France, Anthony and Margery Babington went to Dethick to visit Anthony's mother and stepfather. They travelled on horseback with Henry Dunn and joined a group that travelled to Sheffield and was making the 55 leagues trip in five days. The fourth day the Babington couple and Henry left the group to go to nearby Dethick. After three days in Dethick, Anthony, Margery and Henry went to the Sheffield estate of Henry's father.

Every morning, Anthony and Margery went out for a ride. They used to spend a lot of time around Sheffield Castle, because Anthony wanted to see if he could talk with any of the ladies-in-waiting he had befriended when he was a page of Mary Stuart. He wanted to arrange to become a courier for the prisoner queen. The fifth day, Anthony recognized a lady he remembered was called Jane leaving the castle on foot.

He alerted Margery, 'that's Jane Kennedy, a lady-in-waiting that's very close to Queen Mary Stuart.' Then they both approached Jane.

'How are you Jane? Do you remember me? I'm Anthony Babington.'

'Anthony Babington? Yes, I remember. I can recognize you, but only because you told me who you are. I remembered you as a boy and you're a man now.'

'A married man. This is my wife, Margery.'

Anthony dismounted and then helped Margery to dismount lifting her out of her sideways saddle.

'I'm very pleased to meet you Jane,' said Margery.

Jane continued walking accompanied by the young couple. They were taking their horses along by their reins. After a few minutes of inconsequential talk, Anthony went to the point.

'We were in France a few weeks ago and two men asked me

to become a courier for your queen. I don't trust these men but I want to find out if the queen needs a courier or her needs in this regard are already covered.'

'Oh yes, we badly need a courier. We had one, but he doesn't come any more. One day he came to me and whispered "I'm being followed and cannot continue delivering". I haven't seen him since.'

'Then, I'll contact the French Embassy to see if they have letters for Queen Mary. If they do, I'll bring the letters to you or to another of the ladies at Sheffield.'

'Oh no, don't do that. All the girls are very nice, but one of them might be a spy. Deliver the letter only to me or to Elizabeth Curle. She's the only one I can trust completely. And only one letter at a time. It's dangerous if we talk frequently. I'll think of some place where you can hide the letters, so that I can take them to the queen. In the same place I'll leave the letters the queen writes in reply. Now you should leave. It's dangerous for you to spend too much time with me.'

Having accomplished what he wanted, Anthony started his ride back to London with Margery, joining a group leaving Sheffield the next day. Henry stayed another week with his parents.

'I have excellent news Sir Francis,' said Jones after entering the large office of the Principal Secretary.'

'Is this about the criminal you're recruiting for us?'

'He has already been recruited and I'll give you full details in a moment Sir, but the good news is that I've just arrested Father Ralph Sherwin. We were tipped by one of our informers, Fred Raffer. Sherwin was preaching in the home of a fellow named Nicholas Carrock. I took twenty men there and arrived when the meeting had just ended, but no one had left yet. We arrested 15 men and Sherwin.'

'Congratulations, Jones. See that Raffer gets a good bonus. We must set an example to end the tolerance that many Protestants have for the Catholics. We can hang Sherwin just for being a Catholic priest, but I want him drawn, hanged and quartered for plotting to overthrow Queen Elizabeth, to invade England with foreign armies and to enthrone Mary Stuart as Queen of England. Now tell me about the criminal.'

'I had six murderers to pick from. I elected one that seemed brighter and had worked for a noble family, but just in case, I requested the Lord Mayor to keep another two without trial in reserve. The one I took to Berkshire is called George Eliot and is a murderer and a rapist. I know that he'll repeat his crimes, but he understood quite well that if he does it while working for us, he'll be taken to the Tower to be tortured every day of his life until he dies of old age. I talked to Sir Edward Unton, High Sheriff of Berkshire, and he's arranged to watch Eliot closely until he does his job. Also, he'll be given assistance when he arrests Campion. I believe Eliot will behave until he completes his job. He was so thrilled about the assignment of arresting a priest that he will not throw away this chance.'

'Very good, Jones. After arresting Campion and being released, Eliot will return to his old habits, but not in England. We'll give him some money and a passport to a foreign country. Let me think. We'll send him to Spain. But we can only release him after the trial since we'll need him to testify against Campion. In the interim between Campion's arrest and his trial, we must keep Eliot in the Tower. We must be sure he doesn't commit any crime until we don't need him anymore.'

When Anthony arrived in London after his trip to Sheffield, his friend Thomas Salisbury went to visit him in the evening.

'I bring bad news Anthony.'

'What happened?'

'Father Sherwin was arrested by Walsingham's men two days ago. He was preaching in the house of Nicholas Carrock and Walsingham's men barged in, in the same way they irrupted here last year when Father Campion had just started mass in the attic. I would have liked to attend the meeting in Nicholas home, but fortunately for me I couldn't because of a previous engagement.'

'There are spies everywhere. I was in Sheffield and talked with one of the ladies-in-waiting of Mary Stuart and she told me that one of her companions might be a spy.'

'In the case of Father Sherwin, perhaps no spy was needed because he was taking too many chances of being arrested preaching to Protestants.'

'Yes, but tolerant Protestants that wouldn't betray the confidence of the friend that invited them to a Catholic meeting. Spies that pretend to be our friends are the problem, like the two Englishmen that offered me in Paris a letter to deliver to Mary Stuart. Fortunately, my French cousin realized that it was totally unnecessary that I should take the risk of introducing that letter in England. The French Embassy in London has a numerous staff with members that are constantly travelling between Paris and London, that always carry confidential papers with them that cannot be checked by English authorities.'

'Did your trip to Sheffield work out well? Did you make contact with one of the ladies-in-waiting that had befriended you when you were a page?'

'Yes, and now I'll go to the French Embassy to start working as a courier for Mary Stuart.'

Anthony Babington became a regular courier for Mary Stuart. He was careful and visited the French Embassy only once, arranging for a drop place in a London park where the Embassy left letters for Mary Stuart and picked up the letters from Mary to French destinations left there by Anthony.

Likewise, he contacted Jane only one more time and arranged for a drop place in a Sheffield park. Each round trip to Sheffield on horseback took 8 to 10 days and every time he was staying two days in Sheffield. As a result of being out of London more than ten days every month his law studies were seriously affected.

In early 1581, the secret society for the protection of priests received another blow when Father Alexander Briant was arrested. Anthony got the news at Lincoln's Inn from another member of the society, his friend Charles Tilney.

'Our society is no match for Walsingham's net of spies,' said Charles. 'We saw suspicious movements in the neighborhood where Father Parsons was going to preach and advised him in time to get away. Then they arrested Alexander Briant and tortured him to find out where Parsons was hiding. Under torture, he gave his real name and Walsingham's men realized they had captured a priest.'

'And what do you propose we do?'

'We should help Fathers Parsons and Campion to get out of the country. I think it's time to close our secret society.'

A few months later, Anthony and Charles met again. Anthony was near Westminster Abbey with his friend, Thomas Salisbury, and waved to Charles Tilney.

'I'm pulling out,' said Charles when he reached them, as if these words were a greeting. 'I talked extensively with Father Campion in Oxfordshire and couldn't convince him that he had to leave the country immediately. Now, only a month later, he's been arrested in Berkshire by a spy called George Eliot, who derisively paraded him in the streets of Berkshire riding a donkey backwards, bound hand and foot and with a paper stuck in his hat indicating SEDITIOUS JESUIT. Father Parsons has now accepted our advice, but only after the arrest of Father Campion. We have to find a cooperative fisherman with a boat strong enough to cross the Channel. Edward Jones and Jerome Bellamy are working with me on this subject and we need you two to help us. You should also call your friend Henry Dunn. This is urgent since Father Parsons has had another narrow escape yesterday.'

'How was Father Campion arrested?'

'He was in a very large Manor House at Lyford, Berkshire, the home of a gentleman called Francis Yates, who's currently in prison in London for his Catholic beliefs and sent word to Campion that his family needed support. When Eliot came to capture him with 100 men he got from the High Sheriff of Berkshire, Campion was hidden in a small secret chamber. When he couldn't be found, Eliot, who had seen Campion giving mass in the house before calling for help from the authorities, gave instructions to break walls until a secret hiding place could be found. Several times the soldiers wanted to give up the search but Eliot never allowed it. Campion's hiding place was found 13 hours after the search was started. It's incredible that a spy would be interested in continuing a search for such a long time.'

Father Campion, with clothes that had become rags, disheveled, hands bound, entered the Tower of London escorted by two of Walsingham's men. A yeoman of the guard, wearing the typical military uniform of Tower Guards, was sitting at a desk in the small office at the entrance. Next to him there was a gentleman standing.

'Is your prisoner Edmund Campion?' the gentleman asked the two men.

'He is,' said one of them.

'I have an order from the queen,' he said showing a paper.

'I've checked the order,' said the yeoman of the guard, 'and he's in charge of the prisoner now.'

The gentleman signed the papers for the transfer of the prisoner Walsingham's men had with them and the men retired.

The guard cut the ropes tying Campion's hands and spoke to him.

'Another guard will show you where you can take a bath and change to the clothes this gentleman brought for you'.

'I'm George Stanford,' said the gentleman while shaking hands with Campion. 'I've orders to take you to Leicester House to talk with Sir Robert, but before that you have to look like a normal person again.'

A guard escorted Campion out of the small office and about half an hour later he returned with an elegantly dressed, well-groomed Campion.

'Fine,' said Stanford when Campion returned.

'I don't feel exactly normal,' said Campion. 'I've never worn such fine clothes as I'm wearing now.'

'Since Sir Robert has about the same built that you have, he gave me the last set of clothes, still unused, he had bought for himself. It fits you perfectly.'

Stanford and Campion went out of the Tower and Stanford made a sign with his arm to a coachman in a nearby carriage. The carriage moved to the place where the two men were standing and they boarded it. Twenty minutes later the carriage stopped at the entrance of Leicester House, the house that had been recently built in the Strand by Sir Robert Dudley, Earl of Leicester, as his London residence. Despite of the fact that most of the time, when he was in London, Sir Robert resided at Whitehall Palace, the Royal Palace in London, the earl also needed his own home in town.

'I haven't had breakfast this morning yet,' said Stanford, 'and Sir Robert may not be available to see you for at least an hour, so that perhaps you'll be so kind to join me for breakfast while you wait for him.'

Edmund Campion was starving. He hadn't eaten anything since the High Sheriff of Berkshire delivered him, two days ago, to a party of Walsingham's men led by George Eliot and was happy to accept.

'I'll be most glad to accept your invitation, Sir.'

He appreciated the tactful way he was offered food, without any mention of his arrest and the harsh treatment he received afterwards.

After he had eaten a hearty breakfast, Campion was led by Stanford to a small hall, where not only Sir Robert Dudley was waiting for him, but also Queen Elizabeth, sitting on an armchair.

Some background information is needed to understand the interest in Edmund Campion shown by Sir Robert Dudley and Queen Elizabeth.

In 1560 Campion had delivered the funeral oration at the reburial of Amy Robsart. Campion was then an ecclesiastical Oxford student. Amy was the first wife of Robert Dudley. Both Robert Dudley and the queen were deeply moved by Campion's words because they came at a crucial time in their lives. In 1556, when the two of them were 23 years old at the court of Queen Mary I, they had fallen in love but couldn't marry because, when Robert was only 16 years old, his father had made him marry Amy Robsart. Two years later, in 1558, Mary I died and Elizabeth became the Queen of England. At that time Amy Robsart, who Robert respected but did not love, was suffering from a painful illness and it was highly probable that she would die soon. If that should have happened, after a reasonable mourning period Robert Dudley and the queen would have married.

But in 1560 Amy Robsart died in an accident with no witness present. No one knows why, but she had sent her servants away for the day. She was found dead with a broken neck at the foot of a flight of stairs. Robert Dudley was suspected of killing his wife to marry the queen. Under such circumstances it became impossible for Elizabeth to marry him. Robert pressed for an enquiry to clear his name, Amy's grave was opened for a second examination of her body and the coroner's finding confirmed the results of the first medical examination that indicated accidental death.

Robert Dudley continued to be the queen's favorite and expected that after a few years his wife's accident or suicide would be forgotten and Elizabeth would accept to marry him. 19 years after Amy Robsart's death, in 1579, Robert Dudley married Lettice Knollys because it was obvious the queen would not accept to marry him and he wanted to have legitimate children to inherit his title and his properties. Robert did not tell Elizabeth about his marriage. When Elizabeth found out she banished Lettice from court.

For the funeral oration Campion gave at Amy Robsart's reburial he was held in high esteem by Sir Robert and the queen, who followed his career with great interest. Campion was a brilliant student at Oxford. When in 1564 Campion completed his studies and was ordained as a deacon in the Church of England, he took the Oath of Supremacy, accepting Queen Elizabeth as Supreme Governor of the Church. He started to study as a Catholic during the reign of Mary I and continued to study after Elizabeth changed the school to the Church of England.

The queen attended a debate in Oxford in which Campion debated against four other deacons and was very impressed by Campion's debating skills. She discussed about Campion's future with Sir William Cecil, at the time Principal Secretary, and decided Campion had the brilliant mind the Church of England lacked and needed.

What the queen did not know, was that Campion was in anguish about his decision to leave the Catholic Church and join the Church of England. Campion was sent to Dublin, Ireland, to work with Sir Henry Sidney, Lord Deputy of Ireland, in the reopening of Dublin's University. Campion used that time to write a History of Ireland. In 1570, when Campion was in Ireland, Pope Pius V excommunicated Queen Elizabeth generating a backlash anti-Catholic feeling in England. In 1571, after two years in Ireland, Campion returned secretly to England to look at the new situation of the Church of England from the outside, not as one of its clerics. He then decided not to fight his anguish anymore and went to France to become a Catholic priest. Afterwards he joined the Jesuit Order and he was sent to England.

48-year-old Queen Elizabeth kept a youthful figure, but her attractive face was covered with white makeup. Elizabeth got smallpox when she was 29 years old. She had named Regent her friend Robert Dudley to govern in her place during her illness. She had been on the verge of death but she recovered. However, her face was marred by pockmarks left by smallpox and since then she used heavy white makeup to cover the pockmarks.

Robert Dudley, with a thin moustache and a small beard covering his chin was probably even more handsome at 48 than when he was in his twenties.

'Your Highness,' said Campion while he was kneeling in front of the queen, 'I can't believe you've come to see me.'

Elizabeth extended one hand to be kissed by Campion.

After kissing the queen's hand Campion looked at Robert Dudley. 'Sir Robert, it's an honor to be summoned to you house.'

'Both Sir Robert and I feel great affection for you,' said the queen, 'and we wish to talk to you to see if there is anything you can do to extricate yourself from your present situation. As you know, you're being accused of treason to the crown.'

'I'm your loyal subject, Your Majesty. I came to England only to support the English Catholics that are prevented from practicing their faith.'

'I can't debate the theological differences between the Church of England and the Catholic Church with you,' said the queen. 'To me there's only one Christ, Jesus, one faith, all the rest is a discussion over trifles. It wouldn't matter if the discussions were kept in academic circles, but they are taken to the common people that are not able to understand the differences but take sides. Then, different sides make war against each other.'

After a brief silence, the queen continued. 'I know that the differences that don't mean anything to me mean a lot to you. I know that you were in anguish about having left the Catholic Church, becoming a deacon in the Church of England. Perhaps it was because of decisions I made that you felt that anguish. I just want to see if perhaps I can give you a different point of view, explaining my motivations to you. I can even go further to my father's motivations.'

Edmund Campion did not say anything and just looked at the queen expecting her words, so that she went on.

'I'm told that the Catholic Church is presenting my father's request for the annulment of his marriage to Catherine of Aragon as something immoral that the Church could never grant.'

'Your Highness, I'm aware that Pope Clement VII did not grant the annulment for purely political reasons. The troops of Emperor Charles V had just sacked Rome when Henry VIII presented his first request. Catherine of Aragon was the Emperor's aunt. If Henry VIII had presented his request for an annulment a few months earlier it would have been granted immediately. He had recently granted the request presented by your aunt, Margaret Tudor.'

'I'm also aware,' continued Campion, 'that when you were crowned Queen of England, your only option was to make the Church of England the official church of the kingdom, since the Catholic Church had declared you were an illegitimate daughter of Henry VIII and therefore unfit to be the Queen of England.'

'In fact,' said the queen, 'the Church of England had concurred with the Catholic Church in declaring I was illegitimate, but I had previously been legitimate and as Supreme Governor of the Church of England I could recover my legitimacy.'

'Being aware of this situation, I remained in Oxford and continued my studies to become a Church of England Deacon and as such I took the Oath of Supremacy swearing allegiance to you as Supreme Governor of the Church of England.'

'I'm glad that you mentioned the Oath of Supremacy' interrupted Elizabeth, 'and let me ask you a question. Is this Oath of Supremacy the same that had to be sworn during the reign of my father?'

'No, the Oath of Supremacy used for Henry VIII declared him Supreme Head of the Church of England. Obviously, Parliament considered Supreme Head of the Church to be too much of a title for a woman.'

'You're wrong in what you consider to be obvious. I made the text of the Act of Supremacy of 1559 and Parliament accepted it without changing a coma. I'm the monarch of this realm,' said the queen imperatively, with a glint of anger in her eyes, 'with exactly the same prerogatives of a male king. I left the position of Head of the Church of England opened for negotiations with the pope. You should remember that at that time Catholic King Felipe II of Spain wanted to marry me.'

'Excuse me for interrupting, Your Majesty,' said Robert Dudley. 'May I mention a point here?'

'Go ahead, Robert.'

'I've noticed an expression of skepticism in Father Campion's face. There's a very close precedent for what the queen has just said. In the 1516 Bologna Concordat signed by Pope Leo

X and the King of France François I, although the pope remains as "Head" of the Catholic Church in France, "Government" of the church was transferred to the King of France. Leo X signed this Concordat to prevent François I from repeating in France what Henry VIII had done in England. I'm convinced that Felipe II would have obtained this solution and I advised the queen to marry him.'

'In any case,' said the queen, 'although the official religion of England changed from Catholic to Anglican when I succeeded Mary as Queen of England, the only practical effect on the people of England was to stop the persecution and execution of Protestants. Officially only Church of England services could be performed, but the law was not enforced because I believe in freedom of conscience. I didn't persecute Puritans either, just kept them in check to prevent their efforts to make the Church of England more radically Protestant. I wanted a Church of England acceptable to both Catholics and Protestants and I succeeded. You're the proof of my success. You didn't leave your ecclesiastical studies in London when I was crowned. You continued and became a Deacon of the Church of England.'

Elizabeth went on. 'Regrettably in 1570 Pope Pius V decided to excommunicate me and to instruct English Catholics that they didn't owe allegiance to their Protestant queen. Just at that time, we had in England a refugee deposed Queen of Scotland who as my closest relative would have been treated as my successor in my court. Instead, she elected to declare herself a Pretender to the throne refusing to accept me as the legitimate Queen of England. Obviously, the objective of the excommunication was to incite Catholics to depose me and enthrone Mary Stuart. Did I execute hundreds of Catholics in retaliation? Many monarchs would have acted this way. Did I send Mary Stuart to the scaffold to be beheaded, like the majority of my Privy Council recommended? No, I only took measures against the most blatant cases of Catholic activism that put my crown in danger and kept Mary Stuart as a luxury prisoner in a castle. I just took the minimum measures necessary to protect myself and to protect my kingdom from religious turmoil. Are you aware that the plans to depose me include a foreign invasion and that across the channel there's a large army in Flanders that the King of Spain is ready to send to plunder England?'

'Everything you say is right and I admire you. But if being a queen you see that developments are out of your control, what can I do being a simple priest? I can do nothing to change events, I can only assist those that require my help and obey the orders I'm given as a Jesuit priest'.

'Well, I require your help to lift the excommunication. You could travel to Rome as my delegate to negotiate with Pope Gregory XIII.'

'If I should appear in Rome as your delegate, I would be thrown in jail immediately to suffer, as a prisoner of the pope, the same kind of punishment I can receive in London as a prisoner of Sir Francis Walsingham.'

'Don't go to Rome then. Arrange to meet a Cardinal in neutral territory, ruled by a prince that can be trusted by both sides.'

'You don't need my help Your Majesty, you want to help me. But I'm beyond help now and I must face my destiny.'

'I would understand your resignation to accept death if you had been risking your life because England was ruled by a tyrant,' interrupted Robert Dudley, 'but Queen Elizabeth is no tyrant. You must take advantage of the fact that she wants to help you and devise some excuse, any excuse, to save your life. And you'll be executed if you go back to the Tower of London. Even if Walsingham's plans to condemn you for plotting to assassinate the queen should fail, you can be executed for giving religious services as a Catholic priest and also for failing to abide by your Oath of Supremacy. You don't have to decide right away. Stay here tonight as my guest. Think about it and sleep on it.'

'It's no use, Sir Robert and Your Majesty. Events totally out of our control have put us at this crossroads today. Each one must follow his way. Walsingham will also follow his way and he will not fail. He will have me condemned for plotting to assassinate the queen. But I've received great comfort today learning that Your Majesty knows that the accusation is not true and that both of you want to help me.'

'Let's call a spade a spade. Perhaps we've been too subtle in this conversation. The Queen needs you in the Church of England. Come back to the Church of England to a brilliant ecclesiastical career and your problems are over.'

'I understood clearly. My answer remains unchanged.

In the Tower, Campion was interrogated and requested to sign a confession under torture on the rack several times. Also he was challenged to four separate debates on theological matters.

The queen hoped that theologians might make Campion understand he could return to the Church of England and requested the debates. His adversaries believed that without previous study of the subjects to be debated and weakened by lack of food and torture on the rack he would be unable to perform satisfactorily.

They were wrong and Campion conducted himself at the debates as well as he always did.

Campion was tried for conspiring to raise sedition in England and dethrone the queen. He declared himself innocent of these charges but was declared guilty on the strength of testimony of false witnesses, including George Eliot. He was condemned to be drawn, hanged and quartered.

Near the end of 1581, Edmund Campion was tied on a wooden plank that was tied to a horse and dragged on that plank from the Tower of London to the Tyburn gallows, near the present "Speakers Corner" of Hyde Park. Tied together to another plank, were Alexander Briant and Ralph Sherwin, drawn to Tyburn behind Campion. The three priests were hanged and quartered there.

CHAPTER V
THE THROCKMORTON PLOT

Sir Francis Throckmorton was feeling great. He would be returning to England after having spent three years in France. Francis was 29 years old and single. He was tall, had dark hair and eyes and a rather long nose. He used a thin moustache and a small, pointed beard. Initially he was educated in Oxford and later had moved to London where he studied law at one of the four Inns of Court, the Inner Temple. He had practiced law for three years in Paris and with that foreign experience and his wide family connections he expected to do very well as a lawyer, back in London.

He was on his way to the English Embassy to check that all his documentation was in order. At the Embassy, he was always treated with the utmost consideration since his late uncle, Sir Nicholas Throckmorton, had been the English Ambassador to France for several years. An elderly clerk that used to work for his uncle always took care of his needs when he had to go to the embassy.

Near the embassy entrance Sir Francis was approached by two men that apparently had been waiting for him there. One was tall and thin, the other stocky and rather short; both wore elegant clothes, totally black.

'Excuse me Sir, but are you Sir Francis Throckmorton?'

'Yes, I am, but I'm busy now. I've an appointment at the embassy.'

'Let me introduce us, my name is Thomas Morgan and my companion is Charles Paget, we're assistants to James Beaton, Archbishop of Glasgow, who's the Ambassador of Queen Mary Stuart to the King of France.'

'Glad to meet you, but I must go now.'

'We'll be drinking beer for the next hour or so at the Rai

d'Or, in the next block. We'll be glad to invite you for a drink, if you're free when you leave the embassy.'

'I'll think about it, goodbye.'

Francis went on to the embassy. After he had gone over his papers with his contact, William, he asked him. 'Do you know two Englishmen called Morgan and Paget?'

'Yes, they're two well-known English conspirators. A brother of Paget is a Lord and has had trouble in England because of his brother's activities in France.'

Francis decided not to have any contact with the two men that wanted to talk with him but when he was walking in front of the Rai d'Or, he changed his mind, considering that he wanted to have a drink and that it was harmless to accept the invitation.

The two Englishmen were glad to see that Francis had accepted their invitation. For a while they talked about current events in Paris and the fact that King Henri III was becoming quite unpopular. Then, Morgan went to the point.

'We believe that you're a Catholic, like us, and we were hoping that you would do us the favor to give a message from us to the Spanish Ambassador in London, Don Bernardino de Mendoza.'

Paget completed the request. 'We sent yesterday a long letter to Don Bernardino, through the Spanish Embassy in Paris, but from past experience we know that it'll take about two months for that letter to reach him. The main point of our letter is that Queen Mary Stuart prefers the support of the King of Spain rather than that of his cousin, Henri, Duke the Guise. If you would just go to Don Bernardino's private residence and give him this message, Queen Mary would be most grateful. We usually send our letters to London through the French Embassy there but could not do it with this particular letter. We believe it might be read by the French.'

'Gentlemen, I'm a Catholic in France but I'm an Anglican in England. You two, are well known conspirators that are against Queen Elizabeth. I don't believe it's wise for me to take any messages from you to London.'

'But this is just a verbal message to a most pleasant gentleman who could be a valuable contact for you in London.'

'I'll think about your request when I'm in London, but I don't promise anything. If you should find another traveler to take this message, go ahead. It's been quite pleasant to have a drink with you, gentlemen, but now I must say goodbye.'

The Spanish Ambassador received a letter from Thomas Morgan advising that Sir Francis Throckmorton had just returned to London after three years in Paris. The letter said Sir Francis was a member of a very influential family and one of his uncles, Sir Nicholas Throckmorton, had been Queen Elizabeth's Ambassador to France and Scotland. The letter also said that both Morgan and Paget believed Sir Francis would be a suitable contact for the Spanish Embassy that may eventually be helpful to the cause of Mary Stuart. For this reason, they had given him a verbal message to transmit to the ambassador to his private residence, as a pretext to put him in contact with Don Bernardino. It was added that Sir Francis had not promised to contact him but, if he should do so, it would be convenient to try to develop a friendship.

Don Bernardino was puzzled by this letter. He had a low opinion of both Morgan and Paget. He considered that they were adventurers that had become assistants of Archbishop Beaton just to have access to the large fortune of Mary Stuart in France, managed by the Archbishop. He was aware that the adventurers kept correspondence with Claude Nau and Gilbert Curle, Mary's secretaries in her castle prison in England. Don Bernardino was convinced that the two assistants of Archbishop Beaton and the two secretaries of

Mary Stuart, were working together to divert as much as possible of Mary Stuart's French assets to their own pockets.

Don Bernardino decided that, regardless of his personal opinion of the adventurer that wrote the puzzling letter, he would ask his secretary for background information on Sir Nicholas Throckmorton. After evaluating this information, he would decide how to treat Sir Francis Throckmorton if he should eventually contact him.

Two weeks after his arrival in London, Sir Francis Throckmorton decided it would be interesting to meet Don Bernardino de Mendoza and therefore one evening went to his private residence. An ambassador was always a good contact for a lawyer.

He introduced himself to the butler and asked him if he could see Don Bernardino. He was led to a hall and asked to wait. After a few minutes, a smiling Don Bernardino came in and extended his hand.

'Sir Francis Throckmorton, I'm Don Bernardino de Mendoza. Are you a relative of the late Sir Nicholas Throckmorton?'

'Yes Sir, he was my uncle,' answered Sir Francis shaking Don Bernardino's hand.

Don Bernardino was a wiry short man in his early forties, with very dark hair and a thin moustache. His English was excellent.

'To what do I owe the pleasure of your visit?' asked Don Bernardino.

'I've just returned to London after a three year stay in Paris. A few days before I left Paris I was contacted by two Englishmen that claimed to be assistants of Archbishop Beaton, the Ambassador of Mary Stuart in France. They said they've sent you a detailed letter through the Spanish Embassy in Paris and that you would appreciate to learn in advance that Mary Stuart prefers the support of King Felipe

II to that of her own cousin, Henri de Lorraine, Duke de Guise.'

'Yes, that's important information. I greatly appreciate receiving it. I don't have a high opinion of Morgan and Paget, but it's only through them that I can contact Mary Stuart.'

'Well, I'm pleased I've done something useful for you, Don Bernardino and I'm most glad that this minor service gave me an opportunity to meet you.'

Sir Francis extended his hand again to say goodbye.

'Oh, you shouldn't leave right away. I'm expecting someone in an hour, but since you're here early in the evening perhaps you can join me for a drink.'

'Of course I'll stay. It'll be an honor for me to stay and join you for a drink.'

'I've travelled to many places and I've tasted different drinks, but it's here, in England, where I found the best drink there is. It's not English but comes from Scotland. It's Aqua Vitae, Water of Life, commonly known as Scotch whisky. It's new in England, but the Scots have been drinking it for centuries. We, Spaniards, are experts in alcoholic drinks and I can guarantee you that Scotch whisky will become popular all over Europe.'

The two men talked for about half an hour and Sir Francis congratulated Don Bernardino for being very well informed about current events in Spain.

'In general terms I try to remain well informed about what's going on in Spain, while I'm away as an Ambassador. But I'm not a politician; I'm a military man in diplomatic duty.'

'I know, you fought in Flanders for more than 15 years under the orders of the Duke of Alba and you've been appointed a member of the Military Order of Santiago.'

'I can see that you've taken the trouble to learn about me

before coming to see me, Sir Francis. I'm flattered. I'll tell you something else about me that very few people know, I write. I've written a few poems but basically, I write about military matters, a subject I know well. The Art of War changes in every century and I want to leave a record for posterity of war tactics in the middle of the 16th century.'

After a few seconds of silence, Don Bernardino talked again.

'Now you must tell me about current events in Paris, Sir Francis.'

'I understand that you travel frequently to France,' said Sir Francis.

'I don't travel away from England too frequently, but I go to France once in a while and I have developed good contacts with many French military men.'

'I've a different line of work, in the legal profession. I don't suppose that you know any French lawyers. I used to work with an important lawyer called Jules Chiron.'

'I don't know Chiron but since it's always important to know good lawyers I've developed an excellent relationship with several French lawyers. I now remember one French lawyer that speaks English just as well as you do. His name is Jacques Babton.'

'I know Jacques Babton very well. He's a very good friend of mine. If you know Jacques, you probably also know his associate, Pierre Reveille.'

'Yes, I do know young Reveille. We've many things in common, Sir Francis'.

'That's right, but you must know that I've really enjoyed our conversation and hope we'll continue seeing each other.'

'Certainly, Don Bernardino, it'll be a great honor for me.'

After Sir Francis Throckmorton left the residence of the Spanish Ambassador he found himself facing a well-dressed gentleman accompanied by two men. The gentleman recognized Sir Francis and talked to him.

'Sir Francis, my name sake. How are you doing? How does it feel to be back in England again?'

'Sir Francis Walsingham, I'm flattered to be recognized by you since we met very briefly at court.'

'I've a very good memory for faces and names. Furthermore, the day I met you everyone at court was looking at you. You were accompanied by your beautiful cousin, Elizabeth Throckmorton, the new lady-in-waiting of Queen Elizabeth.'

'Anyway, I'm very impressed to be recognized by the Principal Secretary of Queen Elizabeth.'

'I'm coming to visit Don Bernardino de Mendoza, the Spanish Ambassador. Did I see you just leaving his residence?'

'Yes, we've common friends in Paris, Jacques Babton and Pierre Reveille. They had asked me to send their greetings to Don Bernardino.'

Francis Throckmorton was glad that during the conversation it came out that he had two common friends with the Ambassador. It was a misfortune to be seen by the top investigator of treasonous plots in the kingdom leaving the residence of the ambassador of a not particularly friendly country. He definitely could not tell he brought a message from two conspicuous conspirators. Sir Francis thought it was really bad luck to be seen by Sir Francis Walsingham leaving the residence of Don Bernardino.

Six months later, Sir Francis Throckmorton had several offers of London law firms that wished that he should join them. He finally had accepted one offer. At 10 o'clock in the morning, when he left his house to attend a meeting with his new associates, he was intercepted by several men.

'Good morning Sir Francis. My name is Jones and I work for the Principal Secretary. I regret to tell you that you're being arrested by order of the queen. Two of my men will take you to Whitehall Palace to be interrogated by Sir Francis Walsingham. In the meantime I've an order to search your house. If everything is in order you'll be released immediately, of course, but now please accompany my men quietly.'

Jones went on with the men to search the house without waiting for an answer from the flabbergasted Sir Francis. Two big and obviously very strong men were left with him and one of them addressed the arrested man.

'Kindly come with us, Sir.'

Sir Francis Throckmorton was thinking that this should be a mistake arising from his chance meeting with Walsingham just at the time he was leaving Don Bernardino's residence. He was told by that fellow called Jones that he would be released immediately if everything was in order. Since nothing in his life was out of order and nothing that could be found at his home could be regarded as subversive in any sense, only a few hours of discomfort would follow, but his prospect associates might not want to go ahead with the association they had offered. It was a bad mistake to have had a drink in Paris with two conspicuous conspirators and even a worse mistake to visit the Spanish Ambassador at his residence.

When Sir Francis Throckmorton entered the impressive large office of the Principal Secretary, he walked towards the heavy oak desk behind a window. Sitting at the desk reading papers was Sir Francis Walsingham. He continued reading for several minutes without lifting his eyes to look at the nervous man standing in front of him. When he finally set the papers aside and looked at Throckmorton, he spoke.

'Sir Francis, I'm shocked. Judging by the evidence collected by my people that I've just read, there's no doubt that you're a traitor.'

Throckmorton was on the verge of a nervous collapse after seeing the way this meeting was starting, but he was no coward and decided it was important not to show to this man that he was afraid. Certainly, Walsingham was not going to be moved if he should ask for mercy and he decided to talk calmly.

'Sir Francis, that's a terrible accusation. I'm not a traitor and any evidence to the contrary must be false. I trust that I'll have the right to a fair trial.'

'I'm afraid that I can attest, personally, that at least one of the accusations is true. You were under surveillance by my people and you made many visits to the Spanish Ambassador, Don Bernardino de Mendoza. I made only one visit to Don Bernardino since he was appointed ambassador and in that only visit I happened to see you leaving his residence.'

'That was just a coincidence. It was also the only time that I ever visited Don Bernardino. I'm sure that he'll confirm what I say.'

'Don Bernardino is no longer welcome in England. I'm afraid that as a result of your activities we're technically in a state of war with Spain. Don Bernardino will be expelled from England. It will not be necessary to recall our Ambassador in Madrid since we don't have one.'

'All this conversation is absurd. I'm a Throckmorton. My family has a very special relationship with the Tudor dynasty since the time of Henry VII.'

'Henry VII was a Catholic. Mary I was also a Catholic and she was supported by your father, Sir John Throckmorton. During the reign of Queen Elizabeth, your father had to be removed from his office as Chief Justice of Chester because of his Catholic convictions.'

'You must have been misinformed, Sir Francis. My father resigned from office for health reasons and died a few months later. Both my father and my uncle, Sir Nicholas Throckmorton, accepted Anglicanism during the reign of Henry VIII and again when Elizabeth ascended to the throne.'

'Nicholas Throckmorton was a friend of Mary Stuart and participated in the Norfolk conspiracy.'

'He was accused and incarcerated but it was proved he had nothing to do with the Norfolk conspiracy. He was released and died soon afterwards. He was always an Anglican. During the reign of Queen Mary, he participated in the Wyatt Rebellion, not against the queen but against her marriage to Felipe II. He encouraged Queen Elizabeth to support the Huguenots. The Duke de Guise imprisoned him for being a Protestant, regardless of his diplomatic immunity while he was the English Ambassador in France. Catherine de Medici also imprisoned him for helping the Huguenots and had to release him later. In Scotland, he tried to convince the Protestant nobles to restore Mary Stuart as queen following orders from Queen Elizabeth. She sent him because he was a friend of the Protestant nobles. It's absurd that you can believe our loyal Anglican family is a rebellious Catholic family.'

'I'll tell you what my agents have found out about you. Your frequent visits to the Spanish Ambassador aroused their suspicions and you've been followed closely.'

'Sir Francis, I'm a loyal subject of Queen Elizabeth. You've received false accusations against me and my family. Please tell me the accusations so that I can defend myself.'

'Coming from a Catholic family you fell under the influence of the doctrines preached by Edmund Campion at Oxford that reinforced your Catholic convictions.'

'That's not only absurd but against the facts. My family was Anglican and Campion left Oxford before I entered Hart

Hall.'

'As a student in London you joined a secret society of Inner Temple law students to help and protect Catholic priests.'

'This society must have been very secret since I never heard about it.'

'After your father died you went to Paris, traveled to Italy and Spain and consorted with papists.'

'Guilty on all counts, but I must point out that it's not illegal nor immoral to travel to Europe, that there is no Church of England in France, Italy or Spain and that the population there happens to be papist. Also, I must tell you that after traveling and getting to know Europe, I started to work as a lawyer in Paris. I was a visitor there and I was due to return to England after a few years. England is my home.'

'This year you returned to England as the agent of an elaborate conspiracy to depose Elizabeth and install Mary Stuart as Queen of England. This would be accomplished by a French army led by Henri, Duke de Guise, with the help of a Spanish garrison from Flanders.'

'The Duke de Guise has a large army. Why would he need the help of a Spanish garrison?'

'For political support from Felipe II.'

'And why should this French plot need the large number of meetings between the Spanish Ambassador and me that my accusers claim that have taken place?'

'You'll be asked that question under torture when you're taken to the Tower, so you should start thinking about your answer. I recommend you to confess immediately to reduce your suffering to the minimum possible.'

'Please evaluate this absurd plot that has been invented against me. It will not be believed by anyone.'

Walsingham smiled and looked at his prisoner. After remaining silent for almost a minute he said: 'People only know what they are told.'

He then rang a bell and two men came in. 'Take this gentleman to the Tower,' he said.

Sir Francis Throckmorton was tortured on the rack in the torture chamber of the Tower of London to extract a confession but he refused to talk. After six hours of torture, he fainted. He was removed from the rack and thrown to the floor of his cell.

The next day he was given a small amount of water and taken to the torture chamber again.

'You don't look too well... We can start all over again, if you wish,' said the interrogator, 'or you can go to your cell and wait for your trial there, if you just sign the written confession that has been prepared for you. We're in October now and the date of the trial has been set up for April. I've orders to torture you every day until you sign the confession and also to stop the torture after you sign. I can torture you every day for the next six months. And I don't have just the rack to torture you. I can give you a free tour of everything available here and you'll see that every other method of torture is even more painful than the rack.'

'Give me a few minutes to think.'

'No problem. I can start session number two in half an hour. If you wish to go ahead with it, I promise you it will be much longer than yesterday's session.'

Sir Francis evaluated his situation. Perhaps he could resist another day of torture. Perhaps he could even resist a week, but he could never resist a month. Even if he resisted a month, they had five more months to torture him. Even if he resisted until the trial, they could forge his signature and present a signed confession at the trial.

They were not asking for information. Walsingham had invented an absurd plot with no proof to confirm it. He was supposed to be working to prepare a French invasion of England meeting frequently with the Spanish Ambassador. He did not meet frequently with the Spanish Ambassador, but even if he did, he could not do any significant work to help an invasion. The accusations against him were pure madness. It would be better to conserve some strength and energy for the trial. But he had no illusions about receiving a fair trial. As a lawyer, he knew he would be taken to a Star Chamber trial where all those accused were found guilty.

'I'm ready to sign the confession,' he told the interrogator.

Walsingham was at the office of the Lord High Treasurer of her Majesty, Sir William Cecil, Lord Burghley.

'To what do I owe the pleasure of your visit to my office, Francis?'

Sir William Cecil was a tall man over 60 years old, with intelligent black eyes, an aquiline nose, gray hair, moustache and beard. His beard was quite long. He treated Walsingham with familiarity, by his first name, since it was under his wing that the Principal Secretary had been raised to his present position of power.

'It's because of the Throckmorton plot.'

'This is incredible, a Throckmorton plot. Are you sure that this young man is guilty?'

'Absolutely, Sir William. Jones always follows for a few weeks everyone that returns to England after a long stay abroad and his suspicions were raised by Francis Throckmorton's frequent visits to Don Bernardino de Mendoza, the Spanish Ambassador. His house was searched and damning evidence was found there. There was an unfinished coded letter for Mary Stuart, a list of his connections headed by Henri de Guise, that included the names of his two brothers in law, Sir William Catesby and Sir Thomas Thresham and a map in which several coves in the

Channel's coast are marked as being suitable for surreptitious landing of invasion forces. He has confessed and given us full details of a plot, including a two-pronged invasion of French and Spanish forces under the leadership of Henri de Guise.'

'What a shock. Until now I was convinced that the Throckmorton family was an exemplary loyal Anglican family. But this is your investigation and I don't see how I can help you in any way.'

'The help I need does not concern this particular plot, but what seems to be a constant flow of plots, Ridolfi, Norfolk, Campion and now Throckmorton. Only by sending Mary Stuart to the scaffold to be beheaded can we end these plots.'

'You know quite well that I've advised the queen to do exactly what you just said since the Ridolfi Plot was discovered.'

'That's why I believe that you'll accept my present idea. Obviously, Francis Throckmorton will be condemned as a traitor, while nothing will be done to Mary Stuart on the basis that she knew nothing about this plot. But she would have certainly benefited from the plot if it had taken place. Her cousin, Henri de Guise, would have placed her on the English throne. We should elaborate a document, to be signed by everyone in the Privy Council and by everyone important in the kingdom, including Mary Stuart, condemning anyone that may profit from a plot to kill or depose our Queen.'

'That's a very intelligent idea. It wouldn't matter if the person that receives a benefit participated in the plot or not, what matters is the benefit. I can write that document. I'll call it Bond of Association. The motive of the document should not be obvious because Elizabeth wouldn't allow it. I'll prepare a draft in perfect legal English that Mary Stuart will not hesitate to sign without realizing she's signing her own death warrant. But after I make the draft, we should write together the final text. Your law studies at the University of Padua make you particularly sharp about legal documents with hidden meanings.'

'Thank you, Sir.'

'I'll let you know as soon as I've prepared the draft. You can go back now to your office of Principal Secretary.'

'That title of Principal Secretary is inappropriate. The title should be changed to Secretary of State. It was perfect to use the title of Principal Secretary while you held that office, but it should have been changed when you were made Lord High Treasurer.'

'It's pompous to use titles as Principal Secretary and Lord High Treasurer for functions that should be called Secretary of State and Secretary of the Treasury. We're approaching the 17th century but are still using pompous 13th century titles. But these titles will eventually be changed. What's important is to do the jobs well and in this regard I'm very proud of you, Francis.'

During the months preceding the trial Sir Francis Throckmorton had plenty of time to think about his situation. He reasoned that he had been framed by Walsingham because he filled two requirements. One, he was a member of a very important family. Two, he returned to England after staying three years in France so that he could be accused of contact with Henri de Guise. Walsingham was not interested in him as a person but needed to attribute a plot to someone important so that he could take action against Mary Stuart.

In the same line of reasoning Francis analyzed that the first plot to kill Queen Elizabeth and install Mary Stuart as Queen of England was the plan devised by Italian banker Roberto Ridolfi and discovered by William Cecil when he was Principal Secretary. Francis continued to recall the events.

The Ridolfi plot was a real plot but reached only the planning stage. The idea was to send to England the large army that Spain had in Flanders to depose Elizabeth and enthrone Mary Stuart. The plot was discovered because too many people abroad heard about it when Ridolfi travelled to get the support of the Duke of Alba, in charge of the troops that would attack England, Pope Pius V and King Felipe II. Inevitably, some people considered it was an outrageous plan and wrote to the English authorities informing about it.

Sometime later, Walsingham entered the picture, discovered that Thomas Howard, Duke of Norfolk, had started to implement the plot together with Mary Stuart and requested that both of them should be executed. Francis realized that it was quite possible that Norfolk had been falsely accused by Walsingham who was trying to get Mary Stuart condemned to death. Elizabeth accepted Norfolk's guilt and he was beheaded but she believed Mary was innocent.

Another plot based on Ridolfi's scheme was the Campion plot. Everyone knew that Campion's guilt was based on the testimony of false witnesses.

And now Francis had been framed and was being falsely accused of another plot. Walsingham was making quite a reputation for himself discovering plots invented by him. What would happen when a real plot was made based on Ridolfi's scheme?

In April 1584 Sir Francis Throckmorton went to trial in the Star Chamber accused of high treason.

The Star Chamber was a court of law located in the Royal Palace of Westminster. In this trial the judges were all the Privy Councilors and three more judges elected by Walsingham. They all had been previously convinced by the Principal Secretary that the accused was guilty. Star Chamber sessions were closed to the public.

Proof presented at the trial were the papers claimed to have been found at the home of Sir Francis Throckmorton and the confession signed in the torture chamber of the Tower of London. Although the accused explained he was forced to sign a false confession under torture and that false proofs had been presented that he had never seen before, he was condemned to death. The sentence was to be drawn, hanged and quartered. He was executed in July 1584. Titled nobles, like the Duke of Norfolk, were beheaded if condemned for high treason, but Sir Francis Throckmorton was a knight, not a titled nobleman.

The two brothers in law of Sir Francis Throckmorton were not sent to trial on the basis that they had not yet been told about the plot before the arrest of the plotter.

Soon after the trial Sir Francis Walsingham obtained the Bond of Association signed by all members of the Privy Council and everyone important in England. To obtain this document, that he was planning to use to obtain the execution of Mary Stuart, Walsingham had invented the Throckmorton plot.

In October 1584 Anthony Babington went to the hiding place for correspondence in a Sheffield park. Instead of letters sent by Mary Stuart he found the letters addressed to Mary that he had left in September. He took the letters, went to the nearest pub and started a conversation with the fellow sitting next to him.

'How awful this recent Throckmorton plot. Fortunately, it was discovered before any damage was done. And in this town, you have the beneficiary of the plot, Mary Queen of Scots.'

'Not any more. Now Sir Ralph Sadler is in charge of her. He took her to Wingfield Castle.'

Anthony left the pub as soon as he finished his drink. He went straight to the estate of Henry Dunn's parents, where he was staying as a guest. Anthony thanked Henry's parents for their monthly hospitality over a period of four years and told them that he would not be returning every month for the time being.

He then went to the main fireplace of the large house and threw all the coded letters addressed to Mary Stuart to the fire. This was the end of his activity as a courier which had now become extremely dangerous. He could now dedicate himself to study to become a lawyer. Henry Dunn was already working as a lawyer while he, because of his duties as courier, needed at least two more years of study before becoming one.

Anthony Babington left the Sheffield area the next day.

PART II
THE PLOT

CHAPTER I
THE BEER BARREL

Anthony Babington and Henry Dunn were sitting at a table in the Horse and Unicorn Pub where they started to eat a light lunch of fish and vegetables.

'I talked with Margery yesterday about our idea of a second trip to France and she doesn't object.'

'I knew she wouldn't mind. Let's travel in the spring.'

'Excellent. I'll get the passages to cross the channel as soon as we get our permits.'

The day after he contacted Savage, Gifford introduced him to Captain Fortescue.

'Captain, this man is John Savage, who was a soldier in the army sent to Scotland by the queen in 1560. He was recommended to me as someone who can do all sort of home repairs. I believe he could be useful to you. Yesterday I was at the room where he lives. I visited him unannounced and I can tell you his room was clean and neat, so that he's a man that can live at this house if you two reach an arrangement.'

'I'm glad that you've come to talk about working with me, soldier. Your appearance looks familiar. Have we met before?'

'Yes, we did, 25 years ago. We met during the siege of Leith. You wouldn't remember me because I wasn't serving under you but under Lieutenant Hudson. But I remember you, because you were the most popular officer in our force. Black

Foskew the soldiers used to call you, affectionately.'

'They've called me Black Foskew since I was a young boy. Even my mother used the expression. But you're wrong about believing that I wouldn't remember you. After you called me Black Foskew I realized I do remember you Savage, because you're just as black as I am.'

Both men laughed heartily after this last phrase. Following with the conversation the captain told a joke about a red headed soldier and Savage then told a funny anecdote about a pale and freckled soldier. They continued laughing for a while. Captain Fortescue knew how to charm someone talking with him.

'Well soldier, now I want you to take a look at this house that has fallen to some degree of disrepair,' said the captain.

Savage examined the house very carefully and even went to the roof, regardless of the fact that it was raining lightly. To get to the roof he used a ladder that was stored in a shack of the backyard. He did not talk until he finished examining the house.

'This house is not in as bad a shape as it looks. The roof leaks can be repaired easily. The walls are sound and only the plasterwork must be repaired. Plenty of work, but not difficult. I can make inexpensive plaster myself. Papering or painting all the walls after repairing the plasterwork would be expensive, but I have a suggestion, whitewashing paint, basically just white lime mixed with water. I have my own formula with a couple of additives to make it last longer, but it's very inexpensive. White walls and ceilings make the interiors very luminous and clean looking. I can do all this work. If I live in this house there'll be no trouble with the guilds. Everyone has the right to repair the place where he lives.'

'Then it's settled and you'll come to live in the room of your choice in this house. When can you start?'

'Not so fast, Sir. We haven't discussed my salary yet.'

'That will not be a problem. How much do you want to earn?'

'I'm earning 16 pence a day right now. Of course you can pay me less if I live here.'

'I'll pay you 50 pence a day and I'll pay you one week in advance, soldier. Since you're going to live here I want you to buy new clothes so that you can look better. You must dress as well as our friend Gilbert, here.'

'That's right,' said Gifford. 'I'll bring many friends here and you must be one of us.'

'And I must teach fencing to both of you. My fencing partner may have a problem and might not continue to fence with me.'

'I'm a worker and I dress as a worker, not with the elaborate clothing you use, gentlemen, but I certainly need new clothes. In regard with fencing, I'm quite good with a knife but I've never learned how to handle a rapier,' said Savage.

'I'm not sure about your friend's problem, Captain,' said Gifford. 'I may have confused someone else with him.'

'This is very mysterious, but it's not my business,' said Savage.

'There's nothing that needs to be kept secret,' said Gifford. 'I came from France a few days ago and men from Walsingham came on board the ship I travelled. They checked some passengers and went away. One of Walsingham's men looked like the Captain's friend. This friend might be a Walsingham informer. It's no crime to be a Walsingham informer. Informers are at the service of the queen and I understand they're very well paid, but it's not nice to have an informer around.'

These words made a great impact on Savage. His face became red with anger and for a couple of minutes he remained still, breathing heavily. Then he calmed down and talked, looking at the captain.

'Walsingham's informers are the lowest kind of vermin that you can find in London. I certainly hope your friend is not one of them. If he is of this kind, I'm glad to know that you intend to ask him not to come around any longer.'

'It seems from your words that that you may have had a problem with a Walsingham informer, but that's not possible. No one with that kind of problem remains alive,' said Gifford.

'I'm lucky to be alive. Six years ago I had to teach a lesson to a drunken bastard in a pub knocking him down. But he was a Walsingham informer and in revenge he accused me of being a Catholic that knew in what house a Catholic priest would celebrate mass a Sunday evening. They took me to Whitehall Palace that Sunday for interrogation by Walsingham. Since I knew nothing I couldn't tell anything and was sent to a torture chamber. They put me on a rack and started to stretch me while asking me about the house where mass would be celebrated. I realized I was going to be tortured every day for several days until I died from the pain. That was the revenge of the informer that I knocked down in the pub.'

Since Savage remained silent, submerged in his memories, Gifford prompted him to continue.

'What happened then? How did you get free?'

'I'm not proud of this. I finally figured out someone to accuse. I suddenly remembered a friend told me in a pub that a man sitting at a table was called Jonathan Darcy and was the son of a traitor executed by order of Henry VIII. He was dressed as a gentleman and I figured he might have a house in London, near the pub. I told the torturer the mass would be given at the house of Jonathan Darcy. The torturer didn't stretch me anymore but left me in agony on the rack. A party was sent to raid Darcy's house. I expected to be killed when they came back since Walsingham would be furious after finding out I had lied, but instead after going to

Darcy's house he ordered I should be set free.'

'And what happened to poor Master Darcy?'

'I was very concerned about this. Under the pressure of torture I had accused innocent people. I had been just as mean as the informer that sent me to be tortured. The next day I found out the address of Jonathan Darcy and went there. I made enquiries in the neighborhood and I was happy to learn that nothing happened to him or his family, except the shock and fear of being raided by Walsingham's men.'

After a full minute of silence the captain talked.

'I don't believe that my friend is an informer. It's not in his character. I'll continue to fence with him and I'll teach fencing to both of you. No one likes informers and, since you had a bad experience, you dislike them more, soldier. Now let's go back to the main subject. I want you to start working here as soon as possible. When can you move here?'

'I can move here tomorrow evening, but I'm not certain I can start working in the house repairs the day after tomorrow. I've to make arrangements with my present employer. Probably he'll let me change employment after I do my work tomorrow, but if he asks me to work a few more days I must accommodate him.'

'That's fine with me.'

'When I start working I'll bring an assistant. Since you're paying more than what I'm getting now, I'll pay the assistant myself.'

'Certainly not. If you need an assistant hire him, but I'll pay for the work done in my house.'

'You are very generous, Captain. I'm delighted at the prospect of starting to work for you and of living here with you.'

'I'll see you tomorrow evening then, when you come with your belongings.'

'This is the right man for us, Father. And I'm not talking of fixing your place but about our mission.'

'I was concerned and thought you were being indiscrete when you explained the problem we have with Bernard Maude, but now we know he dislikes Walsingham's informers.'

'And I have the feeling that he didn't tell us the full story of his interrogation under torture. His first reaction showed an intense hatred. But he is thrilled by you. You can make a good Catholic out of him. We can probably organize a team with many idealistic young men, but few of them will be tough. Savage is tough and we need men like him.'

'The Providence is guiding us. We brought here a man to fix this house and he happened to be a key man for our mission.'

'I certainly hope you can recruit him for our mission. Pay him a month in advance rather than a week, to make him even more delighted to work for you.'

Several days later Anthony Babington and Henry Dunn were dining with Jacques and Suzanne Babton at their Paris home. Anthony was staying with the Babtons while Henry was staying with his father's friend, Louis Chatenau.

'Anthony told me that he had been acting as a courier delivering letters from France to Mary Stuart. However he's not doing that any longer since the new warden of Mary Stuart keeps everyone in her staff prisoner in the castle with Mary, making impossible any communication,' said Jacques.

'That's right and I'm glad,' commented Henry. 'Because of all the time that Anthony spent travelling from London to Sheffield during the last four years he hasn't been able to study to become a lawyer. I entered Lincoln's Inn at the same time as Anthony and I have been working as a lawyer for more than a year.'

'As you already know, Jacques,' said Anthony, 'before becoming a courier for Mary Stuart I belonged to a secret society that helped protect the Catholic priests that were working in England. Henry was another member of this society. Today Henry and I accidentally found in Paris our good friend, Thomas Salisbury, who was another member. Thomas told us that five more members of the society are here in Paris with him. They visited Archbishop Beaton, Ambassador of Queen Mary Stuart in France. The archbishop arranged for them to be granted a private audience with Pope Sixtus V if they should travel to Rome. This is as a reward for the work they did for the church protecting priests. They have accepted and Henry and I decided to join them. We'll be starting our trip to Rome within a week.'

Gilbert Gifford was pleasantly surprised when he found that the entrance hall of the house rented by Father Ballard was neatly painted white on nice even walls and had new furniture.

'Now it looks like the kind of place that Captain Fortescue would rent, not the place a Jesuit priest with poverty vows would rent.'

'You had an excellent idea bringing John Savage to repair this house,' answered Ballard. 'His work is very good and he does everything just with the help of a small boy that comes every day. He spent the first three days fixing the roof leaks. Then he fixed the walls of my bedroom, the walls of this hall and then of a big room I plan to use for the meetings of the group we must organize. When he finished with the walls of these three rooms he said my bedroom walls were sufficiently dry to be painted. After my room he painted this place. It looked so bare after being painted white that I realized I had to buy some furniture and he took me to the furniture factory where he used to work. There I got at a very low price everything that you see here. The few old things that were here were taken to other rooms.'

'It seems that now is the right time for you to suspend your fencing lessons until your Fencing Hall is fixed. You need at least two free weeks to go to Chartley with me.'

'Chartley? Why should I go to Chartley with you?'

'I've been very busy while Savage was repairing this house and I have plenty of news to discuss with you. I travelled to Tutbury, where Mary Stuart is imprisoned, to see if there's any way we can get in contact with her. We can only proceed with our plans if we can get in contact with her.'

'Why is contact with Mary Stuart so important? We just want to make her free. She's not going to object to that.'

'Of course she's not going to object. If we go to Tutbury Castle with an army of five thousand men we can rapidly set her free and she'll have no problem to accept her freedom. But we're thinking of sending in total secrecy a small group of 6 to 8 men to free Mary Stuart. Unless we're in contact with her and know exactly how to get the group in and out while she's waiting for it, we have no chance to succeed.'

'You're right We must plan carefully and in detail. We have an idea of something big, to overthrow a government. And we want to do this with a very small group, in which I've been ordered not to participate. It's an extremely difficult task. We want to produce a small flame to ignite a tremendous fire. Only a very precise flame can do it.'

'Let me tell you what I found out. Not only cannot Mary Stuart leave Tutbury Castle, but no one in contact with her can leave the castle, even if they work for her jailer, Amyas Paulet. Therefore no one can take a message or a letter to her. I spent days looking at the castle from the outside to see if the total isolation of Queen Mary was really implemented and I detected a single possibility for contact. There's one person from outside the castle that talks to one of the ladies-in-waiting of Queen Mary once a week. He's the beer supplier that every week withdraws an empty beer barrel from the castle and delivers a full one.'

In the 16th century water pure enough to be drunk was available only in very few places, so that beer was the standard beverage used.

'Do you see a chance of communication then?'

'I saw a chance and decided to find out about the beer supplier. I encountered that he's a Puritan and as all Puritans hates the idea that Mary Stuart should be next in line to succeed Queen Elizabeth. Therefore he wants to see her dead.'

'Then we have no chance at all.'

'I didn't give up and established contact with several men that work for Sir Amyas and go to the Tutbury pubs for relaxation. They don't have contact with Queen Mary but Sir Amyas sometimes talks to them about her.

This Puritan jailer is upset because the deposed Scottish queen, as he calls her, has fallen ill and all her ladies-in-waiting are pestering him requesting that she should be transferred to a better place. They claim that the unhealthy conditions of Tutbury Castle are the reason for Mary's ill health. However, he doesn't want to move her to another place.'

'That's terrible. Mary Stuart will die if she continues to be held at Tutbury.'

'I've been told that Sir Francis Walsingham also believes exactly what you said. He also believes that if Mary Stuart should die of illness, he'll be accused of having poisoned her. Now Walsingham is the one pestering Sir Amyas to move her out of Tutbury. He has even suggested a new location, Chartley Hall.'

'Is that why you want to go to Chartley with me?'

'Exactly. If Walsingham wants Mary Stuart to be the prisoner of Sir Amyas in Chartley Hall and not in Tutbury Castle, she'll be moved to Chartley Hall. Sir Amyas also knows that, but he's a stubborn person and will delay the transfer. The situation provides a good chance for us to establish contact with Queen Mary. We can go to Chartley to meet the beer supplier that's closest to Chartley Hall. We can move around in Chartley with total freedom rather than with all the precautions I had to take in Tutbury. And you have to come. I'm good to investigate but I don't have your knack to make friends. I've no idea of who's the beer supplier closest to Chartley Hall, but he must become our friend.'

'I agree with you and I understand the crucial importance of establishing an excellent relationship with Chartley's beer supplier.'

'To establish contact with the beer supplier, who'll be the only person to talk with the people that attend Mary Stuart, is our main objective at present. But we must not forget there are other matters that also require our attention.'

'I know and I've been thinking about the very pressing matter of what to do about Bernard Maude. Another important matter is to recruit John Savage to our cause. I've given him several hints showing I'm a Catholic and he was never shocked about it. He's very devoted to me and I got the impression that he likes the fact that I might be a Catholic. And I wish to connect these two matters. Bernard has to be followed for several days to see if he goes or does not go to Whitehall Palace to receive instructions from Walsingham. You and I cannot follow him unnoticed since he knows both of us. If I recruit John Savage his first assignment will be to follow Bernard. I've taken care to keep both of them apart from each other.'

'There's something else I have to tell you, very good news.'

'Go ahead.'

'I've received a letter from Charles Paget, the assistant to Archbishop Beaton. Six members of a secret society that used to help the Jesuit priests sent to England contacted the archbishop while visiting Paris. Beaton had previously arranged with Pope Gregory XIII that if any members of this society visit Rome they should be granted a private audience with the pope. Gregory XIII died and Sixtus V is the new pope, but Beaton is confident the agreement continues with any pope. Those six members have been joined by two more and all eight of them are on their way to Rome right now. When they return to Paris, Beaton will tell them to contact you once they're home. Eight men plus Savage and I make ten. With just a few more our small group will be complete and surely the newcomers can recruit other former members of the secret society.'

'These are excellent news, but please write to your friend Paget to tell him not to give any letters to these men. It was very foolish of you to bring a letter addressed to me. If it had been discovered on you they would have tortured you until you told them where to find me and now both of us would be imprisoned at the Tower awaiting execution. An absolutely silly thing to do since you could have collected at the French Embassy the letter that you presented to me, just as you collected the letter with the news you've given me.'

'You are right. I realized I had made a mistake when Walsingham's men boarded the ship that took me to England from France. I must admit that I was scared to death.'

'Why did you tell me I had to suspend the fencing lessons for two weeks? I'm just getting enough pupils to call this place a fencing school. A one-week interruption is reasonable but if I interrupt for two weeks most pupils will leave.'

'We need two weeks because Chartley is almost 50 leagues away from London.'

'Perfect. We can ride 25 leagues a day. Two days to go, two days to accomplish our objective and two days to return. We even have an extra day for contingencies. Riding 25 leagues a day will be good for you. When we get back you'll be a better rider and probably thinner.'

As Father Ballard said, he arrived at Chartley with Gilbert in the evening of the second day of riding.

'Let's take a look at Chartley Hall,' said Ballard.

'Shouldn't we first look for an inn where we can relax for a while first?'

'We're here to work, Gilbert, not to relax.'

After requesting directions the two men reached Chartley Hall and were surprised to find out it was uninhabited and undergoing a substantial reconstruction. It was a large mansion surrounded by a moat.

'This place is being refurbished as a suitable place for Queen Mary Stuart,' said Ballard. 'Your information was right Gilbert, congratulations. Sir Amyas might or might not know this yet, but Queen Mary will be moved from Tutbury Castle to Chartley Hall.'

The next day Ballard and Gilbert went out of the inn where they had slept during the night and walked in the general direction of Chartley Hall. Not far from the inn they found a very large pub called The Red Dragon.

'Let's go inside,' said Gilbert. 'Here they must surely know about the suppliers of beer barrels.'

They approached the counter where a big, fat man with a red face, a bushy gray moustache and long sideburns was talking with two customers.

'Good morning,' said Ballard. 'You've a very nice town and a superb pub. I wish I could find something as nice in London. Can we get something to eat and plenty of beer?'

'You sure can get plenty of the best beer in England, since we make it right here. My main business is to make beer for Chartley and most of the nearby towns. The pub is a side line, mostly for my entertainment. I own the beer factory and I have to keep an eye on it but I don't have to work in it.' The fat man laughed heartily and then added. 'I don't have to work here either, but I own this place too and I like to talk with customers. I gather you two are from London.'

'My friend here is a Londoner but I'm from Black Pool and have been living in London for only a few months. I'm Captain John Fortescue, at your service, and my friend is Master Gilbert Gifford.'

'My name is Thomas Jones and, as I have already told you, I produce the best beer in all England.' The fat man laughed again.

The three men sat at a table and the talkative fat man did most of the talking while the other two were eating. After he finished eating, while drinking beer Ballard took the conversation towards the matter in which he was interested, Chartley Hall.

'Last evening we saw a very large house, surrounded by a moat, which apparently is being refurbished.'

'That's right. It's Chartley Hall. The mansion of the Barons Ferrers de Chartley used to be Chartley Castle. When the baron, Sir Walter Devereux, Baron Ferrers de Chartley died alongside Richard III in the Battle of Bosworth in 1485, the castle was abandoned and is a ruin now. Sir Walter had died fighting against the new king, Henry VII, and his family was out of favor. The family moved to a much smaller place, Chartley Hall, which was new and had a good defensive moat. Another Sir Walter Devereux, grandson of the Sir Walter that fought against Henry VII, regained the favor of the crown helping to crush the rebellion of the Catholic nobles of the north of England. As a reward Queen Elizabeth made him Earl of Essex, in addition to his title as Baron Ferrers de Chartley.'

'Did he stay in Chartley Hall?'

'The family did, but he volunteered to go to the Irish Province of Ulster to subdue the Irish rebels at his own expense, expecting to get very rich with this venture. He departed to Ireland with twelve hundred men. Anyway he was a poor leader and rapidly lost nearly one thousand men because of sickness, famine and desertion. Then this nobleman with centuries old lineage showed his true nature of a pig. He behaved as a traitor against his own deputy and massacred defenseless Irish, mostly women and children, several times. When he returned to Chartley Hall nine years ago, instead of being chastised by the queen for his behavior he was sent to Dublin as Earl Marshall of Ireland. The good news is that he got sick and died in Dublin, only two weeks after his arrival. Chartley Hall has been empty since then and was in very poor condition after being uninhabited for almost ten years, until last week. Now, workers are fixing it.'

'What about the Earl's family. Didn't the wife and children stay in Chartley Hall?'

'That's the juicy part of the story,' said the fat man and he laughed heartily afterwards. 'The Earl was married to a beautiful woman, Lettice Knollys, related to the Boleyn family and therefore to the queen. When she became a widow she was made lady-in-waiting of the queen and went to live at Whitehall Palace. Two years later she was married secretly without knowledge of the queen. Can you guess why she couldn't tell the queen?'

'I've no idea,' said Ballard.

The fat man winked an eye and laughed heartily. 'Because she married the queen's favorite.'

He said favorite in a picaresque way, winking an eye again. 'She married the Earl of Leicester. Quite soon someone told the queen and she mounted in anger.'

At this point the fat man was laughing so much he could not continue. When he recovered he went on.

'She banished Lady Lettice from court and kept Leicester there, but no longer as a favorite.'

He said favorite winking an eye again and in the same picaresque way as before and started laughing again.

One employee called Jones to consult him about something, so that he left Ballard and Gilbert alone for a few minutes.

'This man does not have much respect for Queen Elizabeth,' said Gilbert.

'And he called a pig the nobleman that helped quell the Catholic Rising of the North,' said Ballard. 'I wouldn't be surprised if he turns out to be a Catholic.'

Shortly afterwards the talkative Thomas Jones returned to the table where Ballard and Gilbert were drinking beer.

'Now the second Earl of Essex is coming to live in Chartley Hall. I hope that he's a better person than his father.'

'Why do you say so? Do you have any information?' asked Gilbert.

'No information is needed. Sir Walter had a son, Robert, that must be about 20 years old and Chartley Hall is being fixed after ten years of neglect. Obviously, Sir Robert Devereux is taking charge of his estate.'

'What do you think, Captain?'

'I think that Master Jones must also consider other possibilities. For example we were told that Sir Robert's mother has displeased the queen. It would be convenient for Sir Robert to lend Chartley Hall to the Crown, to make sure the queen's displeasure doesn't reach him.'

'Oh sure. This way, staying at Chartley Hall the queen can visit this pub to look for a new favorite.' The fat man laughed heartily.

'It's commented in London that Mary Stuart may be moved from Tutbury Castle to a more pleasant place. The remodeled Chartley Hall will be a very pleasant place.'

The fat man got suddenly serious and talked in a low voice rather that loudly as he had been talking up to then. 'You fellows know something?'

'We don't know anything, we're just speculating idly while

we are drinking your excellent beer, the best in England, no doubt.'

'Your powers of speculation astonish me, but I'm sure that you wouldn't speak of something of such great importance unless you knew what you say. And I'm glad. It's a shame that Queen Mary Stuart has been kept a prisoner all these years. And I've been told that Tutbury Castle is a horrid place. But let's talk about less serious matters. I envy you Captain. You must be about the same height and age I am, but you keep the figure both of us had in our early twenties while I now weigh twice as much as you do. Did soldiering keep you in shape?'

'No, hard farm work did it. I wasn't a soldier for long, only in the army sent by the queen to Scotland.'

'And how do you avoid getting fat in London?'

'I teach fencing in London.'

'Fencing, that's good. It means that the rapier at your side is not just a dress sword you carry to look elegant but a real weapon that you know how to use. You're a dangerous man Captain. I wouldn't want to make you cross at me.'

'Fortunately, we, dark men, look dangerous and since I look dangerous I never had the need to fight strangers.'

Ballard laughed after these words and the other two joined the laughter.

'But I wouldn't say you're dark, you have black hair, a black moustache and black eyes. Also you're tanned after riding from London, while your friend got kind of red. Sun red, not beer red like me.' They all laughed.'

'I'm English and some of us can be as dark as many men from the Mediterranean countries.'

'The Captain is very confident that as a dangerous man no one will mess with him. We came here from London in only two days, just the two of us along solitary roads.'

'I'm sure you are safer with the Captain than with five young men like you.'

'It's not just the safety. Every bone in my body aches today while he is just as fresh as any day.'

'I don't have that risk. No horse can survive a 25-league ride with me on top.'

The three of them laughed a long time.

'It's almost noon now. I must eat. We're having a good time and you two must join me. It's my treat.'

The three of them were then served a hearty lunch with more beer.

'I was thinking about your soldiering experience. You fought in Scotland to support the Protestant nobles that wanted to take over the country.'

'I had no religious motivation. I just wanted to be an army officer.'

'Sir Walter Devereux went to Ireland to massacre Irish Catholics.'

'Unfortunately, we, English, have been massacring the Irish for a long time and we used to be Catholic when we started.'

'But when English Catholics are being prevented from practicing their faith, our Protestant queen should be more careful about the message given to the English by her wars outside England. Under Queen Mary Stuart, Catholics and Protestants were treated in the same way in Scotland. That's not the case now under the rule of the Protestant nobles. And speaking of Mary Stuart I'll say that I'm sure that what you call speculation is information and that Queen Mary will be taken here.'

'If that should be the case, you'll be in a unique position,' said Gilbert.

'Why would I be in a different position than everyone else in Chartley?'

'Mary Stuart is in total isolation from outside the place where she's being held prisoner. No one around her can have any contact with anyone from the outside, with only one exception, the person that every week delivers a barrel of beer and withdraws an empty one. That person has a few minutes a week to talk to someone at the service of Mary Stuart.'

Thomas Jones remained silent thinking about what he had heard. After several minutes he talked.

'You fellows want to help Mary Stuart, are certain that she'll be brought to Chartley Hall and you want to help her through me. I'm a Catholic that cannot practice his religion and I would love to help Queen Mary, but a few minutes a week are just enough time for very brief messages. My memory is quite limited. I can only give very short messages and probably would make mistakes retelling the messages I receive. I cannot take any letters with me and I cannot accept any letters sent by Queen Mary because that would be suicidal. I would like to help but it doesn't seem worth it because it's too risky for very little help.'

'Short messages would do,' said Ballard. 'The short messages would make a world of difference to poor Queen Mary, compared to total isolation. You're a good man Master Jones. God will reward you.'

'How long will you stay at Chartley?'

'We're planning to start our way back to London the day after tomorrow at 6 o'clock in the morning.'

'Then come back tomorrow morning. I need to think carefully about your request before giving you an answer.'

Ballard and Gilbert went to look again at Chartley Hall from the outside. On the way they talked about their meeting with Thomas Jones.

'It's dangerous to go back to the pub,' said Gilbert. 'The fat man may have denounced us to the authorities. We might be arrested as soon as we enter.'

'Denounce what? That he said he was a Catholic? That he said he would be willing to help Mary Stuart?'

'He can denounce us for being spies that have learned that Mary Stuart will be moved to Chartley Hall.'

'Men that work for Sir Amyas Paulet are talking about this matter in pubs. That's how you found out. You consider yourself a spy, but many people have heard what Paulet's men are saying openly in pubs.'

'Perhaps you're right. But why did he tell us to come back? Why didn't he answer right away?'

'Because it's an extremely dangerous matter to get involved in anything made to help Mary Stuart. And very brief messages that are sent once a week can appear to be a most insignificant help for which it's not worth it to risk so much. It's most reasonable that he wants to think carefully about it. You must notice that he didn't ask us to return this evening for supper, but tomorrow morning. He wants to evaluate the matter most carefully tonight.'

'Why didn't you tell him that brief communications are necessary to arrange how to get in and out of Chartley Hall to free Mary Stuart as well as to tell the day and time to do it.'

'I didn't want to say anything in the first meeting. If he says again that he would do it but the small support given by short messages makes his help irrelevant, I'll explain to him that short messages will be most relevant. Relax Gilbert. Our visit to Chartley has been a success.'

When they reached Chartley Hall they walked around the entire perimeter of the mansion.

'The moat makes the place very suitable for keeping prisoners. We need a boat just to get to the walls of this mansion,' said Ballard.

'All the windows in the ground floor have bars, so that no one can go in and out through them. We need a big ladder to reach the second-floor windows. To support such ladder the boat we use must be quite strong and rather large.'

'No one would have to climb the ladder. Mary Stuart should be on the arranged date, at the arranged hour, at one window she designates. The rescue team that goes in the boat would have men with the mission of keeping the boat stable using hooks to keep it attached to the wall beneath the designated window. Other men should have the mission of keeping the ladder firm and stable. Queen Mary, dressed as a man, should go down the stairs to get on the boat. Then the boat crosses the moat and Mary is given a horse to mount. Finally Mary rides away with a few men as escort and goes to the castle where she'll take refuge until the day she's taken to London to be crowned as Queen of England.'

The next morning Ballard and Gilbert were back at the Red Dragon pub. Gilbert was still afraid to go back.

'I have very good news for you fellows,' said Thomas Jones as soon as he saw them. Once they were seated at a table he explained.

'If your information is correct and Mary Stuart is moved to Chartley Hall, I can deliver and withdraw several letters every week.'

'But it's very risky for you to have such letters in your pockets.'

'The letters will not be in my pockets. The letters will be in the beer barrels.'

'How's that possible'?

'Beer barrels have a hole on the side, near the bottom. On that hole we place what we call a stopper. We plug the stopper in the hole before we fill the barrel with beer. When we pull the stopper out the beer pours out and can be collected in jars. If I have letters to deliver I'll place the letters in a watertight leather pouch that I'll tie to the stopper so that it would not float in the beer when I fill the barrel. When the barrel is empty the pouch can be taken out. Any letters Queen Mary may wish to send to her followers can be put in the leather pouch, again tied to the stopper of an empty barrel.'

'You're a genius Master Jones.'

'Not a genius, a beer brewer. And my father was a beer brewer too so that I know this trade quite well. I'm doing this because I'm a Catholic that cannot practice his faith and I don't like our Virgin Queen.'

The fat man said virgin with a sneer.

'But this is very dangerous business and I'll only receive letters from one of you two. Likewise I'll only deliver letters to one of you. You must be part of a group of followers of Queen Mary but I don't want to be part of that group and I don't want to meet anyone else. I trust I made myself very clear about this. I will not accept anything from anybody except one of you. I'm risking my life and the least I can do is to demand the maximum secrecy possible.'

'You are helping Queen Mary beyond anything we had ever hoped. You'll be rewarded for your help.'

'I'm not interested in any eventual reward. I'm interested in not being caught.'

CHAPTER II
JOHN SAVAGE

Back in London after their trip to Chartley, Gilbert and Father Ballard were exultant about having succeeded beyond their most optimistic expectations.

'Your spying at Tutbury was brilliant Gilbert, and allowed us to obtain full communication with Mary Stuart regardless of the tight measures taken by Sir Amyas to keep her in total isolation.'

'My spying would have been meaningless if I had gone to Chartley alone. We succeeded because our new friend, Thomas, likes you. Perhaps I should say he likes Captain Fortescue, the very likeable character you created as your cover. The real you, the humble Father Ballard, might be a better man than the captain, but not as likeable.'

'You just made a very profound observation. Captain Fortescue is more than a cover. I've become flamboyant Captain Fortescue while remaining introverted Father Ballard inside. The priest must struggle to keep the captain in line. Now that the captain enjoyed himself riding a hundred leagues the priest must talk with Savage. I must find out if he'll continue to be just a good worker that makes our place pleasant or a member of our most intimate group.'

'I have to work too. I must prepare a letter for Archbishop Beaton to tell him that we can deliver letters to Mary Stuart, without telling anything, of course, of the means that we'll use. Then, I'll go to the French Embassy to deliver that letter and to arrange to receive the correspondence for Queen Mary without having to go to the Embassy to get it. Walsingham may have spies looking at the people that enter the Embassy. Since I already went there a few days ago I'll use a false beard this time.'

'That's right. We must be very cautious, since we have a

formidable enemy with spies everywhere. If I manage to recruit Savage, his first assignment will be to check if Bernard Maude works for Walsingham.'

The next day Ballard went to see Savage at the room he was whitewashing with his child assistant.

'Please come with me John, I must talk with you.'

'Yes, Captain, right away. You go on with your work Tod.'

When they were at the room that was prepared as his study, Ballard closed the door and sat at the desk.

'Please take a seat John. How do you feel about working for me?'

'I'm delighted. I'd never worked for someone as considerate with me as you are, Captain. You don't treat me as a hired hand but you make me feel as your soldier and even your friend.'

'Well, I thought that perhaps you could feel uncomfortable in one aspect. You know that I lived in France for many years as a Frenchman and that the French are Catholic.'

'I have wondered if you were a Catholic. For years I've tried to contact Catholics but I've never met anyone that admits to be one. Are you a Catholic?'

'Yes, I am. Why do you want to meet Catholics?'

'Well, you know that a Walsingham informer falsely accused me of a being a Catholic. Also that to save myself I falsely accused someone that might be Catholic of making his house available for a Catholic Mass. I'm ashamed of myself and I feel I owe Catholics some kind of reparation for the harm my weakness may have caused.'

'You acted to relieve the pain for a while when you were under torture. You don't have to reproach yourself for anything. There's something you could do for me however, but only if you wish to do it. You're under no obligation to do anything.'

'I'll consider myself fortunate if I can do you a favor.'

'As you already know, our friend Gilbert suspects that my fencing partner, Bernard Maude, might be a Walsingham informer. Gilbert believes he could have been a member of a party of Walsingham's men that boarded the ship in which he returned to England from France. But he's not sure.'

'Show me this man in such a way he doesn't see me. I can follow him everywhere he goes. If he's a Walsingham spy, he must report to him in Whitehall Palace periodically. If in one week he never goes to Whitehall we can consider he wasn't the man seen by Gilbert in his ship. But, since you have reasons to keep your life confidential, if he does go to Whitehall we must find out if he's been ordered to watch you or if he's watching everyone and just happened to become a friend of yours.'

'You're certainly right. I've something to hide and I must find out if I've already been discovered, since in that case I must leave the country at once.'

'Before you ask me to do that kind of task, you must fully understand the seriousness of the matter. If this man works for Walsingham I must interrogate him. If I interrogate him he must die. It'll make no difference to his fate if he's spying specifically on you or on anyone else. If I leave him alive after the interrogation, he'll realize he was questioned because someone close to him has something to hide. Then he'll report to Walsingham everyone with whom he's in frequent contact with.'

'But I like Bernard. He's my friend. I can't order his death.'

'An informer's only friend is his payment and you wouldn't be ordering me to kill him. You would just ask me to check if he's a Walsingham spy or not. But you must evaluate the full consequences of checking such an important matter. If he isn't a Walsingham spy he'll continue to be your fencing partner. On the other hand, if he's a spy that will eventually denounce you, you can't just ask him to stay away from you. It's him or you. His life or your life. I would imagine you aren't checking on him just because you're a Catholic. Walsingham does not intend to kill every Catholic in England. You've got something else to hide and you don't have to tell me anything about it. But you must realize the eventual result of checking your fencing partner. What's your decision?'

Ballard did not know what to answer. Since the day he met Gilbert and was told by him that Bernard might be a Walsingham spy, he realized that such suspicion had to be checked. Nevertheless he had never thought that if Bernard was a spy he had to be killed even if he was not spying on him. The only possible way to avoid killing Bernard was to cancel the operation and flee the country if Bernard did work for Walsingham. All the preparations would be lost even if Bernard had never realized that Gilbert and he were working against the queen. Convincing reluctant Father Auger to allow him to carry out the plot to replace a Protestant queen by a Catholic one, the careful cover of being a retired captain with a fencing school and the arrangements to have correspondence with Mary Stuart, everything accomplished would be thrown away. Too much was at stake. It was essential to check if Bernard was a spy and, if he was one, he had to be interrogated to find out if Walsingham had already found out that he was a Catholic priest. After a long interval to ponder the situation, Father Ballard gave Savage an answer.

'It's very important to learn if Bernard Maude works for Walsingham. If he does, he must be interrogated. I'll greatly appreciate it if you would take care of this matter.'

'Is he coming here today?'

'Yes, I expect him this morning at ten and he should be leaving around 11 o'clock.'

'I can watch him unseen through a partially opened door

when he's waiting for you. When he leaves I'll follow him wherever he goes. I'll follow him for a week. If he doesn't contact Walsingham in one week, we can safely assume he's not a spy. If I return before the week is over, it's because he contacted Walsingham or his men and I've come to report the result of my interrogation. But you must tell me everything you know about this man.'

'He's the youngest son of a gentleman farmer. He worked at the farm until his father died. He never worked afterwards. The father made arrangements for the brother that inherited the farm to give him a modest annual sum. He married a widow ten years older than him that died two years ago. She had inherited a small but nice house in London from her late husband and she also received an annuity from her own farmer brother. When his wife died Bernard inherited the house and he lives there but of course receives no annuity from his brother-in-law. He has no children and hasn't married again. After becoming a widower he has kept only a man servant and a cook at his house.'

That day Savage followed Bernard from a safe distance. Bernard went to his house for lunch. He was satisfied about his fencing practice with Captain Fortescue because, unlike most other days, he had been much better than the captain. After lunch he took a nap and did not leave his house until it was dark. Savage had been watching the house, standing on the street at one corner, walking a little and then watching from the other corner. He carried bread and a bottle of beer in a small bag hanging from a shoulder, so that he could take a bite every now and then without leaving the watching.

When Bernard left his house he went to a nearby neighborhood and at one point started to walk very slowly, hiding in dark places whenever other people were walking on the street, until reaching a particularly dark place where he remained a long while. Then, at a time the street was totally deserted, he dashed out of his hiding place, crossed the street and knocked at the door of a house. Obviously, he was waited there by someone, since the door opened immediately and Bernard went in.

Savage had expected that the man he followed would spend the night at his own house and planned to use the interval to go to his room to sleep a few hours himself, but he had to remain alert since he had no idea when the man would leave the house. Because of the precautions taken, he figured Bernard was visiting a married woman while her husband was away travelling. At around three o'clock Bernard dashed out of the house into the empty street and walked back to his own home. Savage then decided it was safe for him to go back to his room to sleep for an hour, to get some more bread and to replace the beer in his bottle.

Savage returned to his watch at dawn and stationed himself at a place he had selected the day before from where he could observe unseen the entrance to Bernard's house. At around eleven o'clock that morning, Bernard left his house and walked to the nearby Black Lion pub where he joined a group of friends. Savage sat at a table near the entrance where he drank beer and ate some fish while Bernard and his friends had an abundant meal.

Bernard left his friends at around four in the afternoon. Savage got quite excited with the chase when he saw the man he followed was approaching Whitehall Palace. From a safe distance he saw that Bernard entered the palace. Two hours later he came out and walked jauntily to his house, obviously in very high spirits.

Bernard came out of his house when it was quite dark and walked in the direction of the house he had visited the night before. Since he was obviously going to the same house of the day before Savage rushed, walked fast passing Bernard, reached the street of the house and hid in the same totally dark place where Bernard had hid the night before.

As Savage expected, Bernard went to hide in the same place a few minutes later. Bernard's happy mood turned into terror when he felt a strong arm grabbing him, an unseen man behind him and a dagger at his neck.

'Don't move and don't utter a sound.'

After being silent for several minutes Bernard asked a question in a very low voice.

'Is it you, Roger?'

'No, I'm not Roger. Is Roger the cuckold husband of the lady you're visiting across the street? I'm not your enemy. I just need you to answer a few questions and, if you answer truthfully, I'll let you go.'

Bernard seemed relieved since his body, that had become rigid the moment Savage grabbed him from behind, relaxed a bit.

'What questions?'

Bernard then realized the nature of the questions he would have to answer and his body became rigid again.

'You know very well you're doing something dangerous. I want to know exactly what you do. Whom did you visit today at Whitehall Palace?'

At the time he made this question Savage pressed his dagger more strongly against Bernard's neck, piercing his skin a little. Bernard's heightened senses detected a streak of warm blood running along his neck.

'I visited Sir Francis Walsingham, Principal Secretary to her Majesty. I'm under orders to keep my eyes and ears wide open so that I can report on anything dangerous to the queen. But I haven't seen anything to report yet. A few times I've been called to assist inspectors that board ships bringing people from France, but no arrests were ever made on ships I boarded. I've been paid good money regardless of the fact that I haven't reported anything yet. I don't have much money on me now but I could bring you money.'

'What kind of activities were you told would be worth reporting?'

Savage pressed his dagger more strongly than before.

'Catholic activity. A Catholic Mass, for instance.'

'You must have suspicions about some of your friends. Tell me what friends.'

'I don't suspect any of my friends. I was told I just had to be alert. I was especially warned against making false accusations for personal petty reasons.' At this point Bernard's voice became very feeble and gave Savage the impression he would start to cry. But Bernard recovered enough to talk again. 'You can tell Roger I would never invent false accusations against him to get him out of the way.'

Savage realized that the only person that Bernard thought might be interested in his activities as an informer was called Roger and was probably the husband of Bernard's mistress. There was no more need of running the danger that strong Bernard Maude might break the hold he had on him and he slashed his throat. Bernard died instantly.

Savage wiped his dagger clean against the dead man's clothes and searched him. To give the impression that he was killed to be robbed he removed the bag where the dead man had some money.

When Savage got back to the house where he was working and living, he knocked at the door of the room that was prepared as the study of Captain Fortescue.

'Come in,' answered Ballard from the inside.

Savage found him sitting on an armchair and reading by the light of a small unornamented bronze oil lamp of the relatively new type that had a special reservoir to regulate the flow of oil to the wick. When Ballard saw that it was Savage that entered, he got pale.

'I see that you didn't have to watch Bernard for a full week, John.'

'That's right, Captain. He went to Whitehall Palace today.'

'Take a seat and tell me everything.'

Savage then told Ballard everything that happened since he started watching the movements of Bernard Maude.

'May God forgive me for sending you on this mission, John. But this had to be done. If Bernard had kept coming here, very soon he would have reported to Walsingham about a group of young men meeting at this place. You see John, I'm not just a Catholic but a Catholic priest.'

'You... a priest! I can hardly believe it. But now I understand. I was wondering why you never brought any women here at night. I've walked with you on the streets and all women, young and old, look at you admiringly. And you like women when they're young and pretty, since you look back at them. But you don't want to be involved with women of loose morals and since Catholic priests cannot marry you restrain your feelings towards all women. That's wrong, you know, you should marry and have children.'

'It's not a matter of Church regulations in my case. I can decide to put my own life in danger being a Catholic priest in Protestant England, but I would have no right to put a wife and children in danger.'

'You're right, Captain. You're the master of your own life and I had no right to make any comments. But can I ask you a question?'

'Go ahead, John.'

'Did you know Father Campion and the two young priests that were sent to the gallows with him?'

'Yes, I knew the three of them quite well. I'm a Jesuit like them and Father Campion was a very dear friend.'

'And now you want revenge and cannot have a Walsingham spy around while you're preparing it.'

Ballard was shocked about Savage's bluntness, but accepted that he was that kind of man, with no subtlety and very frank.

'I would say I want "justice", rather than "revenge", but perhaps I should admit the difference is only a matter of choice of words.'

'Well its destiny that made our paths cross, Captain, and I have no qualms about saying that I want revenge. When I was on the rack and my torturer told me Walsingham had given orders for my release, that he didn't approve, I didn't know if he was only giving me hope to increase my pain or if he was telling the truth. I then swore to God that if I did get released I'd kill three people, my torturer, the man that made the false accusation against me and Queen Elizabeth. I killed the first two a few years ago but I need help to kill the queen. The three priests were accused of plotting to kill the queen and since then I've been trying to get in contact with Catholics because I want to participate in a plot like that.'

'The accusations against the three priests and all the other priests executed later were false. If they ever capture me they'll make the same accusations against me and therefore I might as well work to make that kind of plot.'

'The two of us together will make a great team.'

'As a priest, I can't be an assassin, but since it has been approved by the pope that Catholics may participate in a plot to replace Protestant Queen Elizabeth by Catholic Queen Mary Stuart, I can assist a group of Catholic men that plot to do that.'

'Do you have any men already?'

'Eight young men, currently in the Continent travelling to see the pope, will be sent to me soon. Adding Gilbert and you, I'll have ten men. With ten men I have enough for two teams, one to kill Queen Elizabeth and another to set Queen Mary Stuart free. Of course I could certainly use one or two more.'

'Any men like you among the eight you're expecting?'

'I haven't met them yet and I might have a surprise, but I can understand your concern since both Gilbert and I have the same concern. I don't expect any of the eight or any of the additional one or two men that might join us later to be a tough man like you and me. When I requested this mission I wanted to lead the group that'll go to kill the queen, but I was given strict orders that I can only advise but can't have an active role in the implementation of the plan. Without your participation the chances of success were very slim. I started to believe we had a chance of success only after you told Gilbert and me you had been tortured after being falsely denounced by a Walsingham spy. You're the man I needed to lead a small group, you and four strong men, which must infiltrate and hide inside Whitehall Palace. You would come out surreptitiously in the middle of the night to kill the queen during her sleep and escape.

Setting Queen Mary free is difficult but does not require the same type of toughness as killing Elizabeth. It's a task that five or six idealistic young men should be able to perform.'

'Do you have any idea of how my men and I could get into the palace?'

'We'll have to find a courtesan with a grudge. You can be certain that there are many that fit that description. We have an extremely ambitious plan, to replace one monarch with another, working in total secrecy with a small group of young idealistic men untrained in this type of action. I started with only one man, Gilbert. Just the two of us have accomplished something much more difficult than finding a courtesan with a grudge. We established the means of exchanging correspondence with completely isolated Mary

Stuart. Last but not least we found you, someone that can lead the group that'll kill Queen Elizabeth.'

'Yes, Captain. I'll be a member of your Catholic team, but I don't want to be involved with religious issues. To maintain the team spirit I'll participate when you give masses for the group, but don't give me spiritual advice until I'm ready to ask you for such advice. I can't see you as a priest, Captain, but I'm ready to take your fencing lessons.' Savage smiled while saying the above words.

'I won't press you to become a Catholic, but I'm most happy to have you as a member of our ambitious team. Now I'm starting to believe that our plan will not just be a matter of making a forceful statement, but something that can actually succeed.

CHAPTER III
THE PLOT THICKENS

Early in August 1585 Anthony Babington and his friends arrived in Paris, back from Rome. Anthony, as in his previous visits to Paris, stayed at the home of his relative, Jacques Babton. The day after their arrival Anthony and his seven travelling companions went to see Archbishop Beaton to thank him for the arrangements he had made for the audience granted to them by Pope Sixtus V.

'Welcome gentlemen,' said the Archbishop, greeting them. 'I trust that you were given an audience with the pope as I had arranged.'

'The pope devoted to us almost a full hour of his time,' answered Anthony. 'We had no idea that the work we did was considered so important by the church.'

'Your nephew, Monsignor Beaton,' added Thomas Salisbury, 'took excellent care of us during the entire week we spent in Rome. We visited the Sistine Chapel with him and he took us to see the most interesting places in Rome.'

For over an hour the eight Englishmen talked with Archbishop Beaton about their visit to Rome.

'I'm very glad,' said the archbishop, 'that you enjoyed the long trip to Rome so much. When you get back to England I want all of you to get together and visit someone with whom I'm in permanent contact by correspondence, Captain John Fortescue. I would have liked you to take him a letter for Queen Mary Stuart, since I understand the captain might be in a position to have it delivered to her. However it has become very dangerous to enter the Port of London with compromising papers. Anyway, we can send the letters to the French Embassy and a very reliable assistant of Captain Fortescue, Master Gilbert Gifford, will take these to the captain. I've written the captain's address in London in this paper. Memorize it and destroy the paper. You'll enjoy the visit because he's a charming person and he runs a fencing school at the address I've given you. Perhaps you'll take lessons at his school and shall become able swordsmen, like him.'

'It's great that he can have letters delivered to Queen Mary Stuart,' said Anthony. I was a courier for the queen for several years until she was removed from Sheffield Castle to Wingfield Castle. It became difficult to make contact with her under the care of Sir Ralph Sadler. Just a couple of months later she was sent to a new prison, the horrible and unhealthy Tutbury Castle. A short time later, Sadler was no longer responsible for Mary Stuart and another new warden, Sir Amyas Paulet, has made it impossible for her to receive any letters.'

'I don't have confirmation yet, but the Captain is making arrangements and he's confident that he will succeed. You'll know more about this when you visit him. I must also tell you that today I've learned something that makes England particularly dangerous to Catholics. Queen Elizabeth has just signed a treaty with the Protestant Dutch to help them get their independence from Spain. We had a situation of undeclared war between England and Spain, but I've no doubt King Felipe II will consider this treaty a formal declaration of war from England against Spain.'

Three weeks later Gilbert Gifford was talking with Father Ballard at his study in the large house he was using in London.

'Father, I've received several letters for Mary Stuart from the French Embassy, a letter for you from Archbishop Beaton and a letter for me from Charles Paget.'

'Tell me about the letter that you received.'

'It says that the eight members of the secret society that protected priests have already left Paris. Archbishop Beaton requested them to contact you in London. I checked the whereabouts of the leader of the party, a man called Anthony Babington, and found out that he returned to his London home two days ago. He left immediately for Dethick, where his wife is waiting for him with their daughter at her parents' large estate in the country. They'll probably remain there for at least a month before returning to London. It's unlikely that the others will contact you before he returns.'

'Why do you say that he's the leader?'

'After the secret society was dissolved he became a courier for Mary Stuart, remaining an active rebel against Queen Elizabeth whilst all the others continued with their ordinary lives, either studying or working. When he returns to London he'll have to persuade the others to take an active role on behalf of our faith again.'

'We still have a lot to do ourselves. Right now you have a long trip to Chartley to deliver the letters to our friend Thomas.'

'I'll have to make a trip like that every month, since Thomas will only take letters delivered by you or me and you must stay in London. What actually remains is just one thing. We must find a guard that can let Savage and a few more men inside the palace so that they can assassinate the queen. I've been watching Whitehall Palace for months and I've never seen a guard with the familiar face of someone that I've met before. Eventually we must find someone with a grudge so that we may persuade him to work with us. But to start we must at least find someone with whom we can talk and learn about life in the palace.'

'Yes, we should need to talk to many guards and courtiers before we can find someone with a grudge against the queen. First we must wait for the arrival of those that travelled to Rome for an audience with the pope. Then, if possible every day, you should take two of them for the type of watch in which you've become an expert.'

'Since now it's evident we'll have to wait several weeks before the eight travelers contact us, I suggest I should try with another palace, Nonsuch Palace. When Elizabeth signed the Nonsuch Treaty to help the Protestant Dutch, I found out that currently she's staying at Nonsuch Palace much more often than at Whitehall Palace.'

'But Nonsuch is not a Royal Palace. Queen Mary sold it, unfinished, to the Earl of Arundel.'

'The current Earl of Arundel is Phillip Howard, the eldest son of the late Duke of Norfolk. Perhaps he's trying to get favors from the queen by lending her the palace that was finished by his grandfather, Henry FitzAlan.'

'It's more likely that the queen just decided she should use it. When Henry VIII instructed his architects to make this palace following the latest Italian fashions, they told him they would build a palace so beautiful that none such another palace would exist on Earth. That's why Henry named it Nonsuch Palace. But he died before it was finished and Mary I sold it.'

'The fact is that now Elizabeth prefers to use this palace, out in the country but very near London, rather than the Whitehall Royal Palace, in London. I'll start watching the guards of this palace as soon as I return from Chartley.'

'We don't know when Thomas will be able to deliver the letters. I'm concerned about leaving him in possession of a very large amount of compromising material.'

'No one finding these letters, written in code, will be able to read anything. Of course coded letters are compromising, but it's most unlikely that Thomas' papers would ever be searched. It's more dangerous for you or me to keep the letters. The letters for us are in plain English, since we don't have the code, so that these must be destroyed immediately after being read.'

'You must arrange to have the code sent to us by your contact, Paget. We must be able to receive and send coded letters.'

Two weeks later Gilbert was talking again with Father Ballard in his study.

'I've seen someone I used to know rather well years ago, that's now an officer in the guard Elizabeth has taken to Nonsuch Palace. I saw him again hours later at the Woolf and Lion Pub in Ewell, the closest village to the palace. He was there in uniform and I guess he might be in the habit of going to the pub when he finishes his guard. If you come with me we can pretend to have a chance encounter with him there.'

'Did this officer use to have any Catholic sympathies?'

'None whatsoever. He used to be a straight Church of England faithful and as an officer in Her Majesty's Guard he must continue to be one. He's not the man we need, but we'll at least get some information if we talk with him.'

'Tell me about him.'

'Usher George Tyndell, of the Queen's Body Guard of the Yeomen of the Guard, comes from Chillington, Staffordshire, like me. He's 25 years old, like me, and we used to be good friends until I left Chillington ten years ago to go to the continent. I lost many friends when my family was exposed as a Catholic family and my father was jailed for recusancy, but George didn't care. I don't know anything more about him, but as a non-commissioned officer of the guards he must have joined this force shortly after my departure. I made a few enquiries about the guard and it's a force of only 300. About one hundred are stationed at Nonsuch Palace, another hundred at Whitehall, while another hundred are spread out at various places in England.'

'Can you come with me to Ewell early tomorrow morning?'

'I expected you'd want me to do that. In this satchel I brought a few things so that I can spend the night here. I came on horseback and left my horse in the same stable where you keep yours. We can rise early and enter Ewell's pub as soon as it opens at 6 o'clock.'

'You're pure gold, Gilbert.'

When the Woolf and Lion Pub opened the next morning, Father Ballard and Gilbert were the first to enter and they ordered a hearty breakfast. They did not have to wait long to see the man they wanted to talk with. At about 8:30 A.M. several colorfully dressed Yeomen of the Guard entered the pub. Their uniforms were bright scarlet red with flat black hats. The uniforms differed from those used by the guards of the Tower of London only because they had wide shoulder belts to carry heavy harquebuses. The off-duty yeomen entering the pub did not carry harquebuses but only their side swords. Gilbert rose and walked towards a shaved faced husky red headed yeoman with a golden V shaped corporal insignia on his right sleeve.

'George Tyndell! Do you recognize me George?'

'Gilbert Gifford! How are you, my friend? I believe you left the country at least 10 years ago when you were still a boy.'

'How good to find you. I'm here with a friend. Could you leave your companions and join us at our table?'

'Certainly. Just give me a minute to talk with my mates and I'll join you at your table.'

When Usher George Tyndell joined them Gilbert introduced his friend.

'George, I want you to meet my friend, Captain John Fortescue.'

'Oh, a captain! There's only one captain in our force and he's the top man of the Yeomen of the Queen's Body Guard.'

'I was a young lieutenant sent to fight the French in Scotland by Queen Elizabeth. When the captain above me was killed in action I was promoted to replace him. There are many promotions in the armies at war.'

'I don't envy the soldiers in the armies at war. They have a rough life even if they're officers. In our force, instead, we live in a palace, we have a generously paid great life and even the lowest paid guards live like gentlemen and are gentlemen. Our responsibility is great, because we guard the queen's life, but since there's always about a hundred of us around, her safety is in our numbers and we don't have to do anything because no one will dare to approach the queen with ill intentions.'

'Does that mean that you perform only ceremonial duties?'

'No, I haven't explained myself correctly because I was emphasizing the difference we have with an army at war. We must be constantly alert because history teaches us that mad men have killed other sovereigns in the past. I was promoted from guard to usher because my superiors consider I'm always alert, but in nine years of service I never had to take any action.'

'Do I understand that you live at Nonsuch Palace?'

'That's right, the Yeomen of the Queen's Body Guard always live at the palace or castle where they perform their duties. There are no barracks for us and Nonsuch Palace is the best of all palaces. As a guard, I used to share a room with a mate, but after my promotion to usher I have a room for myself. And I must add it's no servant's room but a nice regular palace room, fit for a gentleman like me.'

'I'm glad to see that you've done so well in life, George. Are you still single?'

'Yes, Gilbert. How about you two?'

'Like you, we're still playing hard to get. It's easy for me but difficult for my friend, since not only is he handsome, but he's also economically well off and lives in a very large house.'

'I need the large house because I give fencing lessons.'

'Fencing lessons! Are you a master?'

'Not a master, just a good swordsman. Many young men that wish to improve their skill with a sword can't afford to have lessons with a master. Since my fees are reasonable, I have many pupils.'

'I'm interested. We're given fencing instruction at the guard. I never thought I could get private instruction, because it's so expensive. How much do you charge?'

'For you, a childhood friend of my friend found after 10 years of separation, I'll charge the same as for my friend, nothing. I only hope that you'll come to take lessons more often than Gilbert.'

'I certainly will. With private lessons I should become the best pupil at the lessons we take at the guard. And this is important to me for further promotions since I expect to become an Exon.'

'Is Exon the top position for a noncom at the guard?' asked Gilbert.

'No, Gilbert, the top position is Clerk of the Cheque, but there's only one clerk of the cheque for the entire force, just as we only have one captain. Here, at Nonsuch, we have 92 yeomen, 8 ushers and 4 exons. The Clerk of the Cheque usually stays at the place where the queen is staying, which is Nonsuch most of the time. We also have two officers here, an ensign and a lieutenant. The Clerk of the Cheque has seniority over the ensign. As Clerk of the Cheque, instead of a promoted Exon often we have had a retired colonel. There's only one captain of the force that follows the queen everywhere. But now that you know everything about me, I want to know about you, Gilbert. What about your life?'

'I've enjoyed myself a lot these years travelling all over France, holding different jobs. My goal was to travel, not to have a career. I also spent three years in Italy. Now I've returned to England and I want to settle and have a family. At present I'm working for Captain Fortescue, in whom I have found a real friend.'

'And what are you doing in Ewell?'

'I might buy a house in Epson and I wanted Gilbert to look at it before making a commitment. We're expected there at noon and so we decided to come to Ewell for breakfast, hoping to take a look at famous Nonsuch Palace from our horses before going on to Epson.'

'Not a chance if you go by yourselves. The palace is surrounded by a large well-guarded park. But since I'll be taking your free fencing lessons I can take you to the park with me and we can go around the palace. Unfortunately, I cannot take you inside the palace.'

'All we wanted was just to have a look at the palace from the outside, so your offer is excellent and we're most pleased to accept.'

'Let's finish our beers then and go to our horses.'

Usher Tyndell, Gilbert and Father Ballard, on their way to Nonsuch Palace reached a high place where they stopped to get a view of the magnificent building. Although his view was from a considerable distance, Ballard was discouraged when, from what he saw, he believed the palace was actually a castle with a defensive square wall and four watch towers, one in each corner of the wall.

'From here we have a beautiful view of the south frontage of the palace,' said Tyndell.

'You mean a view of the south defensive wall?' asked Ballard.

'No, that's not a defensive wall, that´s the palace itself. We're not as far away from the palace as you seem to believe. It has four wings making a square surrounding a large patio.

You'll have a better view when we get inside the park and we go around the palace.'

They continued riding until they reached the gates of Nonsuch Park. Tyndell dismounted and went to talk with the guards at the gate. Several minutes later Tyndell returned and mounted his horse.

'You can enter Nonsuch Park with me but you must leave it within half an hour,' he told his two companions.

The visit to the park was made in late September and since the chill at the end of the English summer had started early that year, on that sunny morning the park looked beautiful with the colorful red and yellow leaves of all the trees, both inside and outside the park.

Tyndell rode towards the south face of the palace and reined in his horse at a place where they had a good view of that face.

'As you can see, the second floor room in the center of this wing of the palace is the only room with a terrace, since the ground floor protrudes from the building line only there. For that reason, the queen chose that room as her own bedroom. It's a very large room, since before Queen Elizabeth started using this palace it was a dining room rather than a bedroom. I've seen her many summer evenings in my rounds, all alone at her terrace, looking at the sunset.'

They continued riding around the palace and stopped again at a place where they had a good view of the north face of the palace, obviously its front.

'You can see that this is the front of the palace and the only wing with three floors instead of two like the three other wings. Again the building line at the center advances forward, but here it includes both ground and second floor. There's no third floor room above this special room, because instead we have an ornamented high construction crowned by a clock. The entrance is not in the center but at the left and, as you see, it's large enough to enter with a carriage to the inner patio.'

They finished the ride around the palace and returned to the park gate within 15 minutes of having entered.

'Thank you so much for allowing us to see well this magnificent palace, Usher Tyndell,' said Ballard.

'It's the most beautiful building in all England and I'm as proud of it as if it were my own,' replied Tyndell. 'When can I go to your London school to take my fencing lessons? I haven't forgotten your offer.'

'Any time you want, from 8 in the morning till 5 in the evening. I'm there most of the time every day, but if by any chance I'm not there when you come, ask for Master John Savage, my assistant, who'll take good care of you, including your first lesson.'

'I intend to go as soon as I can and as often as I can, Captain. It was a real pleasure to meet you. And I'm positively delighted at having encountered you again, Gilbert, after so many years. Luckily neither one of us sports a beard, since in that case we wouldn't have recognized each other.'

'I'm most glad with this reunion and once you start a routine of going to fencing classes I'll try to go on the same days, so that we can become again as close friends as we were at 15.'

Ballard and Gilbert started their ride back to London.

'This reunion with Tyndell has been a complete success,' said Gilbert. 'We don't have to get Savage inside the palace and therefore we don't need any friendly courtesan or guard.'

'That's right. We know which is the room used by the queen. Savage must sneak into the park on a dark night. We've many dark nights with a drizzle in the London area. He can easily get to the queen's terrace using a rope with a hook. From there, after having removed the rope, he enters the queen's bedroom in the dark, goes quietly towards her bed and cuts her throat. If she has company in her bed, he cuts two throats. Back in the terrace he replaces the rope, goes down to the ground and sneaks out of the park to go back to his horse.'

'I can be there watching his horse at one of the woods near the park. We don't need the new recruits to do this. Savage can do this basically alone and I'm the only support he needs to watch his horse, just as an extra safety measure to get away. Savage should do this right away the next dark and rainy night we get. Let's do this now, when we can finish our business before we do anything that can be detected. Mary Stuart is next in line even if she's a prisoner. And we don't know for how long Elizabeth will continue to use this palace, that's not a royal palace really.'

'No, Gilbert, if Elizabeth is assassinated while Mary is in prison, Mary will be immediately killed by her jailers. Then Mary's son, Protestant King James VI of Scotland will become King James I of England. And, unlike Elizabeth, James is a Presbyterian, a real Protestant. Such a change would make matters much worse for Catholics than now. We must proceed as planned. Mary should be freed the same night Elizabeth is murdered so that we Catholics can rise. If it can be arranged to get foreign Catholic troops to help our rebellion, fine. We should wait for foreign help a reasonable time, to improve our chances, but not forever. I'll wait until August of next year. July of next year would be the ideal time. In warm summer nights the terrace's door will be left open during the night, making everything real easy for Savage.'

'But what happens if the Earl of Arundel starts using this palace again next year.'

'Sovereigns don't borrow palaces, they take them. If Arundel makes any move to recover the palace he'll be beheaded.'

In late October 1585 Anthony Babington was back in London

with his wife and child and one by one went to see the seven travelling companions that had been in Rome with him.

Archbishop Beaton had told them that they should visit a man called Captain Fortescue who was going to send correspondence to Mary Stuart. Anthony arranged for all his companions to go to his house the following Tuesday, at four o'clock.

That Tuesday some of his friends were a bit late, but all were at his place at a quarter past four. They went walking to Captain Fortescue's house, which was quite near to where Anthony lived. When they arrived they were received by Gilbert Gifford at the entrance hall and were asked to wait for the captain who was busy with a fencing lesson right then. Half an hour later, Gilbert led the eight visitors to the room that Ballard had prepared for meetings with the conspirators with a large rectangular table in the center.

'Gentlemen, I'm Captain John Fortescue and my companions are my two trusted assistants, Master Gilbert Gifford and Master John Savage. Please introduce yourselves and state the purpose of your visit.'

'I'm Anthony Babington and my friends are Henry Dunn, Thomas Salisbury, Robert Barnewell, Edward Jones, John Charnock, John Travers and Robert Gage.'

Anthony gave the list of his friends slowly and each one who was named nodded with his head when his name was given, so that he could be identified by the captain and his assistants.

'We're here,' continued Anthony, 'because Archbishop Beaton asked us to. He said he's in frequent contact with you by correspondence and that he expects you to find a way to establish contact, through letters, with Queen Mary Stuart. Have you established contact, Captain?'

'Not yet, but I'm certain that I shall establish this contact within two or three months. The Archbishop gave me your names and I'm glad I finally met all of you. He also told me that you were members of a secret society that protected priests preaching in England, that the Holy Father highly appreciates the work you did and that as an indication of this appreciation he granted you a private audience. I imagine that you came to see me because you wish to continue working for our church. He also wrote me telling that Master Babington became a courier for Mary Stuart after the secret society was dissolved. Unfortunately, when the Earl of Shrewsbury ceased to be in charge of the prisoner queen, measures were taken to make any communication with her impossible.'

'That's correct, Captain, and I hope that within two or three months I'll be working as Queen Mary's courier again.'

'Perhaps, Master Babington, but my hope is that I'll have the option of giving you much more challenging work on behalf of our church. Since you're concerned about the welfare of Queen Mary Stuart, I expect you to be interested in rescuing her from prison. Archbishop Beaton believed that you gentlemen, all eight of you idealistic young men, would be willing to set free the legitimate Queen of England.'

Anthony and his seven friends were shocked and surprised when they heard Captain Fortescue's words. Thomas Salisbury was the first to react. 'Count me in, Captain,' he said. All the others immediately expressed their willingness to participate.

'Thank you gentlemen. I must warn you that this is a most dangerous enterprise, considered high treason by the crown. The penalty for high treason is death. If we lose we'll go the gallows, but if we win, England will be a Catholic country again. Should any of you wish to withdraw from this group we're forming now, you're perfectly entitled to do so. I want all of you to think carefully about this matter tomorrow. Our next meeting will be the day after. If any one of you doesn't come, we'll understand, consider he's perfectly justified and forget he came today. Total secrecy is of maximum importance since the lives of all of us depend on it. No word of what happened today can be told to anybody. You cannot speak about it with your wives or any friends, male or female. This must be absolutely clear. No one, means no one at all, with no exceptions.'

'Captain,' said Anthony, 'I've got two friends that I believe should belong to this group. Can I ask them to come to Thursday's meeting?'

'Not to Thursday's meeting because we're going to talk about matters that should be heard only by those fully committed, but you can bring them to see me tomorrow. Don't tell them anything, only that you wish they should meet me. If they cannot come tomorrow we should forget about them.'

'I'll do my best to bring them tomorrow, Captain.'

'With regard to the series of meetings we'll have, starting Thursday of this week, we must set an hour suitable for all of you. Our cover is that we've got a fencing school here. You'll come every Tuesdays and Thursdays to take fencing lessons. Don't be concerned since you're not going to be charged for the lessons. But to make our cover realistic, you'll have to apply yourselves to learn how to use a sword. I'm a good teacher. Our friend John Savage, here with us, had never used a sword until June of this year and now, with less than five months of practice, he's so good that he can act as my assistant. Of course he's a very strong and agile man, but you gentlemen are young and youth is a great advantage to learn anything. Every time you come you'll be here for an hour and a half. Forty five minutes to an hour for fencing classes and the balance for our meetings.'

The eight visitors huddled together for about a quarter of an hour and then Anthony talked for the group. 'We'll come here every Tuesdays and Thursdays at seven o'clock in the evening.'

The next day, at three o'clock in the afternoon, Anthony

arrived with two friends at the large house used as a fencing school. An old lady, employed by Ballard for house cleaning and cooking, opened the door and left the three young men waiting at the entrance hall. A few minutes later Captain Fortescue and John Savage came looking for them.

'Captain, these are two very good friends of mine that were members of the secret society formed for the protection of English priests that came here to assist us, Catholics, Charles Tilney and Chidiock Tichborne. Unfortunately, they didn't come to the continent like the other members of the society that you met yesterday. If they had come, they would have attended the audience granted to us by the Holy Father.'

'Very pleased to meet you, gentlemen. I'm Captain Fortescue and he's my assistant, Master John Savage. Let's go to our meeting room.'

Once there, the five men sat at the table in the center of the room.

'These two men are the intellectuals of our group. They are poets. Both of them write beautiful poems and Charles has written an elaborate play, called Locrine, in which the founders of ancient England were exiled Trojans and London was called Troynovant. Charles finished his play about two years ago but, being a perfectionist, instead of presenting it to one of the companies that perform plays, like Leicester's men, he's revising it constantly. I'm one of the few that read it and I think it's great.'

'I like to read in my free time,' said the captain. 'Could I borrow a copy from you?'

'I make a new copy every time I make a revision. I need my fourth copy because I'm working on a fifth version. I can give you the third version, which is the same one read by Anthony. In the first one the verse was too stilted because I had to concentrate on the rather elaborate and tragic plot. My other versions are better, but not good enough for me. The fifth version might be the final one.'

'These two men are not only intellectuals, but men of action as well. Six years ago Father Campion was giving mass in the attic of my house when Walsingham's men burst in. I had to receive the men coming to search the house, while Charles and Chidiock were moving over a hundred people from the attic to the cleavages between the roof of the house and the roofs of the two adjoining houses. It wasn't my house then, but that of my uncle, Jonathan Darcy. I inherited it after he died. Well, Charles and Chidiock managed to get everyone on the roof and Walsingham's men went away.'

'That's not what happened,' said Chidiock. 'I played a very minor role. Charles did a bit more, but if it wasn't for your two big friends, Peter and Michael, we couldn't have emptied the attic in time.'

'I must interrupt this conversation, Master Babington,' said Savage. 'I'm the man who told Walsingham that he should search the house of your uncle because a mass was being given there.'

Anthony, Charles and Chidiock couldn't believe what they were hearing. Had they fallen into a trap and were they at the mercy of Walsingham's agents?

'Let me explain, gentlemen,' said the captain. 'John told me everything about this, months ago. One September Sunday in 1579 Walsingham learned that a Catholic mass would be celebrated in London, at a large private house. An enemy of John happened to be a Walsingham informer and he falsely accused our friend of being a Catholic activist that would know the address where the mass would be celebrated. Since John wasn't a Catholic he couldn't give any address and was put on the rack. He wanted to invent something to stop the torture and remembered having heard in a pub that Jonathan Darcy was the son of an executed traitor. He then told his torturer that the mass was being given at Jonathan Darcy's house. He had no idea that, just by chance, what he had invented to stop the torture was true.'

'I was lucky because everyone attending the mass managed to hide on the roof,' said Savage. 'Apparently Walsingham was amused about having bothered relatives of a traitor because of something I invented and let me go free. Since this happened, I feel I owe a debt to Catholics in general. On top of that, now I know I owe a debt to you, Master Babington.'

'I'm interested in the two big and strong friends mentioned by Master Tichborne,' said the captain. 'I would like to have them as members of the team we're forming.'

'So would I,' said Anthony. Michael Hussley and 'Peter Thornwell are dear friends of mine. They are Catholics, but they are loyal to Queen Elizabeth. They believed I was taking an unwarranted risk being a courier for Mary Stuart. When we discussed, they pointed out that they shared my religious convictions but not my political ones.'

'I see. They wish to remain Catholics, but faithful to a queen that forces them to pretend they're members of the Church of England, under penalty of losing their titles, their property and their freedom.'

'They're lawyers and able to present their case differently. I always find I cannot argue with them. Anyway, they travelled to Rome and became very good friends of a Tuscan nobleman and his beautiful daughter. They met them in Avignon when father and daughter were stranded there. Peter and Michael were invited to stay in Siena with them to watch a traditional Italian race on bareback horses. Peter participated in the race and won. Michael did even better and married the beautiful daughter of the Italian Baron. I attended a large reception given by his father, Lord Dethick, to introduce his son's wife to his English friends. Six months later Peter married a French lady.

'Anthony, your friends must be confused with this conversation. May I call you Anthony?'

'Certainly, Captain.'

'The fact is that we've formed a group for the liberation of

Mary Stuart, whom we believe is the rightful Queen of England. We're starting our meetings tomorrow and you were invited because Anthony believes you belong in our group.'

'I believe so too,' said Charles.

'So do I,' said Chidiock.

'Gentlemen, I'm pleased to welcome you to our team, but I must warn you that this is a most dangerous enterprise and that we're facing a death sentence just for talking about it. Since the lives of all of us are in danger, you cannot tell anybody, not even your wives, or your dearest friends, what you heard today or anything about this matter you may hear in the future. Think about it before coming here tomorrow for our first meeting. If you're not here at 7 PM, no one will think anything ill about you. We'll just forget you were here today and you should forget about us. But if you come, there's no return, we won't stop until we've got a Catholic England again or we go to the gallows.'

CHAPTER IV
THE PLOT IS IN MOVEMENT

Anthony, the seven friends that came with him two days earlier and the two friends that came with him the day before, were already at the house of Captain Fortescue almost half an hour before the scheduled time of 7 P.M. Anthony was the first to arrive. John Savage and Gilbert Gifford received all of them, one by one, and left them waiting for Captain Fortescue, who was busy with a student.

'Welcome, gentlemen, I see that none of you had second thoughts about coming today and I'm glad and proud of you,' said Captain Fortescue when he arrived, two minutes before seven. 'Please follow me to the largest fencing hall we have.'

They all moved to the large hall that had been prepared for large collective lessons and had never been used before.

'At this hall we'll have collective lessons. Those that advance sufficiently will get personal lessons later. My friend Gilbert Gifford has already taken several classes, but he'll join you as a pupil, since a refreshment course will be good for him. My friend John Savage will assist me as a teacher.'

'In our first lesson,' said John Savage, 'we'll teach you the eight basic fencing positions and the advance and retreat steps of rapier fencing.'

The pupils were provided with rapiers and everything needed for the lessons and underwent 45 minutes of intensive fencing training with no mention of anything they had discussed about Mary Stuart and her liberation. All the newcomers were fascinated by the feline and elegant movements of Captain Fortescue.

After the lesson they washed and went to the meeting room.

'Well,' said the Captain, 'you've had your fencing class with

Captain Fortescue and now you'll have a discussion meeting with Father Ballard.'

After a couple of minutes of complete silence, Chidiock Tichbourne asked a question. 'And where is Father Ballard?'

'Right here,' said the captain. 'I'm Father Ballard.'

'How's this possible?' asked Henry Dunn. 'You're Captain Fortescue.'

'I was knocked unconscious when I was taken prisoner by the French. When I recovered I had lost my memory and the French took me to France. I was given the name Ballard in France. Depending on how you pronounce it, the name sounds French or English. When I recovered my memory I was already a priest. To be reunited with my family I joined the Jesuit Order and requested to be sent to England. In the Jesuit Order Father Campion was my best friend, but I also knew well every other priest that was sent to the gallows by Queen Elizabeth.'

'To what part of England were you sent?' asked John Travers.

'I was sent to my home town, Black Pool, in the northwest of England. There I was received as the prodigal son, not only by my parents but by the entire town. In Black Pool I worked at the family farm and also as a priest ministering to the large Catholic population of the area. Many Protestants must also have known that I was a Catholic priest, but the Protestants of that part of the country don't send their friends to the gallows. After my parents died, I travelled to France to report to my order. I was given the option of staying in France or of returning to England to minister exclusively to a small community of devoted Catholics that may wish to discuss if England should remain as a Protestant country, or should be a Catholic country again. I took the second option and started with an extremely small community of two, Gilbert and John. Now, you ten idealistic young men have come and the small community of devoted Catholics is complete.'

'We expect you to be our leader when we rescue Mary Stuart from prison,' said Robert Gage.

'I was strictly forbidden to participate myself in what must be done to make England a Catholic country again, and for good reason. As Robert pointed out, one thing absolutely necessary is to rescue Mary Stuart from prison so that she can be crowned as Queen of England. I believe all of you agree.'

The ten men voiced loudly their agreement.

'Well there's something else that must be done at the same time. Can any of you ten new men in this community of 12 tell me what we need?'

There was complete silence.

'The English throne must be vacant if we want Mary Stuart to become our queen,' said Father Ballard.

Everyone remained in silence.

'You're all idealistic young men and to liberate a beautiful queen that's a prisoner in the country she should be ruling appeals to your idealism, but to assassinate another queen does not. I'll release immediately anyone that doesn't want to participate because he didn't realize what was involved. I'll only need that he swears not to tell anything he heard in this building, but he must make his decision right now.'

Everyone continued to remain silent. It was a long silence because Father Ballard spoke again only after looking straight to the eyes of each one of the ten new men.'

'I expected up to five of you to leave now, but I'm happy that no one did. You can understand that as a priest I cannot participate directly in an assassination, but as your advisor I must tell you this is necessary if you want Mary Stuart to be the new Queen of England. Also, I must tell you that the pope has explicitly declared that it's not a sin for a Catholic to kill the present Queen of England.'

'I was shocked,' said Anthony, 'because I hadn't thought of it, but I now realize that nothing is accomplished freeing Mary Stuart from her castle prison, unless Elizabeth is killed the same night.'

'I agree,' said Thomas Salisbury. All the others uttered similar phrases.

'All of you know your companions quite well because you met several years ago and you've worked together in the protection of Catholic priests. Now I must tell you about my two assistants, since they'll be working with you. Gilbert, who's about your same age, is a Deacon of the Catholic Church. He was ordained in Rheims by Cardinal de Guise and, like you, he was sent to me by Archbishop Beaton. He's been most efficient in finding a way to communicate with Mary Stuart. To take her out of her prison it's absolutely necessary to communicate with her. John is not a Deacon. In fact he's not even a Catholic.'

There was a murmur of surprise, but no one interrupted Ballard.

'He's a mature man of my own age, rather than yours and, as a former soldier, a man of action. I recruited him when he confided in Gilbert and me and told us that he had sworn to God he would kill Queen Elizabeth and he's the kind of man that can succeed in something so difficult.'

'A few of you know what happened to me,' said Savage. 'I was tortured by order of Queen Elizabeth just because I was suspected of being a Catholic. People should not be persecuted, tortured and killed because they prefer to go to one type of religious service rather than another. You must also understand that if Mary Stuart persecutes Protestants like me after she becomes Queen of England, I'll be against her.'

'I've told John,' said Ballard, 'that I agree with him and that when Mary was Queen of Scots she never persecuted

Protestants. In fact, since the Church of England has gone only half way from Catholicism to Protestantism, I believe that, since Mary Stuart has the necessary political experience, she'll also have the political ability needed to prevent the sort of religious wars that afflict France.'

'You're our spiritual guide,' said Anthony, 'and we'll take the spiritual positions that you indicate.'

'You've received a shock today,' said Ballard, 'and that's enough for our first day of discussions. Next Tuesday you'll have another fencing class with Captain Fortescue, followed by a discussion meeting with Father Ballard.'

'I'll be unable to attend next week's meetings,' indicated Gilbert, 'because I must travel to deliver letters sent to Mary Stuart from France. These coded letters will be kept by someone that will be in a position to deliver the letters to Mary Stuart.'

'Now we'll move to another room in which Gilbert has prepared an altar and I'll celebrate mass. We'll end all our Tuesday and Thursday meetings this way. It's too dangerous for you to come here on Sundays to attend mass, but it's safe to do it when you must come to your collective fencing lessons.'

After mass, Anthony and his friends left and Gilbert gave a letter to Ballard.

'Father, one of the letters I picked today is for you.'

Ballard cut the envelope with a knife he carried in his belt, opened it neatly and read the letter rapidly.

'It's from Archbishop Beaton. He makes reference to your request for the code used for correspondence and considers it's not convenient to send the code through the French Embassy. He tells me a militant Catholic has infiltrated the assistants to Sir Amyas Paulet. His name is Thomas Philips and he can be contacted by you or me to get the code. He got it from Gilbert Curle, one of the two secretaries of Mary Stuart. He has informed Queen Mary, through Curle, where to look for the correspondence that'll reach her when she's moved to Chartley Hall.'

'Do you want to go yourself to Tutbury to get the code, Father?'

'No, I must remain here to attend the ten new men we have. You're the right man to go since you know Tutbury well. You can go to Tutbury from Chartley. But there's another matter I must discuss with you.'

'Tell me, Father.'

'I've been giving you funds for your travels, but since you're working full time for our enterprise I should be giving you a salary, rather than just travel expenses. The ten new men either have independent income, like Anthony, or are working in their usual jobs. Savage is getting a salary and I believe I must give you a salary twice as large.'

'I'm glad that you mentioned this, Father. I've saved some money during my years in the continent, but my funds are getting quite low.'

'I should have thought about your need for money months ago. You've been working with me since January and at first I didn't realize that you were involved full time with our venture. It's October now, so that the first payment should be ten months' salary.'

'Thank you, Father. I'm a humble man and when all this is over I intend to become a priest, but for the time being I must keep appearances, dressing reasonably well, having a good horse and renting a suitable place to live.'

'Would you like to move here to lower your expenses?'

'No, we must avoid anything suspicious. Your fencing school is a great cover, but it should be kept as just a school. It's reasonable that Savage should live here because he was doing repairs and now he's your assistant for fencing lessons.

But your pupils aren't supposed to live here.'

The following Tuesday the ten new men came back. That day they had a full hour of intensive fencing training given by Captain Fortescue with the assistance of John Savage. When they started the discussion meeting with Father Ballard, he started telling about the imminent transfer of Mary Stuart to a new place of detention.

'Mary Stuart's health has seriously deteriorated at the horrible castle where she's a prisoner right now, Tutbury Castle. Walsingham is afraid that she'll die soon if she continues to remain there and he's preparing a new place for her detention, Chartley Hall. This place hasn't been used for many years and is currently being repaired. The work is almost finished and it would be quite convenient if you go to take a look at it now, when the mansion is empty and therefore there are no guards in the area. Mary Stuart will have to be rescued from that mansion, which is surrounded by a moat.'

'How did you find out?' asked Edward Jones.

'People working for Sir Amyas are talking openly about this transfer in Tutbury. You should also look, from a distance, at Nonsuch Palace, where currently Queen Elizabeth usually lives. Those of you that can take the time to go to Chartley can arrange to travel with Gilbert, who goes there every month. I expect all of you to go to look at Nonsuch Palace, which is quite close to London. John Savage can take you there and show you the location of the queen's bedroom. It's a room with a balcony and the palace guards have seen her alone in her balcony many evenings. John was there with me yesterday and you should arrange your visit to Nonsuch with him.'

'And what's the next step?' asked Charles Tilney.

'We must set two teams, one that goes to Chartley to rescue Mary Stuart and another to go to Nonsuch to do what's necessary. The second team will only have four members and since John Savage and Gilbert Gifford must participate in this team, you'll have to supply only two members to support them. You'll use the ancient method of drawing straws to determine those that must support John and Gilbert. Two straws will be longer and those who get them will be in the team that goes to Nonsuch Palace. The other eight will of course be the Chartley team and will have to develop a plan to rescue Mary Stuart. Gilbert and I have some ideas and we'll tell you about these ideas, but neither Gilbert nor I will belong to the Chartley team.'

'Shall we make the teams right now?' wondered John Charnock.

'No. All of you prefer to be in the Chartley team and we need ideas from all of you to come up with the best plan to set Mary Stuart free. Three of you will not draw straws. Anthony Babington will be the leader of the Chartley team. Edward Jones and John Charnock must also belong to that team because both of them are very strong and their strength is needed in Chartley.'

Anthony felt he was at the top of the world when he heard that Father Ballard had selected him to lead the team that would set Mary Stuart free. Jones and Charnock were smiling widely since they were very pleased too.

'How will you send correspondence to Mary Stuart?' asked Robert Barnewell.

'It's not necessary for our venture that each of us should know everything. What we're doing is extremely dangerous and if anyone of us should be captured, he'll be tortured to be interrogated. When someone is tortured he talks. Here's our friend John Savage, who knows about torture because he was tortured. When interrogated about things he didn't know about, he had to invent to talk.'

'And what do we do after we take a look at Chartley Hall?' asked John Travers.

'Gilbert and I have a basic plan, but after I explain it to you, you'll have to develop a complete plan to rescue Mary Stuart. Then you'll have to find a place with quiet water where you can test and practice your plan and you'll have to practice a lot. I'll check how well you can do your rescue work. When I'm satisfied you can execute correctly your rescue plan, we'll be in a position to advise Mary Stuart that at a certain hour, a certain day, she'll be rescued, so that she can be ready to escape.'

After a short silence Ballard spoke again.

'We're in mid-November now. On December 1st I'll leave London so that I can be with my family in Black Pool. As part of our cover, twice a week you'll continue coming to your collective fencing lessons. These will be given by John Savage. I expect to be back early in January.'

John Ballard felt a pang of pain when he talked because, although he would be pleased to see Helen Fortescue and her husband as well as his Black Pool friends, he was longing to see his own family. But to visit them would be to put them in danger. Except for very few people, everyone believed his real name was John Fortescue and Ballard was the name he was given in France when he lost his memory. Anyway, he wasn't going to be in Black Pool more than one or two days at most. The real purpose of his trip was to visit all the noblemen that had pledged to rise in arms to support Mary Stuart as the new queen. He'd been in contact with them when he returned from France and now he had to see them to tell them the plot was already in movement. The most important man to see was a lord with a castle relatively close to Chartley, who must be told that Mary Stuart would be taken there after her escape. He was the only one who knew the lords that would rise immediately. None of the members of his little community of conspirators needed to know.

The meeting continued with many questions about the reign of Mary Stuart in Scotland and the problems she faced that forced her to escape to England. Ballard had a great deal of information, but there were some questions that could only be answered by Mary herself.

Ballard gave mass after the meeting and when everyone was leaving he asked Anthony to stay.

'Anthony, I've put you in charge of the liberation of Mary Stuart. It's a great responsibility and I expect you to put body and soul in this enterprise.'

'You will not be disappointed, Father. With your guidance, I'm sure we can make her the next Queen of England.'

Two weeks later Gilbert went to see Ballard at mid-morning.

'Good morning Father. I bring good news.'

'Nice to have you back in London, Gilbert. Give me the news.'

'Mary Stuart will be moved to Chartley Hall on Christmas day. I got this information directly from Thomas Philips, who gave me the code. Starting on Christmas we may communicate directly with Mary Stuart.'

'Fine. As I had already told you, I'll travel to Black Pool. When I return, Mary Stuart will already be settled in Chartley Hall.'

'Have you already told Anthony that he'll be heading the Chartley team?'

'Yes. He was thrilled, of course, and the others accepted this well. As you told me, he's the natural leader of his group. Now we have to see if he can lead a team in action. The rescue plan must be thoroughly rehearsed. If the team doesn't perform well by June, Anthony will have to be replaced by you.'

'That shouldn't be necessary. We're giving an easy plan to the team. Let's hope they find a place where they can test it. If they don't, I'll lead Anthony to the place we found, so that he can believe he found the place himself. And he has six months to train his team. In six months they should be able to do it blindfolded.'

'I'm concerned about the six months. We haven't been detected yet, but a lot can happen in six months.'

'Like you, I would like to take action as soon as possible. You convinced me that we cannot assassinate Queen Elizabeth before Mary Stuart is set free. We can set Mary Stuart free on February. Let's proceed with the plan on February.'

'Archbishop Beaton tells me King Felipe II, of Spain, will send a large Spanish Army as soon as we tell him we're ready. You must take the ten men to Chartley to show Chartley Hall to them and you must supervise their rehearsals of the plan. Hopefully, when I return from Black Pool I can write to the archbishop to tell him we're ready. If Felipe II is true to his word, he'll be in a position to send an army in July or August. If we don't wait, rely only on the forces raised by English Catholic lords and these forces are crushed by English Protestant forces allied to Scottish Protestant forces, our plot would have only served to give a bloodbath to England. On the other hand, if we wait and get the Spanish Army to help us, the forces of the English Catholic Lords will face only token opposition from Protestant forces.'

'When you put it this way we cannot advance with the plan thinking in terms of our own safety.'

'The problem is that regardless of the intentions of Felipe II, the Spaniards will be facing great difficulties when they try to send Flanders troops to England. Now the English have sent troops to Flanders. Dutch and English warships will attack any Spanish ships that try to leave the coast of Flanders. Felipe II would have to send the Flanders troops from the French coast. The Duque de Guise would be happy to help Felipe II, but the King is Henri III, who considers de Guise to be his enemy. My view is that lengthy negotiations would probably be needed to convince Henri III to allow

Spanish troops to cross through French territory. Summing up, we must postpone our plan waiting for an army that cannot leave Flanders. I'll wait, but only until August 20. On that date we'll kill Elizabeth and liberate Mary Stuart.'

The next day Ballard left London. He had to tell the Northern lords that had accepted the plan that August 20 was the date that had been provisionally set for liberating Mary Stuart. The date would be advanced, of course, if the expected Spanish troops should disembark in England. The rebel lords had to be told that the date of August 20 had been set because it was unlikely that any foreign troops would arrive to help the rebellion and they should have to decide if they still wanted to participate in it.

Fearless Ballard travelled alone. He was quite confident that his expertise with pistols, swords and knives, could match that of any bandit that might try to attack him on lonely roads. Bandits knew that men that travelled alone at full gallop did not carry much gold and were well armed, so that no one bothered Ballard.

All the lords said they would rise in arms to crown Mary Stuart as the new Queen of England or at least to establish her right of succession, regardless of the lack of any foreign troops to support them. Many said that they would actually prefer that no Spanish troops should be involved. All of them found the August 20 date better than an earlier date. It was a date that allowed time to talk with those that would be requested to raise men for an army. The lord whose castle would become Mary's home was delighted and thrilled with the honor.

Ballard spent December 24 at the Fortescue farm and left the next morning to visit the lords in the area. He was back there on December 31 and started his trip back to London early in the morning of January 1st, 1586.

Gilbert Gifford was visiting Ballard's house every morning to check if he had returned so that he was able to see him his first full day in London. After the customary Christmas and New Year salutations he talked about the matters that interested the priest.

'Anthony Babington has shown to be an excellent action leader. His people obey every order he gives and he shows remarkable good sense giving orders. And he found a place to practice Mary's liberation that's even better than the one we found ourselves. For four days he visited on horseback every lake, large and small, near London. He found a small lake in Kent with a two story high old house right next to the water. It was in a derelict state and so he was able to rent it as a place to go fishing with his friends for practically nothing for a full year. John Savage, who's become quite fond of Anthony, is repairing it, doing an excellent job like he did on this house.'

'And what about the ladder that has to be placed on the boat? Did he need any advice from you?'

'I was ready to help him but he didn't need any advice. He purchased a flat bottom boat of the right size to be used in the Chartley moat. I told him that you would refund all his expenses and he was pleased to learn about this, but he wasn't expecting any refund, just spending for the cause. You can write to the archbishop to tell him we're ready to go ahead with the plan and we're just waiting for the support troops to arrive. Did you take advantage of your trip up North to contact any Catholic lords?'

'Not yet. It's very dangerous to talk about our plan with anyone outside our small group. Anyway, the Catholic lords don't need us to tell them what to do. The moment they learn that the throne is vacant and Mary Stuart is free, they'll rise to support Mary. And I'm pleased to learn that Anthony performed so well.'

Months went by and everything was working in line with the plans of Father Ballard. The cover was working well, since all ten newcomers had become good swordsmen. Anthony was particularly good because he applied himself very hard to do well and took many extra lessons. Gilbert found it necessary to travel twice a month to Chartley to keep up with the intensive correspondence of Mary Stuart with her powerful first cousin, Henri, Duke de Guise, with Don Bernardino de Mendoza, who had been appointed Spanish Ambassador in France after being expelled from England and with Archbishop Beaton and his two assistants.

Every Saturday Anthony went fishing with his friends to the house he had rented next to the small lake in Kent. John Savage frequently joined them. Gilbert went there once in a while and of course Ballard went several times to check that they kept rehearsing Mary Stuart's rescue properly.

Early in July, Ballard was surprised to receive from Gilbert a letter from Mary Stuart addressed to Anthony Babington. He asked Anthony to share this letter with his confederates. The ciphered letter was decoded and Anthony allowed everyone in the conspiracy to read it. It was a very flattering letter for Anthony, since Mary said she had been informed by Archbishop Beaton that Anthony, who had been her courier for several years, was the leader of the team that would rescue her. She said she remembered him very well from the time he had been her page and that she was looking forward to a long relationship with him after being set free.

Anthony felt he was in heaven and all Ballard's followers were obviously happy and had smiling faces, except for Gilbert, who had a somber expression. Anthony noticed and took him apart.

'What's wrong, Gilbert? I can't believe you're jealous. You know the letter is addressed to me but is meant for all of us.'

'No, Anthony. I'm very happy to see you getting recognition, but I'm sad about you and your friends. You see, Ballard is a priest and I intend to be one. We don't mind if we die. Savage doesn't mind either. But you and your nine friends are full of life and want to live. Mary Stuart has only praise for you now, when she needs you for her liberation. But once she becomes the new Queen of England she'll have to pacify the Protestant majority mourning late Queen Elizabeth. Since we would be the ones that killed her, she would have every right to send us to the gallows. After liberating her we might be executed for reasons of State.'

'Mary Stuart would never do that. Other queens perhaps, but never Mary. Now I have to answer her letter. In my answer I'll make it very clear that we must eliminate the usurper. She'll have to approve or disapprove.'

Anthony wrote a long letter including this paragraph:

"Myself with ten gentlemen and a hundred of our followers will undertake the delivery of your royal person from the hands of your enemies. For the dispatch of the usurper, from the obedience of whom we are by the excommunication of her made free, there be six noble gentlemen, all my private friends, who for the zeal they bear to the Catholic cause and your Majesty's service will undertake that tragical execution."

When he finished the letter, he showed it to everyone in the group. Ballard did not make any comments, although he did not like telling Mary Stuart that those that were planning to free her were also planning to assassinate Elizabeth. There was a risk that she might write back forbidding the assassination. If the ten idealistic young men should accept this, he would have to attempt the liberation himself, with Gilbert's help, while Savage would have to act alone to kill the queen.

All the others were surprised by the numbers given for the two teams that would act.

'Why do you say "myself with ten gentlemen" and later "six

noble gentlemen"?' asked Henry Dunn, saying what everyone was thinking. 'You're adding three men to one group and two men to the other. And from where do you think you can get one hundred followers to help us?'

'To keep our plan undetected it's been necessary to keep our numbers low. I'd have wanted to add every friend of mine to our small group, but Father Ballard said no one else should join after accepting Charles and Chidiock. We're very few for safety reasons, but to make Queen Mary Stuart sure about her liberation it's necessary to exaggerate a bit. Anyway so many will join our rebellion once we have a new queen, that we'll have no problem to supply not only the names of five immediate collaborators, but also of the hundred supporters.'

With Gilbert's help Anthony got immediately to work converting his letter in English into a coded letter.

The next day, Anthony, who was very pleased with the letter he had written, decided to go back to Ballard's house to read it again before destroying it. He decided to read it with a critical eye, putting himself in the position of Mary Stuart. He was sure the letter was excellent, a masterpiece, but wanted to try to guess how it would be received by someone not involved in the plot and learning about it for the first time.

When he read his own letter from a deliberately critical position, he was shocked. He realized he was describing a crazy plan. Just twelve men led by a visionary priest that did not care if he lived or died, with only vague promises of support from large armies, were going to try to change the history of England. The possibilities of success of the plot were minimal, but even in that case a very long war of succession would follow, during which all those involved in the murder of the queen would be hunted like animals. What would happen then to his wife and daughter?

How was it possible that only a few hours ago he was so sure that he was a leader that was going to make history? When he posed that question to himself, he immediately knew the answer.

He had been dazzled by the personality of Captain Fortescue – Father Ballard. A strong, tall and extremely good looking gallant retired army officer that was also a devoted priest risking his life for his church. His nine friends, as well as Gilbert and Savage, had been dazzled too.

Blinded by the strong light emanating from the charismatic priest, twelve otherwise intelligent men were ready to follow him anywhere. He had to get away from these men. But perhaps that would not be necessary. Fortunately, Gilbert, who was confident that the plan would succeed, believed that Queen Mary, instead of rewarding the plotters would send them to the gallows as murderers of Queen Elizabeth. Because of that obviously wrong belief he wrote the letter telling about the execution that was going to take place. It was more than likely that compassionate Mary Stuart would reject the plan. Once the rejection was received, the plan would be abandoned.

Late in July, Gilbert brought another letter from Mary Stuart addressed to Anthony. Gilbert and Anthony proceeded immediately to decode it. The letter included the following paragraph:

"For divers great and important considerations (which were here too long to be deduced) I cannot but greatly praise and commend your common desire to prevent in time the designments of our enemies for the extirpation of our religion out of this realm with the ruin of us all.

For I have long ago shown unto the foreign Catholic princes—and experience doth approve it—the longer that they and we delay to put hand on the matter on this side, the greater leisure have our said enemies to prevail and win advantage over the said princes (as they have done against the King of Spain) and in the meantime the Catholics here, remaining exposed to all sorts of persecution and cruelty, do daily diminish in number, forces, means and power. So as, if remedy be not thereunto hastily provided, I fear not a little but they shall become altogether unable for ever to rise again and to receive any aid at all, whensoever it were offered them. For mine own part, I pray you to assure our principal friends that, albeit I had not in this cause any particular interest (that which I may pretend unto being of no consideration unto me in respect of the public good of this state) I shall be always ready and most willing to employ therein my life and all that I have or may ever look for in this world."

To Anthony's dismay, Mary Stuart had accepted the plan he presented.

Furthermore a postscript of the letter said:

"I would be glad to know the names and qualities of the six gentlemen which are to accomplish the assignment, for that it may be, I shall be able upon knowledge of the parties to give you some further advise necessary to be followed therein; and even so do I wish to be made acquainted with the names of all such principal persons as also from time to time particularly how you proceed and as soon as you may for the same purpose who bee already and how far every one privy hereunto."

When the letter was read to all the members of the conspiracy, everyone celebrated the acceptance of the plan by Mary Stuart. Even Anthony was forced to smile to pretend he was happy.

'You aren't really happy Anthony,' said Robert Barnewell. 'You have to give six names in your answer and you only have four.

'That's right. Seven of you will have to draw straws now. I'll give four names and say the other two will be designated later.'

Robert Gage was the first one to draw a straw and he happily showed it was a short one. Robert Barnewell was next and he got a long one.

'Now I have three names,' said Anthony. Who's next?'

Thomas Salisbury, Henry Dunn and Charles Tilney pulled out short straws.

'I'll let you draw first, Chidiock,' said John Travers.

'No John, I prefer to settle for the last straw that nobody picks,' answered Chidiock Tichborne.

Travers went ahead and got a short straw that he showed smiling.

'Just to check,' said Chidiock after pulling out the last one, taking a look at his long straw.

CHAPTER V
THE PLOT IS IN TROUBLE

The day that Mary Stuart's reply to Anthony´s letter was read, when everyone left after the customary mass Gilbert remained to talk with Father Ballard.

'Father, we're very near the August 20 deadline now. I would like to go to Paris to check with Don Bernardino de Mendoza if any action is being taken to send Spanish troops from Flanders to England. It's most unlikely that they're doing anything, but it would be irresponsible not to check before taking the matter into our own hands. I'll be back as soon as possible, not later than August 5 or 6, two weeks before our deadline. It's not necessary to continue with the correspondence for Mary Stuart. When we get to Chartley in a few days, we only have to advise her through Thomas Philips the date and the hour she must be waiting for her liberators at the selected window. But we have a problem. I'm afraid I might be needed to head the Chartley team. Anthony should have been tremendously happy after the success of his letter. Instead, his spirits were low. I had never seen him in such state before.'

'You're right, Gilbert. It seems that writing his letter Anthony realized for the first time that it's a very risky plan. If Anthony falters and abandons the plan, certainly Thomas and Henry will also leave. The effect on the others will be devastating. We must consider the possibility of rescuing Mary Stuart alone, just you and me.'

Father Auger (7) had forbidden his participation in the plot, but Ballard was now facing a crisis and had decided to disobey, if necessary.

'That would be all right for me, Father. You can do the job of seven young men better than they can. And Savage can do his job alone.'

'Anyway, I must talk to Anthony to try to raise his spirits.'

The next day, Anthony went to Ballard's house.

'Good morning, Father. Will Gilbert be coming here later? I would like to work with him on the reply to Mary Stuart's letter.'

'Don't worry about the reply, Anthony. Think in terms of replying verbally. We're getting close to the date to take action. Does that make you very nervous? Don't be embarrassed if you feel fear. Everyone feels fear when approaching a dangerous situation. A leader like you can feel fear and still lead his men to do what they're expected to do.'

'I would like to work with Gilbert on the verbal reply. When can I see him?'

'After a few days. I've just sent him to Paris to check with the current Spanish Ambassador the information we have on the Spanish and French troops that may help the rebellion. The Ambassador is Don Bernardino de Mendoza (8), who used to be in London but was expelled because of the Throckmorton Plot.'

'Then I'll see him in a few days. I must go now. Goodbye, Father.'

Anthony rushed out because he did not want to give Father Ballard any information about how he felt, nor any chance to talk him out of his decision to get out of the plot. He did not believe that Ballard had decided that Gilbert had to go to France. It was much more likely that Gilbert had suggested the assignment to get out of danger. The execution of the plan was obviously imminent, since Ballard said no more correspondence would be sent to Mary. Anthony thought it was a great idea to get out of England like Gilbert did. He would also go to France to help to get the foreign troops that were needed in support of Mary Stuart. Her last letter, approving the plan described by him, also insisted it was most important to wait for the arrival of foreign troops. He would not leave the plan. Instead, he would travel to Paris to support the plan following Mary's wishes. Of course he would not ask for Ballard's permission. He would send him a message to be delivered after his boat's departure.

Then he realized he could not travel immediately. He needed a travel permit. Surely, he thought, Gilbert had applied for his permit long ago, to make sure he could get rapidly out of danger. But perhaps a little money in the right hands would help. There was a man recommended by Thomas Salisbury he used for his last trip to Europe when he got his permit in two days, paying a very reasonable amount.

His name was Robert Poley. He had access to an office that workaholic Walsingham kept at his home to process papers because he worked for Sir Philip Sydney, husband of Frances, Walsingham's daughter. Sir Philip lived with his wife at Walsingham's home. All Poley had to do was to look for Anthony's application for a travel permit and put it among those at the top of the pile so that it would be processed promptly.

Anthony applied for his travel permit and in the evening went to the Ivory Panther pub where Poley went every day to be contacted by his many customers. He went to the pub and soon he saw Poley, talking with several friends.

'Good evening, Poley, do you remember me?'

'Excuse me mates, I must attend business,' said Poley to his friends. 'I remember your face quite well, Sir, but I don't remember your name.'

'I'm Anthony Babington and last year you helped me to expedite my travel permit application.'

'Yes, Master Babington. Now I remember you well. You're a friend of Thomas Salisbury. What can I do for you this time?'

'Just the same as last year. The need to travel for business came up and I would need to go to France as soon as possible.'

'Have you filed an application already?'

'Yes I have, this morning, almost at noon.'

'Good. But you must know that the number of permits presently issued is much lower than last year and therefore the fee for expediting has increased.'

After a little bargaining, the price was settled and Anthony gave Poley half the amount.

'You'll give me the other half when I bring you the processed application, hopefully in two days. As last year, I must tell you that I have no influence on the decisions taken on the applications and that you must pay me the other half regardless of the outcome. You're paying me only to expedite the matter.'

'Yes, I understand.'

Two days later, in the evening, Anthony returned to the pub to see Poley.

'I'm sorry, Sir, but your travel permit has been denied. You still have to pay my full fee and you shouldn't feel you've wasted your money. It's much better for you to learn right away that you cannot travel than one or two weeks later.'

'But I must travel. Is there anything that can be done?'

'Nothing at all. Sir Francis Walsingham reviews personally each application. If this was a matter left to assistants it would be possible to get a different assistant to review the application. A different assistant might make a different assessment. But Sir Francis is the only one that gives travel permits and he has already made his decision about your application.'

'This is a most serious inconvenient for me. I'll miss the chance to earn a substantial amount.'

'I'm very sorry, Master Babington, but thanks to me you got this information in advance and you must pay me my fee. I'm not supposed to help those that wish to travel and I run a serious risk helping you.'

'All right Poley. Of course I'll pay you. I understand then that the only possibility would be to talk with Sir Francis and persuade him to change his mind.'

'Perhaps you can change his mind and perhaps you cannot. It doesn't make any difference because it will be impossible for you to talk with him.'

To make sure to remain in friendly terms with Poley, Anthony paid him and only afterwards went on with the conversation.

'It might be possible to change Sir Francis mind if you should arrange a meeting for me,' said Anthony.

'And why would I do such a crazy thing?'

'To earn money, of course.'

'You don't understand, Master Babington. You're in trouble. If your permit to travel has been denied by Sir Francis, it means you're in some kind of trouble. I don't care what kind, but I don't want Sir Francis to find out that I've anything to do with you.'

'Here, in this bag, I have 50 gold angels. That's 25 pounds. I can give you 25 angels now and the other 25 when I get the appointment.'

The mention of the gold coins, plus the fact that Anthony had the coins with him now, made go-getting Poley think. He decided he had to get the 50 gold coins right away. Master Babington was in a very weak position if he really needed to travel and he was practically asking to be relieved of the 50 angels. Poley kept thinking for a long interval and he finally answered.

'I'll probably regret accepting to try to get a meeting for you, but since you're a friend of Sir Thomas Salisbury, with whom I've done business for many years, I'll make you a proposal. You'll give me now the 50 coins you brought with you and I'll request Sir Francis to grant you a meeting. If I don't get the meeting for you I still keep the 50 coins, you don't owe me anything and we depart as good friends. But if I get you a meeting you'll give me 150 gold angels more. The 50 coins are a very low price for the risk I'm taking requesting a meeting for someone in trouble and the 150 coins would be a very low price for getting the impossible, if I should get it.'

Anthony thought about the proposal for several minutes. It was a big risk to give 50 gold coins to a man without receiving anything in return. But the only alternative would be to try to make arrangements to be transported illegally to France and he had no contact with anyone that could do such a thing. Ballard had clearly said there would be no more correspondence with Mary Stuart, so that the plot to kill one queen and to liberate another would be put in action very soon. If he remained in England he had to participate in the crazy plot about which he had been so irrationally enthusiastic until a few days ago. Therefore, he decided to accept Poley's proposal, hoping that his greed would make him try to get another 150 coins. If he obtained the meeting, he would offer Walsingham to become his agent in France.

'Here you have, Poley; the bag with 50 gold angels is yours. How will I know about the meeting?'

'Come here every evening. Just wave hello from a distance and don't approach me. If and when I have a meeting for you, I'll approach you and ask you to bring the 150 coins we have arranged for. After I have the coins I'll give you date, time and place.'

When Poley left the pub he was extremely happy with his 50 gold coins. He offered the deal to Anthony with the idea of doing nothing except, of course, to keep the coins. However, as Anthony expected, the 50 coins already in his possession wetted his appetite for the other 150 coins that his customer was prepared to give him.

Poley wondered what kind of trouble Babington would have to make Sir Francis deny him the right to go to the continent, perhaps just a very long stay in the continent last year. He could check about Babington's trip of last year sneaking in the morning into the office Sir Francis kept at home. All foreign travel records were kept there. Poley reasoned that if Babington stayed abroad too long last year that would obviously be the reason for the present denial. It would not be then too compromising to ask for something in his behalf.

The next morning Poley sneaked into Walsingham's home office while the Principal Secretary was at Whitehall Palace. The records he was looking for were not as easy to find as the pile of travel applications on top of his desk, but Poley found the records within half an hour.

Once he could leaf through these records, in a little over ten minutes he located the Babington file in which he found that the young man's stay in the continent had been quite long last year. Poley decided to try to get the appointment wanted by Babington when Walsingham returned home in the evening.

That day, Babington and his friends had one of their usual collective fencing classes at 7 o'clock in the evening followed by a discussion meeting.

Anthony asked for a personal lesson with Savage at 5 o'clock, telling Ballard that at 7 he had to leave to get together with his father in law, who was visiting London for two days.

Having checked that Anthony Babington had had a very lengthy stay on the continent last year, Poley was convinced that Sir Francis had denied him a new permit to travel for that reason. He decided he could try to get the 150 angels without running too great a risk if he was careful presenting Babington's case.

When Sir Francis Walsingham returned home every evening at around 7 o'clock, he always ordered dinner for him and his daughter Frances. Frances husband, Sir Philip Sidney, was currently in Flanders with the English troops headed there by Sir Robert Dudley, Earl of Leicester. Until the meal was ready, Walsingham used to continue to work at the study he kept at home. That evening, Poley was alert and knocked at the door of the study immediately after Walsingham got in to avoid annoying him once he was immersed in his work.

'Come in,' said Walsingham, just after sitting at his desk. 'Oh, it's you Poley. Are you bringing me news about my son in law?'

'No Sir, no dispatches from Flanders arrived today. I just wanted to inform you about a man that approached me in the pub yesterday. His travel permit to visit the continent had been denied. He approached me to request a meeting with you. I refused his request but I wanted to inform you about the fact that he had the nerve to request a meeting with you. His name is Anthony Babington.'

'So that Anthony Babington wants a meeting with me? That should be fun. Do you believe you could find him?'

'I'm sure I can find out about his whereabouts in the pub.'

'I'll give you his address but it'll be better if you can find him casually. Tell him that in spite of your denial you decided to talk in his favor and that I finally granted him an audience at this office, in my home, at half past seven in the evening of August 3. Will you do that for me?'

Walsingham gave Poley Anthony's address, only to be used if he could not meet him casually, and Poley left his office.

Poley walked in the direction of the Ivory Panther pub in case his customer had gone there today, although he did not expect him to come there to talk with him until the next day. While walking to the pub Poley was congratulating himself for having dared to tell Walsingham the matter of Babington's request for an audience with him. He did it very tactfully and now Sir Francis was asking him, as a personal favor, to arrange the audience.

When he arrived to the pub he was pleased to see Antony eating supper at a table.

'Good evening Master Babington. I have very good news for you,' said Poley, sitting at Babington's table.

'Good evening, Poley. Do I understand that you managed to obtain a meeting with Sir Francis Walsingham for me?'

'I certainly did. It was an impossible task, but I finally managed to overcome Sir Francis reluctance and he granted you an audience. Fortunately for you, he has a very good opinion of my judgment and accepted my words of praise for you.'

'On what date will I see him?'

'As previously arranged, I'll give you this information tomorrow, after you give me the 150 gold angels.'

'It won't be necessary to wait until tomorrow. I also have a very high opinion of your ability so that I brought the angels with me.'

Anthony took out from inside pockets in his clothing three bags full of coins and placed them on the table he was sharing with Poley who looked at the bags with extremely opened eyes. His initially surprised expression gave way to one of great pleasure and then turned into fear when he looked around to see if anyone had noticed the bags on the table.

He seemed satisfied that no one had noticed anything and rushed to put the three bags in his own pockets. Then, one by one he pulled the bags out to open them a bit and peek inside for a second to check if the coins were gold angels.

'I'll trust you with the number of coins now but I'll count them at home.'

'You can relax, Poley. I counted the coins before bringing them with me,' said Anthony with a smile of amusement at Poley's conduct.

'Your audience is at Walsingham's own home at half past seven in the evening of August 3. He has a private study at his home and he'll see you there just before supper.'

'August 3,' repeated Anthony. That meant he should have another meeting with Father Ballard and his co-conspirators before the audience. In his present state of mind no such meeting was even possible so that he decided right away to stay in bed the day of the fencing class followed by a meeting telling his wife and servants he was feeling ill. A servant could go to Captain Fortescue's fencing school to explain he was feeling very ill and could not leave home.

'All right Poley. I'll be at Walsingham's home at least a quarter of an hour before half past seven in the evening of August 3. I know the address. I'm most grateful for your service and you've certainly earned the 200 coins I've paid you.'

On August 3 Anthony knocked at the door of Walsingham's home exactly at a quarter past seven in the evening. Just before, he had been walking in the area for over half an hour, waiting for the right time to see Walsingham. Poley opened the door and accompanied Anthony to a waiting room. There, Anthony waited for over half an hour before hearing Walsingham's voice shouting to him from his desk.

'Open the door and come in, Master Babington.'

When Anthony opened the door Walsingham did not even look at him. He was writing at his desk at one end of a very large room and continued to do so. After five minutes, while he continued writing, Walsingham talked to Anthony again without raising his sight from the paper on which he was writing.

'Take a sit on one of the chairs, Master Babington.'

Anthony sat on one of two chairs placed on front of the desk while Walsingham continued to write. Then he finished and moved a lever placed at his left on the desk.

When he did it a bell ringing in the next room was heard. Jones came in from a side door.

'Did you call, Sir Francis?'

'Yes, Jones. This letter has your instructions for tonight. After you do what's indicated here you should go on with the instructions I gave you earlier, but there's no rush, you should have a leisurely dinner with your team first. Have all your men arrived?'

'Yes, Sir Francis. All of them are in the next room.'

Fine, Jones. I must talk with Master Babington now. When I finish and I call you, come in with all of them. Don't take this paper with you yet. I'll keep it on my desk in case I wish to add anything, but don't forget to take it with you when you leave this house.'

'I'll be waiting for your call, Sir Francis.'

When Jones left, Walsingham looked at Anthony for the first time since he had entered the room.

'Master Babington, you've certainly changed since the time we met, seven years ago. At that time you had a shaved face and looked very young. You're still quite young, only 24 I believe, but with your moustache and your pointed blond beard you look mature.'

'I'm flattered to see that you still remember me after so many years, Sir Francis.'

'You shouldn't be. It's not good for a suspect to be remembered by the authorities.'

After the cavalier treatment Anthony had received from Walsingham, ignoring him while he was sitting in front of him, he had started to realize he made a big mistake requesting an audience with the Principal Secretary. Instead he should have used his gold coins to try to find an illegal transport to France across the Channel. Walsingham's last words stressed his mistake, but now he had no alternative except to go on with his original plan.

'Sir Francis, I heard rumors of a conspiracy against the queen being prepared in France. I decided to travel to France to check those rumors and to bring information to you if anything was true. However, when I applied for a permit to travel abroad it was refused. I requested to see you to offer to work for you to investigate in France. Since I've travelled before, I have many contacts in France and can do a thorough work there in your behalf.'

'You can relax Master Babington and disregard any rumors of a conspiracy. There's no possibility of any conspiracy taking place. The reason is the severe penalty for high treason. Do you know about this penalty?'

'Yes. The penalty for traitors is to be drawn, hanged and quartered.'

'Have you watched any high treason execution?'

'I'm afraid I haven't watched any personally.'

'I'll explain the details to you. This penalty was made law centuries ago. I don't remember the exact date, but certainly not later than the 13th century. We're very civilized now, but in the 13th and 14th centuries they were very cruel. They were so cruel that immediately after hanging they revived those hanged, so that they wouldn't miss the next part of the sentence, the quartering part. But they found that quartering was too messy, so that previous disembowelment was needed to be neat. The result was that those sentenced to be drawn, hanged and quartered died during disembowelment, an atrocious way to die. We're much more civilized now, but we're English. Tradition is at the root of English culture. Out of respect for tradition we send to death traitors today exactly in the same way they were sent to death in the previous centuries. You can then relax and disregard any rumors of a plot to commit high treason.'

Anthony felt dizzy. He had always assumed that those sentenced to be drawn, hanged and quartered were hanged until dead, but he had never watched any execution for high treason.

Since Anthony remained silent, Walsingham continued to talk about the subject.

'Of course in the case of the Duke of Norfolk an exception was made and he was beheaded with an axe as corresponds to a nobleman. No exception was made when Sir Francis Throckmorton was executed. Sir Francis was a knight and he belonged to a noble family, but he was no titled nobleman himself. One type of execution or another wasn't important in this case. The important result needed was the Bond of Association. In any further plot Mary Stuart can be condemned to death for profiting from the plot, even if she knows nothing about it. Of course to overcome any objections the queen may have it'll be much better if she knows about the plot.'

'Thank you for your explanations, Sir Francis. Is it still possible for you to be interested in the work I may do for you in France?'

'Not right now, but I appreciate your gesture and I'll think about it. What about working for me right here, in London? I need men like you in London. Do you accept my offer?'

'I certainly will think about working for you in London, Sir Francis, but I'm only an average Londoner.'

'Not so average, young man. You know many influential people from the North of England. Also I understand you're a good friend of Sir Thomas Salisbury.'

The mention of his friend's name preceded by the word Sir made Anthony remember Walsingham's comments about the sentence of Sir Francis Throckmorton. Perhaps these comments were conveying the message that his friend would not get any special treatment for being Sir Thomas.

Since Anthony seemed lost in his thoughts and did not answer to accept his proposal, Walsingham moved the lever at his left, the bell rang in the next room and Jones entered the study followed by ten men.

'Jones, Master Babington has just told me that he might start working for me. In that case he'll be one of your team. Since the crown is treating all of you to an exceptional dinner tonight before you start the new operation, I believe it would be a good idea to take him along to have dinner with you. This way he'll get to know the men he'll be working with. After you go out, ask Poley to go along with you too, since he's a friend of Master Babington.'

'Fine, Sir Francis.'

'And don't forget to take this paper with you. This is your first assignment for tonight, after dinner of course.'

When they were out Jones talked to the group.

'We'll go to the Horse and Unicorn pub. They know me there, I can sign for our dinner and they'll take the bill to Whitehall Palace to get paid. The food and the beer are quite good there. You can eat all you want, but be careful with the beer since we must work after dinner.'

One of the men talked to Anthony. 'I see that you carry a side sword. Do you know how to use it?'

'I certainly do and I'm quite good with it,' said Anthony

dryly.

'We used to have a gentleman like you working with us a few months ago. He also carried a side sword and he was very good with it.'

'He couldn't use it anyway when someone with a sharp knife got to him in a dark corner,' said another man.

A third one got in the conversation. 'Not only was he a good swordsman, but he was tall and very strong. His perdition was that he was too good looking and a womanizer. He got involved with a married woman and her husband ambushed him and cut his throat when he was about to enter the house where the unfaithful wife was waiting. It could have been a big scandal, but since he was one of us Sir Francis arranged for everything to be hushed up.'

'Well, I might be a better replacement. I'm not too tall, only average looking and I don't get involved with married women, except my own of course.'

Everyone laughed at Anthony's comment.

When they reached the pub, Jones, who was evidently very well-known there, asked for a private dining room for his men. They were taken to a large room, just for themselves, with only a door leading to the main area of the pub. There was a long table at the center where they all sat, with Jones at the head of the table.

Pub female attendants started placing mugs of beer before everyone while they were taking their places.

Once seated, Jones took out the paper Walsingham had given him when they left his study, since he had not looked at it yet. After reading it, he gave it to the man at his left, who smiled widely while reading it. Anthony looked without paying much attention and he continued talking with the man at his right side. However he noticed that the next man to read the paper did not just smile but laughed heartily and then looked at him. Anthony pretended not to notice and continued to chat with the man sitting next to him.

When the next man reading the paper laughed and looked at him, Anthony decided he had to steal a look at the paper. Poley was next and he did not laugh, but was dead serious, placing the paper flat on the table so that it could be read by the next man.

Anthony stood up, beer mug in hand and went to the head of the table where Jones was sitting. Instead of taking the shortest way he went all around the table so that he could read the paper on the table when passing by Poley's side. Just a glance was enough for him to realize it was an order for his arrest, as he had deduced from the attitude of those that read it. When he was standing next to Jones he raised his mug high in the air and talked loud to be heard by everyone at the table.

'Congratulations, Master Jones. You've excellent men working for you. I'll be proud to work with them.'

Those that had read the arrest warrant laughed heartily and Anthony joined the laughter to give the impression he was not aware that he was supposed to be arrested after dinner.

Anthony drank from his mug and then spit.

'I come often to this place and they have much stronger beer. This is for women and children. I'll see that they send the good stuff here.'

Anthony went out of the room, ostensibly to order stronger beer.

'Stay with him, Poley,' said Jones. Poley rushed behind Anthony.

Once they were in the main part of the pub, Anthony turned around to face Poley, mad with rage.

'You're a traitor. I paid you to help me and instead you set me up so that I'm sent to the gallows.'

'I swear to you I knew nothing about this. I put the paper flat on the table so that you could take a look at it. You understood and came around as I expected. I'm your friend and because of that I'm in trouble. I warned you that you were in trouble. You could have escaped but instead you insisted that you wanted a meeting with Walsingham.'

'I have one thousand pounds in gold coins stashed away. They'll be yours if you find a way to extricate me from this problem. Take this bag with some gold in it. It's all that I have on me. Go back to the special dinner and say you lost me in the crowd. Fortunately, the place is full and that's possible.'

Anthony had been walking while he was talking. When he finished he was next to the street door, dashed out and started running before Poley had time to react.

Anthony knew that part of London very well and zigzagged as much as possible in different streets to make it difficult to trace his steps for anyone trying to follow him. He did not stop running until he realized he was running slower than what he usually walked. He stopped to get his breath back and to think. Obviously, the plan had been discovered and he had to warn Thomas and Henry, at least. He was relatively close to Thomas house, so that he should go there immediately. When he arrived he knocked at the door. Thomas opened.

'We've been discovered, Thomas. Bring any gold you have at hand. Rush because Walsingham's men will be here any minute now. I'll wait for you in the dark across the street.'

A few minutes later Thomas Salisbury joined Anthony. They went immediately to the house of Henry Dunn, but from a distance they could see the house had already been raided by Walsingham's men, so that they had to think of someone else to warn.

177

Walsingham was enraged when he was told by Jones that Anthony Babington had escaped.

'I serve you the leader of the conspiracy in a plate and you let him escape. You're an idiot. And as an excuse you tell me you told Poley to watch him. I'll send Poley to the Tower but you should have ordered one of your own men to watch Babington. Poley (9) is not one of your men. He doesn't even work for me but for my son in law. He joined you for the dinner only as a friend of Babington. Now you must split your men to immediately raid his home and the homes of Salisbury and Dunn. You'll probably find all three of them are gone. As soon as you finish these three raids you must raid Ballard's house with all your men. You have a copy of the key. Enter without making any noise since you've got to catch Ballard and Savage asleep. If you wake them up they'll probably kill you and your ten men and escape afterwards. You have a sketch of the house in which the locations of the bedrooms of the men you must apprehend are clearly marked. Also marked is the bedroom of the cleaning woman. After you take Ballard and Savage wake her up and tell her to take care of the house until we decide what to do with it.'

CHAPTER VI
WILD SAVAGE

In the early hours of August 4, 1586, Father John Ballard woke up with two clasped hands on his mouth preventing him from uttering any sound, and two strong arms immobilizing his own arms and placing him in a standing position. He did not put any resistance until he was standing and then kicked his bed with the full force of his right leg. The bed was a simple timber frame with a rope latticework to support a mattress of coarse fabric stuffed with straw and came down without much noise. However the noise was enough to wake up Savage, as Ballard intended. Jones was supervising personally the capture of Ballard and Savage and hit Ballard in the head with the butt of his pistol rendering him unconscious.

John Savage, asleep in his room, woke up because he heard an unusual sound. Since he was quite aware Captain Fortescue and he were in a very dangerous situation, he jumped out of his bed immediately and looked out of the window. He saw a couple of men standing on the street watching the house. He immediately realized the house was being raided and that several men had been left on the street to catch anyone trying to escape from the house. Savage was prepared for the situation he was facing now. After killing Bernard Maude he had realized he was in a very dangerous path and moved to another room of the large house used for the fencing school. He picked the one next to Ballard's room. It had two windows and he built a wall converting it in two rooms with one window each.

He made a secret door, almost impossible to detect, to go from one room to the other. This way he had a secret room where he could hide in case of danger. He had offered to Captain Fortescue to make a similar secret room for him, but he had refused. Within two minutes from his sudden wakening only a bare mattress on his bed and a few belongings in the scant furniture were in his room and Savage was well hidden in his adjoining secret room.

In Ballard's room Jones talked to the five men he had there.

'We should have split. Three of you should have gone to Savage's room, while I should have entered here with only two. Savage may have woken up with the noise made by Ballard. The result might be a fiery fight when we enter his room. He may be waiting with a pistol, ready to shoot at the first man entering his room.'

'He might still be asleep. The noise wasn't too loud and he's in another room,' said one of the men.

'Do you want to bet and be the first man to enter his room?' asked another man.

'Don't argue with each other,' ordered Jones. 'Let's quietly push the door open from a side. Then we'll take a look inside without exposing ourselves. If he's still on his bed we'll go and catch him. You, Red, stay here and tie Ballard up.'

Jones had left another man in the corridor leading to the bedrooms of Ballard and Savage.

'Did we make too much noise in there?' asked Jones to the man in the corridor.

'Some, but not enough to wake up anyone sound asleep.'

Regardless of the encouraging words of the man in the corridor, Jones opened the door of Savage's bedroom from a side with utmost care, without exposing himself. He placed a small oil lamp on the floor in front of the door giving a feeble light in the room. He looked inside from a side of the door and saw an empty bed with a bare mattress. Savage might be lurking in a corner with pistols in his hands, ready to shoot. Jones had to make a quick decision.

'The room appears to be empty. He might have gone out tonight or he might be hiding somewhere in the room. All five of you must go in together and search the room carefully.'

The five men entered the room and searched.

'There's no one inside this room. None of the furniture is large enough for anyone to hide inside. Obviously, he went out tonight.'

Jones shouted a series of expletives and finally gave orders. 'Come with me. We'll wake up the old cleaning woman and we must search the entire house.'

An hour later, after a thorough search, Jones left five men in the house to arrest Savage if he should return and went with the others to take Ballard to the Tower in a cart.

When Jones and his men left the house taking Ballard as their prisoner, Savage realized that several men had been left in the house, but no one on the street where he would be seen by anyone returning to the house. He left the house climbing down to the street from his first floor window taking all his money with him. He always kept his money in the secret room.

He also took with him the rope tied to a hook he had prepared to climb to the terrace leading to the queen's bedroom in Nonsuch Palace. Obviously, the plot had been discovered and Mary Stuart would not be rescued, but he could still play his part in the plot. He had been told the location of the queen's bedroom in Nonsuch Palace, so that he could go in to kill her. But he had to take immediate action, before Walsingham had time to take protective measures.

This night the weather was excellent for Savage's plan. There was a light drizzle and it was a very dark night. In spite of the light rain it was a warm August night and there was a good chance that the bedroom door leading to the terrace would be left open. He went to the stable where his horse was kept. He examined the place closely before going in, in case Walsingham should have sent men to wait for him there. When he was satisfied that only the half asleep man that was on duty that night was in the stable, he went in and requested his horse. The man on duty knew him well and gave him his horse immediately, saddled for riding.

In the lonely night Savage rapidly reached the area of Nonsuch Palace. He went to a wooded area not too far from the palace, dismounted, removed saddle and reins from the horse and hid these among leaves and branches. Then he let his horse go free. In the dark night he ran towards the palace.

When he was near he went around the palace, keeping a reasonable distance, until he was in front of the terrace Captain Fortescue had indicated that it had a door leading to the queen's bedroom. He lay down, with his belly against the ground, watching to determine how the palace was guarded.

After a while he saw a yeoman of the queen's guard, armed with a harquebus, walking around the palace counter clockwise. About one minute later another yeoman that was walking around the palace clockwise came into sight. Two minutes later the first yeoman he had detected making the rounds came into sight again. After the second yeoman passed again, Savage burst into action and ran towards the palace. He threw the hook with the rope that caught firmly at the banister of the railing at the edge of the terrace. He easily climbed the rope, reached the terrace, removed the rope and approached the door of the queen's bedroom. The door was locked but with his knowledge of locks he easily opened it with his strong knife making almost no noise. Very carefully he opened the door just enough to get in. The interior of the bedroom was pitch dark.

He entered slowly carefully moving on his hands and knees and then stayed still. When his sight adjusted to the interior of the dark room, he still could not see much beyond the distance he could reach stretching an arm. He advanced very carefully on hands and knees on a wooden floor. After a while he reached a carpeted area and almost immediately found a chair standing on the carpet. Looking very carefully it appeared that at both sides of the chair other chairs were aligned with it.

He stood erect and extending one arm he verified what he had guessed; a large table was ahead of the line of chairs. Walking alongside the line of chairs he was convinced he was not inside a bedroom; he was in a very large dining room with a long table in the center. It was not an ordinary dining room but one for special banquets with many guests.

He was alone in this room; the queen was not sleeping here of course. Captain Fortescue had been deceived by Usher Tyndell almost one year ago, last October, when told that this room was the queen's bedroom. Savage realized that Walsingham could have arrested everyone involved in the plot a year ago.

Well, thought Savage, Walsingham made a big mistake showing him an easy way to get into Nonsuch Palace. He was inside the palace now and no one knew this. He would explore and find out the royal bedroom. Tomorrow night he would enter there to kill the queen.

He was glad that anticipating problems he had released his horse after hiding reins and saddle. If his horse would be found tied up near the palace, Walsingham would immediately realize he was already inside the palace. Now he had to fix the lock of the door leading from terrace to banquet hall and he had to hide the rope with a hook.

When Savage finished fixing the lock the sky had already started to clear. The sun had not come up over the horizon yet, but it was not drizzling anymore and soon a fine summer day would start. It was still rather dark inside the banquet hall, but after closing and locking the terrace door Savage could walk around without bumping into anything. He quietly opened a door at the end of the banquet hall. It led to a deserted corridor and he started to walk silently along it carrying the rope with him. He passed a stairway going down to the ground floor and heard noises from a kitchen already in operation. He tried a door near the stairway. It was unlocked and opened easily. Since it led to an empty room he entered. It was some sort of storage room with the walls lined with shelves.

He hid the rope in a place where he found tools and the rope did not look out of place. He thought he might find some food there but, apart from the few tools, there were only clothes. They were men's clothes in the colors of the queen's livery, the clothing worn by the dozens of lackeys moving around in the palace. Upper-hose and nether-hose had a deep purple color while the doublets were green. A hundred years later upper-hose like that would be called breeches while the nether-hose would be called stockings. The doublet was the garment used above the waist. Savage took off his own clothes; he carefully hid them under a pile of ten doublets and put on a lackey outfit that fitted him well. The doublet was tight fitting, had long sleeves and a deep V-waistline.

He smiled at the thought of wearing purple and green clothing to be inconspicuous. In fact, he normally would feel conspicuous just using breeches and fine stockings, since he used loose pants reaching below the knee, called slops, and long knitted socks reaching above the knee, called cannions. What he really appreciated of the outfit he had procured for himself were the good quality black leather shoes, which felt very comfortable in spite of being new.

Savage had to walk along the corridors to find the location of the queen's bedroom. It should be easy to detect since it would have guards at the door. Of course he would not enter through the door but through a window, but he had to locate the room. The disguise he was wearing was fine in case he was seen by any non-servant members of the household, but he had to avoid to be seen at close range by any servant. Servants should only see him from a distance, since if they saw his face they would realize he was an intruder, posing as a servant. Because of the early hour the corridors were deserted now. If a maid or any lackey should come in his direction he planned to turn around. But the palace was shaped as a square and the corridors had sharp corners.

After turning one of these corners Savage found himself face to face with a man about sixty years old dressed in a liveried uniform. He was tall, heavy set, with a shaved face and a large, hooked nose. His doublet was as purple as the hose, but below the doublet a wide green belt could be seen. Savage figured he would be the butler, wearing a more elegant uniform than the lackeys.

'Thank God I finally find a lackey that rises at a reasonable time. What kind of training have you people got in this palace? I see that you're not tall, not handsome and not even young. Tell me that I'm lucky and that you work here because you're a good runner.'

'I'm a pretty good runner, Sir.'

'Don't Sir me; I'm not a nobleman, only your superior. I'm Master Jenkins to you. By God, you had to call Williams Sir. No wonder the queen decided to transfer me here from Whitehall, sending Williams to Whitehall to replace me. What's your name?'

'John, Master Jenkins.'

'Just John; don't you have a surname?'

'John Wildman, Master Jenkins.'

'Wildman; is that an Irish name?'

'I don't know, Master Jenkins. My father was from Liverpool, where I was born. I never met my grandfather since he died before I was born.'

'We're wasting time. The queen is leaving for Hampton Court in a few minutes in her carriage and you must run along ahead of it to warn the driver of roots or trunks that may overturn it or upset the ride in any way. Come with me. We must hurry.'

When they reached the stairs that led to the ground floor in the front part of the building, Savage followed Jenkins down to the inner open court. There a large carriage with four horses was waiting. Jenkins talked to the driver.

'Bill, John Wildman will be running along with the carriage to warn you about any problems on the road.'

'It's a 10 league ride to Hampton Court, Bill, a full day's ride,' said Savage. 'Where are you stopping so that Her Majesty can rest a while?'

'We'll stop at a castle just north of Fulham, where we can get a bit to eat.'

'That's good, it's about half the distance to Hampton Court. I gather we'll start passing through Tollworth.'

'You're right, John. Do you know the road?'

'I know every road around London, Bill. I can take you to Battersea Castle and Hampton Court Palace. Just follow me.'

'You're right again. Battersea Castle is precisely our first and only stop. I'm glad you're already familiar with the roads we'll travel today.'

At that moment, the queen came along accompanied by one of her ladies-in-waiting, everyone saluted with deep reverences, the two ladies boarded the carriage and it departed going through the palace's main gate with Savage running alongside dressed in the queen's livery.

Ten mounted men of the Queen's Body Guard of the Yeomen of the Guard led by the Guard's Captain, followed to insure the queen's safety.

Savage realized that Bill, the driver, must have believed that Jenkins, the new butler, had brought him along with him from Whitehall as his favorite lackey to run along with carriages, presumably because he was very good for this type of service.

Through Bill, he had now been introduced to the servants as the excellent lackey brought from Whitehall. And he was a good runner that could run for hours along with a carriage and he would do his best to demonstrate to Bill he was good enough to be considered by the new butler as an indispensable lackey. When they returned to Nonsuch Palace he would be able to walk around everywhere unmolested.

The royal carriage had a primitive system of chain suspension that gave a better ride than other carriages of the time, but not of the type developed in Hungary with suspension, called coach, that had started to be used in the continent. Using it the queen had to travel at the leisured pace of only 10 leagues a day to be comfortable. This was good for Savage since in his excellent physical condition he had no problem in running in one day two stretches of about 5 leagues each. He was sure very few of the lackeys working in Nonsuch Palace could have done this work.

Savage took special care to examine carefully the road where he was running to point out not only the obvious obstacles the carriage had to avoid, but anything that could result in an uncomfortable bump.

Bill was very happy since he was getting a smoother ride than normal from the carriage. Furthermore, since this was an unexpected trip he had not been able to study the maps as carefully as he always did and was afraid of perhaps making some mistake, but he just had to follow the lackey running ahead of him.

The carriage arrived at Battersea Castle in just four hours and it was only 10 o'clock in the morning when they arrived.

'Congratulations Bill,' said the queen. 'You rode much faster than usual and nevertheless we had a particularly smooth ride.'

'Thank you, Your Majesty, but most of the merit corresponds to John Wildman, the lackey running ahead to point out the obstacles that make a bumpy ride. He also directed me through a couple of shortcuts since he knows well all roads in the vicinity of London.'

'Thank you very much, John. But I don't like the word lackey. Politicians use it derisively against each other. Footman is the right word to designate the type of service you give, John.'

'I greatly appreciate your kind words, Your Majesty,' answered Savage. 'I was a footman in the army you sent to fight the French in Scotland, several years ago, and I've always been proud of having been a soldier.'

'Do you see, Bill? Make sure that this conversation is known in Nonsuch Palace.'

At that moment, the Lord of the Manor came to welcome the queen, all flushed up after having to rush to put on his best clothes to receive the unexpected guest of the highest possible rank. Savage, Bill and the other coachman riding as his companion were invited to enter the kitchen where they were served beer and food.

Walsingham was very upset. He had planned that in a swift operation all the conspirators should be captured and taken to the Tower of London the night before.

Not only had Babington escaped when he was surrounded by all his men of action, but he had taken Salisbury with him. Also a man called Robert Barnewell had escaped. Worse than that, one of the only two really dangerous men in the plot, Savage, could not be found anywhere. He was sure that after a few days his men would capture the three gentlemen, but what about Savage? High placed men like Babington and Salisbury could only hide in the home of a friend. It was just a matter of raiding the homes of every friend they had until they were found. But Savage was different. He only had to move to another town, change his name and get a job. He would never be found and the man that had planned to kill the queen would escape punishment.

Suddenly Walsingham had another thought that made him pale. Perhaps Savage would not want to escape. He really was not a member of the conspiracy to replace a Protestant queen with a Catholic one. Savage was not a Catholic and was not interested in Mary Stuart. He just wanted revenge against Queen Elizabeth. He wanted to kill her and joined the plotters just because they would show him a way to get close to her.

The thought tormented Walsingham. It was his fault entirely because he had made a series of mistakes. After interrogating Savage he was convinced he knew nothing about any Catholic mass, but anyway sent him to be tortured. And afterwards he pardoned Savage's life. A tortured man had to be killed always, guilty or innocent.

And after learning that this determined and dangerous man had joined others in a plot to kill the queen he had shown him a way to get into Nonsuch Palace. He would never be able to forgive himself if Savage should actually kill Queen Elizabeth.

Jones was standing in front of Walsingham awaiting his orders.

'Stop the search for Babington and Salisbury. Our priority now is to find Savage and I want all your men looking for him.'

'But I have no idea where to look for this man, Sir Francis.'

'Nonsuch Palace. That's where I want you to go with all your men. I'll go too. I'll direct this search personally.'

'Some of my men are here with me in Whitehall Palace. Others are searching the home of Michael Hussley.'

'I'll go to Nonsuch Palace with the men you have here. Get horses for all of us. I don't want to waste time going in a slow carriage. Go to Hussley's home, get the other men and take them to Nonsuch. We'll meet there.'

Walsingham arrived at Nonsuch Palace to look for Savage at 11 o'clock in the morning of August 4, at the same time that Savage was eating a hearty lunch at Battersea Castle as a footman of Queen Elizabeth on her way to Hampton Court Palace. The butler, Jenkins, was called as soon as Walsingham and his men arrived at the palace.

'Good morning, Sir Francis. What can I do for you, Sir?'

'Good morning, Jenkins. I'm surprised to see you here. Didn't they have a fellow called Williams as butler?'

'The queen got used to me after so many years in Whitehall Palace. Since she now spends most of her time here, she brought me from Whitehall and sent Williams there.'

'Good for you, Jenkins. Take me to see the queen. I must speak with her urgently.'

'I'm afraid you'll have to wait a couple of days to speak to the queen, Sir Francis. She's on her way to Hampton Court now. She'll be there all day tomorrow and she'll return the day after tomorrow, arriving in the evening.'

'I'll stay here to conduct a search. If I finish my search before her return, I'll leave. There's a large terrace facing south on the first floor. I must go there with my men. Kindly show us the way.'

'Yes, it's the terrace of the large dining hall. Please follow me.'

'Certainly, Jenkins. Bring along one of your lackeys. When we get there just leave the lackey with us and go back to your duties. We'll ask the lackey if we should need anything.'

'Come with us Jim. You'll stay with Sir Francis and do whatever he orders. The rest of you, go back to your chores.'

Jenkins started his way to the large dining hall followed by

Walsingham and his men. Jim, the lackey designated by Jenkins, followed.

'This is the entrance to the large dining hall, Sir Francis. Now I'll go back to the ground floor.'

Jenkins left realizing Walsingham wanted to be left alone to do his search.

'Wait here at the door, Jim,' ordered Walsingham to the lackey.

Walsingham went straight to the door leading to the terrace to check if it had been opened. If it was opened, that would show that Savage had entered the palace. But Walsingham found the door locked from the inside.

'George, do you know anything about locks?' asked Walsingham to one of his men.

'No, Sir Francis, but William does. Come here, William.'

'Do you need me, Sir Francis?'

'Yes William. Would you say it's difficult to open this locked door from the terrace?'

'Not too difficult. It's not an outside lock, designed to keep people out, but an inside one, just designed to provide some privacy. I could open this lock from the terrace with just a knife.'

'Could you lock it back from the inside, afterwards?'

'I would probably break it, opening it with a knife, but many would be able to open it without causing too much damage, so that it could be fixed and used again as new.'

Walsingham was upset. The locked door did not prove anything. He had to continue to believe that Savage might be inside the palace.

'Search this hall thoroughly. See if you can find a rope hidden here,' ordered Walsingham and then he signaled one of the men to approach him. 'George, after the search for the rope is finished I want you to take the men outside the palace to inspect carefully all the woods around. Perhaps in one of these woods you'll find a horse tied to a tree.'

Walsingham sat on a large chair without leaving the dining hall. After his men left to search the woods, having found no rope in the dining hall he summoned the lackey waiting outside.

'Get me something to eat here, alone, while I wait for my men. Also see that they all get something to eat when they return from the search they are conducting in the woods around the palace.'

The search in the woods lasted all day. Jones arrived around 1 o'clock in the afternoon with the rest of the men and after eating a bit they replaced George and his men in the search in the woods. Just before 3 o'clock all of Walsingham's men were searching the woods.

At 3 o'clock in the afternoon Walsingham requested the lackey assigned to him to summon the butler.

'Jenkins, I'll be leaving now, but I'll be back tomorrow, with my men, rather early in the morning. I've discovered a plot to kill the queen. All the plotters have been arrested today, with the exception of four. We're on the track of three of them, but there's a possibility that the fourth man has hidden himself in Nonsuch Palace.'

'This is impossible. This place is full of soldiers guarding the queen.'

'It's not impossible, only unlikely. But since the consequences of anything unlikely taking place are so terrible, my men must conduct a thorough search of the palace tomorrow. The absence of the queen provides an excellent opportunity of conducting this search without upsetting her. For this search I'll need plans of the palace, a drawing of all three floors of the palace in which all occupied and unoccupied rooms are clearly marked. Please see that such plans are ready for me tomorrow morning at 8 o'clock.'

At the time Walsingham was leaving Nonsuch Palace, Savage was feeling extremely tired after having run seven and a half hours that day. He was in excellent physical condition but he was not used to running for so many hours. The sleepless night was a further cause for tiredness. Nevertheless, with his strong will power he kept running at the same speed, since he wanted to establish his credentials as the special lackey runner that the new butler decided to bring from Whitehall. When half an hour later the two coachmen and he were provided with a room with three beds, he collapsed on his bed and almost instantly fell profoundly asleep.

He dreamed that he had entered the totally dark bedroom in which the queen was sleeping, that he advanced on hands and knees towards her bed, got inside the bed curtains and slashed the queen's throat while covering her mouth with his left hand to prevent her from screaming.

Jenkins had to go to the London residence of Phillip Howard, Earl of Arundel, that afternoon to get the plans of Nonsuch Palace requested by Walsingham. He learned that the earl was a prisoner in the Tower of London because he had converted to Catholicism and tried to leave England. The queen had ordered the Countess of Arundel to leave London and she was moving to Essex, but the plans Jenkins needed were there. Taking the drawings cluttered with measurements and construction information, Jenkins went back to Nonsuch Palace where he arranged to have simple copies of the three floors made. These copies had no confusing annotations. Late at night, with the help of several lackeys and maids he clearly marked in the copies which rooms were occupied and which were unoccupied.

The next day Walsingham conducted a thorough search of Nonsuch Palace with the plans provided by Jenkins. Since Savage was resting peacefully at Hampton Court Palace, the thorough search showed no results. Walsingham left the palace late in the afternoon and decided it would be unnecessary to return and bother the queen with his suspicions.

The return trip from Hampton Court to Nonsuch was much better for Savage, since now he was a trained long distance runner. He still needed to accomplish a trick once he reached the palace used by the queen most nights. He had to be provided with a room, but Jenkins should not be aware of this.

'John,' he said Bill, the coachman, after they arrived at the palace, 'you're the ideal lackey to run before the coach. You're much better than any that have run with me before. You're a true footman like the queen says. But I'm sure you're good at anything you do and I don't want to share you with the pretentious older lackeys that Williams had as his top assistants. I want you to be my permanent helper. Would you mind if I introduce you to the staff as my personal helper? I outrank the older lackeys and I have an empty room, next to mine. I can assign that room to you. For the time being you'll have the room just for yourself.'

'I'm delighted by your suggestion, Bill. I'll bring my things later, but I'll be glad to use the room next to yours right away to freshen up and rest a while.'

'Excellent and give me your dirty livery. I'll give it to a maid to send it to be washed. She'll get you a clean set of the same size.'

Later, in the evening, Thomas Mullberry, the senior lackey in the palace, approached Jenkins.

'Master Jenkins, I must present a complaint against Bill Cochram, the coachman. He has appointed a lackey, John Wildman, as his assistant.

'Bill has seniority over you, Thomas.'

'Yes, in his field, coaches and stables.'

'It happens that the queen has told me that Bill and John make an excellent team that gave a very fast and smooth round trip to Hampton Court. If the queen considers that these two should work together and they get along so well, I won't interfere. Have I made myself clear, Thomas?'

'Yes, Master Jenkins.'

'There's another thing that the queen told me. She doesn't like the word lackey, so that footman is the word we'll use in Nonsuch Palace. Then, from now on your title is First Footman, Thomas.'

'Thank you, Master Jenkins.'

The next day Savage spent all morning working with the two coachmen, leaving the carriage impeccably clean and shiny.

'You're not only a good runner, John,' said Bill. 'You're a hard worker too.'

'This isn't hard work, Bill. It's just that I'm good with my hands and my work gets results.'

'It would have taken all day for Pete and me to leave the carriage like this. Don't you agree Pete?'

'Only with half of what you say, Bill. We've never left it so shiny.'

'We'll go to have lunch now and we're free for the rest of the day.'

Savage had lunch at the large table presided by Master

Jenkins, who sat at the head of the table. Their lunch was after the queen lunch. Savage soon realized that he was treated with great respect. Since everyone believed he was the favorite lackey that Jenkins brought from Whitehall Palace, he was also considered to be a likely candidate to become soon an under-butler, so that everyone wanted to be in good terms with him. He also found that all the servants were talking about the visit Walsingham and his men had made to Nonsuch Palace.

'Am I hearing that Sir Francis Walsingham visited the palace with his men?' asked Savage to the lackey sitting next to him.

'Yes, he did. It seems that a criminal who had planned to kill the queen was discovered but escaped arrest and Sir Francis was afraid that he might have come here to go ahead with his criminal plans.'

'Walsingham is very clever. If he believes that the criminal came here, it's quite likely that he did. What do you think?'

'I believe that the idea that the criminal would come to a place full of armed guards after his plot failed is absurd. I'm sure he's as far from London as possible. But Master Jenkins arranged for a drawing showing every room in the palace to be made. In the drawing all occupied rooms were clearly marked with a large X, while all unoccupied rooms were left with no mark. All unoccupied rooms were searched yesterday, but of course nothing was found.'

'Is it possible that the criminal would remain undetected moving from an unsearched room to another already searched?'

'That would be impossible with the turmoil we had yesterday. Anyway he could never know which rooms had already been searched. And he escaped several days ago. Where would he eat? Do you think he would be invited to sit here to eat with the servants? Or perhaps he would dine with the queen? The mere idea that a criminal could get inside this palace is absurd.'

'Anyway Walsingham may come back and I have now been assigned a room that is marked as unoccupied. I must arrange to have my room marked with a large X in case he returns to make a second search.'

'When we finish lunch I'll take you to talk with Mrs. Cove. The drawings are kept in a third floor hall, in the North Wing. She has the key and she can mark your room with the large X.'

After lunch, Mrs. Cove took Savage to the hall where the palace drawings were kept. When they entered, Savage saw that all the drawings were displayed on top of a table.

'We're keeping the drawings on display in case the gentlemen that want them return,' said Mrs. Cove. 'Please point to me the room that was assigned to you, John.'

'It's this one, Mrs. Cove.'

Mrs. Cove made a large X on the sketch of the room pointed by Savage.

'Now the gentlemen won't bother you if they should return.'

'Which is the room used by the queen, Mrs. Cove?'

'This one, John. It has always armed guards standing at the door, even when the queen isn't there.'

Savage saw that the queen's bedroom was in the center of the North wing, on the second floor, with a window on the central court of the palace. This room and a twin adjacent room had long separate corridors leading to them. This way, although the two rooms were adjacent, there was a long walk from the entrance of one to the entrance of the other. There was no large X on the room adjacent to the queen's bedroom.

Savage left Mrs. Cove when she was closing the hall with her key. He was wondering about the strange design of the twin rooms, of which one was the queen's bedroom. The palace had been built according to instructions given by Henry VIII, who had six wives and an undetermined, but large, number of mistresses. Savage thought it was quite likely Henry requested the twin bedrooms with the idea that one would be for himself and the other for the mistress of the day. In such case, there must be a secret door to go from one bedroom to the other. Savage decided to enter the unoccupied bedroom to look for the secret door.

Savage went down to the second floor, walked along a corridor lined with bedroom doors on either side, until he had to turn right and then left and passed in front of another corridor at the end of which several armed guards were stationed at the door of the queen's bedroom. He went on along the corridor making a series of turns, passing in front of what appeared to be storage rooms, until he got to a place in which he had to choose between a corridor to the left and another to the right. He took the left one, made a number of turns and reached a locked door.

This was the door of the twin bedroom, adjacent to the queen's bedroom. He would have never realized this if he had not seen the drawings showing all rooms and all corridors of the palace.

Savage easily opened the locked door using his knife, entered a luxurious bedroom and quietly closed its door. He examined carefully the wall at his left looking for the telltale signs of a secret door. It was much easier to hide these signs in a decorated wall than in a bare whitewashed wall like that of his room in the fencing school. It took Savage over ten minutes to find the secret door, but once he found it he knew how to open it. He pushed at what he considered to be the right place and the door moved almost imperceptibly. He immediately put back the secret door in the fully closed position. Tonight, he thought, he would enter Queen Elizabeth's bedroom through this door to kill her.

Savage went to the livery storage room where he had hidden

his own clothes, which he retrieved and took to his room. He rested there until supper time when he joined the servants at the table headed by Master Jenkins. After supper, he went to the empty bedroom with a secret door leading to the queen's bedroom. He locked the door from the inside and waited in the dark until it was quite late. While waiting in the dark he reviewed his escape plan. When looking at the drawings he had selected an empty room on the second floor of the South Wing, with a window to the inner court. After killing the queen he would return to this room and, after closing the secret door, would put on his own clothes and leave through the window.

He would climb to the roof and go to the South Wing to climb down to reach the window of the empty room he had chosen. He would re-enter the palace through that window and go to the large dining hall and from there to the terrace. If possible, he would retrieve the rope. After checking the movements of the guards he would use the rope to climb down and escape running through the fields, invisible in the dark night.

After a long wait, Savage figured it would be about two in the morning, a suitable hour to enter the queen's bedroom and kill her. He closed the curtains of the room where he was, to make sure it was completely dark. No light should enter the queen's bedroom when he opened the secret door. He then proceeded to open the secret door just enough to go through it. The bedroom was very dark, but not quite as dark as the room Savage had just left, since a large window was wide open and some light entered through it. Savage went down on hands and knees and remained absolutely quiet, listening and looking at the darker shapes that indicated the position of large pieces of furniture. He detected a large shape, obviously the canopied bed where the queen was sleeping. He also detected he was not the only one in the room outside the large bed. He heard the faint noise of someone moving. The sound lasted just an instant, but he was sure someone was guarding the sleeping queen inside the room. The window must have been left wide open waiting for him to come into the bedroom through it. There was another faint noise that Savage attributed to someone shifting his position on a chair or armchair. He also started hearing the heavy breathing of that person.

Suddenly moonlight invaded the room and Savage clearly saw a big man sitting on an armchair facing the window and holding a pistol in his hand. Fortunately, the man was looking at the window, since if he had looked inside the room he would have seen him on his hands and knees next to a wall. Clouds covered the moon and it was quite dark inside the room again, but Savage knew exactly the position of the man waiting for him, while that man was not aware he was already inside the room.

Savage evaluated two options; to sneak silently behind the man on the armchair and cut his throat or to leave him watching the window while he went to the canopied bed to cut the queen's throat. He decided to go ahead with the second option. If the dying man made a noise, the queen would wake up and call for help, saving her life. If the dying queen made a noise, he would be captured, but his mission would have been accomplished.

The assassin proceeded to advance on hands and knees towards the canopied bed he had clearly seen during the few seconds of full moonlight inside the room.

When Savage reached the bed he got inside the bed curtains and stood erect with his knife firmly grasped in his right hand. He could hear the sleeping queen breathing softly with the paused breathing of someone profoundly asleep. But Savage had a problem, the bed was large and it was completely dark inside the curtains of the canopied bed. To have a chance to escape he should cover the mouth of the woman with his left hand, while simultaneously cutting her throat with the dagger held in his right hand.

Moonlight in the room helped Savage a second time. It was still very dark inside the curtains of the canopied bed but he could clearly see a dark shape on the bed and in a swift movement he covered the mouth and cut the throat.

Not a sound was heard but something was terribly wrong. Savage realized his left hand was not covering the face of a woman but that of a bearded man.

CHAPTER VII
A ROOK CAPTURES THE QUEEN

Savage could not see the man he had just killed, but he figured he probably had a pistol in one hand while he was waiting for him. His two hands followed the contour of the man's arms and found he was still holding a pistol in his right hand. Savage took the gun and figured the man had fallen asleep while waiting for hours in a soft bed. He probably thought Walsingham was wrong thinking someone would get in to kill the queen and never believed he was in any danger. Savage realized that since Walsingham was correctly assuming he was inside the palace, not only he had failed to kill the queen, but it would be quite difficult to escape capture.

Savage retraced his way back to the secret door, but this time he was holding a pistol in his right hand, in case the man watching the window should aim his own pistol towards him. He passed through the secret door and closed it once inside the adjoining room. He took off his lackey liveried uniform and smiled remembering that now the queen had ordered that lackeys should be called footmen as a result of his excellent performance as a runner. He hid the uniform under the large mattress of the canopied bed of this room, identical to that where he had killed a man, and put on his own clothes. He was going to try to escape running through the fields, but was aware that any minute now the man he killed would be discovered and hell would break loose. He had to forget about recovering the rope. It was not important, since there were many places in the exterior of the palace where an agile man could climb down easily. Just before leaving through the window he heard a commotion in the adjoining room and recognized Walsingham's voice shouting expletives. The palace would be soon surrounded by the yeomen of the guard. Savage decided he could not escape running in the fields. He had to go back to his room where, as requested by the coachman, Bill, he had his first lackey uniform, washed and ironed. But guards were everywhere. He saw guards in the large court inside the palace and he could not enter his room. He was sure other guards would be outside the palace to prevent anyone from escaping.

Savage climbed to the roof of the palace. He could not climb down to escape running through the fields, or to enter his ground floor room. It was dangerous to stay on the roof too, since Walsingham would soon order to search it. Savage decided to get inside the vacant room he had elected in the south wing. After the turmoil was over he would be able to climb down to the patio and enter his room. The next morning the queen would travel by carriage to Whitehall palace and he would be the footman running in front.

Soon Savage was inside the room he had selected and locked from the inside the window he had just opened with his knife to enter. Suddenly he heard a key had been inserted to open the door, so that he hid under the bed. It was not a canopied bed but a regular comfortable large bed.

'Come in here Your Majesty. You'll be safe here. The assassin has just been detected in the north wing and he'll be arrested in a few minutes.' Savage recognized Walsingham's voice.

'Don't rush me Walsingham. You told me you discovered a Catholic plot to replace me by Mary Stuart but an assassin had escaped. Also that you had checked this palace properly and were satisfied he didn't come here. A few hours later you came to the palace and made me sleep in the bedroom of one of my ladies-in-waiting, just in case the assassin should be in the palace. Then you wake me up and bring me to another bedroom, in the south wing, because you believe the north wing is dangerous and finally you now tell me you detected the criminal but haven't captured him yet. Tell me what happened and why you say you detected the assassin.'

While the queen was talking Walsingham checked the bedroom window to see if it was properly closed.

'My intuition saved your life tonight, Your Majesty. I left an armed man on your bed, in case the assassin should come. Also I left your bedroom window wide open and another armed man watching the window from a dark corner. A few minutes ago we found the man on your bed was dead, his throat cut; his pistol was gone. The man watching the window didn't see anyone coming through the window and swears he never fell asleep.'

'Do you mean I would be dead now if I had stayed on my bed, even with one of your armed men guarding my sleep hidden in a dark corner of the room?'

'That's right, Your Majesty. The body of the man we found dead was still warm, so that he had been killed only minutes before. We're searching now the entire north wing.'

'Your assassin has escaped, Walsingham. He's either running in the fields or hidden in the palace in a secret place where you can never find him. I'm very tired right now. I'll try to sleep a few hours and tomorrow morning I'll move to Whitehall until everything is settled here. Please see that someone wakes me up tomorrow morning at 8 o'clock.'

'I'll see to that immediately, Your Majesty. I'm leaving six guards standing at the door of this room; call them if you hear any strange noises. Good night.'

'Good night, Walsingham.'

Savage heard the noise of the door opening and closing. Then he moved under the bed to a place from where he could see part of the room. The queen was seated in front of a mirror removing the make-up covering her face that she had hastily put on when wakened by Walsingham in the middle of the night. Savage got out from his hiding place, stood up and a second later was standing behind the queen, covering her mouth with his left hand while his right hand held his dagger against her neck. Just a small movement of his right hand would immediately end the queen's life.

Savage had come to Nonsuch Palace to kill the queen. In the

dark he had already slit the throat of a man lying on the queen's bed, believing he was killing the queen. But one thing was to kill the symbol of oppression in the dark and a very different thing to kill a trembling fragile woman while looking at her in a mirror. Her eyes were full of tears and she was trembling of fear.

Savage decided he had already satisfied his thirst for vengeance. He had not shed tears of fear because that was not in his nature and he could not tremble tightly stretched on the rack. But he had felt the same fear the queen was feeling now, believing he was going to die without knowing why.

Looking at this trembling woman in the mirror he felt more the need to comfort her rather than that to kill her.

'Listen to me, woman, I came here to kill you, seeking revenge. I've been in your power, just as afraid to die as you are now. It was much worse for me because I was suffering great pain. I was tortured under your orders while I'm inflicting no pain to you. Perhaps I'll spare your life. I'll keep my knife against your throat but I'll remove the hand on your mouth if you gesture promising not to shout. You must avoid making neither any noise nor any sudden movement that may startle me, since in such case I would react cutting your throat. Do you understand and promise to be quiet?'

The queen assented with her head and Savage removed his hand from her mouth but kept his knife against her throat. She started to cry inconsolably, but softly, for about five minutes until she gathered the courage to speak, looking at her assailant in the mirror.

'You're going to kill me. You're letting me stay alive for a few minutes just to play with me and enjoy my fear, as a cat plays with a mouse.'

'I'm not a cat. I'm a fair man. I've killed men in revenge and also for my safety. I've killed a man in the dark believing I was killing you. But looking at you in the mirror, as afraid for your life as I was on the rack, I decided I already got the revenge I was seeking and I don't have to kill you. But I'll kill you for my safety if you make any noise that may attract the guards standing at the door of this room.'

Savage's words calmed down the queen and after a couple of minutes she stopped crying.

'Why do you Catholics hate me so much?'

'I don't know. I'm not a Catholic. You should go to one of your torture chambers and ask that question to a Catholic. I worship Jesus Christ in the Church of England. A Catholic friend of mine has tried to convince me I should convert to Catholicism, but I'm not an educated gentleman. I'm a working man and I don't see any difference between the two faiths. I can only understand that one church is ruled by you, as Queen of England and the other is ruled by an Italian Pope. I have a personal grudge against you, but I'm an Englishman and not an Italian, so I prefer the Church of England. But you have no right to persecute Catholics. Likewise a Catholic king, or queen, would have no right to persecute those Englishmen that, like me, prefer to worship in the Church of England.'

'I fully agree with you. I don't believe that the fine theological points that divide Protestants and Catholics are really important. I think no one can be certain of having the right answer in matters of faith. The problems are really about power, not faith. I just needed an official church that would accept me as the legitimate successor of my father, my brother and my sister. The Church of England accepts me. I wanted to be tolerant with Catholics and succeeded for several years, until the Italian Pope excommunicated me.'

'I should leave before I start to like you, Queen Elizabeth, but you're right, politicians seeking power, like Walsingham, make the religious divisions.'

'I have a low opinion of most politicians but not of Walsingham. His most important concern is my safety. He's not a likable person and I don't enjoy his company, but as Principal Secretary he's devoted to my safety.'

'He has fooled you making you believe what you say. He invents plots against you and then pretends to discover them. Everybody knows that the plot attributed to Father Campion never existed.'

'I liked Father Campion but he refused my help and he was found guilty by a court of law.'

'The courts of law accept any false witnesses supplied by the authorities. All those condemned for plotting against you were innocent. I'm not innocent. Our plot is real but Walsingham knew everything about it at least a year ago and probably earlier, but it's like a game of chess to him. You're his white queen. The queen is an important piece in chess, but it's an expendable one. Walsingham is the white king in his game, the only piece that really matters. You realize you wouldn't have been in any danger if I had been arrested a year ago.'

Elizabeth remained silent looking at Savage's face in the mirror in front of her. After a brief interval, having received no answer from the queen, Savage continued talking.

'A year ago Walsingham, through one of his white pawns, instead of arresting me, showed me an easy way to get inside this palace.'

The queen remained silent.

'Please don't be afraid, since I don't want to hurt you, but with my knife I must make a mark on your neck.'

Before Elizabeth could fully understand Savage's words he had made a small nick on her neck and a few drops of blood stained the pale neck.

'Show this blood to Walsingham and tell him a black rook captured the white queen. Since we're playing a game I don't have to kill you to prove I'm a good rook. I trust he considers me to be at least a rook and not a pawn. But even if I'm a pawn, I captured the white queen.'

The queen started to cry again looking at the drops of blood that continued to pour out of the small nick. Although her assailant said he wasn't going to kill her, she thought he might change his mind and kill her to really prove his point to Walsingham.

Savage put out the light from the oil lamp. Elizabeth thought that now her assailant was going to kill her, as he had killed a man in the dark believing he was she.

'I'm going to remain standing behind you, with my dagger ready to strike and kill you if you cry for help. Eventually I'll leave, but I'll stay quite a long while standing behind you before leaving.'

Regardless of his words, Savage went immediately to the window, left the room through it and climbed to the roof. From there he could see about fifty yeomen of the guard surrounding the palace, but none in the inside court. He climbed down to the court in front of his room, entered it and relaxed on his bed.

He knew it was a big mistake to talk to the queen looking at her in the mirror while she was looking at him in the same way. Once he decided not to kill her, he should have put out the light and scared her so that she would remain silent and he could leave the room. If he had done that he could have been her footman this morning running ahead of her carriage to go to Whitehall Palace from where he could leave unmolested and disappear forever. But he could not do that now because he would be immediately recognized by the queen.

Now, he would probably be captured and executed as a traitor. But it felt really good to talk to the queen from a position in which he had all the power, with his knife against her neck, and she had none. And he felt particularly good about the message he left for Walsingham, that the black rook had captured the white queen. Walsingham had won the chess game capturing Captain Fortescue, the black king, but he had sacrificed Elizabeth, the white queen, in the way he played the game. Now Elizabeth knew.

But he still had a chance to escape. Suppliers came in every morning to the kitchen of the palace to bring in the food to be consumed every day. He had to be alert near the kitchen to go out of the palace with the suppliers in his ordinary clothing, as if he were one of them.

Very early in the morning many suppliers were lined up in front of the south wing door of the castle leading to the kitchen. Savage was hidden in the small room of the first floor where the liveried lackey clothing was kept. From there he could hear all the noises in the kitchen.

When he heard that suppliers were entering and discharging his wares he left the room, descended the stairs that led to the kitchen and walked out of the kitchen among those that were leaving. When he walked out of the kitchen he felt a pointed sword against his chest.

'Good morning, John. I guess this is the only way I can beat you in sword play, when I have a sword and you don't have one.'

Usher Tyndell had spoken and was smiling in front of Savage.

'Good morning, George. Regrettably, I cannot say I'm glad to see you.'

'Take him as a prisoner,' said Tyndell to the two yeomen of the guard standing by his side. Search him since I'm sure he's armed.'

'He has a pistol and a knife.'

'Give me his weapons, take him holding one of his arms each of you and follow me.'

They went around the palace to enter through its main door,

in the north wing. Tyndell placed himself next to the two men holding Savage, so that he could talk to him.

'With the fencing lessons I received from Captain Fortescue and you I'm already the best swordsman among the guards and I was certain I would become an exon, in due time. But now, after capturing you, I'm sure that eventually I'll be the Clerk of the Cheque. Furthermore, I'm sure that Sir Francis will reward me generously with gold. I'll be able to afford fencing lessons with an Italian master now, to become as good a swordsman, or better, than Captain Fortescue.'

'Good for you, George.'

'I figured that the best way for you to leave the palace was pretending to be one of the suppliers leaving the kitchen. I was the only one that knew you well and could identify you, so that I placed myself at the door of the kitchen.'

'And you were smart enough to bring two men with you. Otherwise I would have shot you down with my pistol before you could use your sword.'

'That's right, John. As an usher I command a few men. Maybe I should have brought four men with me, but I was afraid that you would notice us if we were too many and then choose another escape route.'

'Well thought, George, you deserve to be the Clerk of the Cheque of your force. If you had come with only one man, I would have killed him with my knife after shooting you down. Two men, plus you, were just right.'

They went on, entered the inside court through the main gate in the north wing and went to a group of several men. Walsingham was there giving instructions to his men.

'Good morning, Sir Francis. I'm Usher George Tyndell. You recruited me last year to work for you. I bring you a prisoner, John Savage, whom I believe is the man you're looking for.'

Walsingham looked at Tyndell and Savage with wide open eyes and a look of disbelief. Then he appeared to be obviously relieved and smiled widely.

'Usher Tyndell, many thanks and congratulations for your resourcefulness. I'll see that your captain gives you the credit you deserve. You'll also receive an adequate reward from my secretariat. John Savage, you don't look a day older than when we met, seven years ago. When I wake up the queen I'll tell her you've been captured. She'll be relieved.'

'She didn't spend the night in her own bedroom but in the south wing bedroom with that window,' said Savage pointing at the window with his chin, since both his arms continued to be held by the guards.

'You can't miss it going through the corridor since it has six guards standing at the door.'

Walsingham got so pale that Jones, the leader of his men, thought he was going to faint. He reacted after about half a minute and run towards the entrance of the palace. The men were left wandering what had happened.

'You've killed the queen when I was on duty in the palace,' said Tyndell looking at Savage with wild eyes, showing his fear.

'Of course not, George, but you know Walsingham; he has a taste for the melodramatic.'

Walsingham run up the stairs to the second floor and then run along the corridor that went along the four wings of the palace. When he reached the door where the six guards were stationed, he opened the door and dashed inside.

After crying for hours, afraid to move, Elizabeth had fallen asleep sitting in front of the mirror, with arms and head on top of the table where she had her toiletries. Awaken by the noise made by Walsingham entering the room, Elizabeth regained her usual regal stance, lost when she had the deadly edge of a sharp knife blade against her neck.

'Walsingham, how do you dare to enter my bedroom without my permission? Don't you know how to knock a door?'

'I'm sorry, Your Majesty, if I offended you, but I'm greatly relieved to see that you're alive.'

'Not thanks to you, Walsingham. The assassin came into this room and gave me a message for you.'

'What message, Your Majesty?'

Pointing at her neck, now covered with dried blood, Elizabeth gave the message.

'A black rook has captured the white queen. He trusts that you give him enough credit to consider him a rook, rather than just a pawn. He made me see I was another expendable piece, the white queen, in the silly chess game you were playing. And I know exactly why you didn't arrest him over a year ago, when you learned that he wanted revenge against me and planned to kill me. You had to extend the game because you had to capture the black queen, Mary Stuart. Her capture was much more important than my safety.'

'Pardon me, Your Majesty. I believed I had everything under control, but this man escaped when I gave orders to arrest him and proved I had been a fool.'

'Fortunately, rather than kill me right away he wanted to talk to me to tell me he had come here wanting revenge. You had him tortured, although he was innocent, and he blamed me for what you did. During our conversation I asked him why do Catholics hate me so much and he told me he didn't know, because he wasn't a Catholic.'

'Yes, I know, he joined the Catholic plot because he wanted to kill you.'

'I've never been so afraid in my life, not even when I was sent to the Tower. I lost all dignity crying and trembling in front of one of my subjects, but I never begged for my life. He didn't kill me because I know how to talk with my subjects, even with a knife against my neck. But you failed me. As part of your strategy, instead of arresting him you showed him an easy way to enter the palace.'

'I failed you, Your Majesty, and you have every right to send me to the Tower for a Star Chamber Trial, but please let me finish first with the Babington Plot against you. The assassin that entered this room has just been captured. All the conspirators have already been captured except for three, Babington himself and two of his friends.'

'And I'm sure you finished this game now, because you believe you can prove you can involve my cousin, Mary Stuart, in the plot.'

'That's correct, Your Majesty. She wrote a letter to Babington approving his plot, unaware that I had intercepted her correspondence.'

'Go ahead and finish this mess, Walsingham. I'll see what to do about you later. But I'll give you a most clear and direct instruction now. The man that was in this room and you've captured now, should not be tortured. He was already tortured when he was innocent, so that there's no need to torture him again. If this instruction is not followed I'll see that you're tortured to extract from you information about which you know nothing at all. Have I made myself clear?'

'Absolutely, Your Majesty. Let me tell you that I believe that torture should be limited to only those cases where we know someone has information that we need. But our system of justice is based on torture. Until Parliament changes the system, there's nothing I can do to change it, although, of course, I can arrange for an exception in a particular case, like the one you just requested.'

'And why this man, that you sent to be tortured, blamed only me and not you for suffering at the hands of the authorities?'

'Because I pardoned his life. He invented a lie to stop the

torture and sent us in a wild chase with no results. I admired his inventiveness and set him free. Soon afterwards, he killed the man that falsely accused him of knowing the place where Father Campion would give a mass and later he killed the man that tortured him. I should have been next on the list, but since I pardoned him, he pardoned me. You realize that the resourceful man that managed to enter this palace, remain in it for several days, kill the armed man waiting for him in your bed and finally enter this room to put a knife against your neck, could have killed me easily if he wanted to do it.'

'And how did it happen that this resourceful Protestant man that wanted to kill me got in contact with Master Babington and his fellow Catholic plotters? Was it you that put them in contact?'

'Yes, Your Majesty, and I'll accept this responsibility when I'm sent to trial.'

'I'll see about that later, Walsingham. Now clear up the mess you made with your chess game. And if I should decide to pardon you, to avoid a scandal, never again use me in any of your schemes, since in that case I'll send you to the gallows with no trial. Now order a carriage to take me to Whitehall Palace. I'll stay there until I recover from the ordeal of last night.'

CHAPTER VIII
ESCAPE, CAPTURE AND TRIAL

When Walsingham's men left their house, Michael embraced Lucia, his Italian wife.

'Don't you worry, Lucia; they have nothing against us.'

'I'm worried about poor Thomas and Anthony, but most of all for Anthony's wife and daughter.'

'I overheard that they had to rush their search for Anthony and Thomas here, because they must find someone else first.'

'Anthony and Thomas might be hiding in Peter's house,' said Lucia.

'They might be there or at the home of some other friend, but if they're at Peter's home we must take them to Liverpool. There, Peter and I know a fisherman who could take them to France, where they would be safe.'

'Let's go to Peter's home right away.'

Michael and Lucia gave orders to their servants to get ready the coach they brought from Italy and very soon they arrived at Peter's residence.

'It's good to see you, Michael and Lucia, but I'm afraid you bring bad news since both of you look quite worried,' said Peter.

'That's right, Peter. Walsingham's men raided our home this morning looking for Anthony and Thomas, who're being charged with high treason. They escaped but they are looking for them at the homes of all their friends.'

'An accusation for high treason made by Walsingham is a death sentence, even if they're innocent. But I can believe it's quite likely that if anyone conspiring against the queen invited Anthony and his friends to join the conspiracy they would have accepted.'

'Then we must take Margery and three year old Mary out of the country,' said Lucia, who was speaking very good English with a charming Italian accent.

'Fortunately Walsingham's men are now looking for a very important member of the conspiracy that also escaped capture,' said Michael. 'Those that raided our house rushed out of it when they were summoned to participate in this other search. I'm sure that right now no one is watching Anthony's house. We could go there to take Margery and Mary to Liverpool. Jonathan could take them to France, where they would be received warmly by the Babton family. You Peter, and I should go with them in Jonathan's boat so that we can take them with the Babtons after we reach Boulogne Sur Mer.'

'Yes, we should do that. Lucia and Celeste will have to wait for our return here, in London.

'The road from London to Liverpool is about 75 leagues long' said Lucia. She continued. 'You can make 25 leagues a day, but you need a sufficiently large contingent of riders to avoid an assault by bandits. Michael can take four servants and still leave a couple with me, at the house.'

'I can take three men with me and still leave two men at the house with Celeste and the children.'

Margery should bring her own lady saddle to ride on horseback from the French coast to Paris.'

'We must rush and get started right away. Riding fast we can make quite a few leagues before nightfall. The next two days we'll make 50 leagues. The fourth day we'll arrive to Liverpool with plenty of time to wait for Jonathan's return from his fishing trip of the day. I'll get ready as fast as possible with my horse and my three servants. You must go to see Margery right away, while I go to William's house to tell him he will have to take care of everything at the firm by himself for about a month. We'll meet at your house.'

'Yes, Lucia and I must make Margery understand she must leave the country right away. Then we must go home to get ready for the long trip and to get our four servants ready. We'll wait there for you and your men.'

When Michael and Lucia entered Anthony's home they were told Margery could not see them. They went ahead anyway to an intimate hall where they found Margery crying.

'Go ahead and cry your heart out Margery,' said Lucia embracing her warmly. 'We know that Walsingham's men are looking for Anthony and that he's being accused of high treason, but even if you cry you must pull yourself together for Mary's sake.'

'You must leave the country with Mary right away and stay abroad until you know what's going on.'

'But this must be a mistake. Everything should go back to normal in a few days.'

'If Anthony is innocent of the charges against him and he can prove it, you'll return to London and resume your life with him. But if he's considered guilty, you'll lose all your properties in England and you and Mary will have a miserable life in this country. Furthermore, you'll run the risk of being accused as Anthony's accomplice.'

'Margery,' said Lucia, 'right now this house isn't being watched because all Walsingham's men are needed to look for someone else. Our house was raided by men looking for Anthony, but suddenly they left to look for someone else. This is your chance to escape and stay in France with your child until you know where you stand and what happened with the accusations against Anthony. This is something you must do to protect your daughter.'

'You can take me with you if you think that's what I should do. But I'll never be allowed to travel to France.'

'We'll take you to Liverpool. Up North we've many friends.

Peter and I will take you to the French coast in a fishing boat and from there to the Babton's home in Paris. Mary and you will ride in our coach, until we reach Liverpool. But in France you'll have to ride so that you must bring your lady saddle with you. You must also bring all your jewelry and any gold you may have in the house.'

'Anthony has over a thousand pounds in gold inside a coffer. It's hidden in our bedroom under the floor. Come with me.'

'Excellent, with one thousand pounds in gold and the protection of Jacques Babton you can start a new life in France, if worse comes to worst.'

Three days later Peter and Michael reached Liverpool. They went to an Inn where they took a room for Margery and Mary and another for the seven servants. The horses and the coach were left at a stable.

Peter and Michael went to the area where fishermen left their boats for the night and did not have to wait long for Jonathan Jordan.

'Peter and Michael! I never expected to see you again young fellows. I heard that you're important lawyers in London. And you're not Peter anymore, but Sir Peter. What made you remember the days when we crossed the channel and went to France?'

'Precisely the need to go to France and return, undetected. Does a trip to France interest you?'

'I travel to France once a month. I need two days to get to Boulogne Sur Mer and another two days to return. I stay three days with my French friends so that these French excursions mean that I don't fish for one week every month. But I earn much more selling English woolen worsted cloth in France and French woad dye in England, than fishing. I need fishing as a cover for my real profession as trader. I realize that you must want to take your own cargo to France.'

'We went with you in one of your trading trips when we were 15 and we're glad that you continue with the trade.'

'I've prospered and I'm a relatively rich man now. I plan to retire next year.'

'Luckily, you haven't retired yet.'

'Even if I had retired I would have been able to accommodate you since my two sons are also traders and each of them has his own boat. But you haven't told me about your cargo yet.'

'A young lady and her three year old daughter.'

'Holy God! Excuse my language but I never expected such delicate cargo. But I can't take any of my two sailors in this trip. The boat would be too crowded and, more important than that, I wouldn't be sure about their silence. The first time they got drunk they would tell everything to whoever wants to listen.'

'You don't need your sailors. You've already trained us as sailors and we're much stronger now than when we were 15 years old. We'll pay you well for your time.'

'You don't have to pay me anything. Your friendship is payment enough for me. And since I'm a relatively wealthy man now, I keep a good stock of worsted at home and this'll be a regular trading trip for me. But we must leave very early, so that no one sees the lady boarding the ship. You must be here with them at 3 o'clock in the morning.'

'It won't be a regular trip for you because you'll have to wait for us for perhaps as long as two weeks. We'll have to take the lady to Paris.'

Six days later Peter, Michael, Margery and Mary had entered the Paris home of Jacques and Suzanne Babton and were waiting for them at a hall of the large house.

'Margery!' exclaimed Suzanne when she entered the hall

with Jacques and hugged her. 'What a surprise to see you in Paris! The little girl must be Mary. We're glad to see you Peter and Michael, but where's Anthony?'

Margery started to cry.

'Anthony is hiding in England. Walsingham, Queen Elizabeth's Principal Secretary, accused him of high treason. We crossed the channel in a fishing boat. Regrettably, Anthony and Thomas, who escaped capture with him, didn't seek refuge with us who would have arranged for them to come here undetected. Michael and I decided that under the circumstances we had to bring Margery and Mary here.'

'You did the right thing. I hope that Anthony will be declared innocent and come here to take his wife and daughter back to England, but in the meantime Margery and Mary must remain here in Paris. They are part of our family and we'll take care of them for as long as it's necessary.'

'Come with me bringing your daughter, Margery,' said Suzanne. 'I'll show you the rooms we have available for guests. Pick one for Mary and another for yourself.'

The two women went upstairs with the child and Jacques remained with Peter and Michael.

'I have a box here with gold coins equivalent to 1.580 pounds of English money and many pieces of jewelry. I hope that with this capital and your protection Margery will be able to start a new life in France. In this paper you have an inventory detailing everything in the box,' said Peter.'

'This is excellent and I'll see that Margery makes the most of it. How was your trip from the coast to Paris?'

'Slow, but uneventful. Why do you ask?'

'Because we're now in our eighth religious war. But there's more than that. My friends and I call this war The War of the Three Henries". Henri, Duke de Guise, has an army that's more powerful than that of our king, Henri III. De Guise controls the north and guards the east against the incursions of German mercenary troops that come here to support the Huguenots, financed by Protestant German Princes and your Queen Elizabeth. The south below the castle of Amboise is controlled by a Huguenot, the third Henri, King Henri III of the small Kingdom of Navarre, so that the King of France controls only a small area south of Paris.'

Almost four weeks later Peter and Michael returned to London. The trip from Paris to the small fishing village near Boulogne Sur Mer where Jonathan Jordan stayed in France in his smuggling trips, that he called trading trips, was longer than usual. Peter and Michael could not approach the village for a couple of days because troops of Henri de Guise were stationed very near it. They stayed at an inn and reached the village when the troops left.

Crossing the channel resulted a bit difficult because they were surprised by a storm, but the two strong sailors and the veteran captain handled the rough weather quite well. Jonathan Jordan was handsomely rewarded by Peter and Michael for his help and decided he did not have to wait another year to retire.

When Peter and Michael arrived in London they learned the news they feared. Anthony and Thomas had been found and captured on August 23 at the house of a friend, Jerome Bellamy. While escaping they had alerted another of their confederates, Robert Barnewell, who ran away with them. The three were hidden in the barn of Jerome's house. Walsingham's method of searching methodically the home of every friend of theirs gave good results.

Walsingham decided to split the conspirators in two groups of seven each that would receive separate trials. Two trials gave wider exposure to the conspiracy and would create a wider sentiment against Mary Stuart among the population.

In the first group was Father Ballard, as mastermind of the

conspiracy, Babington, as leader of the conspiracy, Savage, as the designated assassin of the queen, Tichborne and Barnewell, as the designated assistants to Savage and finally Salisbury and Dunn, as Babington's main accomplices. In the second group were the other five conspirators, Tilney, Jones, Charnock, Travers and Gage, as well as a young Catholic, Jerome Bellamy, who had given refuge to Babington, Salisbury and Barnewell and finally someone called Edward Habington, whose name had been obtained by torture.

September 13 was set as the trial date for the first seven conspirators. The prosecution explained that the conspirators were sending letters to Mary Stuart in watertight envelopes inside the beer barrels delivered to Chartley Hall every week. In the same envelopes, Mary sent the answers in the empty barrels that were withdrawn. Agents of the Crown were able to intercept the letters but could not read them, because they were written in code.

The prosecution also presented a bilingual expert in codes, a Frenchman called Thomas Phelippes, who explained that after careful study of the coded letters he had been able to break the code. Most letters were written in French and some were written in English using the same code. After Phelippes broke the code the agents of the crown were able to read every letter sent to Mary before it was received and every letter she wrote before it was delivered.

The correspondence gave reasons to believe a plot to free Mary Stuart was underway until a letter written by Anthony Babington, in his capacity as leader of the plot, explained the full extent of the "Babington Plot", which included the assassination of Queen Elizabeth the same night of the liberation of Mary Stuart. A full scale war would follow to place Mary Stuart in the throne as Queen of England with the help of a Spanish invasion force of tens of thousands of men.

It was stressed that Mary Stuart explicitly approved this plan in her reply to Babington.

None of the accused denied the charges presented. Savage remained silent and never spoke at the trial. Ballard assumed full responsibility for the plot. The others accepted their participation but blamed Ballard for everything. The second day of the trial, September 14, the judges determined that the seven men were guilty of high treason and they were sentenced to be drawn, hanged and quartered on September 20.

On September 15 and 16 the second trial took place. Jerome Bellamy and Edward Habington protested claiming they were innocent and had signed admissions of guilt only to stop their tortures, but the judges determined their admissions of guilt should be accepted as true. The seven men were sentenced to be drawn, hanged and quartered for high treason on September 21, 1586.

CHAPTER IX
WALSINGHAM TALKS WITH BALLARD

With the only exception of John Savage, the men condemned to death were tortured every day from the day they were captured until two days before the trial. Torture was resumed for a few days after the trial. Two days before the execution, on September 18, the torture sessions ended at noon. Father John Ballard was tortured for more hours and more viciously than anyone else.

Walsingham had given orders to force Ballard to give the names of all the noblemen that had promised to rise as soon as Mary Stuart was set free, to make her the new Queen of England. Ballard never talked and always maintained he had never spoken with any noblemen about rising to support Mary Stuart. Several torturers then told him it did not matter if he had spoken to others or not and all he had to do was to give a list of noblemen to make the torture stop. Invariably Ballard gave then the list of all Privy Counselors', starting with Sir Francis Walsingham. The reaction of the torturers was always to increase the pain until Ballard fainted.

Torture of the others was just a matter of routine. They were asked the name of the other conspirators and they all gave the complete list.

They were asked to add the name of Jerome Bellamy and they all added the name to the list they had to give several times a day, every day.

One day one of the tortured men was beaten more than usual. Torturers had instructions not to hit the prisoners in the head, in order to avoid marks that would be seen during the trial, but sometimes they got carried away and left the instructions aside. One prisoner that had been hit in the mouth mispronounced several names once. The torturer then said that he had obtained a new name, Habington. Walsingham's men checked and found there was an Edward

Habington of the same age as most of the conspirators. The young man was arrested and under torture he was forced to admit he was guilty. All the other conspirators were then forced to add the name of Edward Habington to the list of conspirators.

In the afternoon of September 18, Ballard was expecting his second torture session when a guard took him out of his cell. Instead he was taken to an office. Sitting behind a large desk, an elegant middle aged man with a pointed beard was expecting him. He was dressed in black. A tall and obviously very strong man with a bushy beard was standing next to him.

'Good afternoon, Father Ballard. Please take a seat.'

The only available seat in the room was a chair facing the middle aged man, so Ballard sat on it.

'Do you know who I am?'

'Yes, Sir Francis, we've never been introduced but I saw you at the trial.'

'My friend, Master Jones, is here only for my safety. I want to talk to you with no witnesses, but I'm not as strong as you are.'

'You're as tall as I am and I'm not in my best shape having been tortured every day since I was arrested.'

'I must tell you I'm impressed by your resistance to torture, but I don't understand it. I've only once seen someone else like you, Father Campion, needlessly tortured because he wouldn't sign a confession. If I'm ever tortured I'll sign everything they want, I'll tell everything I know and, if they want more, I'll invent.'

'Why?'

'To stop the torture, of course.'

'That may work out, eventually, but only in isolated cases. Usually the men that torture have a real vocation and love their jobs, so that they'll continue to torture regardless of what whoever is tortured says or signs.'

Ballard's words reminded Walsingham that when Throckmorton was arrested he had given direct instructions to the torturer that the prisoner should not be tortured after he signed a confession. He did it because he knew that the prisoner was innocent, but he had not given similar instructions to Ballard's torturers.

'You can't be so negative, Ballard,' said the Principal Secretary.

'You can't be so deceitful, Walsingham. All my young friends signed their confessions and named everyone that participated in our plot, but they still continued to be tortured every day, just like me, who never talked because I had nothing to say.'

'Well, I must say that your friends were just the victims of our legal system that demands that they should be tortured. We had all the information without even the need of questioning them. Your case is different because I really want to have information that only you have. You haven't told the names of the noblemen that were ready to raise armies as soon as Mary Stuart was freed.'

'But I did give a list. Of course I had to invent it, but the torturers told me they didn't care if the list was real or not.'

'Yes, the list that started with my name. I envy your sense of humor, but I've a very serious proposal to make you.'

'I can imagine the proposal. If I give you a list that doesn't include any member of the Privy Council, you'll declare I'm innocent of all charges and I'm sent to France.'

'The proposal isn't quite as good as that, but it's a serious proposal of something that I can arrange.'

'I don't believe you'll make a serious proposal. Surprise me.'

'The day after tomorrow you'll die a horrible death. After

being drawn along the streets of London you'll be hanged, revived from the brink of death and finally disemboweled so that you can be quartered.'

'I'll be honored to suffer the same execution as my friend, Edmund Campion.'

'Yes, but the charges against Campion were fraudulent, so that Campion was a martyr, while the charges against you are totally true; you're a criminal guilty of high treason. Since you're guilty it makes no sense to have such a terrible death. Give me the list I need and I'll make sure that you're not revived after hanging. You'll receive a merciful death.'

'You did surprise me. You're making the most absurd proposal I ever heard. If I'm revived after hanging I suppose I'll have a piece of paper signed by you so that I can sue you when you go to hell.'

'I never expected you to accept my proposal, but I had to try since torture had failed. And I'm glad I met you, Captain Fortescue.'

'I was surprised you never made reference to my two identities during the trial.'

'I don't know which is your true identity, but Captain Fortescue is very popular in the north of England, so that clearly it was much better to try you only as Father Ballard. Every Ballard in England was under surveillance when you left London in December of last year, but since you didn't visit any of them I believe that you're John Fortescue. You visited the Fortescue family but only for one day and I assume that all the other days you visited the noblemen that were going to rise.'

'You can make all the assumptions you want.'

'Then it's goodbye. I believe we'll never see each other anymore.'

'I must tell you a few things before you leave. You made an excellent investigation and detected our group, but not everything you found out is true. Jerome Bellamy and Edward Habington are innocent and should be pardoned.'

'Jerome Bellamy is not innocent; he gave refuge to Babington, Salisbury and Barnewell. On the other hand I know that Habington is innocent. He had the misfortune to have a last name practically identical to Babington, but there was nothing I could do to save him. Of course I couldn't say at the trial that Gilbert Gifford is my agent and had given me the names of all conspirators. Gilbert can still be useful to me, especially after he becomes a priest.'

Ballard was frozen when he heard what Walsingham said. He stood up after a minute of silence and Jones thought he might attack Walsingham, so that he pushed him back to his seat.

'You're lying,' he said to Walsingham. 'Gilbert is loyal to our cause. He even pointed out one of your agents to me. Perhaps that agent gave you the initial lead to investigate me.'

'Jones,' said Walsingham without answering Ballard, 'ask two of your men to bring Savage to this room.'

Jones went to the door, opened it and without leaving the room gave an order.

'George and James go and bring Savage here. He's a very dangerous man so both of you must hold his arms when he's close to Sir Francis.'

'You must wonder why Jones wishes to be so careful with Savage,' Walsingham said to Ballard. 'Unlike you he was never tortured after his capture so that his strength is intact. Even a strong man like Jones cannot handle both a weakened you and a full strength Savage.'

'Why wasn't Savage tortured?'

'The queen ordered me that he shouldn't be tortured. I wish I could tell you why, but we don't have time since it's a very long story. Now I just want him to answer a few questions in front of you.'

There was a knock on the door and a voice saying 'Jones, we have Savage here.'

Jones opened the door and two men came in holding one arm of Savage each.

'Good afternoon, Savage. I requested your presence here because I want Father Ballard to hear the answer to one question I have for you. Who do you believe that told me everything about your plot, so that I could put all of you in prison?'

'My answer shouldn't surprise the captain. Only one of us wasn't present at the trial as a prisoner, Gilbert Gifford, obviously your agent.'

'I gave permission to Gilbert to go to France to check about the possibility of foreign help for our plot. That's why he wasn't captured with the rest of us.'

'I escaped the night you were arrested. I entered the room of Nonsuch Palace that Usher Tyndell, presumably an old friend of Gilbert, indicated as being the queen's bedroom. That information was false. George Tyndell was an agent working for Walsingham and Gilbert was another agent.'

'That's right; I wanted to capture all of you on August 20 catching you on your act of high treason. That would really have been a truly dramatic way to end the plot. Babington ruined everything when he tried to leave the country and abandon the plot. He forced me to take action before the fool realized he could easily escape to France in a fishing boat. The fool requested a meeting with me to offer his services as my agent in France. I offered him a chance to come clean and denounce the plot himself, becoming my agent in London, but he simply answered he would think about my offer.'

Ballard was speechless. He had always considered Gilbert the most useful member of his organization. He was also hurt by the news that Anthony wanted to be out of the plot, but he was not surprised by the news. He had realized that Anthony was afraid and might leave the plot. He had actually discussed this eventuality with Gilbert. Ballard regretted that Anthony did not confide in him since he could have sent him to France with any of a dozen Catholic fishermen of Black Pool that he knew well.

'I must send you back to your cell, Savage, but if you wish to talk with Ballard, I'll give orders to allow you to do it after I leave.'

'Thank you, Sir Francis; I'll greatly appreciate a chance to talk with the captain before our execution.'

The two men working for Jones left with Savage and Walsingham did not talk, waiting for Ballard to recover from the shock he had just received.

'None of them should be executed Walsingham. I'm the only guilty one. There was no Babington Plot. It was my plot.'

'You're totally mistaken, Ballard.'

'I'm not mistaken. Anthony Babington only described my plot in his letter to Mary Stuart.'

'I'm not saying it was a Babington Plot. I'm telling you it wasn't your plot, but my plot.'

'I don't understand.'

'Just think and remember how everything happened. I gave you every idea for the plot through Gilbert.'

'You must have found he was carrying a letter for me and forced him to become a double agent to save his life.'

'I'm paying a monthly salary to agent Gilbert Gifford since June 1580. He moved to France shortly after his father was imprisoned for recusancy. He took some money with him and studied theology at Douay College. Then he went to Rome and entered the English College to continue to study theology. My top agent in Rome, Solomon Aldred, realized that he was running out of money and would welcome a chance to become one of my spies. He worked for me in Rome, informing about English Catholic exiles, until he was expelled from the college towards the end of 1581. I arranged for him to return to France to teach theology in Rheims, with instructions to study to become a deacon. When he was ordained as deacon by Cardinal De Guise I sent him immediately to work with you.'

Walsingham remained silent for a minute waiting for Ballard to say something. Since the priest did not speak he went on.

'No plot to free Mary Stuart was possible, since she had only one channel of communication with the outside world through Archbishop Beaton. All correspondence with her went through this channel and I had control of both ends of the channel. It was extremely easy to get control. I recruited as agents the two secretaries that worked for Mary Stuart, Claude Nau de la Boisseliere and Gilbert Curle, as well as the two secretaries that worked for Archbishop Beaton, Thomas Morgan and Charles Paget. You never met Morgan and Paget, but Beaton told them everything about you since they had to make the arrangements to finance your plot through the French Embassy in England. I learned about you towards the end of 1584 and I immediately put pressure on Gilbert Gifford to become a deacon, so that he could come to you as such.'

'But when he came to me he exposed Bernard Maude as one of your agents.'

'Poor Bernard Maude, as an impoverished widower with a taste for the good life; he was thrilled about receiving a handsome salary from me for doing nothing.'

'Why did you make him your agent?'

'I recruited him as an agent because he was your friend; not to spy on you but to be exposed by Gilbert as my agent. This way Gilbert gained your complete trust. Even now it's hard for you to believe he was always your enemy.'

'And Gilbert found Savage and brought him to me.'

'I knew that Savage had killed two men to get revenge and I suspected he would be interested in participating in a plot to kill Queen Elizabeth so that I instructed Gilbert to bring him to you.'

'And he fitted into my plans like a glove.'

'He certainly did and he killed Bernard Maude for you.'

'And I suppose Thomas Jones was another of your agents.'

'Thomas Jones is the brother of Horace Jones, who's now in this room with us.'

Jones smiled widely when Walsingham mentioned his name.

'I had cut all contact between Mary Stuart and the outside world but after recruiting Claude Nau and Gilbert Curle I had to re-establish that contact. I had Jones with me to provide muscle to my organization, but he showed me he also had brains. When he learned I was about to lift the restrictions I had imposed to prevent communication between Mary Stuart and the outside world, he suggested I shouldn't do it openly and gave me instead the idea of the beer barrels. He knew the beer business well since he used to work with his brother before joining my service. To keep everything confidential I had to move Mary Stuart to Chartley, so that Thomas Jones would be the courier handling the beer barrels.'

'And Thomas Jones had histrionic capabilities that fooled me completely.'

'Of course Gilbert didn't have to travel to Chartley to deliver correspondence; Jones' men travelled. Here in London, Gilbert shared an apartment with Thomas Phelippes.'

'Phelippes was the expert that broke the code used in the correspondence with Mary Stuart.'

'Yes and no; we said in the trial that he had broken the code, but he didn't have to break it because he had made it. He started working for me years ago when Thomas Morgan hired him to create a code for the correspondence sent to Mary Stuart from France. I've always read all her correspondence. When you appeared on the scene I decided I needed Phelippes in London and he came to England with Gilbert.'

'I see, they converted all correspondence written in code to plain English so that you could read it.'

'The correspondence was generally in French and Phelippes converted code to the original language while Gilbert translated French to English. Although I can read French, I like to have English versions of all correspondence. Mary Stuart acted in the same way and all the correspondence decoded by Nau to the original French, was translated to English by Curle.'

'So that you could have tried and convicted me for high treason when I returned to England, but instead you let me organize a group of idealistic young men so that all of them are sent to the gallows with me.'

'You haven't grasped yet which was my plot. Queen Elizabeth is not safe because we have in England, as prisoner, a former Queen of Scotland. But Mary Stuart doesn't recognize her as the Queen of England. She claims to be herself the legitimate Queen of England. Since Mary is Catholic and Elizabeth is Protestant, Catholics like you want to kill Elizabeth and replace her by Mary.'

'Yes, but we want to do it because intolerant Protestants like you persecute Catholics. You invented the Catholic plots that you discovered.'

'I didn't invent the Ridolfi Plot to bring Spanish troops from Flanders to depose Elizabeth and install Mary Stuart as Queen of England. King Felipe II of Spain approved the plan as well as Pope Pious V. The Pope excommunicated Elizabeth to put all Catholics against her. The only way to stop this madness was to condemn Mary Stuart to death, but Elizabeth refused to do it. To make Elizabeth change her mind I invented evidence against the Duke of Norfolk, who had postponed a request to Elizabeth for permission to marry Mary Stuart, until he could be confident that the Protestant Lords that ruled Scotland would accept him as Consort King. The Duke was beheaded, but Mary Stuart remained alive.'

'And then you invented false charges against Fathers Campion, Briant, Sherwin and many other priests and obtained their convictions.'

'These convictions were needed to make the general public realize that it was very dangerous to keep Mary Stuart alive.'

'Then you invented false charges against Sir Francis Throckmorton.'

'I would have preferred a Lord, but Throckmorton was available and important enough to alert the nobility about how dangerous Mary Stuart was. And the Privy Council was so impressed that I obtained the Bond of Association.'

'And the Bond of Association allows you to request the death penalty for Mary Stuart because she would have profited from the Babington Plot, even if she knew nothing about it.'

'But I don't have to use the Bond of Association because Mary Stuart knows everything about the plot and she wrote a letter approving it.'

'Did she write the letter just because you're lucky?'

'You're beginning to understand how I work. I devised a plan to kill Mary Stuart but not just inventing false charges. This time I needed true charges. Savage, Anthony Babington and his friends, Mary Stuart and you were my puppets and had to be induced to act according to my plan. I asked Mary to write to Babington in a letter in which I told her the young man needed recognition from her because he had a jealous personality. I don't remember now if my letter was signed by Morgan or Paget. Then I instructed Gilbert to tell Babington that when Mary Stuart became Queen of England she would be obliged to execute those that made her queen because they were the assassins of Queen Elizabeth. Babington then wrote the letter in which he told Mary the complete plan, including the assassination of Elizabeth.'

'I didn't like that letter. I was afraid that Mary would ask us to discontinue the plan after learning it included the assassination of Elizabeth.'

'You needn't have worried my friend. I was in charge and I had the coded letter prepared by Anthony and Gilbert rewritten by Phelippes omitting all reference to the assassination. Phelippes is a consummated forger, so that if Babington looks at that letter he'll believe it's the same one he wrote. When Mary answered the letter, Phelippes added a postscript requesting the name of the assassins.'

'And you arranged for Gilbert to introduce us to Usher Tyndell.'

'Of course Gilbert had never met Tyndell before, but he fitted the role because both of them had the same age. Tyndell was upset because I ordered him to get rid of his bushy beard and he was very proud of it. But this movement of my puppets was a great mistake. I showed you that Elizabeth wasn't living in Whitehall Palace but in Nonsuch Palace and I showed you an easy way to enter in it.'

'But Savage just said you fed us false information.'

'All false information contains an element of truth to be credible. The room next to the terrace wasn't the queen's bedroom, but it was easy to get on the terrace.'

'And Savage escaped capture, entered Nonsuch Palace and hid inside.'

'Yes, he was a puppet that broke the strings and took control of his own actions. I knew that he fitted your plot but had no interest in Mary Stuart; he just wanted to kill Elizabeth. Although your plot had failed he could go ahead with his own plan to kill Elizabeth. I was afraid that he had entered

Nonsuch Palace and I went there with all my men and searched not only the palace but the surrounding woods, but I couldn't find him. The queen was not in the palace and that gave me the opportunity to search everything. Savage is a very resourceful man and I have no idea how he managed to hide, or how he fed himself, but he stayed hidden in the palace several days until I abandoned the search.'

'But he's your prisoner now.'

'The first day after I had abandoned the search I had a premonition in the evening and went back to Nonsuch Palace. I asked the queen to move to another bedroom for that night. I left one of my men in her bed, with a pistol in his hand. Jones also was put in the room, pistol in hand, facing the open window. I did this because I had an uneasy feeling for having failed to catch Savage, but I didn't expect any results because I believed that Savage had never entered the palace, had escaped to a faraway city and I would never hear of him again.'

Walsingham fell silent.

'What happened then?'

'At 3 o'clock I decided to leave the palace with my men and I entered the queen's bedroom. Jones came with me immediately but the man in the bed didn't seem to hear me. I opened the curtains of the canopied bed and found the man I put there in a bath of blood. His throat had been cut and the pistol was no longer in his hand.'

'I was in the room all the time looking at the window. I never saw or heard anything and I swear I never fell asleep,' said Jones.

'My blood froze in my veins. I woke the queen up and took her to another bedroom at the opposite wing of the palace. I checked the room and left a guard of six men at the door. Early the next morning Usher Tyndell and two of his men brought Savage to me as their prisoner, just when I was in the central court of the palace. He had been caught trying to leave the palace with the suppliers that bring food to the kitchen early every morning. When I told him that the queen would be pleased to hear the news of his capture, he told me she hadn't slept in her own bedroom and that I should look for her in a room he was pointing to me.'

Walsingham fell silent again. Ballard did not say anything and just waited for the Principal Secretary to resume his tale.

'I thought Savage had killed the queen. I almost fainted but I recovered and ran inside the palace, up the stairs and along the corridors to burst inside the bedroom where I had left the queen. I woke her up; she had fallen asleep sitting in front of a table with a mirror. Her neck was covered with dry blood; her own blood; Savage made a nick in her neck and then spared her life. He also left a message for me: "A black rook has captured the white queen." He meant that instead of arresting you I had played a game of chess with you, using Queen Elizabeth as an important but expendable piece. I may have won the game but I had lost the queen. Since it was only a game he didn't kill her, only made a nick to show me he could have killed her.'

Again, Walsingham remained silent for a moment.

'I'm sorry that Savage didn't escape. When he spared the queen's life he spared my own life. I would have killed myself if he had killed her.'

'No, you wouldn't have killed yourself. You're not a Catholic but you're a Christian. Suicide is a sin that leaves no time for repentance.'

'When you're desperate you don't think about such matters.'

'I'm glad that Savage didn't kill Elizabeth. Her assassination only made sense to put a Catholic queen in her place. A terrible persecution of Catholics would have taken place if the Protestant queen had been killed now.'

'I'll leave, Ballard. You'll be sent to your cell but before I leave the Tower I'll arrange for Savage to have a private meeting with you.'

'Thank you, Sir Francis. Perhaps your feelings towards Savage extend to the rest of us, puppets. I would like to talk, individually, with the other twelve men that are going to be executed, since I'm the one responsible for their deaths.'

'Granted. Goodbye forever.'

'Thank you, Sir Francis. Goodbye.'

PART III
THE SECOND PART OF THE PLOT

CHAPTER I
CONFESSIONS AND EXECUTIONS

Two of Jones men escorted Ballard back to his cell and Walsingham talked to his assistant.

'Jones, you must arrange a meeting between Ballard and Savage in a room where I can listen to everything from an adjoining one. If possible, make arrangements for this matter right away, before I go home. I'll wait here.'

About twenty minutes later Jones returned.

'Please follow me, Sir Francis. There are two offices prepared just for what you want. Of course you'll have to remain in complete silence, since whatever is said in one room is heard in the other one. After you take your place, Tower Guards will be sent to take Ballard and Savage to the next room.'

'Stay with me, Jones. I'll leave after I hear what I want to hear, but I wish you to listen to everything said by the other plotters, in case anything is said that you may consider important, in which case you'll tell it to me.'

Shortly afterwards two guards took Ballard to the next room and a minute later two other guards took Savage to join him.

'I'm glad that Sir Francis kept his word and I can see you again, Captain. I'm a sinner and I'm going to die the day after tomorrow. I need the sacrament of confession and you're a priest and can receive my confession. You often tried to convince me to become a Catholic, but I kept my allegiance to the Church of England. Now I'm a Catholic, like when I was a child, and I want you to receive my confession, Captain. Sorry, I must call you Father. After my confession

I'll tell you about my visit to Nonsuch Palace.'

'You can call me captain like you always did, but now I'll be acting as a priest to receive your confession.'

Ballard continued to talk, whispering in Savage's ear.

'I'm sure Walsingham is in the next room listening to everything we say.'

'I know. He's interested in my phantom like movements in Nonsuch Palace. I don't mind if he hears when I tell you such movements, but I don't want my confession to be heard by him.'

Savage then confessed his sins to Father Ballard talking in a whisper, with Ballard talking to him in the same way. Walsingham did not mind since he realized that both Ballard and Savage were quite smart and probably imagined that whatever they said would be heard by him and a confession was something too intimate to be heard by others. He was not interested in hearing the confession. He wanted to know how Savage had killed the man that had replaced the queen in her bed and how he had managed to enter the remote bedroom of the palace where he thought she would be safe.

After the confession was over and Savage had received the absolution, Ballard spoke in a normal voice.

'Can you now tell me how you escaped arrest? When I was arrested I kicked my bed expecting the noise would wake you up.'

'It did. I woke up because I heard a noise. Not a loud noise but something strange. Looking through the window I saw men outside the house and realized we were being raided so I hid and escaped from the house when the raiders had gone, except for a few men waiting inside for my eventual return in case I had left the house before they arrived.'

'Where did you go?'

'To get my horse to go to Nonsuch Palace.'

Savage then told Ballard in detail everything that happened since his arrival to a wooded area near the palace until Walsingham left the inner court running expecting to find the queen's dead body.

'I'm glad you didn't kill Elizabeth, John. Her assassination was needed to create a power void that would build support for the need to put a free Mary Stuart on the throne. But with Mary Stuart in prison, Elizabeth's murder would have only create a power void resulting in chaos and misery for all Englishmen. I'm also glad that although you were ready to destroy a symbol of oppression, like when you killed in the dark the man that had taken the place of the queen, you found it impossible to kill a defenseless woman face to face.'

'Perhaps you're right. I really don't know myself why I didn't kill Elizabeth after having sworn to God to kill her many years ago and having wanted to kill her for so many years. I wouldn't be here if I had killed her. I would have joined the servants to stay with them until I could go away to disappear forever.'

'I'm responsible for your execution and that of all the other members of our conspiracy.'

'Perhaps you're responsible for the others, but not for me. I could have escaped after you woke me up when you were arrested, but I elected to go to Nonsuch Palace to kill the queen. Later I could have escaped after killing the queen, but I elected to pardon her life. I could still have escaped by staying out of her sight, but I elected to give her a piece of my mind from a position of power, with my knife against her neck. And although I'm going to die, I must tell you it felt really good to have power, the power of life or death, over the powerful Queen of England.'

'You must realize that you've created a legend. History will have no record of what you told me, but many have seen the way Walsingham reacted when he believed Elizabeth was dead. The rumor that the queen's life was in great danger because of the Babington Plot will last forever. Well, we must part company now. Walsingham is allowing me to talk with all the other prisoners and I wish to do that. The next time we see each other will be when we're drawn to the gallows.'

'Goodbye, Captain. I'm glad I met you and I'm not afraid to go to a Christian death with you.'

In the next room, Walsingham opened the door quietly and signaled Jones to go out of the room with him. Four guards and an usher were waiting at the door. Walsingham talked to the usher, obviously the man in charge of the small group.

'Very soon the prisoners will be knocking at the door.'

Before the phrase ended two loud knocks were heard.

'The meeting between Ballard and Savage is over. Two guards must take Savage back to his cell and then they should bring Babington here to talk with Ballard. I've given permission for Ballard to talk, alone, with each of the other conspirators condemned to death. After Babington, you should bring Salisbury and that will be all for the day. The other ten will speak with Ballard tomorrow.'

After these instructions, Walsingham talked with his assistant.

'Jones, I'll be going now but you should stay and listen to everything.'

When Walsingham had gone and Jones had re-entered the listening room, the usher opened the door. Savage came out and the usher spoke to Ballard.

'I've instructions to bring prisoner Babington to speak with you after prisoner Savage is taken back to his cell. After Babington finishes, prisoner Salisbury will be taken here. The other ten prisoners will talk with you tomorrow.'

'I'll be waiting for Babington.'

Shortly afterwards, Anthony entered the room.

'What am I doing here with you?'

Anthony was very suspicious of the situation.

'I thought some of you may wish the sacrament of confession before meeting your Maker the day after tomorrow. I requested Walsingham's permission and got it. I just finished a long meeting with John Savage. This first meeting was requested by him and it gave me the opportunity to request the other meetings. John decided to become a Catholic and is now at peace after his confession.'

Ballard continued to talk in a whisper.

'Don't say anything aloud that Walsingham and his men don't already know. One man is listening next door. And if you wish to confess, do it in a whisper since no one has a right to listen to your confession, except your priest.'

'I don't want anyone to listen to us,' said Anthony, whispering.

'They can't hear what we talk in a whisper, Anthony.'

'I do need a confession, Father. But I'm embarrassed about having you as my confessor because I tried to leave the country without telling you anything.'

'Go ahead with your confession and we can talk later, in a normal voice.'

Anthony then made his confession whispering. Then he started to talk to Ballard in his normal voice.

'The day after sending my letter explaining our plot to Mary Stuart I read my letter trying to put myself in the place of someone that knew nothing about it. I wanted to figure out Queen Mary's reaction to my letter. The result of my reading was appalling.'

'Please explain.'

'I realized that we had a lunatic plan with minimal chances of success. Not only that, but even if by a stroke of luck the lunatic plan should come out right, we would have to start a desperate religious war. We had no army to start this war. I imagine you had spoken with Catholic nobles that were ready to raise armies in support of a Catholic queen, but it wouldn't take long for the army of the deceased queen to wipe out all suspicious noblemen. On top of that, the populace that loved Queen Elizabeth would have started to hunt Catholics in order to kill them.'

'I often thought that you had mistaken your vocation; you were not cut out to be a lawyer but a military man. You're intelligent but can't advance in your studies because you're not interested in law. On the other hand, you're an excellent swordsman and have clear qualities of command. You're the natural leader of your group and you've assessed our plan as a military man.'

'I'm pleased by your words, but the truth is that I don't like to study hard; I'm a coward and I wanted to escape to France, like Gilbert did.'

'You're not a coward. You had a chance to tell Walsingham everything about our plot when you offered your services as a foreign agent and he made you the counter-offer of becoming a local agent. And it was an insane idea to elude problems by double-crossing Walsingham. You should have confided in me. I didn't want anyone in the plot that didn't believe in it. If you had told me you wanted to leave the country to leave the plot, I would have arranged for you to go to Black Pool with your wife and daughter and from there to France in a fishing boat. Walsingham wouldn't have learned about your escape to France, since his informer was Gilbert and he was already in France. Walsingham intended to arrest all of us on August 20 acting in Nonsuch Palace and Chartley in accordance with our plan.'

'I can't believe that Gilbert betrayed us.'

'Gilbert (10) betrayed the Catholic cause six years ago when he was studying theology in Rome at the English School and became a Walsingham's agent. Morgan and Paget, the secretaries of Archbishop Beaton, have also been working as

Walsingham's agents for years.The Principal Secretary learned about my intentions through them. I never met them but the archbishop tells them everything that concerns England.'

'Jacques Babton, my French cousin, suspected the intentions of Morgan and Paget as soon as he met them.'

'Regardless of the merits and demerits of our plan, it could never have succeeded because Walsingham knew everything about it. Even if I had never contacted Archbishop Beaton, I eventually would have needed to contact Mary Stuart. Her two secretaries, Nau and Curle, were also double agents. No plan to set Mary Stuart free could have ever succeeded.'

'In fact, I realize now I was doomed the day I accepted Archbishop Beaton's invitation to visit Rome to get an audience with the Pope. Walsingham was lucky to have a priest like you organizing a real plot. But before learning about you he was already inventing a plot to incriminate all of those, like me, who had helped Catholic priests in England. In particular, those who travelled to Rome for the private audience with the pope we got as our reward.'

'I'm sure you're right and that the audience with the pope was Walsingham's idea, planted on Archbishop Beaton by Morgan and Paget. He had invented plots before within the outline created by Ridolfi.'

'Morgan and Paget had tried to contact me the first time I travelled to Paris. I was the target of Walsingham's plans long ago. He was going to invent a Babington Plot to continue to show it's dangerous to keep Mary Stuart alive.'

'When I appeared he had a chance to get a real plot orchestrated by him. He'll continue to invent more plots until he obtains the execution of Mary Stuart, but he believes that right now the correspondence between you and Mary Stuart will allow him to get permission from Elizabeth for the execution he considers to be necessary.'

'And I'll be the one responsible for Mary Stuart's death.'

'Not at all. She didn't receive your real letter but a copy made by Phelippes, the expert in coded letters presented at the trial. The copy she received didn't include the plans for the assassination of Queen Elizabeth. Walsingham feared that if Mary Stuart should have received your real letter she might have answered forbidding the assassination plans. To her letter, Phelippes added the postscript requesting the names of the friends of yours that would murder the queen. If Mary Stuart is executed because of this plot or after a future plot, Sir Francis Walsingham will be the only one responsible.'

'Why did Mary Stuart write to me?'

'Because of a letter sent to her by Paget (11) or Morgan (12) saying you had a jealous personality and needed her personal recognition. Afterwards it was Gilbert's job to convince you it was necessary to get Mary Stuart's approval of a plan that included the assassination of her cousin, Queen Elizabeth. I'm afraid that history will remember you as a man with petty jealousies because of the letter sent to Mary.'

'That's very low in the list of my worries. I'm afraid to die and I'm afraid to behave as a coward during the cruel execution we'll have the day after tomorrow.'

'You don't have to be afraid to die. You're a Catholic; you've been a good Catholic all your life and you know death is not the end for you. And the execution we'll have is the same that was given to saints like Campion, Bryant and Sherwin as well as to other priests that were martyred after capture. It'll be an honor for us to die in the same way they died, even if we can't be considered martyrs because we're guilty. But you'll be executed because you worked for a superior cause, the cause of a Catholic England, following a road indicated to you by your priest, who was following directives given by the pope. As soon as your soul leaves your tortured body you'll find yourself in heaven.'

'But I'll show my fear for pain.'

'Anything we do once we can repeat and we might improve, but we only have one death and we have to get it right. You can overcome that fear thinking of the glorious end.'

'Even if I overcome my fear, when I'm tortured to die by disembowelment the pain will make me cry.'

'That's right, they'll execute us that way to try to take all honor away from us, but it's them that throw their own honor to the dogs using unwarranted cruelty. I have a suggestion; I'll be the first one to die. Look at me when I'm revived to be quartered and keep looking at me until I'm dead. The natural reaction of someone that will suffer in the same way is to look away from what's being done. By looking you'll show you're not afraid.'

'You're right. I was afraid of a dishonorable execution, but I'll die honorably and in accordance with my convictions. It's dishonorable for those that order this execution to make it so gruesome.'

Anthony Babington felt at peace when he went back to his cell.

Thomas Salisbury had his confession with Father Ballard after Babington. The other conspirators confessed the next day. Ballard knew each of them quite well and had the right words for them, leaving everyone convinced he was marching to a glorious moment. Particularly poignant for Ballard was his meeting with Chidiock Tichborne, the poet, who had written a poem after going to prison. He recited it to Ballard.

My prime of youth is but a frost of cares,
My feast of joy is but a dish of pain,
My crop of corn is but a field of tares,
And all my good is but vain hope of gain;
The day is past, and yet I saw no sun,
And now I live, and now my life is done.

My tale was heard and yet it was not told,
My fruit is fallen and yet my leaves are green,
My youth is spent and yet I am not old,
I saw the world and yet I was not seen;
My thread is cut and yet it is not spun,
And now I live, and now my life is done.

I sought my death and found it in my womb,
I looked for life and saw it was a shade,
I trod the earth and knew it was my tomb,
And now I die, and now I was but made:
My glass is full, and now my glass is run,
And now I live, and now my life is done.

Ballard had a hard time restraining his tears after listening to the poem, recited with great sentiment by Chidiock who had written it to leave it to his wife, but cried after the young man left.

Another poignant case was Jerome Bellamy, whom he had met briefly one day he accompanied Anthony to a fencing lesson.

'I'm innocent, Captain. I've been unfairly sentenced to death as if I had been a member of the plot, when all I did was to allow my friends in danger to take refuge in my barn.'

'Call me Father, Jerome; I'm a priest. I know you should have been sent to a separate trial for acting as a true Catholic, being charitable with your fellow men. Walsingham could have requested the death penalty for you in such trial, but it was easier for him to get it charging you as being one of the plotters.'

'As a Catholic I must be charitable, but also all Christians must be charitable with their neighbors, even those in the Church of England.'

'If Walsingham wants you dead, you're doomed. He can invent all sort of devious doings on your part to make sure you get the death penalty in any trial. He has included you with us only for simplicity. But your case is totally different to ours in the face of God. We're sent to death because we're guilty, while you're sent to death only because you're a Catholic. We can trust in the mercy of God because we acted in good faith for a superior cause, but you're a true martyr. Since I'm a priest, I can receive your confession now, if you wish.'

Jerome was happy to have a chance for a confession with a priest before his execution.

The last man to have a meeting with Ballard was someone that he had never met before, Edward Habington.

'Who are you and why have I been brought here?'

'I'm Father Ballard and I've requested to talk individually with all those condemned to death tomorrow and the day after tomorrow. I'm condemned to death myself and I know everyone well except you. We're guilty as charged, all of us except Bellamy and you. Bellamy is only guilty of hiding Babington, Salisbury and Barnewell, but the authorities preferred to charge him as a participant in the plot to get him sentenced to death. Your case is an unjustifiable murder because the authorities know that you had nothing to do with our plot. I pleaded your case directly to Walsingham, but to no avail. A torturer claimed that one of the prisoners gave your name, only because he had been beaten so badly that he couldn't pronounce the name Babington properly. The authorities decided that it was better to go ahead with your execution than to expose the abominable system of torture used to make justice.'

'So that's what happened. I always thought that the only possible reason for which I'm in this mess would be the similarity between the names Babington and Habington. I actually met Anthony once. This is hard to believe, but I met him in court. And I had been so pleased to have been invited to court.'

'Are you a Catholic by any chance?'

'I am. We're Catholics in our family, but only relatives and friends know about it. In public we pretend to conform to the Church of England to avoid the recusancy laws.'

'I thought that you had to be a Catholic. A Protestant like Walsingham is in the Church of England only for political reasons; he's a Puritan at heart. He must have checked this matter thoroughly before deciding not to interfere with the torturers. If you had been a Puritan or a member of the Church of England you wouldn't be here. You're a martyr Edward. You're being sent to death because of your faith. One day the Church may recognize you as one, but even if it never does, you'll be a saint as soon as you die.'

Edward Habington left after his confession. Once alone, Ballard was concerned with his own conscience exam. He had a practice of conscience examination twice daily, about noon and before going to sleep, but he was going to die the next day with the load of the thirteen men he was dragging to death with him. He knew God would be merciful with those men but, what about him? Were his motives as pure as their motives? Savage once told him bluntly, "you want vengeance like me". His answer had been "I prefer to think I want justice". Was his desire for justice any different from a desire for vengeance? Savage was totally redeemed from his desire for vengeance. He had the chance to exact vengeance and decided to have mercy.

What weighed more heavily on Ballard's conscience was the murder of Bernard Maude. Savage had no interest in him but murdered the man following his instructions. The fact that Bernard was a Walsingham agent was the sign that God was giving him to tell him the plot had to be abandoned and he had to return to France. Probably, even if he had followed that sign, Anthony and his friends would be going to the gallows. They would have been accused of a Babington Plot invented by Walsinham who had decided to go on inventing plots until he could obtain the execution of Mary Stuart. But abandoning the plot he would not have committed the horrible sin of ordering Bernard's murder.

And the two poets, Chidiock Tichborne and Charles Tilney had been recruited by him and would not have been included in any plot invented by Walsingham, since they did not attend the audience given by Pope Sixtus V. He was directly responsible for cutting short two brilliant careers. Chidiock was a gifted poet, but the world was going to get just a small peek at his talent. Ballard cried thinking of the volumes of poems he might have written if he could have lived just until his mid-thirties. And Charles had written such an imaginative and ambitious first play as Locrine, with a mythical foundation of London as Trinovantus (New Troy) by exiles from a defeated Troy. In that setting, he wrote the tragedy of King Locrine, who falls in love with the widow of a defeated enemy. Ballard had read the third version of the play and Charles, a perfectionist, was working on a fifth one. Ballard cried again thinking of the series of plays that Charles Tilney could have written if his life had not been cut short because of him.

Ballard never slept a wink that night, praying all night.

The next morning, September 20, 1586, John Ballard, Anthony Babington, John Savage, Chidiock Tichborne, Robert Barnewell, Thomas Salisbury and Henry Dunn were bound to wooden planks and drawn along the streets of London from the Tower of London to a scaffold erected in the open fields in a place called Cup Field, probably very near of what today is Lincoln Inn's Field. Ballard was on a single sled and the others two-a-piece. The scaffold had been erected in the open fields to allow thousands of people to be present and was particularly high, so that everyone could see justice being done. The site was fenced off to prevent horsemen from blocking the view.

One by one the seven men were hanged, immediately revived and then disemboweled so that they could be quartered. They had a painful slow death by disembowelment.

John Ballard was the first man to be executed and when he was taken to be hanged he addressed the spectators that had come to see justice done.

'I wish my blood could spill over my companions to make my death sufficient penalty for all of them.'

When he was revived after hanging he talked again. 'Parce mihi Domine Iesu,' Spare me Lord Jesus. He repeated this phrase several times until he lost consciousness under the knife of the executioner. While his five companions looked the other way, Anthony looked at Ballard's execution to prove he was not afraid.

This way of applying the penalty of being drawn, hanged and quartered, mandatory for traitors, had been used in London many times before. It was this way martyrs Campion, Bryant and Sherwin had been executed, but it was the first time that such horrible and cruel display was repeated seven times. Cheers were heard after Ballard was quartered but the number of cheers decreased in each execution that followed. No one cheered after the last three executions.

The queen did not attend the executions; she never did. This time the men to be executed had planned her murder so that, exceptionally, she had ordered all her ladies-in-waiting to attend. The ladies were not just horrified, but actually sick because of the spectacle they had to witness and told this to the queen as soon as they returned to the palace.

The queen became red with shame and anger and requested to be left alone. Once alone she called a footman.

'Sir Francis Walsingham must be summoned to come to see me immediately.'

The queen had been waiting in Whitehall Palace for the ladies she sent to watch the executions. Walsingham had his office in that palace so that just a few minutes later he was in front of his queen. As soon as he saw her, he realized she was mad with rage and he immediately assumed that she must have received a report of the execution from a witness. He could not believe that any courtesan would have the audacity to tell Elizabeth anything bad about the execution of traitors, but something had gone wrong.

'Good afternoon, Sir Francis. Did you watch today's executions?'

'No, Your Majesty. My function is to send conspirators to the gallows, not to watch their executions.'

'Can you tell me the sentences dictated for today's executions?'

'The mandatory sentence for traitors is that they should be drawn, hanged and quartered. When the traitor is a nobleman, he's beheaded instead, but all those executed today were commoners.'

'I never watch executions, but since the men executed today had planned my assassination I sent all my ladies-in-waiting to watch. They told me that none of the seven men executed today died by hanging, as indicated in the sentences they received. They were hanged as a form of torture, since they were revived after hanging. After being revived they were tortured to death by disembowelment. Can you give me an explanation?'

'What you described is the centuries old traditional way to apply the sentence to traitors.'

'Are you telling me that this is the way my friend Campion was executed?'

'Yes, Your Majesty.'

'You've failed me, Walsingham. You're not the king that can decide that some customs may be followed as traditions. You had no authority to make a decision like this I am the queen and I decide on these matters. The people don't know or care if the execution they watch was also used 200 years ago. They watch abominably cruel executions and consider they have an abominably cruel queen that is ordering such executions. You'll pay for this, Walsingham.'

'I'm sorry I displeased you, Your Majesty.'

'Displeased me? You have dishonored me. And you've disregarded direct instructions I gave you.'

'I don't understand, Your Majesty.'

'I ordered that Savage should not be tortured.'

'And he wasn't tortured during the time he was in prison before the execution.'

'But he was tortured to death, instead of the death by hanging imposed by his sentence. Another seven men will be executed tomorrow and I'm ordering you to make immediate arrangements to ensure that when they're hanged, they're hanged until dead. And you must watch the executions personally, to make sure this is the new traditional way to execute traitors. Did you understand my orders? For your own sake, I hope that you've understood correctly. My ladies-in-waiting will also attend and will report to me. Later, I'll think about what to do with you.'

The next day, September 21, 1586, Edward Habington, Charles Tilney, Edward Jones, John Charnock, John Travers, Robert Gage and Jerome Bellamy were tied to wooden planks and drawn to the Cup Field gallows. Habington was tied to a single sled and the others two-a-piece. Habington was the first to be hanged and had a chance to shout loud and clear that he was innocent and had never conspired against the crown. This time all the men condemned were hanged until dead.

CHAPTER II
THE TRIAL OF MARY STUART

One morning in late September Sir Francis Walsingham went to the Whitehall Palace office of Sir William Cecil, Lord Burghley.

'Good morning, Francis. What brings you here?

'I need your help to protect the queen, Sir William. Babington, the Jesuit priest Ballard and the other conspirators participating in the most recent plot have been executed these last few days, but as long as Mary Stuart continues to be alive the queen's life remains in danger. And we have grounds to arrange for Mary's execution immediately. In the first place, we have the Bond of Association, a legal instrument written by you, with my cooperation. But even if we didn't have it, we have the correspondence between Mary Stuart and Babington that demonstrates clearly that she participated in the Babington Plot.'

'Do you want me to accompany you to discuss this matter with the queen?'

'No, I want you to convince her that Mary Stuart should be beheaded, but you should act alone or with other members of the Privy Council, not including me. I've done my part discovering the plot and sending all the conspirators to trial and execution. You know that she loathes executions. She's already upset with me now. If at this delicate moment I tell her that we must add the execution of her cousin, she'll probably fire me as Principal Secretary and decide to protect the life of her cousin.'

'Then perhaps we should postpone this matter for a few months and talk with the queen about it in mid-January of next year.'

'That would be worse. If we don't take immediate action

now, we'll have to wait for another plot to make the queen understand that Mary Stuart is a menace.'

'Perhaps we don't need to talk with the queen. I'll start talking with Sir Amyas Paulet. As you pointed out a minute ago, I wrote the Bond of Association. I wrote it in such a way that it's a "License to Kill". It's not written in "plain" English but in "legalistic" English. Perhaps this is something that escaped even you, in spite of your Italian legal training.'

'It didn't escape me. I remember exactly the words you used, hidden among those of legal lingo. Anyone signing the bond was swearing to "pursue as well by force of arms as by all other means of revenge anyone plotting to cause harm to the queen." I signed the bond and I've contemplated killing Mary myself, but I can't reach her. Only her guardian, Sir Amyas, can kill her. It's necessary to contact Sir Amyas, as you said, but I don't believe this Puritan will agree with our interpretation of the Bond of Association as a "License to Kill" and use it as such.'

A week after his conversation with Walsingham, Sir William Cecil arrived at Fotheringhay Castle and requested to see Sir Amyas Paulet.

'Good afternoon, Sir William. I wasn't expecting any visitors since I have just moved to this new location.'

'I know, Sir Amyas. I'm sorry if I cause any inconvenience. I'll be staying here only tonight and I'll leave early tomorrow morning, but it's absolutely essential that I speak with you personally on a most important matter.'

'Let's go to my study then, where no one can hear us. David, my butler, will take you to your room afterwards. You should be ready for dinner at 8 o'clock.'

When they were seated on comfortable armchairs in Paulet's study, the host spoke to Cecil.

'We're alone now, Sir William. What is it that you need to talk about with me personally and required you to come here, so far away from London?'

'In the Babington trial it's been exposed that there was a direct correspondence between conspirator Babington and Mary Stuart. She has participated directly in the Babington plot as another conspirator and she must be executed.'

'I'm quite aware of everything you just said since I participated directly myself in the interception of all the correspondence of the deposed Queen of Scotland.'

'But we have a serious problem, the queen's reluctance to execute another queen who is also a close relative and perhaps you hold the key to the solution of this problem.'

'I agree that there have been grounds to take the former queen to trial before and that, if Queen Elizabeth had been willing to get rid of her, she could already be dead. I also know that everyone in the Privy Council has advised the queen to execute the person that Catholics support for her replacement, but in the past it could never be proved that this woman was actually planning to kill the queen. We can prove it now and this matter will be definitely settled quite soon.'

'Very soon we can have Mary Stuart condemned to death, but she can't be beheaded until the queen signs the sentence. I know Queen Elizabeth very well, since for many years I've been speaking with her about matters of state almost every day. I can tell you she'll be in agony if she has to sign the death sentence of her cousin.'

'She'll be in agony and it's natural that she'll delay signing the death sentence, but it's her duty to do it and she'll fulfill her duty.'

'But you're in a position to take action to relieve the queen from the responsibility and agony of having to sign the death sentence of her closest living relative, who inherited a throne, just as she did.'

'I don't understand what your point is.'

'You've signed the Bond of Association. By signing it you've taken a vow to "pursue as well by force of arms as by all other means of revenge anyone plotting to cause harm to the queen." This means you can walk into her room with your sword and put it through her chest. You have the legal right to do this.'

'You're insane.'

'You also have the legal right to shorten the life of the deposed queen by arranging to have her food poisoned. Apparently, she'll die of natural causes. She's been ill so often that no one will suspect anything if she's so upset that she gets ill and dies after the execution of Babington, her friend.'

'You're offending me, Sir William. God forbid that I should make so fowl a shipwreck of my conscience, or leave so great a blot to my posterity.'

Cecil realized he had made a great mistake taking a criminal suggestion to a Puritan.

'Please excuse me, Sir Amyas, for requesting something you find offensive. It's just that I'm so concerned about the agony that the queen will suffer when she has to sign her cousin's death warrant.'

'I understand that you're just following your sovereign's orders.'

Cecil did not know what to answer and decided it was better not to answer anything. If he denied he was following Elizabeth's orders, Paulet might expel him from the castle and become his enemy forever. He just should not say anything and leave Paulet with the impression that he had just told him what the queen wanted him to say.

'I see that you don't want to involve the queen directly in this matter and I respect you for that. You may tell her that my answer would have been the same if she had made the request herself. Let's forget about unpleasant matters. I expect you to tell me the news from London during dinner.'

Mary Stuart attended her trial for the first time on October 15, 1586.

The Commission designated by Queen Elizabeth started to meet on October 7, but Mary refused to attend on the basis that she could not be tried for treason to the English Crown, since she was not an English subject but the sovereign anointed queen of another kingdom. Sir William Cecil finally persuaded her that since the trial would proceed even if she was absent, it was better for her to attend and speak in her own defense.

Very soon she realized that no one was interested in anything she might say in her defense and they just wanted to say that she had been properly tried before her execution. The accusation against her was the declaration given by her secretaries confirming her correspondence with Babington as shown at the Babington trial. She then made the statement repeated below:

"I am myself a Queen, the daughter of a King, a stranger, and the true Kinswoman of the Queen of England. I came to England on my cousin's promise of assistance against my enemies and rebel subjects and was at once imprisoned... As an absolute Queen, I cannot submit to orders, nor can I submit to the laws of the land without injury to myself, the King my son and all other sovereign princes... For myself I do not recognize the laws of England nor do I know or understand them as I have often asserted. I am alone without counsel, or anyone to speak on my behalf. My papers and notes have been taken from me, so that I am destitute of all aid, taken at a disadvantage.

I came into this kingdom under promise of assistance, and aid, against my enemies and not as a subject, as I could prove to you had I my papers; instead of which I have been detained and imprisoned... I do not deny that I have earnestly wished for liberty and done my utmost to procure it for myself. In this I acted from a very natural wish...

Can I be responsible for the criminal projects of a few desperate men, which they planned without my knowledge or participation?

I do not desire vengeance. I leave it to Him who is the just Avenger of the innocent and of those who suffer for His Name under whose power I will take shelter. I would rather pray with Esther than take the sword with Judith."
"Nau had many peculiarities, likings and intentions that I cannot mention in public... For my part, I do not wish to accuse my secretaries, but I can see plainly that what they have said is from fear of torture and death. Under promise of their lives and in order to save themselves, they have accused themselves at my expense, fancying that I could thereby more easily save myself, at the same time, not knowing where I was, and not suspecting the manner in which I am treated... If they were in my presence now they would clear me on the spot of all blame and would have put me out of case.

There is not one, I think, among you, let him be the cleverest man you will, but would be incapable of resisting or defending himself were he in my place."

The Commission appointed by the queen had 36 members, including Walsingham and Cecil. October 16, 1586 was the second and last day of the trial. The Commission reconvened on October 25, declared Mary Stuart guilty of treason and condemned her to death. Only one member, Edward la Zouche, Lord Zouche (13), gave a rare show of independence and courage and voted for Mary's absolution.

On October 29 Parliament met to discuss the sentence of Mary Stuart and voted to request Queen Elizabeth to sign the death warrant of the former Queen of Scotland.

CHAPTER III
ELIZABETH AND MARY

Elizabeth was in agony during the three months that followed Mary's trial. It was her duty to proceed as Parliament requested and to sign the death warrant, but she could not bring herself to do it. Her Secretary, Sir William Davison, a diplomat, received the death warrant prepared by William Cecil but could not get the queen's signature on it.

On February 1, 1587, Elizabeth reached a decision. She would have a secret meeting with Mary Stuart. She would talk face to face with her to learn if it was true that she knew that an assassin had planned to kill her as part of the Babington Plot and that she had approved the murder.

Elizabeth requested the presence of Robert Dudley, Earl of Leicester, who among other duties was her Master of the Horse. Dudley was Governor General of the United Provinces and as such he should have been in the Netherlands, but Elizabeth requested his return to London after the death sentence of Mary Stuart. Elizabeth had been told by Dudley that Mary was the rallying point of any Catholic revolt against the crown and for that reason her execution was necessary for her safety.

'Good morning, Robert. How are you today?'

'I'm quite well, Your Majesty, but I would rather be back in Flanders, where the Dutch need me.'

'You'll go back to Flanders in due time, but right now I need you here. I must travel tomorrow and I must travel fast. Do we have any carriage that can travel 15 leagues a day?'

'I sent a Prussian coach to the palace a few months ago. It has only one horse and springs that give you a reasonable stability even if it's going fast. Leaving very early in the morning you can travel 20 leagues a day. It's not as fancy or comfortable as the carriages you always use, but it's the vehicle to use if you want to ride fast. We'll have to make them in England.'

'Get it ready for me at 6 o'clock tomorrow morning, with the corresponding mounted guard.'

'Wait a moment Elizabeth. I can easily imagine where you're going. Fotheringhay Castle is about 30 leagues away from Whitehall Palace. You want to meet Mary Stuart. You'll be making a great mistake.'

'You decided to get married, Robert. I'm not Elizabeth anymore for you, but Your Majesty, even if no one is listening.'

'Forget the formalities. You'll be making a big mistake that can cost you your life. You told me yourself that the assassin that had been planning to kill you for many years instead of killing you right away decided to talk with you first. After talking with you, he couldn't kill you and that cost him his life. Now you're planning to make the same mistake yourself. You know that I don't like Cecil or Walsingham, but they are right when they tell you that as long as sweet Mary Stuart lives, your life is in danger. As long as she lives, Catholic rebels will plan to replace you with her. You never met her personally before. Now she's been tried by a court of law and sentenced to death. You must sign the sentence and this way there'll be no more Catholic plots. If you should die, the Catholics can only expect the King of Scotland as their new ruler. I'm sure they prefer to keep you as their queen.'

'As your sovereign, Robert, I command you not to say anything about my trip to anybody.'

'I won't say a word, but Walsingham will find out.'

'Walsingham and Cecil are constantly planning measures for my benefit. Don't join them in any plan until I come back. Get me the Prussian coach and the guard tomorrow morning and wait for my return without doing anything. I have a few things to do now. Goodbye, Robert.'

'Since you'll go ahead with your idea regardless of anything I may say, I'll send you an experienced coachman with another one as his assistant. They'll have instructions to take you to Fotheringhay Castle with an overnight stop at Pixhall Castle, near Huntingdon. Lord Pixhall is a good friend of mine and he can be trusted to keep your trip confidential. Goodbye, Your Majesty.'

After Dudley left, the queen requested the presence of her secretary. When he arrived she asked. 'Do you still have the death warrant for Mary Stuart, William?'

'Yes, Your Majesty. I'll bring it immediately.'

Just two minutes later Davison returned with the parchment.

'I'm glad that you finally decided to sign it, Your Majesty.'

'I did not make any decision yet, William. I just want to read it carefully. I'll keep it myself now, since I may want to read it again. You may leave now.'

Elizabeth then went to her study, closed the door and in complete privacy sat at her desk, signed the warrant and affixed the Royal Seal to it. Her desk had three drawers and she placed the warrant in the middle one. She decided that if an attack by rebels or an accident should happen during the trip, causing her death, a very difficult situation for England would take place with an heir to the throne sentenced to death. If anything should happen to her, her papers would be searched and the awkward situation would be solved. After her meeting with Mary, she would decide if she should deliver the signed warrant to the Privy Council or if instead she should destroy it and sign a pardon.

Elizabeth, accompanied by only one of her ladies in waiting, Elizabeth Throckmorton, arrived to Fotheringhay Castle early in the afternoon of February 3. Paulet was most surprised to see her, but was obliged to do his utmost to please his unexpected visitor. He immediately realized the purpose of the queen's visit and was most disturbed by the possibility she might decide to pardon Mary Stuart, after meeting her.

'Good afternoon, Your Majesty. This is a most unexpected pleasure.'

'Good afternoon, Sir Amyas.'

'I'm most sorry I didn't make any suitable arrangements for your visit, Your Majesty.'

'I took the decision to come here only two days ago, so that I had no possibility to let you know I was coming. But no fuss is needed since this is a secret visit. It's most important, Sir Amyas, that you shouldn't mention it to anybody. Sir Robert Dudley is the only one that knows since, as Master of the Horse, he had to make the travel arrangements. None of my ladies-in-waiting knows about the trip, except of course Bess, that's coming down from the coach now.'

'Good afternoon, Bess.'

'Good afternoon, Sir Amyas.'

'Sir Amyas, I must talk to you privately.'

'My study is right here. Let's go in.'

The queen and Paulet entered Paulet's study, which had a door at the entrance hall. The queen spoke immediately before Paulet could offer her a seat.

'No one should learn about this visit. Please don't mention to anyone that I came here. Of course I came to meet the former Queen of Scotland and to talk with her, but this is a matter I don't wish to be public.'

'Of course, Your Majesty. I'll keep this matter in strict reserve but you must realize that the servants have seen you here, as well as the soldiers of your guard.'

'Whatever is said unofficially is not my concern. It will not be too credible. The important thing is that no one should be in a position to say he learned about this visit from you.'

'I'll never mention this visit to anybody, Your Majesty.'

'I'm very tired after the trip, so that I wish you would give me a room where I can wash and change my clothes, and another one for Bess. The clock you have over there indicates its 3 o'clock now. Kindly arrange for me to have a 4 o'clock meeting with my cousin, in total privacy and in a comfortable room.'

'We have in this castle an intimate hall, very suitable for the meeting you wish to have, small and fitted with comfortable armchairs. Also we have several bedrooms ready to receive unexpected guests, so that there's no problem to accommodate you and Bess. My butler will make arrangements for the soldiers of you guard.'

'Thank you, Sir Amyas.'

'Will you join me for dinner at 8 o'clock, Your Majesty?'

'I'm not sure, Sir Amyas. I don't know how I'll feel at 8 o'clock.'

Thomas Philips was resting in his room at Fotheringhay Castle. He was bored. His recent job had been to be a courier between London and Chartley. He had enjoyed that job that kept him riding all day for several days a month. Gilbert Gifford told Ballard he was making these trips, but he did not; instead, those days he worked with Phelippes to write in English the copious coded correspondence of Mary Stuart. Philips retrieved the correspondence that Nau and Curle placed in the watertight leather bags, inside the empty beer barrels and replaced these with the letters that were sent to Mary Stuart before the barrels were filled with beer.

As a second occupation in London, Philips did a series of odd jobs for his employer. But when he was in Chartley between trips, he had to be a spy for Walsingham, visiting taverns and talking with strangers to see if he could hear anything that might interest the Principal Secretary.

Now he worked as a spy in Fotheringhay. He had two carrier pigeons with him, in case he had to report anything urgent, but he had never reported anything at all.

Gilbert Gifford had told Ballard that a Catholic agent called Thomas Philips had infiltrated the staff of Amyas Paulet. He said he had learned about this through a letter sent to him by Morgan. Also that he contacted Philips in Tutbury, so he could tell Nau or Curle about the beer barrel correspondence they would receive after moving to Chartley Hall. Gilbert told this to Ballard following Walsingham's instructions, but Thomas Philips was never told about his supposed role as a double agent.

When Philips heard the noise made by all the horses of the soldiers that were guarding the queen, he opened the window of his room and looked outside. He saw that the soldiers were guarding a strange carriage of a type he had never seen before.

Philips was shocked when he saw Queen Elizabeth descending from the carriage. He had seen her several times when working in Whitehall Palace so that he recognized her immediately. He realized this was most important information for his employer and he immediately wrote a message to be taken by a carrier pigeon. He wrote:

QUEEN ELIZABETH HAS ARRIVED AT FOTHERINGHAY CASTLE TODAY FEBRUARY 3 JUST BEFORE 3 O'CLOCK IN THE AFTERNOON.

The carrier pigeon left right away with the message.

At 4 o'clock Queen Elizabeth was taken to the intimate hall where she would receive Mary Stuart. She sat on a comfortable armchair, but did not have to wait long since just a few minutes later Mary Stuart entered the room. The two of them were alone in the room as Elizabeth requested.

Elizabeth was impressed by Mary's frailty. She was also

impressed by the fact that Mary did not look 44 years old, nine years younger than her, but older than her.

Elizabeth stood up. 'Good afternoon, Mary. We finally meet. I came because I now have a terrible responsibility.'

'I'm so glad to meet you, Elizabeth. I would have preferred to meet you almost 20 years ago, when I arrived to your country, but after waiting for 20 years I'm enjoying it more.'

'My Privy Council never allowed me to meet you. These men still don't want me to meet you, but they don't know I'm here. This is a secret meeting. The only member of the Privy Council that knows I came to meet you is my dear friend, Robert Dudley, whom I have sworn to silence. But he admonished me sternly for coming to meet you.'

'I can understand that. As a queen I was always limited by what the close circle of those that had the highest responsibilities in my government believed I should do. Being women we might tend to think this is a result of the need for domination felt by men, but I'm sure that kings are pressured just as much by their ministers.'

'My father never accepted any pressures and always did what he wanted. As a result he became a tyrant and that wasn't good for England. The right thing is to find a balance and to accept and evaluate advice. And it's important to always follow one's conscience. Let's sit to continue our talk.'

Elizabeth noted, with pity, that Mary wasn't walking firmly towards the armchair next to hers that she was pointing at with her left arm, but stumbled a little. When they were seated, Elizabeth talked again.

'Mary, I've been shown the English version of a coded letter sent to you by a man called Anthony Babington, explaining that he and other men had a plan to kill me and to set you free, so that you could become Queen of England.'

'I never received such letter Elizabeth. I did get a long letter from this man, explaining that he and several of his close friends had a plan to set me free. Of c0ourse I was delighted with the possibility of becoming free, but didn't believe a small group of civilians could manage such enterprise. These men could never get the support of an army. Only a state of war between England and another country could result in foreign troops coming here. My answering letter was a way to thank these men warmly for wishing to set me free, while telling them that their plan could not succeed without the help of foreign troops.'

'There's a state of war between England and Spain right now. English troops are fighting Spanish troops in the Netherlands right now.'

'Countries often fight each other in foreign lands, but aren't willing to do it directly. In my own experience, England fought the French in Scotland, but France never dreamed to send forces to England and you, the English Queen, never dreamed to invade France. In any case, if Spain should invade England, I would be executed immediately. I'm your prisoner and I long for freedom. If a few desperate men believe they can set me free, I'm grateful to them, but I know that they're too few. If the King of Spain would want to set me free and wage war against England to do it, I know that an invading army would be too many. In a nutshell, only you can set me free. Is it too late?'

'You mentioned the war between English troops and French troops in Scotland. That was the first time I sent English troops to fight outside our country. I did it to avoid a direct war with the French. The French already had a powerful army in Scotland. If I had allowed that army to stay there, the French would have built up its numbers until they had an army sufficiently powerful to invade England. Believe me that they did have plans to invade England. Regrettably, English lives were lost in Scotland, but many more were saved when the Edinburgh Treaty was signed, stipulating the withdrawal from Scotland of both the English and the French armies. Furthermore, the treaty stipulated that France accepted me as the legitimate Queen of England. The King of France, Henri II, signed the treaty as well as his son François, the Dauphin. François was only 15 but he was already married to you, who also had to sign the treaty. Why didn't you sign it?'

Mary started to cry. After several minutes she calmed down and answered.

'Henri II, who always treated me as if I were his own daughter, as well as my uncle, the Duke de Guise, made me swear to God that I would never sign that treaty. They said that if I did it, I would destroy the right of my son to be the King of England.'

'Henri II and the Duke de Guise never dreamed at that time that your son would be the Protestant King of Scotland rather than the Catholic King of France. But you should have realized, when you became Queen of Scots and were outside the influence of your French uncle, that by refusing to sign the treaty you were accepting the position of the pope and King Felipe II that declare I'm not the legitimate Queen of England and only you are the legitimate heir to my throne.'

Mary cried for a few more minutes before she spoke again.

'But I couldn't break an oath made to God.'

'You swore not to sign the Edinburgh Treaty. It wasn't necessary for you to sign it. You just had to make a statement accepting me as the legitimate Queen of England. You're nine years younger than me. You could have been my guest as my eventual successor. Instead, you presented yourself as a pretender to my throne. If I had been like my father, or my sister Mary, I would have sent you to be beheaded just after you arrived.'

'I never looked at it that way. I thought you would help me to recover my throne because you're my cousin.'

'You had 20 years of time to wonder why I never wanted to meet you and why my Privy Council wanted to cut your head off.'

Mary started to cry again. When she calmed down, Elizabeth spoke.

'When you arrived here you were accused by the Protestant nobles that were ruling Scotland of conspiring with the Earl of Bothwell to murder your husband, Lord Darnley. They said they had proof, the "Casket Letters" you had written to Bothwell. I helped you to prove your innocence by ordering a trial. The nobles couldn't produce any "Casket Letters" handwritten by you or signed by you. They presented only what they called copies. Of course they had invented these copies that were no proof. You were declared innocent and that was all I could do for you. Scot nobles were always divided into two groups, French sympathizers and English sympathizers. Those that deposed you and governed Scotland were pro English. Why would I sacrifice English lives to fight against them and support a Queen of Scots that was a pretender to the English Crown?'

Mary did not answer and after a few moments Elizabeth continued.

'You placed me in an extremely difficult position. You were my cousin and I couldn't send you to Scotland where the ruling nobles wanted your execution and I couldn't send you to France, where you had a fortune that would allow you to raise an army to invade Scotland supported by your cousin, the Duke de Guise. This duke hated all Protestants, including me and all English Protestants. I've already explained why I cannot accept French troops in Scotland. I did the only thing possible, to keep you as a prisoner, but not in a prison but in a castle where you had your own ladies-in-waiting and your own secretaries. I expected that within a reasonable time you would declare that you were not a pretender to the English Crown.'

Mary Stuart spoke now. 'The situation was much more complex than what you have just said. The Scot nobles had originals and they sent them to Sir William Cecil. These were real letters I had written but in different order and with the insertion of forged incriminatory statements. Sir William discontinued the trial because he decided that this pastiche would never be accepted by future historians. And I wasn't declared innocent. No further mention was made of the "casket letters" and I wasn't sent back to Scotland but I remained in prison. I wrote to Archbishop Beaton (15) and asked him if then I should sign the Edinburgh treaty and he said it would be a great mistake on my part.'

'He advised you in accordance with his own interests, not yours. If you had declared you were not a pretender, I would have invited you to live in my court. You could also have purchased your own castle bringing the funds you keep in France.'

'I always tried to live in accordance with my birth.'

'I see that you believe in the divine right of monarchs to rule.'

'I certainly do. It's the basis for monarchy and for my own life.'

'That's your mistake, the people are supposed to believe that, not the monarchs. The people must believe that we have the divine right to rule them, because they have the power and we want that they should give that power to us. Monarchs invented the divine right of kings to remain in power, but it's the people that have that power we take as our own. The people of Scotland didn't want to be ruled by you, they preferred the Protestant nobles and they gave the power to them. The nobles had your son and he was the right excuse so that the people could still say that they believed in the divine right of kings. If you had no son they would have found another excuse.'

'But you're in power because of the divine right of monarchs.'

'I'm in power because the people didn't accept as queen our

cousin, Lady Jane Grey. John Dudley, who governed in the name of infant King Edward, my brother, had presented her with all the wrappings of the divine right of monarchs, but the people didn't accept her.'

Mary did not speak and Elizabeth continued. 'Another reason is that my sister Mary, who the people wanted as queen and obtained the power, loved me and didn't accept the advice of those that wanted my execution. Do you now understand why I'm here?'

'You can't love me because you never met me before. You came to meet me and you found I'm a total disaster. Now you can go back to London and sign the warrant for my execution with a clear conscience.'

'I just arrived and I already knew that you never signed the Treaty of Edinburgh. I also knew that the people that advised you were not your friends and that your position as a pretender was in their interest, not yours. The only thing new I learned is that you never received a letter telling you Babington and his friends were planning to kill me. I believe you; Walsingham was in total control of the correspondence and he couldn't run the risk that you might not approve the assassination. Your secretary, Claude Nau, has not been jailed. I know this because, taking the example given to me by Walsingham, I have a few agents myself to learn what those in my Privy Council are doing behind my back. Claude Nau is living as a guest in Walsingham's home. What you read and what you dictated differs from what was presented at your trial.'

'I was shocked when I learned that my secretaries had declared against me. I had full confidence in Nau (16) and Curle. I thought they had been tortured or menaced.'

'They were bribed, something less brutal but more effective. Curle has been sent to the Tower but I know he hasn't been tortured, which is something unusual. Curle has to continue to live among Englishmen and Scots. He must appear to receive some punishment so that he can go back to his friends as the former loyal secretary of Mary Stuart.'

'One of my ladies-in-waiting, Barbara Mowbray, married Gilbert Curle (17). I baptized her daughter, Mary Curle, since Sir Amyas wouldn't allow a Catholic priest to come to do it. Furthermore one of my two dearest ladies-in-waiting is Curle's sister.'

'She should continue to be your dear friend. She's not responsible for her brother's sins and of course his wife and daughter are not responsible either. But we should make a break now. Would you join me in drinking some beer? I had a very light lunch so that I'll ask for some toasted bread with the beer, as well as some cheese and ham. If they should have any available I would also like some cold chicken or hen.'

'Lunch is always very light in a household run by Sir Amyas, so that I'll be happy to join you.'

During the break Elizabeth avoided speaking of anything concerning Mary. She told many funny anecdotes because she wanted the poor girl to relax and to be at ease. She regretted having told her that her sister had rejected the idea of her execution because she loved her. She realized that this gave Mary the feeling that she was at another trial and that, if she failed, the death sentence would be confirmed. In this brief meeting she had already learned what interested her; the trial had been unfair, based on false documentation and statements.

When both of them were satisfied that they had compensated the light lunch of the day, Elizabeth started to talk about serious matters again.

'Do you mind if I ask you a very personal question, Mary?'

'Go ahead, Elizabeth, make it as personal as you wish.'

'Why did you marry James Hepburn, the Earl of Bothwell,

who murdered your second husband, Lord Darnley?'

'This is the most personal question that you could have asked me. No one ever asked me that question before. I really don't know what I would have answered. I believe I would have probably refused to answer but I'll tell you the truth. I had to marry him to recover my honor because he had kidnapped and raped me. I fought hard to defend myself. I was young and strong then, but he was much stronger than me. I had experience in resisting unwanted advances of intimacy from Darnley, when he was drunk. He was my husband but I couldn't accept his intimacy when he was disgustingly drunk. He would beat me then, but not as hard as Bothwell. And the fight would take away from him all carnal desires so that after beating me he would go away to continue drinking. But Bothwell was a real beast and beating me increased his lust so that he raped me repeatedly. I hated Bothwell. I never accepted his intimacy, not even after he married me, so that he continued to beat me and rape me until he got confirmation that he had made me pregnant. Only then, he did not molest me anymore.'

'Poor dear, I never imagined you had gone through such hell.'

'And no one else should ever know. I could never stand the humiliation if this is known, even if it's known after my death. I had never told anybody but you made the question at a very special time in my life and I believe that you can understand me.'

'It is known of course that Bothwell kidnapped you, but it was always assumed that you were Bothwell mistress and that the kidnapping was arranged between you two.'

'Rape is the vilest crime that can be committed but, unless the victim is murdered by the rapist, it is always assumed that it's the woman that provoked the man. The woman cannot denounce the crime. If she does, she is dishonored and the man is considered the victim of her enticement. You are a woman, but you were convinced that it was my fault that Bothwell kidnapped and raped me. We live in a male dominated society with a male dominated culture. It will continue to be like this for centuries. We can only hope that very gradually humans will be more civilized and women will be equal to men.'

'You made me realize that I've been very wise remaining single. I didn't want a husband that could interfere in my policies to govern England. I witnessed what had happened to my sister Mary. Her Spanish husband got Spain in a war with France and to support him Mary entered England in that war. As a result England lost Calais, for centuries the English foothold on the continent. But I never imagined that husbands could take advantage of their strength to abuse their wives, except in the lower classes.'

'That was my belief too, until I married elegant Henry Stuart, Lord Darnley, my handsome first cousin.'

'You should have married Robert Dudley, Earl of Leicester. He would have helped you to be a great Queen of Scotland. Idiotic Henry instead was your perdition.'

'How could I marry Leicester? He didn't want to marry me; he wanted to marry you.'

'If I had decided to marry, I would have married him. I loved him and he's the best possible husband any woman could have.'

'Why didn't you marry him?'

'That's a very personal question that no one ever dared to ask me before. Since you told me your own most personal secret, I'll tell you mine, but you must swear not to tell anybody.'

'Of course I swear to God not to reveal your secret.'

'Robert and I fell in love when we were 23 years old and my sister Mary was the queen. Both of us had been sent to the Tower. The queen's advisors wanted my execution because I could be considered the Protestant pretender to the crown, but my sister released me after a brief period in the Tower. Felipe II, who then was Consort King Philip of England, agreed with my release. Furthermore, Robert had been sentenced to death because of his part in his father's plot to make Lady Jane Grey the Queen of England. King Philip requested his wife to pardon him and his brother since it was their duty, not their fault, to help his father. I must be grateful to Felipe II all my life for this action. Robert and I had known each other since we were children and when we met again after extreme danger we fell madly in love. We couldn't get married however because his father had arranged for Robert to marry when he was 16 years old. We became lovers but we had to take many precautions so that I wouldn't get pregnant.'

'And then you became Queen of England.'

'Yes and Robert had been my lover for almost two years, but our encounters were very limited since I dreaded becoming pregnant. Amy Robsart, Robert's wife, was very ill, so that I had decided to marry Robert after her death. I still kept correspondence with foreign monarchs that wanted to marry me, but that was strictly for political reasons. I loved Robert and I was going to marry him.'

'And then Amy died under mysterious circumstances.'

'That's right and I couldn't marry Robert because there were rumors that he had killed his wife to marry me. Amy was alone in her home, after giving all her servants permission to leave. That was something very unusual that seems to indicate she was waiting for someone that didn't want to be seen. While she was supposedly alone she fell down the stairs and died. I always suspected William Cecil, the Principal Secretary at that time, of arranging Amy's murder because he was opposed to my marriage with Robert. He wanted me to pick a foreign ruler as a husband. Robert and I were devastated by Amy's mysterious death since we had planned to marry once Amy died consumed by her serious illness.'

'But you kept William Cecil working for you.'

'Of course I did. I had suspicions but these could be wrong since Robert had many enemies. Furthermore Cecil was the most brilliant member of my Privy Council, and he still is. Except for my suspicions about Cecil I believe that, as gossip, you have already heard everything I told you so far.'

'That's right, but it was only gossip. I feel privileged for hearing this from you.'

'Well, you'll be more privileged now because I'll tell you something nobody knows. I didn't tell anybody but I decided to marry Robert anyway. I decided to have relations with Robert as frequently as possible and without any of the precautions I used to take to avoid getting pregnant. I expected that once I got pregnant, I would tell Cecil and he would be the one that would make the announcement of my marriage to Robert. Furthermore, he would have to announce it to England and to the world.'

'And why did you change your decision?'

'I never did. I just never got pregnant. I'm sterile. Since I wasn't going to have a child with Robert I didn't have to marry him. I had Robert as my lover, without giving him the power he would have as Consort King. He's the best man there is and a great lover, but it's been much better to keep him as a subject rather than as a Consort King that would resent any limits to his power.'

'Did you explain your position to your lover?'

'I never did explicitly tell my position to him and for many years he thought I would marry him. He got madly jealous when the brother of Henri III, François, Duke d'Anjou and Alençon, visited England to woo me. It was silly of him because I had no interest in getting a husband, although I was of course flattered by the attentions of a powerful man 22 years younger than me. But Robert really resented me when I proposed you should marry him. I was making a great sacrifice offering him to you. He wasn't a former lover as you might have believed, but my one and only lover at that time. I was giving him a chance to become Consort King of Scotland and you a chance to have a politically experienced, intelligent and honest husband, to help you govern a country where you had many things going against you. Neither Robert nor you appreciated my gesture.'

'And does he continue to be your lover?'

'Not any more. I still love him, but I don't allow him in my bed any more. I was always faithful to him but he didn't reciprocate. But my problem weren't his escapades; I could forgive love affairs, although he had an illegitimate son with a secret lover, but I couldn't forgive him when he was secretly married.'

'I know, he married one of your ladies-in-waiting.'

'Yes, Lettyce Knollys, the widow of Sir Walter Devereux. I brought her to court when her husband died in Ireland. I can understand Robert; he wanted a legitimate son that could inherit his title and his properties. I expelled Lettyce from court, but I kept Robert with me because I love him too much to let him go. Furthermore I need him. I keep with me people I don't like, as Cecil and Walsingham, because I need them. I also need Robert, whom I like so much. But now he has to keep his distance like any other member of the Privy Council.'

'A while ago you said that Leicester was your only lover at the time you proposed he should be my husband. Does "at the time" mean that you have another lover now?'

'Only in my dreams. I'm in a most difficult position since I always considered Robert as my husband before God and our romance started before I was a queen. It's been for political reasons that I couldn't marry him when his wife died and that later I didn't accept him as my husband before men. When he got married, he actually divorced me. Now

I've become a solitary woman. For political reasons I'll never get properly married and I've contemplated taking a lover. There's a handsome courtier that got my attention some time ago spreading his cape over the mud when I was entering Whitehall Palace. He took that crazy action so that my shoes could remain clean. He's brash, but not brash enough to make a proposal to me. I often use a palace in the outskirts of London that has an adjoining room with its correspondent secret door. It was designed by my father so that it has a very complex corridor and no one realizes this room and mine are adjoining rooms. Should I invite him to that palace and suddenly present myself in his room in the middle of the night? That would be too undignified for a queen.'

'That's what kings do.'

'Yes, men are supposed to take the initiative, but I'm not a man.'

'Bothwell was more than brash enough but I hope you'll never get that kind of suitor.'

'God forbid, but some men that seem attracted to us might be actually attracted to power, not us. That might well be the case of the handsome man with the muddy cape. We have many things to talk about and I don't wish to interrupt our conversation to dine with Sir Amyas. If you agree, I'll order that dinner for the two of us should be brought here.'

'I certainly agree.'

After the interruption for ordering dinner, Elizabeth restarted the conversation.

'Lord Darnley, your second husband, was your perdition. Not only did he mistreat you, but he prepared a stage in which Bothwell mistreated you more and at the same time he made you antagonize the people. You told me a while ago that Bothwell made you pregnant. I didn't know that.'

'Yes, my two pregnancies were most difficult to me. During

the first one I was beaten three times by the baby's father. After the third beating I expelled him from the royal palace I was using. I had intended to give him the crown matrimonial with parliamentary approval, but changed my mind after the beatings. Darnley became then an assiduous customer in brothels and got infected with syphilis. When I was in my sixth month of pregnancy one evening he entered the palace with a group of rebel nobles that bribed my guard. I was having dinner with friends and they interrupted our meal and brought my secretary, David Rizzio to the dining room. They accused him of being my lover and had him killed in front of me. He was stabbed 59 times by the nobles. The rebel nobles had taken over my palace, Holyrood Palace, and said that Darnley was now the king and that I would be judged and executed the next day. I was locked in my bedroom. I managed to escape through a window after making a sort of rope tying up a series of bed sheets. Loyal servants got me a horse. Accompanied by a group of servants I fled to Dunbar, where the majority of the nobles pledged to support me. I thought I would have a miscarriage but kept my baby. I returned to Edinburgh and gave birth to my son James in June 1566. My son reached his 20th birthday last year.'

'After you escaped from Holyrood Palace, the people supported you. With the people's support you had legitimate power and the majority of the nobles had to support you. But Lord Darnley had to be tried for treason.'

'Darnley was the father of the future king and I decided not to do anything about him, except to keep him away from me. His syphilis got worse and he had to remain in bed.'

'It would have been a scandal to condemn the Consort King to death for high treason, but it was necessary to do it. After his death sentence you could pardon him, condemn him to exile and request the annulment of your marriage to him to both the Presbyterian Church of Scotland and the Catholic Church.'

'I thought about it but I couldn't request the annulment of

my marriage to my son's father nor accuse him as a traitor. I couldn't accuse the rebel nobles without accusing Darnley. I simply accepted the repentance of the rebel nobles and Darnley and let matters stand with no fuss. Perhaps I didn't live up to the position God had given me to rule Scotland.'

'You reacted as any 23 years old young woman who just had her first son. I told you that there's no such thing as a divine right to rule. Of course I support the idea, in my own benefit, but I don't believe in it. I'll tell you of someone else who didn't believe in it, my grandfather, your great grandfather, Henry VII. He lived in France since he was 3 years old. His family had to move to France during "The War of the Roses" because they were supporters of the Red Rose House of Lancaster that was defeated by the White Rose House of York. By blood, Henry Tudor was distantly related to the House of Lancaster because his great great grandfather was the third son of King Edward III. Just on that basis, he claimed he was entitled to the English Crown from the Lancaster side. And this claim was accepted after his army defeated the army of the ruling king, Richard III, who died in the battle.'

'I understand your point now. Richard III, of the House of York, was not supported by the people. It was believed he had assassinated his two nephews to become King of England.'

'That's right. And my grandfather was wise enough to marry the surviving niece, Elizabeth of York. This way he united the House of Lancaster, of the red rose, with the House of York, of the white rose, creating the House of Tudor of the red and white rose. He pacified England after the long "War of the Roses". People prefer to have peace rather than war and supported him. Henry Tudor proclaimed himself Henry VII and no one examined his ancestry to check if there were any nobles more closely related to Edward III. Believe me, there were certainly many nobles much more closely related to Edward III than our ancestor.'

Elizabeth and Mary had to interrupt their conversation at this point because servants requested permission to enter to lay out the table for their dinner.

During dinner, Elizabeth conducted the conversation to make it light so that Mary could relax and feel at ease. After an abundant dinner, of a type that Mary had not seen for a long time, Elizabeth started again on the subject of Mary's life, interrupted with the comments about Henry VII and his disregard for the divine right of kings.

'What happened after your son James was born?'

'My husband returned to Edinburgh. I didn't accept him at the palace with me, so that he settled at nearby Kirk o' Field, with a servant, in a Royal Palace that had been an old abbey. He was ill and staying in bed and I visited him there, out of pity.'

'And Bothwell and other nobles murdered him there. The plot was so obvious it was a disaster.'

'I have already told you that, not only I was not Bothwell's lover, but I hated him. He didn't plot to kill Darnley. A group of nobles had made a plot to put my dear brother, Morey as Regent, after killing me. Bothwell had to instrument the plot. Darnley also had to be killed so that no one could say that after my death he should be king. I was staying at the palace in Kirk o' Field, where I had gone to visit my son's father, Henry Stuart, Lord Darnley, who was ill in bed there. When Darnley and I were in the same palace was the ideal time to kill both of us. They filled the basement of the palace with powder to make it blow when both Darnley and I were sleeping there. Bothwell was the leader of the plot to kill me. Fortunately, I was invited to a party and wasn't in the palace when it was blown apart. Darnley was warned by his servant and escaped from the palace. Both of them were strangled on another property after leaving the grounds of the palace. I ordered Bothwell to go to trial by Parliament, but his friends were a majority in Parliament and he was declared innocent.'

'And then Bothwell thought he had total power and could do whatever he wanted.'

'That's right and he decided to betray Moray and take power as king himself. To do it he decided to marry me and have a son or daughter with me. I now believe that once the boy or girl was born, he would kill me and my son James, crown the new born and govern Scotland in his name as Regent. He accused himself of infidelity and divorced his wife. Then he kidnapped and raped me. Finally, he married me.'

'And the people didn't accept this marriage and turned against him and you. No one realized you were a victim. You shouldn't have thought of your honor as a woman. You were the Queen of Scotland and you should have refused a marriage that would consolidate the power of a murderer over your kingdom. But I don't blame you; you reacted as a 23 year old woman with a just born baby. I can see what you should have done when I'm 53 years old and have nearly 30 years of experience as a queen, but at 23 I might have reacted just as you did.'

'But I wasn't free to make any decision. I became Bothwell's prisoner. As you say, the people have the power. The people had always loved me and supported me as queen. That's why I always had a majority of the nobles supporting me. The Scot nobles are not like your English nobles loyal to the crown. They are constantly forming different alliances to increase their own power. I wanted a husband to have a man that would help me to have control. Instead, he became another noble to participate in plots.'

'I had never learned that Bothwell had plotted to kill you.'

'When the nobles that supported Bothwell realized that the people were against him, they turned against him and confronted his army. When Bothwell found his friends had deserted him he escaped from Scotland without a fight. The nobles took me prisoner; they placed me at Loch Leven Castle and made me abdicate in favor of my son James. I had a miscarriage and lost twins. My half-brother, James Stewart, Earl of Moray, took power as Regent.'

'Then you escaped from Loch Leven and raised an army but Moray defeated you so that you took refuge in England. I had no idea that your married life had been so miserable. Most women envy you because of your handsome last two husbands, but both of them were wife beaters. And your first husband was just a boy you must have regarded with sisterly love only.'

'You're completely wrong about my first husband, François, the love of my life. I was so happy the years I spent with him that God must have given me the other two husbands as compensation. I never felt sisterly love towards him. I met him when I was 6 years old and he was 5. When we met we were told we were going to be husband and wife, so that I always thought of him as my future husband, not my brother. I had a delightful infancy with the King of France, Henri II, and Diane de Poitiers acting as my parents, but I knew that my father was the late King of Scotland and that my mother governed Scotland in my name, as Regent, since I was the Queen of Scotland.'

'But Diane de Poitiers was the mistress of Henri II. His wife was Catherine de Medici.'

'When Henri II was not working, Diane was his permanent companion. Catherine was in charge of her several children, but Diane was in charge of me. And Diane knew everything about love and taught me everything gradually, starting at an early age. Neither one of my two adult husbands was interested in love, but I had a wonderful year of married love with an adorable 15 year old boy. Henri II had planned that we should marry when François reached the age of 17, but the boy couldn't wait so long until our complete union and begged his father to let him marry with no delay. At 15 this boy was already a very handsome and tall young man. I asked Diane to help us, she did and we were married immediately.'

'And you had a wonderful married relationship with the young boy and an inferno with the two handsome men; just the reverse of what everyone thinks. But from what you've told me I'm now puzzled about the relationship between Diane and Catherine.'

'Diane was older than Henri. She used to take care of him when he was a boy but she was very beautiful and Henri always loved her. Catherine was much younger but Henri didn't find her attractive and hardly ever was intimate with her. That's why after 10 years of marriage he had no children, no heir. Diane suddenly realized the situation and told Henri he had to be intimate with his wife every night. Catherine gave Henri 10 children the next ten years. When Henri died accidentally in a tournament, Catherine expelled Diane from court and I never saw her again.'

'Catherine should have been grateful to Diane for sharing Henri II with her.'

'And how was your own childhood.'

'Change was the only permanent thing in my childhood. I have a faint memory, so faint that perhaps it's only my imagination, of being loved as a child, but my father never loved me and I was told by courtiers that didn't like me that I was a bastard daughter. They said the same of my sister Mary. I remember vaguely the baptism of my brother Edward. From that day onwards Mary and I received better treatment. Mary was the godmother in the baptism and I participated in the ceremony. Then we had a situation in which Edward was the favorite because he was a boy, but Mary and I were not mistreated. We both accepted that it was natural that Edward should be the favorite because he was a boy and he was the heir, while we were only girls and couldn't be loved as much as he was.'

'And you were still a child when your father died and

Edward became King of England.'

'I was 12 at the time. A brother of the late mother of Edward, Jane Seymour, became Regent. His name was Edward Seymour but the important character of this period for me was his brother, ambitious Thomas Seymour. The ambitious man took as wife the widow of my father, a very nice woman called Katharine Parr, who had been my father's eighth wife. Shortly after the marriage, Thomas and Katharine took two girls with royal blood under their care, Jane Grey and I.'

'Did you like to be with them?'

'I certainly did because I was only 13 years old and my caretaker, Thomas, gave clear signs of being romantically attracted to me. I was extremely flattered because I felt I was so attractive that a very powerful man had fallen madly in love with me and that love made him risk everything'.

'He was obviously scheming to make you pregnant, to make his son King of England and govern as Regent.'

'That might have been his plan, but instead of raping me like your Bothwell (18), he kissed and caressed me making me feel wonderful. He also had an alternative plan marrying young King Edward with Jane Grey after winning Jane's total confidence.'

'What happened then?'

'Katharine surprised him embracing and kissing me. She didn't denounce her husband but made arrangements so that I would be transferred to the care of another family, that of Sir Anthony Denny. Shortly afterwards, Katharine died giving birth to a son and almost immediately Thomas sent me a letter proposing to marry me.'

'Did you refuse?'

'I was only 14 years old, but I had seen too many plots and executions around me. I wanted to accept but realized that it would be extremely dangerous to marry Thomas in secret, so that I answered that our marriage would require previous acceptance of the union by the Privy Council. Thomas decided to put his plans aside rather than request permission to the Privy Council, but shortly afterwards the Council requested his presence to question him about some suspicious attitudes.'

Mary remained silent, expecting Elizabeth to continue.

'Thomas should have attended the Council's request, since his brother would certainly have protected him, but he decided to fight fire with fire, making a coup. He attempted to kidnap Edward, was caught in the attempt and executed. In the investigation his correspondence with me was found. The Council interrogated me thoroughly since several members believed I might be pregnant. I assured the Council that I had never been intimate with Thomas, although he tried to make me believe he was in love with me.'

Elizabeth and Mary continued their conversation all night until daybreak.

CHAPTER IV
LAST TWIST OF THE PLOT

Francis Walsingham irrupted suddenly into the office of William Cecil.

'Excuse me, Sir William; I need to meet urgently with you.'

Two assistants of Cecil were at his office discussing a matter concerning the Treasury.

'Do you expect our meeting to be rather short, Francis?'

'I'm afraid not, Sir William. It'll probably take the rest of the day and it's very important. Regrettably, something happened that requires our immediate and undivided attention.'

Cecil addressed his assistants. 'Gentlemen, you've heard what the Principal Secretary just said. We must interrupt our meeting and I'll expect you tomorrow afternoon at 3 o'clock.'

After the assistants left, Cecil talked. 'What's the problem, Francis?'

'I just received a message sent by carrier pigeon. Take a look at it.'

Walsingham showed the message written by Thomas Philips that afternoon.

QUEEN ELIZABETH HAS ARRIVED AT FOTHERINGHAY CASTLE TODAY FEBRUARY 3 AT 3 O'CLOCK IN THE AFTERNOON.

'It's fortunate that you took the precaution of having an agent in Fotheringhay Castle.'

'Fortunate is not the right word. I'm a careful man. I'm sure you'll agree with me that we must take immediate action. Obviously, the queen is talking with Mary Stuart right now. She'll ask Mary her version of the trial. We know her version. She said at the trial that the letter she received from

Babington didn't say anything about assassinating Queen Elizabeth. Our queen, having to choose between the version given by her cousin and that given by me, will believe her cousin. She'll pardon Mary and the deposed Queen of Scotland will continue to be the rallying point for Catholic plots that necessarily will include the murder of Queen Elizabeth.'

'Do you already have a plan to propose me?'

'Yes, Thomas Phelippes must sign the Execution Warrant and we must search and find the Queen's Seal, so that the warrant can be properly legalized and sent to Fotheringhay. We must make arrangements so that the execution takes place the day the queen travels back to London.'

'But the queen will be furious at us for forging her signature on the Execution Warrant. We'll be sent to the gallows.'

'Not you, just me; maybe Phelippes too. Unfortunately by sending Sir Thomas Salisbury to be drawn, hanged and quartered I've confirmed the precedent that knights without a nobility title don't qualify to be beheaded and must be hanged.

Fortunately now the queen herself has set a new tradition and traitors are now hanged until dead. I'll die by hanging, not by evisceration.'

'And if regardless of your good intentions to preserve me I'm condemned to death, being Lord Burghley my head will be chopped off. But perhaps your information is wrong. The queen slept at her rooms here, in Whitehall, the night before yesterday. She can't have arrived at Fotheringhay today, at 3 o'clock.'

'Yes, she can. This is the 16th century, the age of change. There are new types of carriages, widely used in the continent, with springs that give stability and allow a fast ride. I have one myself. Using it I've covered 20 leagues in one day. The palace must at least have another one and Fotheringhay is only about 30 leagues away.'

'Then the queen will need two days to return. You'll have to request your man in Fotheringhay to advise us immediately as soon as she starts her trip back to London. We must send the warrant to him as soon as possible. Also we must arrange for at least two important noblemen to be ready, with short notice, to be present at Fotheringhay Castle to witness the execution of Mary Stuart.'

'I've already sent a message by carrier pigeon to my man in Fotheringhay telling him to advise me immediately as soon as the queen leaves the castle. When we get a reasonable warrant, we'll send it using a messenger rider escorted by soldiers. I have a very good one. He carries papers that allow him to change horses anywhere in England when he needs to do it. He has already delivered papers to my man in Fotheringhay, so that point is fully covered. In regard to witnesses, I suggest Shrewsbury and Kent. Kent doesn't live too far away and Shrewsbury is currently staying at a small castle he has in the same county as Fotheringhay, Peterborough. Philips, my man in Fotheringhay, can advise them to be ready and advise them again when they have to take action.'

'I'll call Davison now to get the unsigned warrant.'

After Cecil rang a bell, a footman came to his office. 'Tom, please ask Sir William Davison to come to see me urgently.'

While waiting for Davison, Cecil and Walsingham discussed other matters unrelated to Mary Stuart but soon they were interrupted by a knock at the door and the entrance of Elizabeth's secretary. After the exchange of salutations, Cecil made his request.

'Sir William, could you please bring us the Execution Warrant that the queen must sign.'

'I'm afraid I can't, Sir. The queen requested it and she hasn't returned it to me.'

'That's very strange. She was supposed to request it to sign it.'

'That's what I thought when she asked for it. I told her I was glad she had decided to sign it when I gave it to her, but she told me she hadn't decided anything yet. She said she wanted to read it and that she was going to keep it in case she might need to read it again.'

Both Cecil and Walsingham remained silent for a long while after hearing Davison. Walsingham was the first to react.

'William, it's most unlikely that the queen would have taken the warrant with her when she left on her current trip. Would you help us to search her rooms to find it and to find her seal?'

'That's completely out of the question Francis. We cannot search the queen's rooms while she's away on a trip. I'm her secretary and guarding her rooms while she's out is my responsibility.'

Walsingham stood up to answer. He spoke slowly in a very soft voice, with a subtle but distinctly menacing undertone. 'William, we've been friends for a very long time and we've been talking to each other on a first name basis for years. However, I must remind you that your position at the palace is that you work for the Principal Secretary. You work for me. I assigned you the task of taking care of the queen as her personal secretary, but you work for me. When I give you an order I don't bark like a Sergeant at Arms. I ask you politely, as if I were asking a friend to help me. But you must understand that I'm giving you an order and you must always obey. Have I been clear enough, William?'

Davison's face became red and after a pause he answered. 'Yes Francis, of course. In fact I was thinking aloud that the queen would make me responsible if she objects to our search when she returns.'

'I'll also be in this search party, Sir William, and that should make you feel at ease. Regrettably, the queen is away at a time when we must take immediate action, so we must act in her behalf.'

'We need a fourth member, one of my men called William, like both of you. He knows a lot about locks. Wait for me a minute. I'll go to the corridor to ask a lackey to bring my William here.'

Cecil, Walsingham, Davison and the man Walsingham called "his William", entered the Whitehall Palace rooms of Queen Elizabeth.

'We must start at the room where the queen has her private papers. Please take us to that room, William.' Walsingham was addressing William Davison. Once in the room that the queen called her study, they noticed a small very elegant desk.

'This desk is the most promising place to start our search. I'll see if I can open the three drawers.'

After trying to open the three drawers and finding them locked, Walsingham talked to "his William". 'Can you open these drawers without causing any damage, William?'

William had brought some tools with him, since Walsingham had sent for him advising him he would have to open locked drawers and doors. Quite rapidly, William opened the three drawers and stepped aside. He knew that he was not supposed to look at what was inside the drawers.

Cecil went rapidly through the series of annotations, on paper, made in the queen's handwriting, but there was no parchment in the first drawer. The second drawer did not look too promising since only white, unused sheets of paper were guarded there, but one sheet appeared to be thicker than the others. Cecil extracted a parchment and after reading it gave it to Walsingham with a triumphal gesture.

'William, please lock the three drawers again.'

Then, the three Williams and Walsingham left Queen Elizabeth's rooms.

'You can go back to whatever you were doing before I called you.' Walsingham had addressed "his William". He and Davison returned with Cecil to his office. Once they were there, Cecil spoke to Davison.

'You have performed a great service to England, Sir William. You looked at the parchment when I gave it to the Principal Secretary. The Execution Warrant has been signed by the queen and it has the Royal Seal on it. It's very important that this warrant should now be in the hands of the Privy Council rather than in a locked drawer. You may leave us now.'

'Goodbye, Sir William. Goodbye, Francis.'

'Goodbye, William.'

Once Davison left, the two highest officers of Queen Elizabeth were alone to discuss how to implement the execution of Mary Stuart while the queen travelled from Fotheringhay to London.

'Well, since we don't have to forge the queen's signature, our lives are not at risk now.'

'I hope you're right, Sir William.'

'She'll be mad at us, since she'll probably come with the idea of destroying the Execution Warrant and signing a Pardon Warrant. But Davison has given us a duly signed and sealed warrant. Besides, we haven't received any specific instructions from her. Therefore even if we're sent to a Star Chamber trial, the only accusation that can be made against us is that we acted in her absence. Knowing how much she dreaded this action, to which she was obliged by a decision made by Parliament, we can say we acted mercifully to limit her agony. We are saving her from the actual action of delivering her signed decision.'

'The first thing we have to do is to arrange for a meeting of the Privy Council to approve the implementation of the Execution Warrant. We must convene that meeting for this evening.'

'One Privy Counselor we must not invite is Leicester. Not only will he never approve that we should take action in the absence of the queen, but he'll do everything possible to convince the other counselors to act like him. As Master of the Horse, he must have made the queen's travel arrangements. I'm sure he knows she's meeting with Mary Stuart as we speak.'

'This very evening we can count on the presence of John Whitgift, Lord Archbishop; Christopher Hatton, Lord Chancellor; Henry Carey, Lord Chamberlain and James Croft, Mr. Comptroller. Adding the two of us we have a total of seven counselors,' said Cecil.

'You're forgetting two good friends of yours, Sir Thomas Sackville, Lord Buckhurst; and Sir Francis Knollys. Both of them are in London today and they can come to a Privy Council meeting this evening. That makes nine, more than half of the 17 members of the Council. We shouldn't inform anyone else. We also have to tell all those that participate in this meeting that they shouldn't mention it to anybody until after the execution takes place.'

'How could I forget Buckhurst and Knollys? Buckhurst is ideal to travel to Fotheringhay to give the news of the execution to Sir Amyas and the deposed queen. You said you've got one of the new carriages that can travel 20 leagues a day. Could Buckhurst use it? Leaving tomorrow, he could be at Fotheringhay on February 5.'

'I believe it's a good idea to send Buckhurst to tell Mary Stuart she'll be executed, but he should be warned that the queen is travelling and that to minimize her agony over this matter, the execution must take place the day she's due to arrive in London.'

'That's right, and the warrant must be sent to your man in Fotheringhay. Chances are that the queen will stay at least two more days with Mary and that Buckhurst will arrive just on time; but he cannot go straight to Fotheringhay Castle. I'll tell him to go to stay with Shrewsbury.'

'Fine.'

'Could we have ten counselors? It sounds much more definite than nine.'

'We can't include Davison; he'll certainly tell the others that the queen isn't in London and that the Privy Council shouldn't act without her consent.'

'I know the right man to reach ten, Darby Cobham. He lives in London and will raise no objections. He always follows my lead.'

'Excellent idea. And we can even make it eleven counselors. We were forgetting about Lord Howard of Effingham, who has even dared to request the prompt execution of her cousin to the queen.'

'Since we don't need eleven counselors you can stay home. We don't need your vote, Francis.'

'What do you mean?'

'We've done a very dangerous thing today and the queen will be furious at us when she learns about it. She'll be particularly angry with you. Go home, say that you're ill and get into bed. Stay in bed claiming you're ill until after the queen returns. I can handle the Privy Council meeting by myself. If you go to a Star Chamber trial and you didn't vote in today's Privy Council meeting, you can't be found guilty. When the queen realizes she cannot take legal action against you, she won't do anything against me.'

Elizabeth spent three more days exchanging confidences with Mary Stuart. As a queen, she had a very good relationship and even a friendship with most of her ladies-in-waiting. However they were not at her level and she had to be reserved when speaking with them. It was different with Mary Stuart. She was like a younger sister, lost long ago.

There was a special empathy between the two of them. Furthermore, since they had only heard about each other but had never met, they had a lot to talk about exchanging confidences.

The first night they did not sleep at all. They spent the entire night talking to each other and did not stop until daybreak. The second day they had to sleep all morning and started at noon with a lunch that had to double as breakfast. The third and fourth day they were together all day from 9 o'clock in the morning till 10 o'clock at night.

In the evening of the fourth day, Elizabeth had to talk about the future, not the past.

'Mary, I have to return to London since I have a kingdom that requires my attention. Tomorrow we'll have breakfast together and then I'll start my return trip. Once I return I'll sign a Pardon Warrant; but what will you do?'

'I'll make a formal statement declaring I recognize you as the legitimate Queen of England, that I have no desire to be your successor and that I hope you'll survive me and not the reverse. I'll also say that if I should survive and Parliament would approve me as your successor, I would maintain the Church of England as the official church of this land and I would propose to Parliament the union of the kingdoms of Scotland and England. If my proposal should be approved, I would abdicate the English throne in favor of my son, James.'

Elizabeth smiled when she saw that Mary had reacted exactly like she believed he would. 'That statement should satisfy Walsingham and Cecil and you can come to live in Nonsuch Palace (19), where I live most of the time.'

The next morning, February 7, 1587, Queen Elizabeth left Fotheringhay Castle at 8 o'clock in the morning. Immediately afterwards Thomas Philips sent a message by carrier pigeon advising Walsingham of the queen's departure. Philips did not have to wait for further instructions from Walsingham since he already had his orders. He prepared his horse, going first to the nearby castle where Shrewsbury had decided to stay until the Mary Stuart matter was over. Buckhurst was staying there as Shrewsbury's guest waiting for Philips' notification. From there, Philips went on to advise Kent.

At 7 o'clock that evening, Shrewsbury and Buckhurst arrived by coach to Fotheringhay Castle followed by many more men on horseback. Philips was waiting at the door and gave the Execution Warrant to Buckhurst.

'Here's the Execution Warrant a messenger escorted by ten soldiers gave me a few days ago. Regarding the Earl of Kent, he told me he'll be here tomorrow morning before 7 o'clock.'

The two noblemen requested the butler to see Sir Amyas Paulet.

'Good evening, Sir George, Sir Thomas; what brings you here?'

'Good evening, Sir Amyas.'

'Good evening, Sir Amyas. I bring the Execution Warrant for Mary Stuart. Sir George has been kind enough to lend me six carpenters, waiting outside, on horseback, to prepare every-thing needed for the execution. The Privy Council has instructed me to request you it should take place tomorrow morning at 8 o'clock.'

Sir Amyas was flabbergasted. That morning Queen Elizabeth and Mary Stuart had said goodbye to each other with the idea of meeting again in London quite soon, acting as if they were the best of friends.

'There must be some kind of mistake, Sir Thomas.'

'There's no mistake. I was present at the Privy Council Meeting that approved the Execution Warrant I bring. Here it is.'

While reading the warrant, Sir Amyas wondered if it could

be possible that Queen Elizabeth would be so devious as to make Mary Stuart believe she was pardoned while she had already ordered her execution.

'On what date did the Privy Council meet?'

'The evening of February 3.'

Amyas Paulet realized that the queen did not know anything about the Privy Council Meeting, since February 3 was the date she had arrived at Fotheringhay Castle. Walsingham had one of his men at the castle, a young man called Philips, who kept carrier pigeons; he must have informed him. Upon receiving the information the Principal Secretary realized the queen would like Mary Stuart and would pardon her. Walsingham and Cecil would have then decided to proceed with the execution during the time the queen travelled back to London. The warrant must have been signed by the queen before the trip. Then she must have repented and resolved she had to meet her before deciding on her fate. He spoke.

'There's no rush. The former Queen of Scotland has been a prisoner in England for nearly 20 years. Let's set a date for next week and decide carefully about the best place to erect properly a strong scaffold.'

'I'm here representing the Privy Council, Sir Amyas, with specific instructions to implement the execution on February 8, at about 8 o'clock in the morning. Outside, we have six carpenters ready to erect a scaffold that's already made and will be rapidly assembled. We also have with us the necessary amount of black cloth to drape it. We have everything, the three steps needed to reach the platform, the block, a cushion and stools for the witnesses. Of course, the executioner and his assistant are among the horsemen that came with us. Sir Thomas has come as an official witness of the execution. Sir Henry Grey, Earl of Kent, will arrive tomorrow morning as another official witness.'

Sir Amyas was very upset about what was going on. He had been expecting a rapid execution of Mary Stuart after she was found guilty in her trial. But an execution decided by the Privy Council during the queen's absence, with strict orders to be implemented during that absence, was obviously an immoral palatial intrigue. It was unlikely that Buckhurst and Shrewsbury should be aware that the Queen of England had spent four days talking with the former Queen of Scotland. Buckhurst had very definite instructions from Cecil, but might decide to wait a few days if he told him about the queen's visit. However he could not tell Buckhurst about the queen's visit because she made him promise he wouldn't tell anybody.

'I see that you have everything perfectly covered. I'll inform Mary Stuart about your visit.'

Paulet knocked at the door of Mary Stuart's suit of rooms. 'Good evening, Madam.'

'Good evening, Sir Amyas. It's very strange that you should come to see me at this hour. I was getting ready to go to sleep early tonight, after staying talking with the queen until late these past few nights.'

'I'm afraid I bring bad news tonight. There's a gentleman that must speak with you immediately, Sir Thomas Sackville, Lord Buckhurst. He comes representing the Privy Council.'

Mary remembered Buckhurst quite well. He was a member of the commission that judged her for high treason and condemned her to death. She knew Buckhurst hated her. His visit representing the Privy Council could have only one meaning, notification of her execution. Her enemies must have been informed that Elizabeth was visiting her. Realizing she was going to be pardoned, they decided to take action while the queen was travelling and could not stop the execution. After a rather long interval, she answered.

'I understand, Sir Amyas. I'll be waiting for him; send him to talk with me.'

Several ladies-in-waiting were with Mary Stuart and she talked to them.

'Dear friends, leave me now. I must receive an unexpected visitor that's been sent by the Privy Council.'

The women left without daring to say anything after seeing Mary's somber expression.

A few minutes later Buckhurst knocked at the door of Mary Stuart's rooms.

'Good evening, Madam.'

'Good evening, Sir Thomas.'

'Madam, the Privy Council has given me the painful duty to inform you that the date for the execution has been set for February 8, that is tomorrow, and the time will be 8 o'clock in the morning.'

Mary was prepared for the words she heard and remained with a serious expression, showing no feeling. She did not want to give her enemies the satisfaction of seeing her distressed.

'In that case, I must speak with an old family friend that lives nearby, Monsieur De Preau. Kindly ask Sir Amyas, who knows his address, to ask him to come and visit me.'

'Yes, Madam. Good night now.'

A few minutes later, Sir Amyas came to see Mary Stuart. He spoke bluntly.

'Madam, I know this is a most difficult moment, but I also know that Monsieur De Preau is a Catholic priest and that you want him to come for your confession. I cannot allow a Catholic priest to enter a household under my jurisdiction. I can offer you the services of my good friend, the Dean of Peterborough.'

'I'm asking you for my friend and you offer me your friend instead. Thank you, Sir Amyas, but I have no interest in meeting your friend.'

'I'm sorry Madam, but perhaps you would accept the visit of the Bishop of Peterborough.'

'I have no interest in meeting the Protestant Bishop of Peterborough.'

'As you wish, Madam. Will you have dinner tonight with your ladies-in-waiting?'

'Just a very light supper, with them of course and as early as possible, if you please.'

'I'll arrange immediately for your supper, Madam. Good night.'

'I wish you can have a good night, Sir Amyas.'

A few minutes later all of Mary Stuart's ladies-in-waiting came to her rooms. All of them were crying and only the former Queen of Scotland remained serene. She went through all her possessions at the castle and distributed these among the ladies, separating a few things for friends abroad.

Sir Amyas knocked at her door again.

'I'm very sorry to have to bother you again, Madam, but I must inform you that I had a serious discussion with Lord Buckhurst about your execution. He had a written authorization of William Cecil to go to the scaffold tomorrow, to tear your dress and leave you in your underwear, so that you could present your neck to the executioner properly. I said I would not allow him to do such thing. If any garment needed to be removed, you had to go to the scaffold with two ladies-in-waiting to help you. After much discussion he accepted. So that you must select two ladies to accompany you. I had to inform you about this so that you can prepare yourself with plenty of time.'

'Thank you Sir Amyas. I see that you acted as an honorable man.'

'Good night, Madam'

'Good night, Sir Amyas'

'You have all heard Sir Amyas. I had been wondering what to wear to go to the scaffold and nothing seemed suitable. Now I know, I'll wear my best dress, a red one I wore only once to go to a party in Kirk o' Field. Going to that party saved my life that time. The palace was blown out to kill me, but I had gone to the party. It's quite suitable that now I should die wearing it. As a party dress it leaves the neck quite widely exposed. On top of it I'll put on my ugliest dress, the black one I use to go to funerals. Elizabeth Curle and Jane Kennedy will accompany me to the platform and remove the black dress. And the malignant spectators that are looking forward to see me half naked in my underwear will be disappointed when they see me wearing my best party dress.'

The light supper, with Mary eating practically nothing, followed. After supper she wrote two letters. The first one was to her priest, De Preau, whom she had only seen once after entering into Sir Amyas care. Suspecting he was a priest, Paulet never allowed a second visit. That letter to De Preau was her confession. The second one was to her brother-in-law from her first marriage, Henri III, King of France. Between the two letters she wrote her will. When she ended, she was dressed by Elizabeth and Jane. At 2 o'clock, she just lay on her bed, fully dressed, without attempting to sleep.

In her thoughts, she was comforted with the knowledge that both her son, James VI of Scotland and her brother-in-law, Henri III of France, had written to Elizabeth requesting her to pardon Mary. Elizabeth had told Mary about these requests. She had not answered the letters yet, but intended to do it after her return to London. It was nice to think that she and

Elizabeth had finally met and that Elizabeth had decided to pardon her. Unfortunately, it was too late to save her from the plans of her enemies. And she was fully aware that it was entirely her own fault, not Elizabeth's, they had not met before.

Mary got ready for the execution quite early in the morning, aided by Elizabeth Curle and Jane Kennedy. Shortly before 8 o'clock she was taken to the Great Hall of the castle, accompanied by the two ladies-in-waiting. Waiting there were Sir James Melville, a Scottish diplomat that was helping Mary as her secretary since she came to Fotheringhay Castle; Bourgoing, her physician; Jacques Gervais, her surgeon; Didier, her faithful porter of many years; Sir Amyas Paulet (20) and the Protestant Dean of Peterborough. On the scaffold, sitting on three stools, were Sir Thomas Sackville, Lord Buckhurst, Sir George Talbot, Earl of Shrewsbury and Sir Henry Grey, Earl of Kent. Standing on the scaffold were the executioner and his assistant, their heads covered by masks. He scaffold that had been erected the previous night was not too high and it was reached by three steps. It was draped in black and in the center was the block, with a pillow for Mary to kneel before it.

Mary was dressed in a black satin dress, embroidered with black velvet. The only note of color was in the purple trim of the black acorn buttons. On her head she wore a white veil, edged with lace, which flowed down her back almost to the ground. Her shoes were of black leather. She held a crucifix and a prayer book in her hand. She had a pomander chain on her neck, a type of chain widely used in those days to carry aromatic herbs. She had also a silver chain with a large "Agnus Dei" medallion.

John Palmer, Dean of Peterborough (21), asked Mary to read her prayers from a Protestant book he was handling her. She refused, opened her own book of prayers and started to pray. Undeterred the Dean competed with her reading aloud at the same time in a louder voice. Mary was very pleased. Palmer was making her a Catholic martyr.

Afterwards, following custom, the executioners asked Mary for her forgiveness. "I forgive you with all my heart, for now I hope you shall make an end of all my troubles" was her answer.

Before the decapitation came the moment Mary was eagerly expecting. She had to remove her outer garments. This had to be a moment of humiliation, instead she smiled and joked saying "she never had such grooms before... nor ever put off her clothes before such a company" She was aided by her ladies-in-waiting to remove her black dress revealing that underneath she was wearing her best party dress. Mary then positioned her neck on the wooden execution block and extended her arms to show she was ready. "In manus tuas, Domine, commendo spiritum meum" (Into thy hands, O' Lord, I commend my spirit) she said just before the axe came down.

The executioner missed the neck and the axe fell on the back of Mary's head. Mary, still alive, whispered in pain, "sweet Jesus".

The executioner gave a second blow that might have killed Mary but did not severe her head completely. Only after he used his axe as a saw to cut a remnant of the neck, did Mary's head fall on the scaffold.

The executioner then went to pick up the head and show it to the audience by holding it up with one hand by the hair, as customary. However, when he grabbed Mary's hair he picked only a wig and the head rolled on the scaffold. The audience could then see that after the years of imprisonment Mary's hair had become gray and she was wearing it very short with a wig on top.

Regardless of the blunders of her enemies, Mary died in a most dignified way.

Anyway Walsingham had succeeded; the last twist of the

convoluted "Babington Plot" had taken place and Mary Stuart was finally dead.

EPILOGUE

Elizabeth arrived at Whitehall Palace at 4 o'clock in the afternoon of February 8, 1587. About an hour later, refreshed and having changed her clothing, she went to her study. She opened the mid drawer of her stylish desk and looked for the Execution Warrant she wanted to destroy, but it was not there. She was certain she had put it right there but, just in case she was confused, she looked in the other two drawers. Since it was not where she thought, she rang a bell to call a footman.

'Good afternoon, Your Majesty. Did you call me?'

'Yes, George. Please ask Sir William Davison to come and see me immediately.'

About ten minutes later Davison entered the study. His face was red because he had guessed the reason the queen was requesting his immediate presence.

'Good afternoon, Your Majesty. What can I do for you?'

'You should be able to clarify a matter that's bothering me. A most important document that I placed in this desk is missing. Do you know if anyone entered my study while I was travelling?'

'Yes, Your Majesty, Sir William Cecil and Sir Francis Walsingham entered the study with me to look for the Execution Warrant of Mary Stuart. Once it was found they took it and left.'

'How could they find it in a locked drawer?'

'Sir Francis brought with him one of his men with special tools to open locked drawers and doors.'

'Do you mean to say that you used your position as my secretary to guide a search party that wanted to find one carefully guarded document that I didn't want anyone to see?'

'I wouldn't put it that way, Your Majesty. The two most important members of your government, Sir William Cecil and Sir Francis Walsingham, were most upset because they didn't have instructions from you about the execution of Mary Stuart and you were travelling. They wanted to know if you had signed the warrant they had given to me. I told them I gave it to you.'

At this point, Davison became silent.

'Go on, Davison.'

The queen was not calling him William, as she always did, but Davison.

'Sir Francis ordered me to help him and Sir William to find the warrant.'

'And you obeyed him because you value his orders more highly than mine.'

'He's the Principal Secretary. His orders are your orders.'

'What you did was worse than disobeying my orders. To satisfy a man that supposedly works for me you violated my intimacy and searched my personal papers in locked drawers, picking the locks with the help of a professional thief. What happened after your crime?'

'I didn't do anything. Sir Francis and Sir William then convened a meeting of the Privy Council, but they forgot to tell me, so I didn't participate in that meeting.'

'Have you learned what was decided in that meeting?'

'Yes, Your Majesty. Darby Cobham told me. The warrant signed by you was presented and the Privy Council had to implement the warrant fixing the place, date and time of the execution. As witnesses, the Earls of Kent and Shrewsbury were designated and a member of the council, Lord Buckhurst was selected to notify the former Queen of Scotland.'

'You haven't told me the date and time.'

'The execution took place today, at 8 o'clock in the morning.'

The queen was devastated by the news she received from Davison, but controlled her expression, deadly serious.

'You'll be punished severely for what you did, Davison.'

'But, Your Majesty, we were aware of how much pain these necessary steps would cause you. We acted in your absence to save you from that pain.'

The queen rang a bell and the footman assigned to her appeared immediately.

'What can I do for you, Your Majesty?'

'Send the captain of the Yeomen of the Queen's Body Guard to talk with me.'

'I'll do it immediately, Your Majesty.'

Elizabeth talked to Davison as soon as the footman left.

'Davison, wait for my orders in the corridor outside, standing next to the door. I can't stand your presence and I don't want to see you ever again.'

Once she was alone, Elizabeth cried her heart out. After crying for about five minutes she started to calm down, since the captain of the guard should be arriving any minute now. After a while she dried her tears, went in front of a mirror and fixed her makeup. Just when she had finished, there was a knock at her door.

'You may come in.'

The captain of the guard entered the queen's study.

'I'm told you want to see me, Your Majesty.'

Yes, Captain. There's a man outside called Davison.'

'I know him, Your Majesty.'

'Take him to the Tower for flagrant disobedience of my orders. He should remain in prison until I decide what to do with him. Ask the footman outside to come in. That's all,

Captain.'

'I'll proceed in accordance with your orders. Goodbye, Your Majesty.'

The captain left the study and the footman came in.

'George, please find the Earl of Leicester and ask him to come to see me here urgently.'

Elizabeth started crying again as soon as the footman left. After a while she recovered and recomposed her makeup for a second time. She was ready just in time when Leicester knocked at the door, but after he came in she could not control herself any longer, embraced her former lover, that she continued to love, and started to cry again.

'I know what happened, Elizabeth. Lord Burghley told me just before lunch.'

'I loved her, Robert. I spent only four days with her, but I considered her a lost sister that I had recovered. Now, I have lost her forever. And she suffered so much in her short life. We talked all the time these four days, that were some of the happiest of my life and surely of her own.'

'That should be your consolation. You gave her four very happy days.'

'And the highest members of my government betrayed me.'

'Perhaps they disobeyed you, but they didn't betray you.'

'Disobedience to the queen is high treason. They must pay for this.'

'They used an Execution Warrant signed by you and with your seal. Did you really sign it? Did it have your signature?'

'It had my signature, but I left it in a locked drawer in that desk. Elizabeth pointed at the desk.

'Why did you do such thing? You hadn't taken any decision yet and travelled to investigate if the trial had been fair.'

'I was going to be travelling along the fields with twenty

cavalry guards. It was unlikely that I should suffer an attack by superior forces since you were the only one that knew about this trip. As you know, I already suffered an unlikely attempt against my life in Nonsuch Palace. If I should die with my next in line condemned to death but not properly executed, an internal war of Catholics versus Protestants would take place. Only in case of my death could my papers be searched. They're traitors because they searched my papers without my permission. Walsingham and Cecil are always making machinations but I trusted Davison to take care of my things. He told me himself he directed the search personally. He's already on his way to the Tower and the other two must follow.'

'Please don't do that. If you do it the entire world, including the kings of Scotland and France, will believe you've invented a situation to get rid of Mary Stuart pretending you had nothing to do with the execution you ordered. It's all right to send Davison to the Tower for his flagrant disobedience. But you can't be seen trying to dissociate yourself from an Execution Warrant signed by you. You could plunge England into the war between Catholics and Protestants that you've always wanted to avoid.'

'I see your point, Robert.'

'Thinking about this, perhaps you performed a service to England signing the warrant.'

'How can you say such a thing, Robert?'

'Because, judging from what you told me about your ordeal in Nonsuch, the entire "Babington Plot" must have been an invention made by Walsingham to kill Mary Stuart. Did Davison know you had signed the warrant?'

'No, I never told him. In fact I told him I just wanted to read it, perhaps more than once.'

'With the excuse of looking for the warrant they were actually looking for the seal. Walsingham has this fellow called Phelippes that can forge anything. If you hadn't signed the warrant, Phelippes (22) would have signed your name. In that case, they would have obviously committed high treason.'

'But Walsingham wouldn't risk his life to have Mary Stuart (23) executed.'

'Why not? Didn't he already risk his queen's life showing a dangerous fellow like Savage how to enter Nonsuch Palace easily?'

'You're very convincing, Robert. I'll go to Nonsuch Palace and I'll try to avoid Walsingham and Cecil for as long as possible. I must go on trying to do the best I can for the people of England.'

'What were your plans after signing her pardon? Were you going to send her to exile in France?'

'No; I was going to keep her in court as my cousin and my successor. She was going to make a formal statement indicating she recognized me as the legitimate Queen of England, that she didn't want to be my successor, but that if eventually Parliament made her queen she would keep the Church of England as the official church of this kingdom. If Parliament approved, she would abdicate the English throne in favor of her son, James.'

'That statement wouldn't stop Catholic plots. It might have worked 20 years ago when she escaped from Scotland, but not now. The people wouldn't believe she meant it. She would be accused of lying to avoid the scaffold. On top of the Catholic plots to kill you, we would have had Protestant plots to kill her.'

'Do you think that my only option would have been to send her to exile in France?'

'Not to France. Mary Stuart in France would have made the religious war being fought there more complex than what it already is. The only solution would have been to have her accepted by her son, King James VI of Scotland.'

'King James VI sent me a letter asking me to pardon his mother.'

'But he could have suggested that his mother should be sent to exile in Scotland and he didn't do that. Henri III also wrote you a letter asking for Mary Stuart's pardon with no suggestion of exile in France.'

'You must help me now, Robert. What can I do? My instinct tells me I must send Walsingham and Cecil to the Tower with Davison (24).'

'Please, don't do that. You would be accused of mounting a farce to avoid admitting what you did. It would have been necessary to do it if they had forged anything, but you told me the warrant had your signature. Avoid Cecil (25) and Walsingham (26) for a while and then talk privately with each of them, making them know they'll have to look for a new occupation the next time you're displeased with them. Keep Davison in the Tower for a long time to remind the other two that he's only a scapegoat for what they did. And you must tell the full story to James VI, but verbally, not in writing. Sir James Melville is the Scottish diplomat that can take care of this mission.'

'I know Melville and I like him.'.'

'James VI sent Sir James to act as Mary Stuart's secretary when she was transferred to Fotheringhay Castle. He's still there, but must return to Scotland quite soon. Send a fast messenger to summon him to see you. When you see him, he must be sworn to silence, except to retell King James VI what you'll tell him about Mary Stuart and you.'

Sir Robert Dudley remained with Elizabeth for nearly two more hours that day.

Elizabeth had to recover rapidly because it became evident that Felipe II, King of Spain, was preparing the invasion of England with a large fleet. Events forced her to work with Cecil and Walsingham almost immediately. That same week, she had to give orders to send Sir Francis Drake with a few ships to attack the Spanish fleet being prepared in La Coruña and Cadiz.

A few months later, Drake attacked. The surprise attack was a great success, 37 Spanish ships were destroyed and the attack of the Spanish Armada had to be postponed for one year.

In 1588 the Spanish Armada attacked, but the English were ready. The troops that were on land to defend the Thames Estuary against any incursion up river towards London were stationed at Tilbury under the command of Sir Robert Dudley, Earl of Leicester (27). On August 9, 1588, Queen Elizabeth was at her finest hour and gave her Tilbury speech to the troops, including the following sentence:

"I know I have the body of a weak and feeble woman; but I have the heart and stomach of a king – and of a King of England too."

The troops on land did not have to fight. The English fleet commanded by Lord Howard of Effingham, Sir Francis Drake and Sir John Hawkins, thoroughly defeated the Spanish Armada commanded by the Duke of Medina Sidonia .

Elizabeth died in 1603 after ruling England for almost 45 years, giving stability to a kingdom that had been shaken by the brief but turbulent years when the rulers were the Regents of her child brother Edward and then her sister Mary.

---------- * ----------

HISTORICAL NOTES

The notes are marked in the text with a number between brackets. To avoid interrupting the flow of the story, it is suggested to read these notes only after the entire novel.

This novel has several fictional characters added to round up a story which is based on true events. Most of the characters are real historical characters and these notes tell what became of those with the most relevant roles in the story. A few notes correspond to places and events rather than people.

(1) Amsterdam's Church in the Attic

The 16th century Church in the Attic that was used for Catholic services in Amsterdam, was moved from one attic to another to avoid detection until 1661. That year, Jan Hartman, a rich Catholic merchant, decided to make something permanent. He bought three adjoining houses, one facing the Oudezijds Voorburgwal canal and the other two around the corner. He unified the attics and built there a large church. He must have counted on the protection of sympathetic Protestant authorities, because he made a permanent church with the type of ornaments seen in any Catholic church. It has great religious paintings, a large crucifix in gold, candles and images of the saints. Since Catholic services were forbidden, care was taken to avoid anything on the outside that would indicate that there is a church inside. It really resulted in a permanent church that today is called Our Lord in the Attic and continues to have services at 11 o'clock on Sundays every week, except during the summer. It also operates as a museum, the Museum Amstelkring, visited by thousands every year.

(2)   The Pilgrimage of Grace

The Pilgrimage of Grace was a popular rising in the north of England during 1536, in protest against Henry VIII's break with the Roman Catholic Church and the Dissolution of the

Monasteries, as well as other specific political, social and economic grievances. Robert Aske was chosen to lead the insurgents; he was a London barrister, a fellow at Gray's Inn, one of the Inns of Court, and the youngest son of Sir Robert Aske. In 1536 Aske led an army of nine thousand followers who entered and occupied York. There he arranged for the expelled monks and nuns to return to their houses; the king's newly installed tenants were driven out and Catholic observance resumed.

The success of the rising was so great that Aske's army reached nearly forty thousand men and the Duke of Norfolk had to open negotiations for Henry VIII with the insurgents. Aske explained that they were not rising against the King but were going in pilgrimage to London to request attention to their problems. He gave his movement the name of Pilgrimage of Grace. Henry authorized Norfolk to promise a general pardon and a Parliament to be held at York to discuss their grievances within a year, as well as a reprieve for the abbeys until the York Parliament had met. Aske was given an audience with Henry VIII in which the king gave the same promises personally. Aske believed the king and dismissed his followers after disarming them. Minor rebellions remained scattered in the north of England and gave a pretext to Henry to disregard his promises and send to jail and to trial Aske and all important leaders of the Pilgrimage, including Baron Thomas Darcy. In all, 216 men were convicted of treason and executed.

(3) La Tour d'Argent

Since it was inaugurated in a famous dinner by King Henri III of France, this restaurant, the first in France in which forks were used, became one of the most exclusive restaurants in the world. It continues to operate successfully to this day.

(4)   Father Edmund Campion

Campion was beatified by Pope Leo XIII in 1886 and canonized in 1970 by Pope Paul VI as one of the Forty

Martyrs of England and Wales. His feast is celebrated on December 1.

The forty martyrs are Catholic men and women executed in England and Wales for their faith between 1535 and 1679, usually falsely accused of high treason. The 14 men executed for the Babington Plot were not included in the list since they had not been falsely accused.

(5)   Father Robert Parsons

Parsons was the Jesuit priest that headed the mission to England sent by the Jesuit Order in the 16th century. He left England shortly after the execution of Campion, Briant and Sherwin. He worked in France, Rome, Flanders and Rome again. In 1588 he was given a very delicate diplomatic mission in Spain by Father Claudio Acquaviva, the Superior General of the Society of Jesus, to conciliate King Felipe II with the Society. Parsons was very successful and used the royal favor to open seminaries in Valladolid, Seville and Madrid as well as residences in San-Lucar and Lisbon. He ended his days as Rector of the English College in Rome, the most important seminar for English priests. He died in 1610 when he was 64.

(6)   Father Alexander Briant

Briant was beatified in 1921 by Pope Pious XI and canonized in 1970 by Pope Paul VI as one of the Forty Martyrs of England and Wales. He was condemned to death for high treason with six other Jesuit priests and he was selected to go to the Tyburn gallows with Campion and Sherwin, who had been tried together.

(7)   Father Ralph Sherwin

Sherwin went to trial and was executed together with Edmund Campion and, like him, was beatified by Pope Leo XIII in 1886 and canonized in 1970 by Pope Paul VI as one of the Forty Martyrs of England and Wales.

(8) Father Edmond Auger

French Catholic Father Edmond Auger, a Jesuit priest, was regarded as one of the most eloquent men of his time. When he entered the city of Valence, France, as a priest, the city was controlled by the Huguenots after the local bishop had become a member of this faith. Auger was taken prisoner and condemned to be burned at the stake by the Huguenots for being a Catholic priest. Standing on the pyre before it was set on fire, he harangued the multitude which became so impressed by his words that they demanded his release. Pierre Viret, a Huguenot leader who was a famous orator, decided to postpone the sentence. He gave Auger a chance to live if he would accept to convert after debating with him. Auger was taken to prison and during the night a group of Catholics set him free and he escaped from Valence. Later, he went to Lyon during a pestilence. He devoted himself to the care of the plague-stricken and made a vow requesting the end of the plague. The plague ended and the authorities of Lyon attributed this favorable outcome to Auger. To express their gratitude they established a school for the Society of Jesus and were astonished when Auger demanded that any Huguenot children that wanted to enter should be accepted. Eventually, Edmond Auger was made Principal of the Society of Jesus in France. He had to resign this position when King Henri III requested that he should become his Father Confessor. The high responsibility demanded full-time attention. The new assignment resulted extremely conflictive. Duke Henri de Guise, the leader of the Catholic League, was constantly working to diminish the power of King Henri III. The Duke's position of Catholic leadership had earned him the support of Pope Sixtus V. The resulting political intrigues included Father Auger's own person. The Duke de Guise repeatedly requested Father General Aquaviva, of the Society of Jesus, the dismissal of Auger. On the other hand, King Henri III always requested the pope to reinstate him. Auger had to put an end to the situation resigning his position of Father Confessor of the King and retiring to a convent in Como. Shortly after Auger's resignation, Henri III assassinated the Duke de Guise. Auger died a few years later in 1591 at the age of 61.

(9)   Don Bernardino de Mendoza

When Don Bernardino was expelled from England, Felipe II appointed him as the Spanish Ambassador to France. In this position he helped Henri, Duke de Guise, in the tug of war between the leader of the Catholic League and the King of France, Henri III. Don Bernardino was very effective helping Henri de Guise to undermine the authority of the king. He was the organizer and coordinator of the May 12, 1588 riot that was called "the day of the barricades" and appeared to be a spontaneous riot. As a result, Henri III had to escape Paris where the government was assumed by Henri de Guise with the title of Lieutenant General of the Kingdom. This was the day when the "War of the Three Henries" became an open war. The three Henries were Henri III, King of France, Henri, Duke the Guise, and Huguenot Henri III, King of Navarre, next in line to become King of France at the death of the current king. Until "the day of the barricades", the leader of the Catholic League and the King of France were supposed to be on the same side. Early in 1599 Don Bernardino resigned his ambassadorship because of ill health. He had become completely blind. He died in Madrid at the age of 64 in 1604.

(10)   Robert Poley

Robert Poley was blamed by Walsingham for Babington's escape the night of the arrests and was sent to the Tower. Since Babington and the two co-conspirators he had alerted were captured shortly after running away, Poley's fault had no consequences and he was released in late 1588. He was without employment, because Sir Philip Sidney, his employer, had died before his release. However, he managed to convince Walsingham he had been imprisoned unfairly and was given a job as courier to take correspondence abroad, working for the Principal Secretary. After the death of Sir Francis Walsingham he continued to work for Sir William Cecil, who replaced Walsingham as Principal Secretary.

Poley was a witness at the inquest made after playwright Christopher Marlowe was killed. In the inquest it was said that a man called Ingram Frizer had killed Marlowe in self-defense after he was attacked by him. Some Marlowe biographers believe he was murdered and others elaborated the "Marlovian Theory", contending that the killing was faked and Marlowe was the real author of many of Shakespeare's plays. Considering Poley's previous conduct, it is reasonable to suspect that his testimony in the inquest might have been false. In 1601 Poley was paid for taking a letter to Paris written by the Principal Secretary. There is no more information about Poley afterwards.

(11)   Gilbert Gifford

The story of Gilbert Gifford has been told in the novel until he leaves London in July 1587. He went to Rheims to complete his studies to become a priest. In March 1588 he was ordained in Rheims as a Catholic priest. However, Walsingham never had the chance to use him again in anything important. Towards the end of 1588 he was arrested in Paris when a brothel was raided. He was found there in bed with a woman and a male servant of the Earl of Essex. Paris was under the rule of the Catholic League. As a priest he had committed what was considered a serious crime. He was imprisoned in the Bastille to await trial. In mid-1589 the trial took place. He tried to extricate himself denouncing Morgan and Paget as double agents. No attention was given to what he said and he was condemned to 20 years in prison for offending the Catholic Church. The next year, the army of Henri IV put siege to Paris and, as always when a city suffers siege, there was famine. Prisoners were underfed in Paris in 1590 and 30 year old Gilbert died towards the end of the year.

(12) Charles Paget

Paget and Morgan, as secretaries of Archbishop Beaton in Paris, together with Nau and Curle, as secretaries of Mary Stuart, managed the funds that the deposed Scottish Queen and former Queen Consort of France, held in that country. After the execution of Mary Stuart each one went his own separate way. Charles Paget had a special problem. His brother, Thomas Paget, was Lord Paget. As to all appearances Charles was plotting against the queen, the English authorities were constantly watching and bothering his brother.. Walsingham could not do anything in favor of Lord Paget without endangering one of his best agents. In 1587 Lord Paget, tired of the persecution against him, escaped from England and went to live in Spain as a Catholic, losing his title and his lands. Lord Paget died a few months after leaving England before Charles could do anything to help him.

In March 1588, a year after the execution of Mary Stuart, Charles Paget started to work for Spanish king Felipe II in Brussels and therefore continued to be very useful to Walsingham. When Sir Francis Walsingham died in 1590, Charles continued to work for the new Principal Secretary of Queen Elizabeth, Sir William Cecil and later for his son, Sir Robert Cecil. When Queen Elizabeth died in 1603, Charles Paget was given the difficult assignment of obtaining support for King James VI as the new King of England among the English refugees in Flanders. He was very successful in this seemingly impossible task, renouncing his employment with Felipe II and splitting the English refugee community. His success allowed him to immediately request the Principal Secretary that his nephew, William Paget, should receive the title of Lord Paget and the lands he would have inherited from his father. In 1604 William Paget received his lands and his title.

Charles Paget's work as a double agent had now ended and he returned to England where he lived peacefully until 1611.

He died at age 65 leaving a considerable estate. Since he had no children, the son of one of his sisters received the inheritance.

(13) Thomas Morgan

When the Babington plot conspirators were arrested, Thomas Morgan was denounced by the Jesuit Order to the French authorities as a Protestant double agent. Morgan was sent to the Bastille, but was released for lack of evidence in 1590. He was free, but no longer useful to be recruited again by Walsingham. He then went to Brussels where he expected to be accepted by the large community of English exiles. However, not only was he not accepted by the English Catholic exiles but he was denounced to the Spanish authorities as a Protestant agent and imprisoned in Truerenborche, a prison much worse than the Bastille. In 1593 many prisoners were released after the death of Flanders' Governor, Alessandro Farnese, and Morgan was free again. It is not clear what happened to him afterwards, but it is apparent he did not get any help from his former associates, Charles Paget and Gilbert Curle who were living in Brussels at the time. Some reports indicate that he managed to travel to Rome to seek help from the pope, claiming to have been falsely accused and that he might have been sent to work with the Bishop of Cusano Milanino. He died in 1606 at age 60, in Amiens, France.

(14) Sir Edward La Zouche, Lord Zouche

Edward La Zouche earned his place in history for the courage and independence he showed when he gave the only dissident vote in the trial of Mary Stuart. He voted against her conviction and death sentence. As told in the novel, Mary Stuart was judged by a Commission of 36 members in which he participated.

Sir Edward studied in Cambridge and graduated as a lawyer but never practiced his profession. He held several diplomatic positions of importance during the reigns of

Elizabeth I and James I, including the post of Ambassador in Scotland. Also he was a Commissioner of the Virginia Company.

He had a very conflictive personal life. He married his cousin, Eleanor Zouche, and had two daughters, Elizabeth and Mary. Shortly after the birth of Mary he obviously thought his wife had been unfaithful since he abandoned her. Although he never accused his wife he never accepted to pay her any allowance. When forced by a court of law to pay her a rather small allowance he preferred to leave England rather than comply. Eleanor died in 1611, 29 years after she was abandoned by her husband. A year later Sir Edward married a woman that had been widowed twice, Sarah Harrington.

In 1621 Sir Edward accidentally earned another place in history. He invited George Abbott, Archbishop of Canterbury, to his mansion in Surrey for a stag-hunt. The guest accidentally shot and killed one of the wardens and became the only Archbishop of Canterbury that ever killed a man. Edward La Zouche died in 1625, at the age of 69.

(15)   James Beaton, Archbishop of Glasgow

Beaton was Catholic Archbishop of Glasgow during the years when Marie de Guise ruled Scotland as Regent for her daughter, Mary Stuart. When Marie de Guise died and the Protestant nobles ruled Scotland, Beaton had to leave his country, went to Paris and was in direct contact with Mary Stuart when she was Consort Queen of France. When Mary Stuart left France to assume her position as Queen of Scotland, she entrusted Beaton with the management of her French assets and named him Ambassador of Scotland in France.

When Mary Stuart was deposed by Protestant noblemen, Beaton continued to represent her as her personal ambassador and to follow her instructions as manager of her French assets.

After the death of Mary Stuart, her son, King James VI of

Scotland, showed his appreciation for Beaton's service to his mother by naming him Ambassador of Scotland to France. In 1598, following the King's wishes, the Scottish Parliament restored all his *"heritages, honors, dignities, and benefices, notwithstanding that he has never acknowledged the religion professed within the realm"*.

James Beaton died in Paris in 1603, at the age of 86, after having witnessed the union of the kingdoms of Scotland and England. This was only one month before King James VI of Scotland was crowned as King James I of England.

(16)   Claude Nau de la Boissiliere

Claude Nau was a French lawyer sent to England as a secretary of Mary Stuart by the de Guise family. When Mary Stuart was accused of participating in the Babington plot, Nau was arrested but instead of going to prison he went to live comfortably at the home of Sir Francis Walsingham. His testimony and that of Mary's Scottish secretary, Gilbert Curle, were the only proof presented at the trial of Mary Stuart. The two secretaries did not attend the trial and only their signed testimonies were presented.

Nau had a wife, a son and three daughters in France. He returned to France, after the execution of Mary Stuart. In France, he managed to convince the Duke de Guise that he had not betrayed the duke's cousin and he lived comfortably with the funds he had managed to deviate from the assets of Mary Stuart to himself. He worked for King Henri III and also devoted himself to writing. He enjoyed the favor of King Henri IV. It is possible that he may have continued to work as an English agent in France, but there is no historical confirmation of such work. Nau died in 1605.

(17)   Gilbert Curle

Gilbert Curle worked for Mary Stuart for more than twenty years starting his service before her imprisonment in England. After the execution of Mary Stuart, he spent a reasonable time in prison to cover appearances and settled in Brussels with his wife, Barbara Mowbray, his daughter Mary (baptized by Mary Stuart) and his sister Elizabeth. He convinced his family that he had always been loyal to Mary Stuart. There is no information about his activity in Brussels. Like Charles Paget, who also settled in Brussels, and Claude Nau, who settled in Paris, Gilbert Curle had an affluent position. His family was always Catholic and his two sons, James and Hypolitus, became priests who joined the Jesuit Order and moved to Spain. Both his wife and his sister were ladies-in-waiting of Mary Stuart and always remained very devoted to her memory. Elizabeth, who never married, had accompanied the prisoner queen to the scaffold. About 15 years after the death of Mary Stuart she commissioned a large oil painting that can be seen today at the Blair Museum, in Aberdeen, Scotland. It is a Flemish School full size portrait of the deposed queen, dressed like she was dressed when she went to the scaffold. She is seen standing erect, turned slightly to the left and holding a crucifix in her right hand. In the background, under her right hand, is a smaller scale insert with the scene of the execution, and on the left in the background another insert with the figures of the two ladies-in-waiting that accompanied her to the scaffold, Jane Kennedy and Elizabeth Curle. The expensive portrait shows that Gilbert Curle was in a position to give substantial funds to his sister. There is no information about the date of the death of Gilbert Curle, only that when his wife died in 1617 she was already a widow.

(18)   Sir James Hepburn, Earl of Bothwell and Duke of Orkney

James Hepburn inherited his title as Earl of Bothwell when he was 22 years old. He also had the hereditary title of Lord High Admiral of Scotland and travelled a lot with ships of the Scottish fleet. At the age of 25, on a visit to Copenhagen, he took a Norwegian noblewoman, Anna Throndsen, as his wife. He married according to Norwegian law, took Anna to

Flanders and spent all her dowry there. He sent her back to Denmark to ask for more money quite aware that Anna's family would not accept this request. Bothwell felt that he was not obliged in any way by a Norwegian marriage and continued to travel considering himself a single man. He went to France and met the royal couple, King François II and Queen Mary Stuart. He was very well received, since both he and his father had been loyal to Regent Marie de Guise, Mary's mother, although they were Protestants. He was honored with the post and salary of Gentleman of the King's Chamber and received 600 Crowns. The following year, 1561, he travelled to France twice. The last trip was as part of the commission formed to take the widowed queen back to Scotland and to make the travel arrangements as Lord High Admiral of Scotland. When Mary assumed power as Queen of Scotland, Bothwell was one of the Protestant lords that supported her. In 1565 Mary married her cousin Henry Stuart, Lord Darnley. The following year Darnley attacked his wife, already six months pregnant, with a band of Protestant nobles. These assassinated her secretary, David Rizzio, in front of her, leaving her as a prisoner in her bedroom. Then the nobles told her Darnley was the new king and that she would be judged and executed the next day. Mary escaped from the royal Holyrood Palace through a window making a rope with her sheets and was supported by most nobles of Scotland. Mary decided not to act against the father of her son and heir. She just kept him apart. Darnley was sick with syphilis and had to stay in bed. James Hepburn was one of the nobles that supported her immediately when she escaped from the rebel nobles. Since no action was taken against Darnley and the rebel nobles, these swore allegiance to Mary Stuart but participated in another plot to kill her and make regent her half-brother, James Stuart, Lord Morey. James Hepburn not only participated in this plot, but he was the leader of its implementation, filling with barrels of gun powder the basement of a palace where Darnley was staying and, for only one night, both Mary and Darnley would sleep. Darnley had to be killed with Mary, since otherwise he would be supported by nobles who might support him as Regent or even king. The plot failed because Mary Stuart was invited to a party and was not in the palace when the powder exploded. Darnley was not inside either since he had escaped alerted by a faithful servant. They had already left the palace grounds and were in another property when several plotters reached and strangled them. Mary decided not to declare she was the victim but sent Bothwell to trial at the Scot Parliament for the murder of Darnley. Most parliamentarians were friends of the accused and acquitted him. Furthermore, a group of Protestant noblemen wrote a statement declaring that the Queen of Scotland had now to marry a Protestant Scot noble. Bothwell arranged with his wife to divorce her on grounds of adultery, his own adultery with a servant woman. He intercepted Mary when she was travelling to Glasgow, took her to his castle and raped her to force her to accept to marry him. He also forced Mary to make him Duke of Orkney and married her eight days after his divorce was granted. The majority of the Scottish nobles, led by Mary's half-brother, James Stewart, Earl of Moray, sent an army against the army of Bothwell and Mary Stuart. Finding himself attacked by superior forces, Bothwell fled and Mary was left alone to surrender.

Bothwell left Scotland with several ships of the Scottish Royal fleet. He was chased by ships of Scottish nobles and to escape a battle and a storm he took refuge on the Norwegian coast. There, his past caught up with him. The family of his abandoned wife, Anna Throndsen, requested his arrest and he was taken to Bergen, her home town. He was sued by Anna for abandonment and managed to settle the matter out of court by giving Anna one of the ships of the Scottish fleet. But Bothwell was now in the hands of the ruler of Norway, Frederick II, King of Denmark, who thought he had a valuable prisoner, wanted by Scotland and England and with a claim to the throne of Scotland. Bothwell was well treated until Frederick realized that he had no chance of becoming King of Scotland and no payment for him would ever be made by Scotland or England. He was sent to prison in Dragsholm Castle. After 11 years in prison he died in 1578, at the age of 54.

(19) Nonsuch Palace

H0enry VIII ordered the construction of this palace, started in 1538. He named it Nonsuch Palace because his instructions were that there would not be such palace elsewhere equal to its magnificence. When Henry died in early 1547, the palace had not yet been completed and Mary I sold it to Sir Henry FitzAlan, Earl of Arundel, who finished it.

As told in the novel, the palace and the title of Earl of Arundel were inherited by Sir Henry's son in law, Sir Philip Howard, son of Sir Thomas Howard, Duke of Norfolk, beheaded after being accused (most probably falsely) by Walsingham of participation in the Ridolfi Plot. In 1585 Sir Philip, who had converted to Catholicism, tried to leave England. He was captured in the high seas and imprisoned in the Tower of London, losing his title and all his possessions, including Nonsuch Palace. Philip Howard died in the Tower of London becoming sick after ten years in prison in solitary confinement. He was beatified by Pope Benedict XV in 1929 and canonized by Pope Paul VI in 1970 as one of the 40 martyrs of England and Wales.

Philip's son, another Thomas Howard, was restored to the title of Earl of Arundel in 1604, during the reign of James I, and received some properties taken from his father, but not Nonsuch Palace, that remained as royal property.

In 1670 King Charles II gave the palace to his favorite, Lady Barbara Palmer, Countess of Castlemaine and Duchess of Cleveland. Twelve years later, in 1682, Lady Barbara, who had already sold the panels and most parts of the palace to pay gambling debts, had the building demolished to pay more gambling debts with the construction materials. Except for Nonsuch Park, nothing remains today of the 16th century palace which was so beautiful there was no such palace elsewhere that could rival its magnificence.

(20) Sir Amyas Paulet

Amyas Paulet was a fanatical Puritan, a Calvinist rather than a member of the Church of England. He hated Catholics. He was the Governor of the Channel Isle of Jersey. In 1576 he was knighted by Queen Elizabeth and appointed Ambassador to France, post where he served three years, returning afterwards to his functions as Governor of Jersey.

In 1576 Queen Elizabeth appointed Sir Amyas as the gaoler of Mary Stuart. He survived Mary Stuart only for a year and a half, since he died in 1588 at the age of 56.

(21) John Palmer, Dean of Peterborough

John Palmer entered history as the Dean of Peterborough that prevented Mary Stuart to read her prayers quietly before her execution. He covered her voice reading in a louder voice from a Protestant book of prayers. He died in a debtor's prison in 1607.

22) Thomas Phelippes

Thomas Phelippes returned to France after the Babington trial. He may have continued to work for England's Principal Secretary, but there is no information on his activities after his return to his country. He died in 1625 at the age of 69.

(23) Mary Stuart, Queen of Scots

The story of Mary Stuart's life has been told in the novel. She was buried with a Protestant service at Peterborough Cathedral. Her son, King James I, ordered she had to be reinterred in Westminster Abbey, in a very ornamented chapel opposite the tomb of Elizabeth I.

(24) Sir William Davison

Davison was a diplomat that served for ten years in Scotland as English Ambassador and later carried out diplomatic functions in the Netherlands. There, the Dutch were supported by England in their fight for independence from Spain. He returned to England in 1586, becoming a Member of Parliament and a Privy Councilor. He was appointed as assistant to Sir Francis Walsingham, the Principal Secretary, who had been his friend for many years. When Queen Elizabeth found out that during her absence from the palace while travelling, the Privy Council had taken action to execute Mary Stuart using an execution warrant guarded among her personal papers she became extremely upset. Since he was acting as her personal secretary, Davison was responsible for the queen's personal papers during her absence, so that her wrath was directed against him. He had a Star Chamber trial. Usually those tried in Star Chamber trials were sentenced to death, but in in this case all the jurors were friends of the accused. They didn't dare to upset the queen declaring him innocent so that they condemned him to pay a fine and to remain imprisoned at the queen's pleasure, which meant until she decided to set him free. Davison was a scapegoat for the wrath of the queen against Cecil and Walsingham, who were badly needed by the queen at the time because of the imminent danger of an invasion by Spanish armies. Walsingham became very ill in 1589 and that might have been the reason the queen decided to release Davison that year, since both Cecil and Walsingham knew that Davison was in prison to pay for what they had done. After his release Davison retired to a quiet life at his London home, where he died in 1608 at the age of 67.

(25)   Sir William Cecil, Lord Burghley

As soon as Elizabeth was crowned as Queen of England she appointed Cecil, 38 years old at that time, as her Principal Secretary. He had already held that position from 1550 till 1553 for King Edward VI when Sir John Dudley, father of Robert Dudley, was Regent. During the five years of the reign of Queen Mary I he served as a Member of Parliament. In 1571 Elizabeth elevated him as Baron Burghley. In 1572 Mary needed a Lord High Treasurer she could trust and elected Cecil for that position, while Cecil's assistant, Walsingham, became Principal Secretary. In 1590, when Walsingham died, he became Principal Secretary again until his death in 1598 at the age of 77.

(26) Sir Francis Walsingham

Walsingham survived Mary Stuart by only a few years and died early in 1590. He was very fond of his son in law, Sir Philip Sydney, the husband of his daughter, Frances. Sir Philip, who died in the war in the Netherlands in 1586, was considered the model of an English gentleman since he was both a learned poet and a brave soldier. When in 1587 his body was returned to England for burial, Sir Francis Walsingham gave him one of the most elaborate funerals ever staged and became almost broke because of the expense. This resulted in economic difficulties at the end of his life. Elizabeth ordered her rich favorite, Robert Devereux, Earl of Essex, to marry Walsingham's widowed daughter Frances, to ease the economic burden on her Principal Secretary. However Walsingham died at the age of 57 in early 1590, before the marriage took place.

(27) Sir Robert Dudley, Earl of Leicester.

Robert Dudley was a son of Sir John Dudley, Earl of Warwick, who led a "coup d'état" against the Regent of King Edward VI, Sir Edward Seymour, Duke of Somerset, making himself the new Regent and assuming the title of Duke of Northumberland.

During the reign of Edward VI the Protestant Church of England was kept as the only church allowed, with tolerance for Puritans and intolerance for Catholics. When Edward became so sick that it was obvious that he would not live too long, the Regent arranged for one of his sons, Guilford Dudley, to marry Lady Jane Grey, a granddaughter of Mary, the youngest daughter of King Henry VII. The Regent hoped that Guilford and Jane would have a son. A male descendant of Henry VII would be more acceptable to the English people as the heir to the crown than the two daughters of Henry VIII, Mary and Elizabeth. The two sisters had the legal right since they had been accepted by Parliament in the Third Succession Act made by Henry VIII. The nobles that were part of the Regent's Government were Protestants and gladly supported Guilford and Jane because Mary was Catholic. However, Jane did not get pregnant, the health of Edward VI deteriorated and he was expected to die soon.

Instead of abandoning the plan, John Dudley convinced Edward that his two sisters, Mary and Elizabeth, were bastards and therefore had to be excluded from succession. The conclusion presented to Edward was that he had to name Lady Jane Grey as the successor to the throne of England.

Four days after the death of Edward, the Privy Council declared that Jane was the new queen. The news was received with dismay by the population of England, which demonstrated on the streets in favor of Mary. John Dudley raised an army of 3.000 men to take Mary prisoner, but her supporters rapidly raised an army of 20.000 men to defend her. The Privy Council realized that naming Lady Jane Grey as the new queen was a mistake and switched sides, naming Mary as the new queen. Supporters of the John Dudley scheme made a Protestant rebellion that was rapidly suppressed. Then all participants in the scheme were condemned to death, including Robert Dudley and a brother.

After the execution of John and Guilford Dudley, Consort King Philip saved the life of Robert and his surviving brother suggesting to Queen Mary that the young men that had to obey their father should be pardoned.

Most salient facts about the life of Robert Dudley have been told in this novel. Apart from his relationship with Queen Elizabeth, he had love affairs, including two very serious ones with beautiful young widows of noble families. At the age of 37 he took as his mistress Lady Douglass. She had an illegitimate son, recognized by him, who was named Robert Dudley. She later married Lord John Sheffield.

The other mistress was Lettice Knollys, the widow of Walter Devereux, Earl of Essex. She is believed to have been Dudley's mistress even before becoming a widow while her husband was in Ireland. At the age of 46 Dudley married secretly Lettice Knollys. She was expelled from court when the queen learned about the marriage. Robert Dudley retained all his titles and functions, but after his marriage he was no longer the queen's favorite.

In December 1585 Robert Dudley was entrusted the delicate mission of leading the troops sent by England to Flanders to support the rebellious Protestant Dutch, who were fighting against Spanish rule. These were the troops pledged by England in the Nonsuch Treaty. He considered insufficient the troops provided by the queen and mortgaged his properties to add cavalry, expecting to be reimbursed by the Dutch after defeating the Spaniards.

The Dutch received Dudley with great honors and on January 1st, 1586 the States General of the United Provinces named him Governor General of the United Provinces. Such a title given by a supporting Council of State to an English subject, would make the Queen of England the sovereign of the United Provinces. Dudley sent a message to Queen Elizabeth asking if he could accept and explaining that it was very important to accept. On January 25, since he had not yet received a reply, he yielded to the pressure of the Dutch and accepted. When the news of Dudley's acceptance without waiting for her decision reached the queen, she mounted in anger. She sent a nobleman to read a letter of disapproval to him in his presence at a formal meeting of the States General. The result was great loss of prestige by Dudley. The Dutch patched up the problem declaring that the people of the United Provinces wanted and accepted Dudley as their

Governor General. This position was accepted by the queen but only after much pleading by Dutch emissaries.

Another blow to Dudley's prestige took place in December 1586, when Dudley returned to England a few months at the request of the queen. In his absence, two high English officers that commanded garrisons defending forts went over to the Duke of Parma, leader of the Spanish forces. Lack of payment to the troops was one of the reasons for the defection so that Dudley had to get deeper in debt to pay the troops with his own money.

Internal politics among the Dutch were complex since not all of them had the same position with regard to the Spaniards. Some of the United Provinces wanted to continue to trade with Spain. Tired of Dutch politics, Elizabeth reached a settlement with the Duke of Parma and recalled the English troops in the Netherlands. As a result, Dudley lost all possibility to recover the funds he had spent financing the war.

After the Tilbury Speech to the troops waiting for the Spanish invasion that the defeated Armada could not implement, Dudley became the queen's almost constant companion, but only two months after the speech, in September 1588, he died suddenly at the age of 56.

Robert Dudley had two sons named Robert Dudley. The legitimate one that could have inherited his title as Earl of Leicester, died in his infancy and the title disappeared.

———— * ————

Printed in Great Britain
by Amazon

53661916R00185